Dear Reader:

Five years after Jason S[...] Baltimore and the Wyndhams (*The Valentine Legacy*), one of the premiere racing families in the area, he wakes up early one morning with Horace's ugly pug face staring him down, and knows it's time for him to go home.

Jason wants to breed and race horses, primarily his own Thoroughbred, Dodger, who's faster than a Baltimore pickpocket. When his twin, James, takes him to Lyon's Gate, a once-renowned racing stud farm near his family's home, Jason knows to his soul that this property is what he wants more than anything.

Unfortunately, Hallie Carrick (*Night Storm*) wants Lyon's Gate just as badly as Jason, and she's fully prepared to fight him down and dirty to get it.

Now life and fate take a hand, and the two of them end up with something neither expected.

Come to Lyon's Gate in 1835 England, visit with the Sherbrookes, and see Jason come back to the fullness and joy of life.

Prepare to laugh yourself silly.

Do let me know what you think of *Lyon's Gate*. E-mail me at ReadMoi@aol.com or write me at P.O. Box 17, Mill Valley, CA, 94942. Do visit my website at www.catherinecoulter.com.

Catherine Coulter

THE VIKING TRILOGY

Lord of Hawkfell Island • *Lord of Raven's Peak* •
Lord of Falcon Ridge

"Coulter's characters quickly come alive and draw the reader into the story. You root for the good guys and hiss for the bad guys. When you have to put the book down for a while, you can hardly wait to get back and see what's going on."   —*The Sunday Oklahoman*

THE LEGACY TRILOGY

The Wyndham Legacy • *The Nightingale Legacy* •
The Valentine Legacy

"Delightful . . . brimming with drama, sex, and colorful characters . . . Her witty dialogue and bawdy, eccentric characters add up to an engaging, fan-pleasing story."   —*Publishers Weekly*

CATHERINE COULTER

LYON'S GATE

JOVE BOOKS, NEW YORK

THE BERKLEY PUBLISHING GROUP
Published by the Penguin Group
Penguin Group (USA) Inc.
375 Hudson Street, New York, New York 10014, USA
Penguin Group (Canada), 90 Eglinton Avenue East, Suite 700, Toronto, Ontario M4P 2Y3, Canada
(a division of Pearson Penguin Canada Inc.)
Penguin Books Ltd., 80 Strand, London WC2R 0RL, England
Penguin Group Ireland, 25 St. Stephen's Green, Dublin 2, Ireland (a division of Penguin Books Ltd.)
Penguin Group (Australia), 250 Camberwell Road, Camberwell, Victoria 3124, Australia
(a division of Pearson Australia Group Pty. Ltd.)
Penguin Books India Pvt. Ltd., 11 Community Centre, Panchsheel Park, New Delhi—110 017, India
Penguin Group (NZ), Cnr. Airborne and Rosedale Roads, Albany, Auckland 1310, New Zealand
(a division of Pearson New Zealand Ltd.)
Penguin Books (South Africa) (Pty.) Ltd., 24 Sturdee Avenue, Rosebank, Johannesburg 2196, South
Africa

Penguin Books Ltd., Registered Offices: 80 Strand, London WC2R 0RL, England

This is a work of fiction. Names, characters, places, and incidents either are the product of the author's
imagination or are used fictitiously, and any resemblance to actual persons, living or dead, business
establishments, events, or locales is entirely coincidental. The publisher does not have any control
over and does not assume any responsibility for author or third-party websites or their content.

LYON'S GATE

A Jove Book / published by arrangement with the author.

PRINTING HISTORY
Jove premium edition / August 2005

Copyright © 2005 by Catherine Coulter.
Cover design by Brad Springer.
Cover illustration by Gregg Gulbronson.
Cover photo by Charles William Bush.
Book design by Kristin del Rosario.

ISBN: 0-515-13897-5

JOVE®
Jove Books are published by The Berkley Publishing Group,
a division of Penguin Group (USA) Inc.,
375 Hudson Street, New York, New York 10014.
JOVE is a registered trademark of Penguin Group (USA) Inc.
The "J" design is a trademark belonging to Penguin Group (USA) Inc.

PRINTED IN THE UNITED STATES OF AMERICA

10 9 8 7 6 5 4 3 2 1

To Yngrid Flores Becker: you are a very special woman, and a delight. I am so pleased you are part of our family. So are Corky and Cleo.

CATHERINE

Chapter 1

✢⸱✢

Baltimore, Maryland
April, 1835

❧ Jason Sherbrooke knew it was time to go home when he rolled away from Lucinda Frothingale, stared into the fat ugly face of her pug, Horace, who growled at him, and suddenly, with no warning at all, saw his twin, eyes sheened with tears as he'd waved good-bye to Jason from the dock at the Eastbourne Harbor. Waved until the ship was too far away for Jason to see him. Jason felt tears choking his throat and an ache so deep he knew his heart was cracking clean in two.

Jason eyed the dog curled up against his mistress's side, then turned onto his belly, listening to both Lucinda's and Horace's breathing. It was true, only moments before he'd felt sated all the way to his heels, and then suddenly he'd been flooded with that particular memory, and the pain of it. Now, just moments later, he was impatient, so restless he could barely keep still. He wanted, quite simply, to jump out of Lucinda's warm bed and start swimming across the Atlantic.

After nearly five years, Jason Sherbrooke wanted to go home.

At eight o'clock that morning, Jason was seated at the big breakfast table in the Wyndham dining room. He looked at the two people who'd welcomed him into their home so many years before, and at their two boys and two girls who had all become very dear to him. He cleared his throat to get everyone's attention. He prayed that lovely, fluent thoughts would flow flawlessly out of his mouth, which, naturally, didn't happen. He said only, a lump in his throat the size of the Crack County racetrack, "It's time."

Jason didn't realize he looked like a blind man who'd suddenly regained his sight. He was wondering why there were no more words, just those two that popped out of his mouth, hanging there in the Wyndham dining room.

James Wyndham, seeing the expression on Jason's face, but not understanding it, raised a dark blond brow. "Time for what? You want to race Jessie again? Haven't you had enough punishment at her hands, Jase? Even riding Dodger doesn't give you all that much of an edge."

Jason jumped at the familiar bait. "Like you've always said, James, she's skinny, doesn't weigh more than Constance here, and that's why she usually beats us. It has nothing to do with skill."

"Har har," Jessie Wyndham said. "Both of you are pathetic, always trotting out the same tired old excuses. Now, the two of you have seen me ride Dodger—Jason's own horse—we're like the wind, so fast we blow your hair into your faces. All Jason can do when he rides Dodger is raise a slight breeze."

That was an excellent slap to the head, Jason thought, and grinned at Jessie.

"Papa's right," seven-year-old Constance said. "Although," she added, looking at her mother thoughtfully, "perhaps Mama does weigh a little bit more than I do. But Uncle Jason, you're just like Papa, you're too big to race, you nearly drag the horse down into the dirt. Jockeys have to be small. Even though Grandmother says it's a disgrace, what with Mama out there aping men and not staying here in the parlor mending, she still remarks on how skinny Mama is even though she's birthed four children, and that isn't a bit fair."

Jonathan Wyndham, the eldest of the Wyndham children at nearly eleven, nodded. "It was a bit rude of you to say it so starkly, Connie, and Grandmother shouldn't speak so badly about Mother, but the fact remains that Mother is a female and females aren't supposed to be racing against men."

Jessie threw her slice of toast at her eldest son.

Jonathan laughed and ducked. "Mama, you know gentlemen can't stand it when you beat them. Once I saw Papa nearly weep when you raced ahead of him at the last moment."

"On the other hand," Jason said, "everyone I know seems to think you were born on a horse's back, you're so good, and who cares if the best jockey in Baltimore has brea—er, never mind that."

"That's exactly what I was thinking, Mama."

"Dear Lord, I hope not," Jason said.

"I hope not too," Jessie said. "No, don't ask, enough said."

Jonathan began picking toast crumbs off his jacket sleeve, and only his little sister Alice saw the wicked gleam in his lowered eyes. "Like I was saying, Mother, you're a bruising rider, mean as a snake when you have to be, but still, isn't a smartly mended sheet much more fulfilling for you, so—"

"I don't have anything else to throw at you, Jon. Ah, look, this nice heavy fork just hopped into my hand." Jessie aimed the fork at her son. "I suggest you retire from the fray or face very bad consequences."

"I'm done," Jonathan said, splaying his palms in open surrender, a huge grin on his face. "Retired, that's me."

"Time for what, Uncle Jathon?" four-year-old Alice asked, lisping charmingly. She was leaning toward him, and Jason knew that if they weren't at the breakfast table, she'd have already crawled onto his lap and curled into him the way she'd done since she'd been six weeks old. When he didn't immediately speak, his brain empty of words, huge tears shimmered in her beautiful eyes. "Thomething wrong, ithn't it? You don't like uth anymore. You want to shoot Mama because she beat you?"

Jason looked at that precious little face and sought for the right words, but what came out of his mouth was, "I love you all dearly. It's not that at all. It's—" And then the truth burst right out. "I want to go home. It's time. I'm leaving Friday, on *The Bold Venture,* one of Genny and Alec Carrick's ships."

Instant and utter silence fell over the breakfast table. Everyone stared at him, including the Wyndham cook, Joshua, who was handing Jessie a fresh piece of toast. As for Lucy, their serving maid, she was so distracted by the awesomely beautiful young master Jason's words that she was in danger of pouring coffee into Mr. Wyndham's lap. James grabbed her hand just in time.

"Home?" said Alice. "But you are home, Uncle Jathon."

He smiled at the little faerie, the very image of her mother, who'd been born after he'd arrived here in Baltimore. "No, sweetheart, this isn't my home, although I've been here longer than you have. England is my home, where I was born, at a beautiful house called Northcliffe Hall. That's where my family lives, where I spent twenty-five years of my life."

"But you're ours, Uncle Jason," nine-year-old Benjamin Wyndham said even as he passed a crisp slice of bacon to Old Corker, the family hound, who'd been born within a week of Benjamin. "You don't belong to them over in that foreign country anymore. Who cares about Northcliffe Hall anyway? We could name our house—make it sound all sorts of grand—if you wished us to."

"We're already named, bacon-brain," Jon said to his brother. "We're Wyndham Farm."

"You've got quite a few cousins in England," James Wyndham said to his son, but his eyes were searching Jason's face. Then he smiled. "You know, it's time for us to pay a visit to England as well. The months and years slip by, don't they? Time simply marches forward, and so very quickly. Nearly five years. That's amazing, Jase. It seems like yesterday we met you at the dock in the Inner Harbor and Jessie couldn't take her eyes off of you, said you were even more beautiful than Alec Carrick, surely the most beautiful man God had ever created. She said you had an identical twin, and that meant there was another one like you. I'll tell you, I was grateful she didn't swoon."

"You remember I said all that?" Jessie said, a dark red eyebrow cocked up.

"Certainly. I remember every word you've ever uttered, my sweet."

Jessie made a gagging sound that reduced her four children to giggles.

James felt both immense sadness and joy in that moment. Evidently Jason had finally come to grips with the past.

"Uncle Jason is prettier than Aunt Glenda," Constance said and grinned, showing a missing front tooth. "When she's not staring at him, she's looking in the mirror, trying to figure out how to make herself look more like him. I told her once to give up. She threw her hairbrush at me."

James cleared his throat. "You'll make your uncle Jason blush, Connie, so let's move along. Marcus and the duchess were here last year, and North and Caroline Nightingale the year before. Yes, it's our turn to go to England and visit with everyone, your family included, Jase. I want to see if my wife swoons when she meets your twin, and you've told the children so many stories about Hollis, I know they're expecting him to deliver stone tablets to them. Ah, and your father and mother, of course."

"But they talk funny there," said Benjamin. "Like Uncle Jason. I don't want to go to this place."

"Think of it as an adventure," said his mother.

"Yes, that's it exactly, Ben," said Jason. He was thinking it would be an adventure for him as well as he sat back in his chair and laced his fingers over his lean belly. "All my family will welcome you as you welcomed me." He paused, looked at James and Jessie, shrugged. "I want to go home. I'll be thirty years old next January."

"That's still only twenty-nine so you're not that old, Uncle Jason," Benjamin said. "When you're as old as Papa, then you can go back there."

"Your father is only thirty-nine, not all that great an age," Jessie said, then paused and blinked. "I'm nearly thirty-one, more than a year older than you, Jason. Good heavens, how the time leaps away from one."

Jason said, "Do you know I have a pair of twin nephews nearly three years old now, and I've never seen them?"

"Yes," Jessie said. "They look like their father, which means they look like you too."

Jason nodded. "My brother wrote that meant yet another generation looked like my aunt Melissande." James had written so amusingly about how it drove their father mad, that Jason easily pictured his twin's smile and his father's face as well. So many letters over the years, and he'd only begun really answering three years before. For the first two years he'd been here, he'd written acknowledgments, nothing important, nothing that really meant anything, if indeed anything did mean anything back then. But things had slowly begun to change. He'd begun to see behind the words in the letters that arrived weekly from his family, begun to feel again what they meant to him, and his letters had grown longer and, perhaps, richer, because he himself was now in them.

"Yes," Jessie said. "We know. I feel we know all of your family very well indeed. It will be like seeing dear friends."

Jason hadn't realized that he'd spoken about his family all that much.

Alice said, "But none of your family have ever come here, Uncle Jathon. Why haven't they come? Don't they like you? Did they thend you away?"

"No, Alice, they all wanted to come to visit me. The truth is, I asked them not to come. And no, no one sent me away." He paused a moment. "The truth is, I sent myself away."

"But why?" Jonathan asked, sitting forward, hands on the table since he had no more bacon to slip to Old Corker.

Jason said slowly, "Some very bad things happened five years ago, Jon, and I was responsible for them. Only me."

"You killed a man in a duel, Uncle Jason?" Ben asked, eyes shining, nearly ready to leap out of his chair.

"Sorry, Ben, no. What I did was worse. I brought evil to my family, and that evil nearly destroyed them."

"You brought the Devil home, Uncle Jathon?"

"That's close enough, Alice. Fact was, I couldn't stay, couldn't bring myself to find anything good in my life there. I couldn't face all the people I'd endangered, and so I asked your parents if I could come here and learn all about running a stud farm."

Jessie knew the children didn't understand—not that she understood all that much herself—and, knowing they had a dozen questions to fire at him, she said quickly, "You've helped us more than we've taught you. And even though James and I have tried our best to fill up this blasted house"—she paused a moment, waving her hand to encompass her four children— "there was more than enough room for you."

"Oh no," Jason said. You've taught me endlessly."

"Don't be a dolt," James said, then raised his hand when he saw that all four children wanted to speak at once. "No, no, children, be quiet. No more arguments to try to make your uncle Jason feel guilty about leaving you. He's obviously made up his mind, and we will all respect his decision. You will not ask him any more questions. No, Jon, I see that busy brain of yours working hard. Let me repeat, you won't ask questions and you won't make him feel guilty about leaving." He paused a moment, smiled toward Jason. "Besides, we'll visit him in England. And you want to know something else? He'll come back for visits. He won't be able to help himself—he has to try again to beat your mother in a race."

"But why didn't you want your family to come thee you, Uncle Jathon?" Alice asked. She was sitting on a pile of six books so she could reach the table, the top one being a huge volume that held an article by Jason's brother, James, Lord Hammersmith, on a huge orange ball of gasses that had glowed brightly in Venus's acrid northern hemisphere three nights running the previous April.

Alice's father opened his mouth to scold her, but Jason said quickly, "No, it's all right, James. That's a good question, Alice, and I want to answer it. I want all of you to understand that my family didn't want me to leave. They didn't blame me for what happened. They should have, but they didn't."

"What did happen?" Jonathan asked and James Wyndham rolled his eyes.

"Just know that it was bad, Jon, that my father, Hollis, and my twin could have been killed, and that it was all my fault. Now, they all wanted to come, but you see . . ." He paused a moment, trying to find the right words. "The thing was, I wasn't ready to see them. To look at them was to see my own blindness, I suppose." Badly said, but close enough.

James said, "No more, children. No more."

Jessie rose from her chair and clapped her hands. "That's right, you will now hold your tongues, as impossible as I know that is. Uncle Jason has made up his mind. Leave him alone about this. All of you know what you're supposed to do after breakfast, so go do it and no complaints, if you please. James, Jason, if you two gentlemen will come with me into the parlor."

Jessie Wyndham faced her husband and the young man she'd come to love like a brother. "Now, Jason, it will be all right. I doubt the children will leave you alone, but feel free to tell them to shut their traps. That's up to you. Now, it's April the fourth. It will take you two weeks to get home. We will come to England to visit you in August. What do you think of that, James? Can we get away then?"

James nodded. "August it is. Funny how both your twin and I share the same name."

Jason nodded. "It made me feel quite odd for a good six months saying my brother's name to another man's face." He searched both their faces now, faces that had become so dear to him over the years. "I don't know if I've really told you how very much you mean to me, you and the children. I am of no blood relation to you, but you didn't hesitate to make me part of your family, to teach me. And you, Jessie, to beat the dirt off my heels in racing, laughing merrily all the while, no concern at all to the continued bruising of my fragile male self."

"That's because James has the biggest fragile male self in all of Baltimore, and yours is paltry in comparison."

James said, "We won't talk about huge female selves. Now, Jason, you became part of the family very quickly, but the rest of that is nonsense. Everything we had to teach you, you learned in the first year. You are magic with horses, they respond to you on an almost human level. It's as if they know you're there for them, that you will do whatever they need." James shrugged. "It's difficult to put into words, but I know any horse racing or breeding you do in England will be a success."

Jason stared at him, nonplussed.

"That's right, Jason," Jessie said. "Now, when you go back, where do you plan to settle?"

"Near Eastbourne, near my father's home, Northcliffe Hall. Since my father forced my grandmother to move into the Dower House five years ago, James and Corrie and their twins stayed on at Northcliffe." He paused a moment, gave James a crooked smile. "So that you will understand why my grandmother's absence from the great house made such a difference, let me say that knowing your mother, James, has made me feel like I never left my grandmother. Undoubtedly my grandmother's removal was an unadulterated blessing. She was very unpleasant to my mother and to Corrie."

"Oh dear," Jessie said with some awe. "Your grandmother is like my mother-in-law?"

"Yes, but she never tried to be subtle like Wilhelmina. She was always a hammer, went after her victims with a good deal of enthusiasm."

Jessie said matter-of-factly, "We are very grateful we only have to see her once a week. She's always hated me, as if you didn't guess that immediately, Jason. She says these horrible things, all thinly disguised to sound innocuous. Sometimes I just wish she'd shoot it all out, like your grandmother evidently does."

James laughed. "Actually, you'd have to be a blockhead not to understand that you're being insulted down to your toes."

Jason said, "Like Wilhelmina, my grandmother hates every woman in the family. The only female she isn't rude to is my aunt Melissande." He paused a moment. "I desperately want to see my parents again. I want to see my brother and Corrie, and my nephews. And the funny thing is that it just came upon me early this morning—"

Jessie's right eyebrow went straight up. "Before or after you left Lucinda's house?"

"Before, actually," Jason said, his voice and expression suddenly smooth and austere. "She was rather surprised when I bounded out of bed like Satan was on my heels."

"We will miss you, Jason," Jessie said as she took her husband's hand. "But we'll all be together again in August. Not long at all."

She smiled up at her husband, blinked back tears, then walked into Jason's arms. "I always wished I had a brother and God finally gave me one."

"He gave me a brother too," James Wyndham said. "One with honor, immense goodwill, and a brain. Whatever happened all those years ago, Jase, it's time to let it go."

Jason didn't say a word.

James quickly added, realizing that Jason wasn't yet ready to let anything go, "I just wish you weren't so bloody handsome."

Jessie leaned back in Jason's arms, laughing. "It's true, all the females between the ages of fifteen and one hundred follow you, Jason. Don't even try to deny it. You would not believe how many ladies have cornered me, every word out of their mouths about you. Oh yes, they all want to be my best friends and visit me." She turned to her husband. "As I said at breakfast, Jason is first, then Alec Carrick. Hmm, I wonder what Alec thinks about that."

Jason said on a sigh, "I wish you would believe me that Alec, like me, thinks it's a bloody nuisance. Who cares about a face anyway?"

That was so stupid, Jessie didn't say anything.

Jason paused, then hugged Jessie again. "The thing is, I always wanted a sister. And do you know what? You have hair just as red as my mother's, and though your eyes are green and hers are blue, there is a great resemblance between you. She's the most beautiful woman I know." Jason touched his hand to her fiery red hair, a thick braided rope falling halfway down her back. "If, that is, beautiful faces make any difference at all." He paused a moment, and his eyes darkened. "Thank you. Thank you both so very much for bringing me back to life."

CHAPTER 2

❧⋅❧

Northcliffe Hall
Near Eastbourne, Southern England

❧ Jason guided Dodger toward the Dower House at the end of the lane. It was a good three hundred feet from Northcliffe Hall, far enough away, Corrie had written, so that his grandmother couldn't flounce in, wreak havoc, and flounce out, grinning with her few remaining teeth. His grandmother was an amazing eighty years old, even older than Hollis. He wanted to see her, hug her, and thank the Lord she was still here to be nasty. Perhaps great quantities of vinegar kept a person healthy.

His father had written just prior to Jason's departure from Baltimore that Hollis still had a surfeit of both hair and teeth. Jason was simply grateful that Hollis, like his grandmother, was still alive.

Jason tethered Dodger, who was so happy to be

home that he couldn't stop tossing his head and sniffing the air. Jason hugged his neck, and the horse whinnied. He'd withstood the two-week voyage well. "You, old man, have more heart and fortitude than any other horse in the world." He looked at the ivy-covered Queen Anne–style house and the beautiful garden surrounding it, which he knew was probably tended by his mother. The windows sparkled in the mid-afternoon sunlight, and there was an air of contentment about the place. He wondered if his grandmother had ever breathed a word of thanks. He doubted it.

He smiled when he hit the brass knocker against the thick oak door.

He couldn't believe it when Hollis opened the front door. The old man stared at him, clutched his chest, and whispered, "Oh dear, is it really you, Master Jason? After all these years, is it really you? Oh my dear boy, oh my precious boy, you're finally home." Hollis threw himself into Jason's arms.

Hollis was so much smaller, Jason realized with shock, holding the old man as gently as he could. He'd known Hollis his entire life; indeed, his father had known him nearly all his life as well. Hollis had strength in those old thin arms of his, thank God.

He breathed in the old man's scent, the same scent as it had been all twenty-nine of his years on this earth, a mixture of lemons and honey wax, and said, "Ah, Hollis, I have missed you. I received your weekly letters, just like from my brother and from my mother and father. Corrie too. I'm sorry it took me so very long to begin to really answer them, but—"

The old man cupped Jason's face in his hands. "It's all right. You will not feel guilty about it, you will not apologize. You've been answering my letters for three years now. That was enough."

Jason felt guilt rip at his throat, but he saw such love and understanding in Hollis's wise old eyes that he nodded instead of throwing himself at Hollis's feet. "Do you know Corrie has been penning letters from my nephews?" He drew in a big breath, then hugged the old man again. "I'm home, Hollis, I'm home now, for good."

"Hollis! What is this? Who is here? I allow you to bring me nutty buns when you take your afternoon constitutional, but look what you've done—you've let someone follow you. You're handing over my nutty buns to some riffraff, aren't you, Hollis? What absolute gall."

Jason recognized that sour old voice. "Some things never change." He grinned as Hollis stepped back, rolled eyes that held both infinite acceptance and a great deal of amusement, and called out, "Madam, your grandson is here, not to steal your nutty buns, he assures me, but to visit you."

"James is here? Why on earth is James here? That wife of his tries to keep him away, I know she does. She's a disgrace, that silly girl, like her mother-in-law, that hussy who's married to my Douglas and refuses to look old like she's supposed to."

Jason looked up to see his grandmother walking slowly and carefully toward the front door, using a highly polished cane with a lovely hummingbird knob. He could see her pink scalp through her snow-white hair, all done up in tightly crimped little curls.

"It's not James, Grandmother. It's me." Jason walked to the old woman whose eyes still shone brightly with both intelligence and malice.

She stopped dead in her tracks and stared at him. "Jason — You're not James pretending to be Jason, are you? I haven't lost my final wit, have I? Is it really you?"

"Yes, it is." He strode quickly to her because she looked to be weaving a bit with shock. He took her very gently into his arms, realized she was even more frail than Hollis. Her old bones felt as if they could easily snap in a strong wind. He felt her dry seamed mouth kiss his neck, then he drew back, and looked down into his grandmother's face, lines scored around her mouth, downward, naturally, since she was always berating everyone around her, never smiling. To his immense pleasure, that seamed old mouth parted in a smile. She kept smiling as she patted his face. "My beautiful Jason," she said, and she kissed his neck again. Her look was suddenly searching as she said in the gentlest voice he'd ever heard from her in his life, "You've forgiven yourself, boy?"

He looked down at that cantankerous old face, and instead of vinegar all he saw was a wealth of concern and love, and it was for him. He couldn't take it in, no more than he could begin to explain why he'd wanted to stop here first, to see her. He'd received two letters from her a year, one near his birthday and one near Christmas.

"You told your father and your brother not to come see you," she said, still patting his cheek. "And then you wrote only niggardly excuses for letters for a very long time."

"I wasn't ready."

"Answer me, Jason. Have you forgiven yourself?"

"Forgiven myself?"

"Yes, that's it exactly. For some reason no one can fathom, except for James, who claimed he understood even as he knew you were dead wrong, you blamed yourself for what happened. It's nonsense, of course. It's probably an excuse for immense self-pity since you're a man, and the good Lord knows that men love to wallow in self-pity, lap it up like cats do milk. Do it so that the women who have the misfortune to love them will spend endless amounts of time to reassure them and to stroke their brows—"

"—and pour tea down their gullets and overlook their indiscretions," Hollis said. "I believe I've learned the litany."

"Ha! You are a great deal too smart, Hollis," the old woman said, and tried to hit him with her cane.

Now this was more like the grandmother Jason remembered. He gave her a huge grin. "Do you have any brandy to pour down my gullet, Grandmother?"

"Yes, but I daresay you'd rather have one of my nutty buns. You were riding by, weren't you, and you smelled them wafting out the window, although the windows are supposed to be shut tight to keep out the noxious vapors."

"Actually," Jason said, "I didn't smell the nutty buns. I haven't smelled a nutty bun in five years. I came because I wanted to see you. Er, may I have a nutty bun now that I'm here and the nutty buns are here as well?"

She actually took several moments to weigh this— he could see it in her bright old eyes.

She yelled, "Hollis, you old stick, bring the nutty buns to the drawing room! Yes, my boy, I've decided that if there are at least a half-dozen, then yes, you may have one too. Hollis, your bony old self was just here. Where have you gone now? Are you doddering somewhere? Trying to stuff a nutty bun down your gullet? I'll wager you are since you think I'll not say anything since my precious boy is finally home." Her grin was bright with spite as she spoke.

The grin fell away as she looked back up at Jason. "So you don't wish to answer me, do you? That's all right for now. Perhaps it's too soon for you to realize what's in your heart."

Hollis, who had just entered the hall carrying the brandy, was having trouble believing his eyes. His mistress was treating Jason with more affection than she'd ever treated anyone in her entire life. He'd heard what she'd said, and was outraged. "You will allow Master Jason to eat one of your nutty buns, madam? You have never before offered me a nutty bun."

The dowager countess looked him up and down. "I have always counted the nutty buns you bring me, knowing that it's always supposed to be half a dozen, but there rarely are. I know you many times filch one for yourself. Don't try to deny it, Hollis." The old lady finally nodded, a curl of silver hair falling over her forehead. "Very well, Hollis, I will not berate you today. Look at your face—it's begun to look like a starving monk's, more than you did just last week when you deigned to come visit me with one nutty bun missing from that lovely covered plate. Hmm. You may also have a nutty bun, but get them now or I will rescind my offer." The old woman released Jason, tapped her cane a couple of times, a prelude, Jason thought, to her tottering off to the drawing room.

Jason watched Hollis, stately and tall, those old shoulders as square as they'd been when Jason had left, walk down the hallway into the nether regions of the house to get the nutty buns. He heard him muttering how miracles did happen, that it appeared he would have one of the dowager's nutty buns before he croaked it. Jason wondered if Hollis realized that two maids were hovering just beyond the staircase, ready for any assistance should he require it, asked or unasked for.

Jason said grandly, "Grandmother, may I offer you my arm?"

"Certainly, my boy. It has to be better than hanging on to Hollis. That old man is as weedy as a dormouse."

CHAPTER 3

❧✦❧

Northcliffe Hall

❧ Silence hung heavy in the drawing room that evening. Tension swirled in the air, thick with bone-deep concern, unspoken worries, and unasked questions. Then Corrie appeared in the doorway carrying a freshly scrubbed twin under each arm, their beautiful small faces alight with excitement and shock because it was so very late and they weren't in their beds, Nanny snoring not six feet away from them.

"Uncle Jason, it's us again!" Douglas Simon Sherbrooke, older than his twin by exactly eleven minutes, broke free of his mother and ran as fast as his legs could carry him to Jason, who caught the little boy when he leapt into the air in his general direction.

"I see that it is," Jason said, nuzzling Douglas's neck. He smelled just like Alice Wyndham, after her evening bath. He felt tears well up. He looked down to see Everett Plessante Sherbrooke tugging at his trouser leg, ready to yell or burst into tears, Jason couldn't tell which. He scooped up the little boy and held both of them close, letting them pat his face, give him wet kisses and talk nonstop, words that weren't really words but rather twin-talk bursting out of those small mouths, just like the incomprehensible language he and James had shared.

Douglas drew back and said, "Everyone said you looked just like Papa and Aunt Melissande, but you don't, Uncle Jason."

"That's true, Douglas. I don't look exactly like your papa, but it's close, don't you think, Everett?"

The other impossibly beautiful little face scrunched up in thought. Everett then announced, "No, Uncle Jason, you look like yourself, and you look like me too. Not Douglas—he looks like Papa. Yes, that's it, you look like me." And that little face wore the same wicked look Jason had seen on his mother Corrie's face.

Douglas said, after another wet kiss on the right side of his uncle Jason's neck, "Grandpapa can't stand that I look like Papa and Aunt Melissande. She always brings Everett and me little almond cookies when she visits. Grandpapa says blessed hell, he'll never be free of *The Face*. What's *The Face*, Uncle Jason?"

Jason heard his father groan, his mother laugh. He turned to his father, brow raised. "Cursing, in front of this little scamp?"

"He's got ears as sharp as you and James had when

you were his age," Douglas Sherbrooke, the earl of Northcliffe said, and poked his wife in her ribs. "Be quiet, Alex. I don't believe a lad can be too young to learn of the Sherbrooke curse."

"I agree," Corrie said. "No, don't you dare disagree with me, James Sherbrooke. Blessed hell is always your prelude when you're ready to cut loose." She grinned over at Jason. "He gets mad at me—only the good Lord could possibly understand why—and I know he wants to throw me out a window, but he has to make do with blessed hell and stomp out of the room."

"A monstrous lie," James said, then loudly cleared his throat when his two little boys turned wide eyes to him. "Jason, do you want me to liberate you from at least one of those imps?"

Both imps wrapped their arms more tightly around Jason's neck, nearly choking him. Jason shook his head. "Not yet. All right, lads, can we settle ourselves down for a moment or do you want me to dance you around the drawing room? Your grandmama can play a waltz on the piano, if you like."

"Let's dance!" Douglas shouted, his feet kicking out.

"I want to waltz too," Everett shouted in Jason's other ear. "What's waltz?"

There was laughter in the air now, the awful deadening stress and anxiety swept under the carpet, at least for the time being. To Jason, it felt wonderful. He began to waltz slowly about the drawing room, tightening his hold on the squirming little bodies, kissing their ears and their chins, and watched his mother pick up her skirts and walk quickly to the piano where she soon was playing a waltz he'd heard at a ball in Baltimore some two months before.

James Sherbrooke, Lord Hammersmith, twenty-eight minutes older than his twin, sat back, aware of his smiling wife's warm self now pressed close to his right side, and looked toward his brother. He wasn't surprised Jason looked as natural as could be waltzing around with two small boys in his arms, since James Wyndham had often written about how well Jason handled his own four children. He wondered if James Wyndham had ever told Jason about all the letters he himself had written here to Northcliffe Hall, at first to reassure all of them, then later detailing Jason's successes on the racetrack, the mares he'd selected for James's breeding program, the wonderful stallion he'd found for his host that had made him a bloody fortune in stud fees.

But all the letters didn't make up for the lost years. He felt his heart fill to bursting. At least his twin had finally begun acknowledging all of them after two years of perfunctory, emotionless letters.

Little Douglas was right; they were no longer identical. Well, they were, objectively, but anyone who knew the both of them wouldn't confuse them anymore. Jason was more—what was the word? More spare, maybe that was it, though they were still of a size. The big changes were on the inside. James could see the suffering deep in his twin's eyes, and it hurt him, even as he understood it.

They'd never been identical on the inside, but they'd been connected, had known what the other worried about, what the other was feeling at any given moment. Their experiences had made them into vastly different men, the advanced age of thirty not all that far distant. He looked toward his smiling father, nearly sixty, his black and silver hair still thick, as he was always pointing out to his wife.

James saw that Hollis was stationed near the drawing room door, his foot tapping to the beat of the waltz. He was smiling, and there was such love and relief in that smile that James felt warmed to his soul. He knew how Hollis felt.

Now James had to find out what was in his twin's mind. But not tonight. His precious, loud, and demanding little boys had saved the evening from being a silent torture, everyone afraid to say anything that could be taken the wrong way, everyone walking on eggshells around Jason. He said to Corrie, "Have I told you recently that you are very smart indeed?"

"Not since last May, I believe it was."

He rubbed his knuckles on her cheek. "You brought Douglas and Everett into nail-biting silence and look what happened. Jason is waltzing with them."

"It seemed the thing to do," she said.

James took Corrie's hand in his. He leaned back, and allowed the warmth of the laughter to flow through him.

Jason was home. At last he was home and that was all that mattered.

CHAPTER 4

❧❧

❧ The two brothers stood side-by-side on the cliff overlooking the Poe Valley.

The silence between them was awkward. James finally said, "We spent so many hours here as boys. Remember the time you hurled my book on Huygens off the cliff, you were so mad at me?"

"I remember throwing the book over the side, laughing when the wind caught it and sent it even farther away, but I don't remember why I was mad."

James laughed. "I don't either."

"I do remember you and Corrie lying on your backs on this hill on clear evenings, staring up at the stars."

"We still do that. The boys have heard me talking about the Astrological Society, listened to me whine about how my telescope doesn't magnify enough.

Unfortunately, now they're demanding to come with their mother and me. Can you imagine? Two three-year-olds holding still for longer than thirty seconds?"

Jason said, smiling, "No, it won't happen. Alice Wyndham, James and Jessie's four-year-old, would be looking up at the stars while sucking her thumb, loudly, and be demanding an apple tart in the next breath. But it won't be long at all before the four of you are stretched out like logs on the hearth looking at the heavens."

They fell silent. Then James couldn't stand it any longer. He grabbed his brother, held on tight. "By God, I've missed you. It's like part of myself simply disappeared. I couldn't bear it, Jason."

Jason held himself stiff, utterly rigid—for about three seconds. Then he saw James's utter relief that he, Jason, who'd nearly cost him his life, was back again. His generosity astounded Jason. Jason couldn't help himself; he pulled away. He felt self-conscious, clumsy, and so very sorry that he wished for the thousandth time that what had happened could be undone, but of course it couldn't. Nothing could ever be changed once it happened. He said, voice thick, "Forgive me, James, it's still difficult for me. I'm so very sorry for what happened. Your acceptance of me now is so very like you."

"Don't you understand? I never *didn't* accept you. I never blamed you, nor did anyone else."

Jason waved that away. "The truth is the truth. You knew I couldn't stay here, not after what I did."

James accepted the rebuff though it hurt him to his soul. "I knew how you felt and I did understand, but I still couldn't bear it. Neither could Mother and Father. It's been difficult without you, Jase." He paused a moment, drew himself together, and stared out over the green Poe Valley. "You're staying home now?"

"Yes. I'll be looking for my own property. I want to own and operate my own stud farm."

James felt a surge of pride. He wanted to tell Jason that James Wyndham had written that Jason was magic with horses, that he would soon be one of the premier breeders in England. He asked, trying his best to sound nonchalant, "Where are you interested in buying?"

"Why, near here of course."

James nearly whooped aloud. He let himself breathe again. He gave his brother a fat smile. "You'll not believe this, Jase, but old Squire Hoverton—remember, we called him the Old Squid, because he always had a hand to catch you no matter how many *thieving little varmints* there were in his apple orchard? Well, he died. You remember his son, Thomas, don't you? He and his father were constantly arguing about the money the squire spent?"

"Yes, I remember. I also remember wanting to throw Thomas in a ditch. What a fool he was."

"He's still a fool. He's wanted to sell out since the minute after his father's funeral. There have been no buyers because Thomas is asking too much, probably because he owes an immense amount to his creditors. I've heard that he gambles at every hell in London."

Jason nodded. "Fortunately Squire Hoverton spent a great deal of money modernizing the stables, the paddocks, and the stalls."

James said, "The house is probably moldering on its foundation, but who cares? Well, a wife would care, but since you're not married, it doesn't matter. What you're interested in is the condition of the stables and stalls, the health of the land itself, and the beech and pine forests. I'm not sure of the acreage, but a thousand acres comes to mind. We'll ask."

Jason couldn't contain his excitement. "What good fortune indeed. Bless the kind Lord for letting such blighters as Thomas appear occasionally. Let's go now, James, let's go see it."

Thirty minutes later, the twins pulled Bad Boy and Dodger into the lane leading to Lyon's Gate, once one of the premier stud farms in southern England. Jason said, "I remember Thomas was a bully, and that's always a disguise for weakness."

"I agree. Thomas must be in desperate need of money by now. I'll wager you'll be able to buy the property at an excellent price. Father's solicitor can deal with it for you if you decide you want it."

"Wily William Bibber?"

"Yes, old Wily Willy is still working his magic. Father says he's like Hollis—he'll probably be dead six months before he stops working. Now, Thomas immediately sold off all the horses. I wouldn't be surprised if he sold off all the furniture in the house, and all the tack as well. His creditors probably made him sell the silver. But look at the stables, Jason, they look solid even from here—some paint, some horses, new equipment, some excellent grooms, good care and management, and—" James shut up. He didn't want to overdo. His blood was surging in his veins. He was praying hard now.

Jason said, looking about, "It doesn't look all that bad, does it, given that it's been sitting here abandoned for what? Over a year, you said?"

"Nearly two years now."

"Thomas is indeed a wastrel and I'm grateful for it," Jason said in a voice so filled with excitement, James wanted to sing.

Jason pulled Dodger up in front of the neat redbrick Georgian home, ivy hanging off in clumps, dead bushes surrounding it, glass from broken windows scattered on the barren ground. "I can see Mother rubbing her hands together, picturing how everything will look when she's finished, ordering around a dozen gardeners, all of them staggering around with buckets of plants."

"Think of the flowers," James said. "She'll have more color cascading out of the flower beds than you can imagine."

Jason rubbed his own hands together. "I hope there's a retainer here to show us about."

"Probably not. I'll wager the front door isn't even locked. We'll show ourselves around."

The house was indeed moldering on its foundation.

Jason doubted it had been touched after Squire Hoverton's wife had died trying to birth her sixth child somewhere around the first part of the century. Such a pity that only Thomas had survived. The house was filled with shadows and smelled of damp. Tattered draperies hung askew over long dirty or broken windows.

"The floors look solid," James said.

"Let's see how bad it is upstairs," Jason said. "Then we can visit the stables."

It was bad, more dank gloom and dirt.

"Lots of white paint should take care of things, Jason, don't you think?"

"Oh aye, at least a half a dozen cans of white paint. Let's get out of here, James, it's depressing."

James buffeted him on the shoulder. "The price has just gone down a good bit."

There were four different paddocks, each fenced with solid oak planks, some needing repair, all needing paint. But the size of the paddocks was perfect and the holding paddock gave directly into the huge main stable. There were a total of three stables, all desperately in need of paint as well, but until two years ago, they'd been prime, and Jason could see that all of them were quite modern. The empty tack room was nicely proportioned, with a goodly sized area set aside for a head groom to work close to the horses. There were half a dozen small rooms for the stable lads.

"It reminds me of James Wyndham's main stable," Jason said.

There were twenty stalls, ten to a side, in the big main light-filled stable, a wide aisle between them. Beautifully built. Moldy hay and equipment parts were strewn on the floor. Jason stood there, right in the middle, sucking in great gulps of air.

"If I close my eyes I can see the horses' heads bobbing over the stall doors, hear them neighing when they know oats are coming. Plenty of breeding and birthing stalls. It's perfect." Jason jumped up and clicked his heels together.

At that moment both Bad Boy and Dodger let out loud whinnies.

"What's this?" James said and strode to the stable's double-door entrance.

A large raw-boned chestnut stallion was pawing the ground, looking at Bad Boy and Dodger, head thrown back, nostrils flared, ready to take on both of them.

A girl's voice called out, "Who are you and what the devil are you doing here?"

CHAPTER 5

⁂

James and Jason Sherbrooke stared from the huge bay stallion, who looked like he chewed nails for breakfast, to the girl astride him, dressed in trousers, a dusty leather vest, full-sleeved white shirt, and an old hat pulled down over her head.

"Blessed hell," James said. "It's Corrie five years ago, down to the fat braid hanging down her back."

Jason said slowly, never looking away from her face, "You look familiar. Do I know you?"

"Of course you know me, you dolt."

Jason's eyebrow arched a good inch.

She pulled off the cap. Tendrils of golden hair had pulled free of the braid and hung in lazy curls down the sides of her face.

"You do look familiar," he said again. "Oh yes,

whoever you are, forgive my ill manners, this is my brother, James Sherbrooke, Lord Hammersmith."

"My lord." Hallie stuffed her hat back down on her head, but didn't give him her name. "I had heard you were twins, identical in every way. But that isn't true. Let me say, my lord, that you most certainly appear the more acceptable twin. You don't really look like this other one at all. Did you know that he would strut down the streets in Baltimore, knowing that every female between the ages of eight and ninety-two would stop and stare at him, dropping fans, parasols, umbrellas, even in the rain, to get his attention?"

James, enjoying this unusual girl who was making his twin feel like a fool said easily, "Ma'am, a pleasure. No, I didn't know this about my twin. To the best of my memory I haven't ever seen him strut. I shall ask him for a demonstration."

Hallie said, "Ladies would lurk in doorways, waiting for him to pass by. They'd throw a handkerchief or a reticule or their little sister in his path to gain his attention. You haven't seen him strut? No wonder, since he ran away from home five years ago, you haven't had the opportunity to witness the strut in all its glory. Conceited oaf."

When Jason didn't respond to this face-smacking, she went on, "I understand you're going to be thirty years old next year. Thus it takes your brain longer to function properly. Or is it that your eyesight is already faulty?"

Jason was more amused than not. He was used to

insults after living with Jessie Wyndham for five years, so he didn't leap on her. He knew he should recognize her, but he simply didn't. Obviously this was an insult of major proportions to her, but there was nothing he could do about it. He shook his head, still looking at her horse, who appeared quite ready to take a bite out of Bad Boy's flank. "You'd best pull that beast back before my Dodger breaks his neck."

"Ha, I'd like to see that." Still, she forced Charlemagne back, one unwilling step at a time. It took skill to make the horse obey. Jason gave her silent credit for it. Who the devil was she? That golden hair of hers was spectacular, certainly he should remember a girl with hair that color.

"I do admire Dodger though. He's a fine racer. Did you ever manage to beat Jessie Wyndham riding him?"

So she'd seen him race, had she? Even though she sounded British, she'd obviously lived in Baltimore.

"No horse stood a chance against Dodger. As for Jessie, that's another matter. If you were more familiar with Baltimore horse racing, you'd know Dodger was the best, most of the time."

Her mouth was opening when James said, "You're an American? But you sound like a Brit. Why?"

"I am English actually. My family lives here half the year and the other half in Baltimore. However, four years ago my parents sent me back here to live year round to get me polished up."

"When will the polishing begin?" Jason said, looking at her from head to toe.

"I've heard it said that cleverness is in the eye of the beholder, and I must say that I'm not seeing much of anything."

"Then how could you see me strut if your eyesight is so bad?"

She tossed her head and nearly lost her hat. "Another pathetic attempt at a clever remark. I live with my uncle and aunt at Ravensworth Abbey. They provide a marvelous home for me when my parents aren't here."

James said, "Burke and Arielle Drummond, the earl and countess of Ravensworth? You're their niece?"

"Yes. My mother was the countess's sister. She died when I was born."

Jason said, "I'm sorry about that."

"But what are you doing here?" James said. "Here, as on the Hoverton property?"

The chin went up, as if she expected sarcasm, argument, a fight even. Jason couldn't wait to see what would come out of her mouth. She said, "I will be twenty-one in December. I am an adult. I love horses."

Jason said slowly, "I remember you now. It was a long time ago, just after I'd arrived in Baltimore. You were that skinny little girl who was forever hanging around the racetracks. There was someone always trying to find you. Jessie brought you home a couple of times, but you stayed with the children. Then I didn't see you anymore. Ah, yes, I remember Jessie saying that you'd come to England to live. You're Hallie Carrick. I came home on one of your father's steamships,

The Bold Venture. Yes, I remember. Your father went to America some fifteen years ago to buy a shipyard and ended up marrying the owner's daughter."

"Yes, that's what happened. I was in Baltimore three years ago, but I believe you and James Wyndham were in New York, buying horses."

She had an astounding memory for his brother's whereabouts, James thought, staring at her. Why?

"Allow me to correct you. My father and Genny— my stepmother—run the Carrick Shipping Line together now. I believe Genny built *The Bold Venture*."

James arched an eyebrow at that. "Really? That is very impressive. Very well, then, Miss Carrick, what are you doing here? By here, I mean Lyon's Gate."

"That's easy to answer. I intend to buy Lyon's Gate. You are very nearly on my property. What are you two doing here?"

Jason came to instant attention. He stood appalled, disbelieving, staring at this absurd girl who had the golden hair of a princess and had suddenly become the enemy. "What do you mean, you intend to buy Lyon's Gate?"

She shot a look at James, who was standing with his back against the stable door, arms crossed over his chest. "Is your brother hard of hearing?"

"No," James said. "He is merely astounded. You're a girl. You shouldn't even be here alone, much less garbed in clothes many stable lads would despise."

"That has nothing to do with anything, and you know it. Unlike my stepmother and father, I have no interest in either shipbuilding or running ships across the Atlantic or down to the Caribbean." She turned to Jason. "If you had paid any attention at all to that skinny little girl—to me—you would have realized that I was more horse-mad than you are, Jason Sherbrooke. Of course, even five years ago, you were a grown man with every woman in Baltimore after you. What was I but a fifteen-year-old skinny rope of a girl who paid you no attention at all?"

Suddenly she grinned, showing lovely white teeth and a smile so beautiful it should have made the sun burst through the overhanging clouds. "Yes, I was shy, and thinner than a windowpane. Tell me, did Lucinda Frothingale, who's never been any of those things in her entire life, ever get you into her bed? Did Horace try to bite you?"

"Do you mind telling me what you know of Lucinda Frothingale?"

"I get letters from my siblings and my parents. Genny occasionally tells me which ladies manage to snag you, if but for a little while, since you're fickle. Well? Did Lucinda finally manage to get a hook in your mouth?" She tossed him another impudent grin, and with that grin, he suddenly saw her father's face. He waved away her words. It was hard to tell if she had his astounding male beauty, but pull a gown over her head, scrub her face, and he would wager she'd be a stunner, a lady to stop the male population of London in its collective tracks.

She said, a wealth of disappointment in her voice,

"I suppose you won't speak of Lucinda. It wouldn't be gentlemanly, even though—"

"It's best you don't finish that thought, Miss Carrick. I believe I can see your father in you now."

"Glory be," she said and rolled her eyes. "But you might as well be honest, Mr. Sherbrooke. My father is the most beautiful man ever born, to my mind more beautiful than you two. As for myself, I gave it up years ago."

James said, fascinated, "Gave what up?"

"Thinking I would ever have even a dollop of the beauty he has."

Jason said, "I suppose you could take off that ridiculous hat again, then we could see."

She didn't say a word, but her horse snorted.

Fact was, Jason thought, she could have looked like an old crone and it wouldn't have mattered. He said, "I'm buying Lyon's Gate, Miss Carrick, not you. It seems to me you'd be better off buying something closer to home. Where is your father's estate?"

"Carrick Grange is in Northumberland. It isn't particularly good horse country."

"Fine, then buy something close to Ravensworth. How about some property in America, near Baltimore? You could race Jessie Wyndham."

"No, it's Lyon's Gate for me. Get used to the idea, Mr. Sherbrooke. It's mine."

James felt his brother stiffen beside him, and since he knew Jason as well as he knew himself, and he knew bloodshed was close, he said before Jason could leap on her, "Do you have step-siblings, Miss Carrick?"

She nodded and shoved her old hat so low on her head, she nearly covered her eyes. "Yes, I have three stepbrothers and one stepsister, the youngest. We're a large family, as the dolt here could tell you if he ever applied his brain to anything other than getting women into bed, and racing horses."

Jason looked ready to leap, James thought, followed by throwing her into the dead flower bed. He said rather loudly, "Then there are step-siblings who will carry on the Carrick shipping tradition?"

"You are certainly nosy, my lord."

"He's trying to keep me from pulling you off that brute's back and throwing you in that horse trough, Miss Carrick."

"It's empty."

"Yes, I know."

"You just try it, Jason Sherbrooke. Charlemagne would pound his hooves into your belly."

James cleared his throat. "I believe you were going to tell me about your step-siblings, Miss Carrick."

"Very well. Go ahead and protect him. He probably needs it. He is on the puny side, isn't he?" Since both men looked at her like she was a moron, which maybe she was in this particular instance, Hallie gave it up. "Very well, my father and mother are building very few sailing vessels now. It's all steamships, and that is a very different thing indeed. Can you imagine, it takes only two weeks to voyage from Baltimore to Portsmouth on a steamship? It was closer to six weeks when I was a little girl."

"Progress is everywhere," James said to his twin. "There are gaslights in most all the public buildings in London now."

"London is behind. Gaslights are simply *everywhere* in Baltimore, my father tells me," Hallie said. Since all she got for that remark was a raised eyebrow from James, she continued. "If you must know, my lord, I have one stepbrother, Dev, only thirteen, but I know he will be a very accomplished shipbuilder by the time he's twenty. My oldest stepbrother, Carson, will run the company one day, and my youngest stepbrother, Eric, is only ten but still, he's sailing mad. My sister, Louisa, wants to write novels. However, she's only nine years old, a bit early to know if her stories will improve."

Jason said. "I know your step-siblings. They are friends with the Wyndham children. Whenever I was close by, Louisa would spin a tale for me. She always told me she wanted me to be the hero of all her novels, and that there would be at least one hundred since she planned to write until she croaks over her quill at the turn of the century. She'll have me perform deeds of derring-do and rescue ladies from villains, starting with her, she hopes, when she grows up."

Hallie rolled her yes. "Louisa doesn't know any villains. The thought of my father letting a villain get near her is about as likely as a week passing in England without rain."

"A novelist, Louisa has given me to understand, can spin villains out of red yarn if she wishes to."

She looked him up and down. "I must write Louisa about losing her perspective over a pretty face, wide shoulders, and a flat belly."

CHAPTER 6

꘎꘎

꘎ "I thought I was a dolt."

Not even a second passed before she said, "That's true enough, but Louisa is small for her age and simply doesn't recognize it as yet."

Jason laughed at that quick, clean shot, and smiled, thinking of Jessie Wyndham.

Hallie felt a glow in her own belly at that laugh and smile. "I'm the only one in the family who prefers four-legged transportation to rudders and wood. I sailed all my life until I came to live year-round in England. Let me tell you, I've run my uncle's stables for two years now. It's time I went out on my own, that's what my uncle finally told me since I was tired of waltzing with chinless young men and lecherous old men who wanted to stare down my gown."

Jason said, "Ha. Did you get your uncle drunk?"

"There was no need to. I had his sons tell him it was time. I'm not stupid. I got them on my side two years ago."

"I should have known. Given that they're young and impressionable, they were easy targets." Jason turned to his brother. "This is the typical behavior of an American female, James. Yes, yes, I know you're English, but you were raised in America for much of the time, and that's what counts."

"That's not true. I spent my first five years traveling the world with my father."

Jason ignored her. "James, American girls plot and scheme and simper and wheedle, all with equal facility. They are a scary lot, particularly those with a modicum of intellect and a pocket full of groats. In Miss Carrick's case, evidently her father has allowed her to dip deep into his pockets. Did I forget to mention spoiled? Another American female trait. Hopefully she isn't instructing our English girls on how to—" He stalled, Judith's face so clear in his brain that he wanted to pound his head with a rock to get her out.

"Trust me, Mr. Sherbrooke, your English girls don't need any assistance from me. The way they can freeze you in place with only a raised eyebrow—" She shuddered. "They are very much in control, your English girls."

James, who had seen the sudden pallor on his twin's face, wanted to tell him not to think about the girl who'd betrayed him, who'd betrayed all of them, but he knew he couldn't. He said, all bland and easy, "So all the gentlemen in London bored you, Miss Carrick?"

"Yes, they bored me senseless, my lord. I told my uncle that I had no intention of marrying, no intention of returning to America or moving in permanently into Carrick Grange, and that announcement helped spur him toward agreement to my buying my own property. Naturally he hied himself off to his study to write my father, but my father won't interfere."

"I can see why your uncle would resign himself," Jason said. "Since you haven't managed to find yourself a husband and are well on your way to your dotage, he doesn't want you hanging about Ravensworth. How many seasons have you had? Five? Six? Of course if your father is providing a big dowry, it wouldn't matter if you were sixty, without a tooth in your mouth. Some fool would be on his knees begging you to make him the happiest of men."

"Not so far into my dotage as you are, Mr. Sherbrooke. May I ask why you bothered to come home? I heard you were content to live with James and Jessie Wyndham and raise their children."

"Didn't you say I only thought about sleeping with women and racing?"

"That too." She frowned as she patted her horse's neck, keeping him calm. Charlemagne loved to fight or gallop with the wind, he didn't care which. She knew he was keeping a hopeful eye on the two Sherbrooke horses, hoping she'd let him go kick them into the fodder bin. She let him rear up on his back legs, fling his great head from side to side, and give a very fine show.

"See to your horse, Miss Carrick," Jason said, "else the gentlemen will have to rescue you."

"As if I would ever expect one of your ilk to rescue me." She sneered.

James felt as if he'd been pulled back in time. He burst out laughing, couldn't help himself. It was a Corrie sneer, one she'd perfected more than seven years before and used with flawless timing to make him so angry his eyes crossed. He wondered if his twin would fall for it, turn purple in the face, yank her off her horse, and wallop her butt.

But Jason merely sneered back at her, a sneer more potent than hers. He'd learned that in America? "Listen to me, Miss Carrick," Jason said slowly, as if speaking to the village idiot, "I plan to buy Lyon's Gate. It will be mine. Go away."

"We will see about that, won't we?" Hallie Carrick wheeled Charlemagne about, let him rear up and paw the air one more time. She smiled as he bugled a clear challenge to Bad Boy and Dodger, whose eyes were rolling, on the brink of pulling free of their tethers.

Jason spoke in a low quiet voice and both horses calmed.

"Wait," James said. "Where are you staying? Surely Ravensworth is too far a ride for you today."

"I am staying at the vicarage in Glenclose-on-Rowan with Reverend Tysen Sherbrooke and his wife." She struck a pose. "Why, I do believe they're your aunt and uncle."

Jason stood there, shaking his head back and forth. "No, that isn't possible. Why ever would they have you there? Rory wrote me from Oxford, not above a month ago, so even he's not at home any longer, and there are no spinsters your age—"

"Leo Sherbrooke is marrying a dear friend of mine, Miss Melissa Breckenridge. I'm supporting her to the altar on Saturday, and that's why I'm visiting the vicarage."

"You make it sound like you're going to have to carry her."

"No, Melissa is actually a blithering idiot when it comes to Leo. She'll probably be running, skirts held high, to get to him as fast as she can. I will precede her, strewing rose petals from Mary Rose's garden, all the while praying that Melissa doesn't gallop over me to get to her groom. Whilst I'm strewing, I will marvel at the stupidity of girls giving over all their freedom, not to mention their money, to a man."

"Their father's money," Jason said.

"Jessie Wyndham would surely shoot you if you said that in her hearing. As would my stepmother."

"That's true," Jason said, surprising her. "There are exceptions, albeit very few."

James's eyebrow arched. "I take it you don't care for Leo?"

Jason said, "I think Miss Carrick would like to serve all men up in the same soup, chopped into small pieces."

She gave him a considering sneer. "Very small pieces. However, for a man, Leo isn't all that bad. I wouldn't care to deal with him every day of my life, but I'm not the one who has to marry him. If he follows in his father's footsteps, at least he won't run to fat or lose his teeth, and that's saying something. Perhaps he laughs as much as his father as well. All in all, I suppose I must admit that if one has to be shackled in leg irons, Leo just might be one of the best of the lot."

James said, "Leo is more stubborn than his hound Greybeard. Does your friend know that?"

"I don't know, but I imagine it's too late to tell her now. She wouldn't believe me. Or if she did, she would doubtless believe it charming."

"Greybeard also sleeps with Leo."

"Oh dear, Greybeard is rather large."

"Indeed," said James. "I see conflict on the near horizon."

"Surely Leo would rather sleep with his new wife than his old dog."

"For a while, at least," Jason said, cynicism dripping from his mouth.

James said, "So Leo is all right, as is my uncle Tysen. I assume you also admire your father and uncle?"

"Well, yes, I suppose I must."

James said, "Well, then, it seems to me you can hardly say we're a bad species."

"You have made a good point, my lord, but the fact is, you could be a rotter and I just don't know it yet. But experience with your twin here suggests that a girl—spinster—better tread warily around him or suffer the consequences."

"What consequences?" Jason asked.

He'd stumped her, both James and Jason saw that he'd left her with not a word to fire back. She opened her mouth, closed it. She looked at Jason like she wanted to ride her beast right over him. She finally managed to get out, "To my mind, calling men a species grants them too much importance."

"That was paltry, Miss Carrick," Jason said, a potent sneer on his mouth. "Let me ask you, what man hurt you so badly that you've painted every one of us with your manure-covered brush?"

She froze in the saddle. Jason watched her force herself to ease, force herself back in control. It was amazing how quickly she got hold of herself again. What he'd said had hit close to home. So, there had been a man who'd hurt her. Would she screech at him like a fishwife? What came out of her mouth was, "I found out about this property from your uncle Tysen. He was telling us about Squire Squid and how he'd spent so much money on the stables and paddocks. And Leo chimed in about the son, Thomas, who was a wastrel and a bully, and how he wanted to sell out to pay off all his creditors. Leo brought me here yesterday and I knew the moment I saw the stables I wanted it. He also agreed to escort me here today, but since he is a man, and since today he managed to drag Melissa along, he clearly had other things on his mind. Since Melissa would try to shoot the moon out of the heavens if Leo wanted it, you can be certain that he's hauled her off to some private place in the woods to frolic."

"Frolic?" Jason's eyebrow was up, the sneer sharp. "What a blurry, watery-as-soup word that is, fit only for females who don't like to speak clearly and to the point." An infinitesimal pause, then, "Or they can't be any clearer since they don't know what they're talking about."

James eyed his twin. What was going on here? Well, it had been five years, and Jason had been living in a foreign country. Perhaps men in America insulted women in this fashion?

James cleared his throat, bringing both sets of eyes toward him. "The house is a disaster. Surely you don't wish to be bothered with such a moldering ruin."

"Who cares? It's the stables, the paddocks, this beautiful breeding room and birthing stall that are important. Did you see the tack room? I will be able to work there with my head stable lad."

Jason wanted to tell her he'd shoot her between the eyes before he'd let her buy Lyon's Gate, but instead, he turned to his brother. "Let's go. I intend to buy this property immediately. You, Miss Carrick, are out of luck. Good day, ma'am."

"We'll just see about that, Mr. Sherbrooke," she called over her shoulder as she galloped off down the drive.

"Leo getting married? I can't imagine Leo married," Jason said, laughing.

"I suppose no one mentioned it in their letters to

you. You haven't seen him in five years, Jase. He's as horse-mad as you are, spent the last three years up at Rothermere stud with the Hawksburys."

"Have you met the girl he's going to marry? This Melissa who's mad for him?"

"She's quite charming, really. Very different as girls go, you could say. I hadn't met her friend here, though."

"Even being British by birth, she still acts like an American, more's the pity. That means what I said before—she's brash, overconfident, doesn't know when to back down . . . Well, that's neither here nor there."

"She's very beautiful."

Jason shrugged. "Why isn't Leo trying to buy this property? How old is Leo now?"

"About our age, maybe a bit younger. Actually, Leo has his eye on a stud up near Yorkshire, near Rothermere and his future wife's family. Oh yes, we're all going to the vicarage Saturday for the wedding, spending the night there, which ought to be an experience given that Uncle Ryder is bringing all the Beloved Ones. We'll be piled to the rafters. Oh yes, Uncle Tysen is marrying Leo and Melissa."

Jason had turned to watch Hallie Carrick ride away, that fat braid of hers flopping up and down against her back. She rode well, damn her. Could be she rode as well as Jessie Wyndham.

"I'm leaving for London within the hour. I will have this property. I will see Thomas Hoverton myself.

It will be done before that girl can begin to sort out a plan of action."

James doubled over in laughter. "This is simply too rich. Corrie isn't going to believe this."

He was still laughing when the two of them walked into Northcliffe Hall, Jason's boots pounding up the front staircase to get himself packed and off to London.

Twenty minutes later when Jason was riding down the wide Northcliffe drive, James shouted, "Don't forget to be at the vicarage on Saturday."

Chapter 7

At first Jason didn't recognize her. He heard a light, lovely laugh, and his head turned automatically in its direction. Was this the bride? No. It was Hallie Carrick. Gone were the old breeches, the ratty hat, the thick dirty braid, the boots as dusty as her face. In their place was a gown of pale lavender, with big billowy sleeves, a neckline that could be more modest, and a waist the size of a doorknob. Very tightly pulled stays, he imagined, but what he was looking at now was her hair. It was golden, no other way to describe the color, the exact same color as her father's—shiny as the satin gown his aunt Mary Rose was wearing—woven into a thick, intricate braid on top of her head with little wisps and curls dangling artistically around her ears. Small diamond earrings sparkled through those myriad wisps, sparkled just like her laugh.

Jason smiled an easy, very masculine smile. She was a girl, despite her boasts and braggadocio. Why not admire her since Lyon's Gate was now his? He could afford to be gracious. He'd won. His ownership hadn't ever been in doubt, even though Thomas Hoverton hadn't been in London when Jason had gotten there. It had taken him only an hour to track down the Hoverton solicitor, Arlo Clark of 29 Burksted Street, who'd nearly broken into tears and fallen on his neck when he'd realized Jason was there to actually make an offer for the Hoverton property. Mr. Clark had the papers right there in a drawer, where they'd moldered for nearly two years. The offer was more than generous, though Jason realized the solicitor would never admit that. One had to play the game. The game was finished soon enough, and Jason had signed his name with a flourish and a sense of deep pleasure. Mr. Clark then signed in Thomas Hoverton's place since he was his legal representative.

Yes, Mr. Clark knew Wily Willy Bibber, the Sherbrooke solicitor, and they would see to the transfer of funds. Everything was right and tight. Jason could take possession of Lyon's Gate as soon as he wished to.

Yes, Jason could be gracious to this American baggage with her British accent and British blood. Now he could even appreciate her virgin blue eyes, her golden hair that surely belonged to a fairy tale princess—an image that didn't suit her personality at all—and a figure to make any man whimper. And that laugh of hers—too free, too easy, far too American—sounded like she didn't have a care in the world. Well, she shortly would when she realized she'd lost to him.

He'd arrived no more than ten minutes before the ceremony and had instantly been surrounded by his huge family. For today at least, there would be no swirling tension in the air because he wasn't the focus of everyone's attention, thank God. No one would ask how he was feeling or if he'd yet gotten over the betrayal that had nearly destroyed his family. His uncle Ryder, a child sitting on each leg and a child on either side of him, had everyone press together so Jason could fit on the same pew. His aunt Sophie was seated between two older children, Grayson next, holding two small children on his legs. Grayson, a born story-teller, was his uncle Ryder and aunt Sophie's only natural child, tall with the Sherbrooke looks, and eyes as blue as a clear summer sky.

Jason's parents, Hollis, James, Corrie, and the twins, twitching and yawning and jabbering in twin talk, were in the pew in front of him. Jason saw that every adult was responsible for one child, including his grandmother, who wasn't frowning at the small human being seated quietly beside her, surely a special gift from God. He saw his aunt Melissande, all of fifty now, seated two rows up. She was still so beautiful she stopped young men in their tracks. She looked more like his and James's sister than their mother's elder sister. Uncle Tony, her husband, was seated next to her, one arm resting on the pew behind her, his fingers playing with a strand of her beautiful black hair.

The church was filled to bursting since all of the groom's relatives had come to Glenclose-on-Rowan for the wedding. The only missing relatives were Aunt Sinjun and Uncle Colin from Scotland and Meggie and Thomas from Ireland. Jason settled in on the pew next to a four-year-old boy who, Uncle Ryder whispered over the top of the child's head, was named Harvey. He looked too old for his years, and he looked afraid, but that would change now that he was with Ryder. He was a very lucky little boy. He would eventually forget all the bad things that had happened to him. Harvey had large, very dark eyes, nearly as dark as Douglas Sherbrooke's eyes, and straight, shiny, dark brown hair. His cheekbones were still too sharp, his body too thin, but that would change as well.

When Miss Hallie Carrick glided down the aisle to support Miss Breckenridge, strewing rose petals from Mary Rose's garden, he caught her eye and gave her a cheerful little wave. Was there a sneer of triumph on his mouth? No, surely he was too well-bred to allow any sort of gloating to appear.

Evidently she didn't consider his little wave and smile gloating because, funny thing was, she looked momentarily surprised, and nearly dropped the lovely bouquet of flowers she carried. Jason would swear she giggled as she had to do a fast step to grab the small ribbon-tied roses. Then she smiled back and returned his little wave.

Harvey poked him in the ribs. "Who is that angel wot's sashshaying down the aisle flingin' rose petals about and eyin' ye?"

"That's Miss Carrick, the bridesmaid to Miss Breckenridge, the bride," Jason said. "She is rather flinging the rose petals about, rather than gracefully strewing them, isn't she?"

"Lawks," said Harvey, his voice loud and crystal clear over the organ music, "she could dump 'em out o' a bucket right on me 'ead. Ain't she jest purtier than the sun shinin' down on a puddle of clean water in Watt's alley? I wants to marry the angel when I grows up."

"No you don't, Harvey. Trust me. She's no angel. She'd chew your ears for breakfast." He took the little boy's hand and drew him closer. There were smiles and some laughter following Harvey's announcement. Harvey opened his mouth, but Jason, well practiced with the Wyndham children, said quickly, "I want you to count the hairs you can see on my arm until you've got them all."

"There ain't many showin'," Harvey said, "an' that's good 'cause I can only counts to four." That was too bad, Jason thought. Four-year-old Alice Wyndham could count to fifty-one. At least Harvey counted with great precision. It kept him quiet for about twenty seconds. Jason looked down the bench at his uncle Ryder, who'd just kissed a child's head. He was nodding at

Jason, smiling. Since his uncle Ryder had been a very young man of twenty, he'd been taking in abandoned children or rescuing them from drunken parents or sadistic masters. It was his aunt Sinjun who'd started calling his children the Beloved Ones.

Jason lifted the fidgeting Harvey onto his left leg, and thankfully soon felt the small body collapse back against his chest. Jason managed for the most part to keep his eyes on his cousin Leo Sherbrooke as he stood tall and proud opposite a heavily veiled girl who was, evidently, Melissa Breckenridge. She didn't leap on Leo, at least until her new father-in-law, Reverend Tysen Sherbrooke told her, a wonderful smile on his face, that the bride could kiss the groom.

At the reception following the ceremony, guests overflowed the vicarage into the lovely vicarage gardens. Reverend Sherbrooke was heard to bless God for delivering up this magnificent sunny day a good dozen times. After three toasts of the excellent champagne provided by the earl of Northcliffe, Tysen cleared his throat to draw everyone's attention. Unfortunately at that particular moment, one of the children shouted, "I have to go behind that bush!" which had everyone dissolving into laughter. Tysen tried again. "My wife has informed me that to keep us all from becoming drunk as loons, eating and dancing is required. The countess of Northcliffe has consented to play if all the young men will assist in clearing space in the drawing room."

Within four minutes, Alexandra had struck up a

lilting waltz with Leo leading his bride to the center of the floor. Jason turned when he heard the catch of a breath. He saw his uncle Tysen staring at Leo, shaking his head in bewilderment, probably because his son was actually now married. He had one arm around Rory's shoulders, all of nineteen, a student at Oxford, nearly a man grown. So many changes, Jason thought, all the cousins getting married, producing the next generation.

He watched his brother lead Corrie onto the floor, the twins in their grandfather's arms, waving wildly toward their parents. His cousin Max, Uncle Tysen's eldest son, gave his hand to a young woman Jason hadn't seen before. He looked down to see Harvey tugging on his trouser leg. "I wants to dance wit' the angel."

"You can't. The angel is dancing with my cousin Grayson, who's probably telling her a ghost story. Why don't you and I show this group how to waltz properly?" Jason lifted Harvey in his arms and began to waltz him around the perimeter of the room in great dipping steps. One of the twins shouted, "Uncle Jason, I want to waltz with you!"

Jason laughed, called back, "Dance with your grandfather." From the corner of his eye, he saw his father, holding a twin in each arm, swing into the waltz, sweeping around the room, not six feet behind Jason and Harvey. Laughter flowed as freely as champagne. Adults and children waltzed. All in all, it was a fine afternoon, Melissa's family mixing well with all the Sherbrookes.

An hour later, Jason was seated on a swing in the vicarage gardens, his right foot lazily pushing off every now and again to keep the swing moving in a nice smooth glide. Harvey, stuffed to the gills, exhausted from dancing, was sprawled on his lap, his head against Jason's chest. A female voice said quietly from behind him, "I don't expect you to congratulate me, but I suppose since I did have the lead in our competition, I should tell you that you probably ran a fine race. However, truth be told, I don't know what you did. You could have simply sat in a ditch and given up, for all I know. Also, you didn't ask me to waltz. I believe every single male at the wedding asked me to waltz. All save you. Surely that doesn't bespeak a gracious loser, and I had high hopes for you after that smile and little wave at the ceremony."

Jason, who didn't want to disturb Harvey, didn't turn, and said toward the graveyard beyond the far garden wall, "I always run a fine race, Miss Carrick. I usually win except when it is against Jessie Wyndham. I kept encouraging her to eat so she would gain flesh, but it never happened. She laughed at me."

Hallie laughed herself, walked around the swing and stood there, eyeing the beautiful man holding the boneless little boy who had chocolate smeared on his mouth. She said, "I watched Jessie race for as long as I can remember. She's a killer, is Jessie." She paused, frowned down at the sleeping Harvey. "He's too thin."

"Yes, a bit. That will change. My uncle Ryder bought him two months ago from a factory owner in

Manchester. He was working fourteen hours a day, fixing machines that knotted thread."

"I heard Melissa's parents speaking about your uncle Ryder and all the children he's taken in over the years. They couldn't quite come to grips with it."

"And you, Miss Carrick? What do you think of the Beloved Ones?"

"That's a lovely name for them. Actually, I've never seen such magic as your uncle has for the children, except perhaps for you. They want to crawl all over him. It's amazing. Did you see all of Melissa's relatives waltzing with the children? I don't think Mellie's father has danced in thirty years, yet he was carrying about a little girl no more than seven. So much laughter today. Quite amazing, really. You wouldn't see that in London, perhaps even in Baltimore. It would be all adults trying to act superior and eyeing each other's jewelry. How many children has he taken in?"

"I don't know. You will have to ask him or my aunt Sophie. There are usually fifteen or so children in residence at any given time."

"I think he is a very good man. He sees and he acts. Not many people do."

"No, not many do. So, we have another man of which you must approve. The list is growing, Miss Carrick."

She struggled a moment, kept quiet, and reached out her hand to give the swing a shove. Harvey snorted in his sleep. "Yet again I've left you speechless."

"Aren't you going to congratulate me, Mr. Sherbrooke?"

"On supporting your friend to the altar? Harvey here was certainly impressed with you."

"I nearly dropped the bouquet." She leaned over, pulled a handkerchief out of a pocket in her gown he couldn't have found even if he'd been looking for it, and, just like Jessie, spit on the handkerchief, and efficiently wiped Harvey's face. She saw him staring at her and said only, "I raised four children, myself. Did you see Melissa grab Leo at the end of the service? I thought Reverend Sherbrooke would laugh out loud."

The vicarage gardens smelled of honeysuckle and roses in the late afternoon, or maybe it was her unique scent, he wasn't sure. He said, "I remember when I was a very young boy, Uncle Tysen rarely laughed, especially when he gave a sermon. His life was dedicated to God, a God who evidently was only interested in hearing about endless sins and avoiding transgressions, always impossible. This God of Uncle Tysen's didn't believe in laughter or in everyday sorts of pleasures. Then he met Mary Rose. She brought God's love and forgiveness into his life and into his church. She brought laughter and peace and infinite joy." He paused a moment, felt his voice thicken as he said, "I didn't realize how much I'd missed my family until today when they were all around me. And my aunt Melissande, who always patted my face and called me her mirror. She didn't this time, she hugged me until my uncle Tony finally pulled her away. There were tears in her eyes." Why had he said any of that to her? After all, he'd beaten her. Shortly she would want to drive a knife between his ribs. Harvey snorted again in his sleep. Jason automatically tightened his hold, rocked him.

"What you said about your uncle Tysen—it was quite eloquent."

He ignored that, feeling something of a fool for speaking of it to her. "Why should I congratulate you, Miss Carrick?"

She'd forgotten her victory, her absolute triumph, but for only a moment. She grinned down at him. "Because, naturally, I am the new owner of Lyon's Gate."

Jason stopped swinging. He looked up into a face that could have given Helen of Troy a hell of a race. "No," he said matter-of-factly, wondering what her game was, "I own Lyon's Gate. If you would like to see it, to ensure I'm not lying, I can show you the deed. I have it in my pocket."

That drew her up short. "Why are you saying that? That isn't possible, Mr. Sherbrooke. I have the deed in my reticule, which is in my bedchamber upstairs. Your joke isn't funny, sir."

"No, I don't make jokes about something as important to me as Lyon's Gate is, Miss Carrick. I went to London, I met with Thomas Hoverton's solicitor, and I bought the property."

"Ah, that's cleared up then." She looked ready to dance and fling about more rose petals, the light of victory back in her eyes. "Not that it was ever in any doubt."

Her grin grew bigger. Jason frowned at her. "What are you talking about? What have you done?"

"I knew where Thomas was—he's staying with his aunt Mildred in Upper Dallenby, only twenty miles from here. I rode over, and he and I came to an agreement. Lyon's Gate is mine."

Now, wasn't that a kick in the ass, was all Jason could think.

CHAPTER 8

❧

It was after midnight. Leo and Melissa were long gone on their honeymoon, their first night of married bliss to be spent in Eastbourne, then they were off to Calais on the morning tide on Alec Carrick's packet, *HiHo Columbus,* named by Dev when he'd been five years old.

The Sherbrookes and Miss Hallie Carrick were seated in the drawing room. Jason knew that every one of them would willingly bash Hallie Carrick on the head, maybe bury her in the garden, so that he, their beloved returned prodigal, would have Lyon's Gate. It was close to Northcliffe Hall, which meant he would be near. They would be a family again, as soon as they got rid of this English-American upstart who'd had the nerve to stick her oar and her money in to steal what their beloved son wanted for himself. But they were all polite, solicitous, his mother going so far as to pour milk, not arsenic, into Miss Carrick's tea, which she doubtless would have preferred.

Hallie said suddenly, breaking the butter-thick silence, "Listen, all of you. I bought the property from Thomas Hoverton himself, not his solicitor. It seems very clear to me that I am the new owner of Lyon's Gate."

Jason said, "Mr. Clark is Thomas Hoverton's legal representative. Mr. Clark showed me the document giving him the power to transact any of Thomas Hoverton's business, with both their signatures on it. It is his right to act on Thomas Hoverton's behalf, and he did. I bought the property before you did, Miss Carrick. The deed is not only duly signed, it is dated, even down to the time of day our signatures were affixed to the bill of sale."

Hallie looked at all those perfectly pleasant faces, knowing full well they'd like her to disappear, perhaps by violence, given the blazing red of Jason's mother's hair. "Thomas is the owner," she said. "No one else. A solicitor, when all is said and done, is still only a solicitor."

Douglas rose, smiled at the group. "This will get us nowhere. I suggest we travel to London tomorrow. Miss Carrick, you may stay with us on Putnam Square since it would not be appropriate for you to open up either your father's or your aunt and uncle's town houses."

"I will stay with Melissa's parents," she said.

James said, "They're journeying directly back to Yorkshire tomorrow."

Douglas continued, "We will all gather together at the solicitor's, and the legal minds will help us sort this out. Now, it's time for bed. I, for one, am still swimming in too much champagne."

Since it was the patriarch who had spoken, everyone dutifully rose.

As James had said, the vicarage was packed to the rafters of the third floor. Jason and six other young men, including the bedchamber's owner, Max, Uncle Tysen's eldest son, were sleeping lined up like logs on thick piles of blankets, collected from Uncle Tysen's parishioners.

Except Jason. He couldn't sleep. All his plans, all the magnificent execution of his plans, what would happen now? He hated the uncertainty of it. He listened to the snoring, the grunts and groans of all his cousins, wondered how wives ever got any sleep, what with all the racket men made, pulled on a dressing gown his cousin Grayson had loaned him, and slipped out of the vicarage. He walked into the moonlight-drenched gardens, pausing by a thick twisting honeysuckle vine to breathe in its night scent.

"Do you know that women snore?"

He nearly jumped out of his bare feet. He whipped around, stepped on a sharp twig, and began dancing on one foot.

The witch laughed.

"Women's snores aren't as earsplitting as men's," he said, rubbing his foot. "Just little mewling sounds, delicate little snorts and whistles."

"I suppose you would know, what with all the women you've put to sleep over the years."

He raised an eyebrow at that. "Is this why you're up, Miss Carrick? You couldn't sleep with all the little grunts and groans?"

"It was almost like I was lying there listening to some sort of strange string quartet. A little wheeze here, a heady sigh from across the room, a deeper rumble from beside my left elbow."

"And you couldn't join in the orchestra?"

"I was lying there, wondering what we're going to do about all this mess. Not that I have any doubt about the correct outcome, naturally, but getting there, the plowing through your very rich and powerful family, who would like to send me to China. In a barrel. Filled with herring."

"Plowing? You think my family would be dishonest? I assure you, Miss Carrick, there is no reason to be since I have the right of it. Thomas Hoverton is a wastrel, a small-minded, womanizing, gambling wastrel, and that is why his solicitor has the power to make financial decisions for him. Thomas initiated it himself to keep him separated from his creditors who would probably like to jerk his guts out through his nose. Besides, you're not some poor little waif. Talk about a powerful family; your uncle, Burke Drummond, the earl of Ravensworth, is a very powerful man indeed. As for your father, he is Baron Sherard. Contact them, Miss Carrick. Until your father arrives, your uncle can represent your interests, he and his solicitor. Stop your whining. Actually, my parents would seriously consider China or perhaps Russia. Somewhere remote."

Hallie sighed. "Yes, that's all true. But it will take days for Uncle Burke to get to London. Was I really whining?"

"Yes."

"Well, that isn't very attractive, is it? No, don't you dare say it's what all American girls do or I'll knock you into those rosebushes."

"All right, I won't say it. The fact is, I'm charmed with the image of you climbing out of a herring barrel after six or so weeks at sea, on a rutted road that will take you to Moscow, in about six months."

"English herring or American herring?"

He wanted to laugh, but he didn't. "British herring are saltier in my experience. Not that I don't like a whiff of salt, naturally."

"You're making that up." She paused a moment, then said, "The fact is I like being more American than British. I have a different perspective on many things. You know, the way I look at people, the way I respond to situations."

"That must mean you're not an insufferable snob yet."

"Is that how you see English girls, Mr. Sherbrooke? As snobs?"

"No, not at all. You're right about American girls—they're more likely to kick a man in the shins if he offends her rather than whimpering behind a potted palm in a corner."

"Are you speaking from experience?"

"Yes, of course. I've seen both. For myself, I'd prefer the attempt to the shin."

"No attempt. I'd do it, fast and hard."

"I suppose you could try. A gentleman is at a disadvantage, of course, since he can't kick you back. You've a sharp mouth on you, Miss Carrick. You've got a vicious streak too, if I'm not mistaken—about the female of the species, I rarely am mistaken." Except one time, he thought, feeling the damnable familiar pain slice through him. One time he'd been so damnably blind—No, he wouldn't think about it. It was long in the past. He was home again, and he knew, knew to his heels, that no one blamed him. It never ceased to amaze and humble him. He wondered if he would ever stop blaming himself and knew he wouldn't.

He looked back at her, wondering what she'd look like with that marvelous hair of hers loose around her shoulders instead of in a single fat braid. If he wasn't mistaken, and he didn't think he was, he thought she looked hurt. Hurt at what? What he'd said? No, impossible, not this tiger of a girl, this baggage whose mouth would have to be taped over to keep her quiet. "Perhaps it would make you feel better toward me if you knew I've never had a girl try to kick me in the shins or sob behind a potted palm."

"That's because every female in the vicinity is hanging all over you," she said quite matter-of-factly. "Enough pandering, else you will become even more conceited than you are now. Listen to me. I'm worried, I'll admit it. I mean, I know that since Thomas Hoverton sold me his property, I am the real owner, but this solicitor business, well—"

"As I said, Miss Carrick, there are many properties for you to buy. This is the only one that is close to my home." He hated going over problems when he could see that each side had some right going for it. He said instead, "Did you know that your name nearly rhymes with my sister-in-law's?"

"Corrie. Hallie. Yes, it is close, looking at the names. She is very smart."

"Why do you think Corrie is very smart?"

"It's obvious. Oh, I see, as a man, you wouldn't notice a female brain if it winked up at you in your soup. She deals well with her husband."

"Yes, she would kill for James."

"Like Melissa would kill for Leo."

"Evidently."

"Your feet are bare, Mr. Sherbrooke. And that dressing gown you're wearing is very tatty and old."

"It belongs to my cousin Grayson. I forgot to pack anything. I arrived home just in time to change clothes and come galloping here. You look like a whipped-up dessert, Miss Carrick, all soft and fluffy and peachy."

"Yes, well, it was a gift from my aunt Arielle when she thought I was going to marry—" She slammed her hands over her mouth, looked horrified that those words had popped right out of her mouth. She took a step back, clutched at the flowing peach silk dressing gown and pulled it so tight over her breasts that beneath that lovely moonlight, he could see through to her lovely white skin.

She knew he was going to blight her: she'd just blurted out some powerful ammunition, but "Hmm," was all he said, nothing more. She still backed up three steps until her back hit against a climbing rosebush. A thorn must have stuck her because she jumped, stepped away.

Then, he saw, she simply couldn't stand it. "Oh, go ahead and mock me about this, I know you want to."

"Actually, I don't. Now, my father will speak to Melissa's parents since they're in charge of you."

"They aren't in charge of me, damn you."

"Very well, but you are their guest, are you not?"

"Yes, I suppose. I was going to leave for Ravensworth tomorrow in any case. But not now."

"No, not now. You will have to come back to Northcliffe Hall with us tomorrow," he said. "Then we will all go to London together. My father will send a messenger to your uncle."

"Yes, all right. I want this to be resolved quickly. I want to move into my new property."

"I don't suppose you planned on living at Lyon's Gate alone? You're a young lady—well, you're more young than not, I suppose."

"I hadn't really thought about it," she said slowly.

"This has all happened so quickly. There must be some spare relative hanging about who could come to Lyon's Gate to live with me. My aunt Arielle is sure to know of someone."

"How about my grandmother?"

"I didn't meet her, but isn't she dreadfully old?"

"Not beyond her eightieth year. She would refuse in any case. She doesn't like ladies, except my aunt Melissande. I was joking with you. However, finding a chaperone won't be a problem since you're not moving to Lyon's Gate."

"I wish you would give it up, Mr. Sherbrooke. I bought the property from the actual owner. It's done."

"I have a feeling that Thomas will prefer the sale going through his solicitor."

"Why?"

"Because the money that goes to Mr. Clark might be a bit more safely hidden from creditors than if it went directly to Thomas Hoverton. Hmm, I wonder what Thomas will have to say if that is true?"

"No, that can't be right. You made that up. The money goes to Thomas in any case."

"We will see, won't we? Go to bed, Miss Carrick." He towered over her. "Jessie Wyndham is taller than you are."

"These things happen. Perhaps James Wyndham is taller than you. We grow big in America."

He smiled down at her. "It's better this way, Miss Carrick. Lyon's Gate is a grand property, its potential can be reached only by a strong man who has a vision. I am that man, Miss Carrick."

"Your foot is bleeding, Mr. Sherbrooke. Brought low by a twig. Some strong man you are."

Jason reached out his hand and lightly touched his fingertips to her chin. A firm, very stubborn chin. "Give it up, Miss Carrick. Go back to Ravensworth. Buy something there."

"Good night, Mr. Sherbrooke. If I am found dead beneath one of Mary Rose's honeysuckle vines, you can be certain you or one of your family members will be blamed for it."

"Oh, were any of us to resort to that, you would simply disappear, Miss Carrick. Don't forget that herring barrel." He gave her a small salute and walked back into the vicarage, trying not to limp even when he stepped on another sharp twig.

CHAPTER 9

❧❧

❧ Jason didn't return to Northcliffe Hall. He rode directly back to London in clothes he borrowed from his twin.

When everyone arrived at the Sherbrooke town house late afternoon of the following day, he was waiting for them in the drawing room.

He wasn't all that surprised when Hallie Carrick ran into the drawing room ahead of everyone, her right hand fisted, blood in her eyes.

He managed to catch her fist before it landed. "You miserable sot." She managed to twist her hand free and hit him in the belly. He grunted as he grabbed both wrists.

She stood on her tiptoes, right in his face, squirming and tugging, but he wasn't about to let her go again. "You paltry cretin, you puling weasel—let go of me so I can hove your ribs in!"

"I might be paltry and puling, but I'm not stupid. I'm not about to let you get loose again, Miss Carrick."

"Let me at you, let me have more leverage, and I'll send my fist into your liver."

Corrie said, "She's been muttering all the way to London about the most satisfying ways to kill you, Jason. Even my best conversational efforts didn't deter her from quite innovative murder schemes, including stuffing you in a herring barrel and sailing you off some place on the other side of the planet." Corrie paused a moment, tapped her fingertips against her chin, and sighed. "But you know, Hallie, in the end, you've let me down."

Hallie jerked around at that. "What do you mean let you down?"

"You obviously are not acquainted with boxing science. When all's said and done, you hit him like a girl—a straight shot, nothing subtle, nothing surprising at all."

James said, "I hesitate to insert myself in the middle of this battlefield, but how the devil do you know anything about boxing science, Corrie?"

"I followed you and Jason to a boxing match near Chelmsley when I was twelve. You, Jason, and a half dozen wild young men from Oxford came down to get debauched and lose your groats on some sweating idiot trying to kill another sweating idiot."

Douglas said, "You never saw her, James? You never knew about this until now?"

"She was always sneaky," James said. He raised his eyes to the ceiling. "Thank you, God, for not letting all the gentlemen present realize she was a girl. You were wearing your britches, weren't you?"

"Yes, naturally. I even won a pound betting on the very sweaty man—now what was his name? Crutcher, I believe. I wagered on him because he had longer arms. I figured that gave him the advantage."

"You're right," Jason said, "Crutcher was his name. No, Miss Carrick, don't try to knock me into the fireplace again. That's better, hold still. Your wrists are staying right where they are. I bet on him too, Corrie. Won a hundred pounds off Quin Parker. I'd never even seen a hundred pounds before that day. James tried to extort a share, but I hid my booty."

James said, "I searched your room at least three different times looking for that money. Where did you hide it?"

"In the gardens, not a foot from Corrie's favorite statue."

"Oh dear, how do you know which is my favorite statue, Jason?"

"It's every female's favorite statue," Jason said.

Jason and James's mother, Alex, said kindly to Hallie even as her husband gave her an astonished look, "They are large, very nicely carved statues of men and women in an unclothed state, very artistic, naturally, and I suppose you would say their subject matter is explicit. They were brought over by one of my husband's ancestors in the last century."

"Explicit what?" Hallie asked.

"I'll show them to you, Hallie," Corrie said. "They are vastly educational."

"But how?"

"Well, they show you all the ways that a man and a woman can be intimate—"

"Intimate?" Hallie asked, her voice lower, vibrating with interest. "What do you mean 'intimate'?"

"Well—oh dear, perhaps we'd best not discuss that here."

Jason rolled his eyes.

"Amen," said Corrie's husband. "Forget about the statues."

Hallie said, "They're naked, you say? The male statues?"

"Well, yes," Alex said.

"Hmm. You can show me these statues, Corrie—I don't suppose the weasel here compares favorably to them?"

"Actually, truth be told, the statues don't compare favorably to the weasel. Or to James."

"Enough!" Jason roared.

Hallie jerked, found that he hadn't let up on his grip at all, and said, "I'll wager you dug up the one hundred pounds as soon as you could and lost it all in twenty minutes in a gaming hell."

Douglas said, "My sons only visited a gaming hell

once, Miss Carrick, and that was with me, their father, when they were seventeen."

Alex said, "Goodness, Douglas, you never told me about that. How I should have liked to have seen it. I could have dressed in a pair of Corrie's britches, perhaps worn a mask, sipped on brandy—"

"It was pretty bad, Mother," James said. "Men were drunk as loons, wagering huge amounts of money as if they didn't have a care in the world. The place smelled, to be blunt about it. As for the man who owned the hell, he looked like he'd willingly shove a knife in your belly if you didn't pay up your losses."

Corrie said to her father-in-law, "That was quite brilliant, sir. You did it as a lesson."

Douglas nodded. "The unknown is a powerful lure. Strip away the mystery and you see the rot beneath. As I recall, my own father took me to a notorious hell when I was about that age."

Alex said on a sigh, "I don't think it ever occurred to my father to take Melissande or me on an educational experience like that one. I'll wager there were gaming hells in York, don't you think, Douglas?"

"Lord give me strength," Douglas said, eyes heavenward.

Hallie jerked once more on her wrists, but Jason's hold was still unbreakable. "This is all well and good, all these educational lessons, my lord, but may we get back to business?"

"What business?" James asked. "Oh, sorry, I forgot. You want to kill my brother."

"No," she wailed, "I want my stud farm! It's mine, it belongs to me, I paid good money for it right into the cupped open hands of the owner himself, not his smarmy solicitor."

"Before we return to that subject," the earl said, "I'm curious about what you did with the money, Jason."

"Do you know," Jason said slowly, "I forgot about it. I think it still must be buried there."

"You forgot one hundred pounds?" Hallie said. "That's impossible. A young man never forgets his money, even one like you with more looks than brains."

"Excellent," Corrie said. "Hallie, you've regained your sense of humor."

Hallie wanted to leap on Corrie, but Jason kept tight hold of her wrists. He did give her enough freedom so she could shake one fist in Corrie's direction. "You have the unmitigated gall to make fun of me?"

Corrie said, unruffled as a sleeping hen, "Not at all. You still want to flatten Jason? I'll teach you to box, Miss Carrick. What do you say to that?"

James's eyes, like his father's, went heavenward. "She saw one boxing match when she was twelve and now she's going to give lessons?"

"Well," Douglas said. "I gave her lessons. And your mother as well." He gave a pirate's grin to his slack-jawed sons.

Jason tightened his grip even more, shot his father an appalled look. "Now, Miss Carrick, enough reminiscing, though it has brought revelations that have shaken my poor brother to his toes. You never saw Corrie in britches. Now, Corrie is right. Simple hits in the gut show no real depth of boxing science."

Hallie said, "I merely wanted to get your attention. Murder comes later."

The earl, who now stood with his shoulders against the mantel, arms crossed over his chest, said, "I wonder where Willicombe is. He should be in here pouring tea down our gullets and—"

"My lord! Ah, Master Jason is home as well. What a delight, what a brave new day it is. Just see how the sun is now pouring in through the large window to shine upon your returned face. I say, Master Jason, why are you holding that young lady by her wrists?"

"Willicombe, this girl wants to lay me out. Her name is Miss Hallie Carrick."

"Shall I fetch Remie to deal with her, Master Jason?"

"Not yet, Willicombe, I'm currently holding my own."

Willicombe turned to Alex. "Refreshments, my lady?"

"Whatever cook can put together would be fine, Willicombe. How is Remie?"

"He pines, my lady, pines until he has become thin as a chicken's leg. Trilby is a lady's maid and she knows all the tricks from her mistress on how to make a young man sweat." He shook his head as he left the drawing room.

"Remie in love," Corrie said. "Trilby? Who is her mistress, I wonder? Did Willicombe say she learned tricks from her mistress? Hmm, I wonder—"

"Corrie, I will teach you all the tricks you need to please me."

Douglas said, "Why don't we all sit down? No more baiting, Jason, no more violence, Miss Carrick. Now, Jason, I tried to explain to Hallie that this wasn't some sort of underhanded trick, that you were simply trying to get things moving. Your mother tried to assure her you were honorable and you simply wanted to get things moving as well. Your brother tried to assure her that moving things smartly forward was one of your special gifts—"

To Douglas's absolute astonishment, the young twit had the nerve to interrupt him. "Ah, yes, everyone was talking about moving things along. What things, I asked, but naturally, no one had an answer to that." She jerked once more, then looked up at Jason. "As for your bloody twin, he turned up his nose at me for daring to accuse you of being a foul creature fit only to have your guts stuffed in your ears. Let me go!"

"All right." Jason released her and strolled over to sit in a high-backed wing chair. He steepled his fingers, stretched out his long legs and crossed his ankles. "Miss Carrick, what did Corrie say? After all, you were telling me how smart she is."

"What's this? You think I'm smart?"

"Be quiet, Corrie," Jason said. "Miss Carrick?"

Hallie was still too angry with him to think straight,

and now he was sitting at his ease in a damned chair. What had Corrie said? She managed to get herself under control. She became aware that all the Sherbrookes were strewn about the large drawing room, looking on, obviously enjoying themselves at her expense. "Corrie said you were one of the more moral men she knew and I was to stop carping."

There was a lovely moment of silence.

"You really said that about me, Corrie?" Jason asked.

"It's the truth," Corrie said.

James said, "Well, maybe she is pretty smart after all. Just look at the twins she produced. You waltzed with them, Jason, saw how graceful and enthusiastic they were. It was Corrie who taught them how to dance."

Corrie laughed. "Yes, they nearly float, they are so light on their feet."

Hallie felt bludgeoned to the carpet. They were all laughing, happy as larks, and her role, which she was playing superbly well, was that of an ill-bred harridan.

Jason looked at Hallie for a long moment. "If you are ready to listen to me now, Miss Carrick?"

"Yes, I am ready."

"It isn't good news."

"I wasn't expecting any," she said.

Douglas didn't like the look on his son's set face. Something was very wrong. It was hard not to leap right in and protect him, but he forced himself to say nothing. He walked to his favorite wing chair and sat down opposite his son. Alex moved to stand next to him, her hand on his shoulder. He looked up at her, smiled, and pulled her down onto his lap.

As for James, he studied his twin's face. Like his father, he didn't like what he saw. He didn't want his brother to be unhappy, dammit, he wanted him to have Lyon's Gate. He wanted him to have what he deserved and that was whatever he wanted. James didn't want his twin to leave again. The excitement in Jason's eyes when he'd walked into the Lyon's Gate stables had made James want to dance. He heard the fear in his own voice as he said, "What is it, Jase? What is the bad news?"

Jason sighed, rubbed the back of his neck. "It turns out Thomas Hoverton had already sold Lyon's Gate to a Mr. Benjamin Chartley of Manchester for a modest sum of money. He hadn't bothered to notify Mr. Clark, his solicitor here in London. When Miss Carrick showed up on Thomas's doorstep, he saw his opportunity and took it. When he heard from his solicitor the following day that he'd sold Lyon's Gate to yet another buyer, Thomas decided it would be best for his health if he left for the Continent that very evening. Of course, what's really important here is that Mr. Chartley now owns Lyon's Gate."

The silence in the room was absolute.

"Well," his father said finally, "I didn't think Thomas Hoverton had the guts for this sort of thing."

Alex said, "He must have been very desperate. And to leave England, that is indeed a surprise."

Hallie said nothing; she walked to the fireplace, stared down at the empty grate, and kicked a log.

Jason said to her back, "I'm sorry, Miss Carrick. I know this comes as quite a shock. It did to me as well."

She turned to face him. "I'm leaving tomorrow morning to find that little worm and shoot him. I will get my money back, and yours as well, Mr. Sherbrooke, since you are the one who discovered what he'd done so quickly." She picked up her skirts and walked quickly from the drawing room.

Alex said, "That was a fine exit, but she doesn't know where her bedchamber is." She regretfully left her husband's lap and hurried after her.

"What are you going to do, Jase?"

"I've already contacted Mr. Chartley. He is willing to sell me Lyon's Gate, but the price has now doubled. He owns three successful factories in Manchester. He knows desperation when he sees it."

Douglas said, a dark eyebrow raised a good inch, "Does the fellow know who you are?"

"Well, he knows that I'm Jason Sherbrooke. Does he know that I'm your son? If he didn't, he probably does now. But what difference would that make in any case?"

Douglas smiled at his innocent boy. "The first thing we need to know is why Mr. Benjamin Chartley, factory owner, is in London. I'm thinking it's very likely he has hopes to enter London society. More than likely he has a daughter of marriageable age. If that is the case, we've got him."

"But I don't—"

"Jason, he will sell you Lyon's Gate at the price he paid for it or he will find every door in London closed to him. Then I'll consider ruining him."

Jason laughed. "Now, aren't I a moron for not thinking of that?"

Douglas said, "You would have, given a couple more hours. You've been in America too long. Do you really think Miss Carrick is off for France to bring Thomas Hoverton to ground?"

"I wouldn't doubt it. I keep telling her that she's more American than English and this certainly proves it. It's exactly what Jessie Wyndham would do. Give her a whiff of a villain and she'd be off. She'd take at least two guns with her, the whip she uses on jockeys who don't play fair on the racetrack, and a knife in her boot, strapped to her ankle." He laughed, couldn't help himself, and shook his head. "What a debacle."

Corrie said, "It is something we never considered. I like Hallie, but let me be painfully honest here. I was perfectly ready to have her kidnapped and removed to the Shetland islands. I fancy she could spruce up one of those ancient Viking huts and be perfectly content raising the local ponies."

The twins' nanny appeared suddenly in the doorway, looking harried, nervous, and resolute. James and Corrie were on their feet. "Yes, Mrs. Macklin? Is something wrong?"

Mrs. Macklin said, "No, no, don't worry, my lord. It's just that Master Everett wants to waltz."

"Waltz?"

"Yes, my lord. With his uncle."

At that moment, they heard a loud yell.

"He is rather insistent," said Mrs. Macklin over another yell that made James's left eye twitch.

Corrie said, "You waltz very well, Eliza. Why don't you take him for a spin around the nursery?"

"Master Everett says I'm not man enough to do it right," said Mrs. Macklin.

"Oh dear," Corrie said. "It's begun already?"

"Master Everett says my feet don't cover enough ground."

Jason was laughing. "Well, who can play the piano whilst I dance with Everett?"

His mother appeared in the doorway, Willicombe behind her, a large silver tray on his arms. Alex said, "I'll do it. Goodness, Everett's gotten bigger in the last day and a half."

"We're off then to the music room. Mrs. Macklin, what about his brother?"

"Master Douglas is currently chewing on Wilson's bone and the puppy is trying to drag it away from him."

Corrie said, "He is only seven weeks old, a Dandie Dinmont terrier, so ugly and precious all you want is to hug him until he creaks. Wilson and Douglas are good friends."

"More ugly than precious," James said. "But he fits quite nicely against my neck at night."

Mrs. Macklin said, "I'm sorry, my lord, but Wilson slept against my neck last night."

"Well, Wilson is in a new house," Corrie said. "We'll see whose neck he seeks out tonight."

"Unfortunately," the earl said, "it would appear that Douglas also likes to eat from the puppy's bowl."

"Oh dear," Mrs. Macklin said, "and here I hid Wilson's bowl underneath Everett's bed."

Smacked in the face at the same time by both the absurd and the ridiculous, Jason thought as he hauled Everett off to the music room, the little boy kicking his legs and waving his arms and singing at the top of his lungs in Jason's right ear. James and Corrie went with Mrs. Macklin to pull the bone out of Douglas's mouth all while slipping the new puppy another one. Neither of them doubted Douglas would be waltzing with his uncle in under five minutes.

As for Hallie Carrick, she was upstairs in a lovely bedchamber, changing into her oldest clothes.

CHAPTER 10

❧⊱

❧ When Hallie appeared thirty minutes later, a single valise clutched in her hand, a lovely dark blue cloak over her shoulders, Willicombe, the Sherbrooke butler, sent his lovesick nephew Remie to inform Jason, who gave Everett and Douglas over to their grandfather for the next waltz. Jason came into the entrance hall where Hallie was giving instructions to Remie, who stood frozen with horror.

"Just a moment, Miss Carrick," Jason said. "I'll need to change before we can leave."

She whipped around. "You think you're coming with me, Mr. Sherbrooke? You think you'll stomp this blighter's liver before I can? No, you stay here and beg and plead with this Mr. Chartley whilst I go fetch our money from Thomas Hoverton. When I return I'll see to Mr. Chartley. In the meanwhile, don't you dare let this man fleece you, do you hear me?"

"You're thinking like an American," he said, picking a spot of lint off his sleeve, suppressing a smile.

"What do you mean by that snide remark?" He saw her right hand tighten into a lovely fist.

"Oh, I don't know. How about you're exhibiting a marked lack of subtlety? Or you're simply forging ahead without pausing even a moment to think things through? There's no need to boil over with rage."

A lovely arched eyebrow went high.

Remie took two quick steps back, hoping to escape.

Jason said, "There's no reason to go haring off after Thomas Hoverton right now. If you still wish to go after him once I've told you some things, why, I'll be forced to accompany you."

"You won't be forced to do anything of the kind. What sorts of things?"

"London is very different from Baltimore, Miss Carrick, surely you learned that. You're a bright girl. As you must know, London society doesn't allow just anyone through its august portals. Money doesn't matter. For example, Lucinda Frothingale's now-dead husband wouldn't have ever been admitted into London society for the simple reason that he owned and operated flour mills. The fact that he would have been richer than many of England's vaunted peers wouldn't have mattered. Flour mills constitute trade, Miss Carrick, and folk in trade, who have no ancient lineage, no powerful family behind them, aren't allowed into the club. Do you understand?"

"Yes, of course, but I still don't see what—" Jason saw the instant she realized what he was talking about. He refused to acknowledge she'd caught on more quickly than he had. She said slowly, "I think I'll go see my uncle's solicitor. He can find out just exactly who this Mr. Chartley is."

He realized, of course, that he should have encouraged her to go after Thomas Hoverton, despite the fact that she was a young lady, quite alone. Did she have any money left after paying Thomas Hoverton for Lyon's Gate? And if she didn't have very much money, would she arrive in Calais and realize she couldn't afford a baguette much less respectable lodging? Jason said, "There's no need for you to do anything, Miss Carrick. My father has already taken care of it. We will know all about Mr. Benjamin Chartley soon enough."

"But I—"

"I'm beginning to believe you have more hair than brains. And I'm thinking your hair is probably lovelier than your brains as well."

To his surprise, she didn't hurl herself at him. She didn't move at all. She stared down at her shoes, the oldest pair she had, which were very fine indeed. "Yes, I suppose you're right. My father was always telling me that I should make it a habit to sit in a corner for three minutes and think before I acted. He said whenever I acted too quickly, he had to clean up the most abominable messes." She looked up at him, a glimmer of a smile lighting her eyes. "I thank you for stopping me before I could make a mess. I should hope that my hair looks better than my brains. That's a horrifying thought, though I've never seen what brains look like. Now that I think about it, I don't have much money either."

"I wondered."

"I don't think my father's bankers would stuff more money in my outstretched hands, particularly after they found out how easily I was swindled. They would believe I was naïve and incompetent, in short, a woman. But money isn't what's important here. I have my pistol, a small riding crop, and a knife, strapped to my ankle. Thomas Hoverton wouldn't ever imagine that I'd come after him. I'd probably find him in Calais, toasting his good fortune. Then I could carve out his gullet."

"Or villains would find you first. Maybe you'd shoot one villain, Miss Carrick, but the second and the third lurking in the alley? With those skirts it would be hard to get to the knife fast enough."

She raised her hand and fisted it.

He laughed.

He realized she was staring up at him, her head cocked to one side.

"What is it?"

"I know you don't like me, Mr. Sherbrooke. I don't understand you. You could have simply let me leave. I would be gone and you could do as you please. Now there will be endless complications."

"I don't want you to get hurt and that's very likely what would happen. I have never trusted the French, particularly after the dealings I had with Mademoiselle Benoit in Baltimore who— Well, never mind that."

"I heard my father say the French believed God didn't intend the Ten Commandments for them since he hadn't written them in French, and that's why the French pox was so prevalent."

Fascinated, Jason said, "He spoke to you about the French pox?"

"No, I was eavesdropping. When I managed to slip French pox ever so skillfully into a conversation, I thought he would explode, he turned so red in the face. Who is this Mademoiselle Benoit?"

Jason wanted desperately to laugh, but managed to hold it in. He didn't want her to pull her pistol, her whip, or her knife out of her boot and dispatch him. He cleared his throat. "Mademoiselle Benoit isn't any of your business. Now, stop fretting. We will work this out."

"How?" She struck her palm to her forehead. "How stupid I am. There won't be any complications at all. If your father threatens Mr. Chartley with social ostracism, then he will sell the property to you. I will have no chance at it."

Jason shrugged, as it was the truth, after all.

"It will be done before I can get my uncle here to do the same thing to him."

"Yes, that's true enough."

"So you've won, Mr. Sherbrooke."

"That's very nice of you to say so, Miss Carrick, but a bit premature. I suggest you hold off on your congratulations until after we find out what Mr. Chartley's hopes and aspirations are in our fair city."

"I'll wager he has an eighteen-year-old daughter he wants to marry off to some bankrupt baron, whose pockets he'll fill to brimming."

"One can but hope."

"I might as well go after Thomas Hoverton, or else my siblings will never let me hear the end of it. I can hear them now. 'Hallie, you say you bought a property and the owner sold it to someone else first then flew off to another country?' 'You knew he was a rotter and you didn't even take any precautions?' 'How big did you say your brain was, Hallie?' And on and on it will go until I garrote myself."

Yet again, Jason wanted to laugh, but didn't. "Let's just wait and see what happens with Mr. Chartley. Regardless of whether or not I end up with Lyon's Gate, I will help you find Thomas." He couldn't believe he'd said that. He fell silent, watching her.

"You're not as angry as you should be with Thomas Hoverton," she said slowly, eyeing him. "Why is that?"

Jason smiled. "Fact is, he didn't get my money. Not because I'm such an excellent man of business, mind you. It was the Sherbrooke solicitor, Wily Willy Bibber, who refused to pay the solicitor a single groat until I had taken actual possession of Lyon's Gate."

Hallie felt like a complete and utter fool. She turned on her heel and went back up the wide staircase. Midway up, she paused and turned to see Jason standing in the entrance hall, staring up after her.

She said, her voice emotionless, "I understand now why Lord Renfrew took Mrs. Matcham for a lover not two weeks before we were to be married. He believed I was too stupid and too infatuated with him to find him out. Do you know what? I didn't find out about Mrs. Matcham until after I had broken our engagement. What I did find out was that his tailor, a Mr. Huff, hadn't been paid for six months. He came to me, you see, hoping I would pay him. He told me not to be surprised if more tradesmen arrived on my doorstep since all his lordship's creditors knew now that his lordship had found a lovely plump pigeon who was so green she'd probably start blooming before spring."

"That's a goodly dose of humiliation," Jason said. "Are you talking about William Sloane?"

"No, William Sloane gambled away nearly all the money before he conveniently died, and his brother, Elgin Sloane, became Lord Renfrew."

"But didn't your uncle meet him? Make certain he wasn't marrying you for your money or—"

"Yes, he did. It was William who had the bad reputation, not Elgin. After all, Elgin Sloane had only been on the London scene for seven months before he met me. No one knew the real state of his finances."

"So only the tradesmen knew the truth about him."

"Evidently so."

"At least you found this out before you married."

"If I'd found out after the wedding, I would have shot him."

"That's an American thing to say." But he laughed. "You would have been hung here. It was then you decided you wanted to own a stud?"

"Yes. I will become independent, and never marry."

"As I've said, Miss Carrick, there are probably many properties for sale as well as many men out there who aren't rotters like Elgin Sloane."

She waved away his words. "Or, I suppose, I could become a nun."

"I can't imagine any mother superior worth her salt taking you on. I strongly doubt you are docile enough to take orders."

She shrugged. "Regardless, I will never marry, not unless I lose my wits entirely and pour my money into another bounder's hands. I believe I'll hire someone to watch me. If I am in danger of falling into that wretched trap again, that person will simply shove me into the herring barrel."

"Like I said, not all men are bounders, Miss Carrick."

She shrugged again, not looking at him.

He felt her pain and hated that he felt it. She turned to go back up the stairs when he called out, "Like you, Miss Carrick, I have also determined that I will never marry. I am fortunate that it isn't my responsibility to provide an heir for the Sherbrooke line, so it won't matter."

She said nothing, but he knew her attention was focused on him. Still, he wasn't about to say anything more, and was horrified at himself for saying this much. Never would he speak of it, never— "It happened to me nearly five years ago." He shut his mouth. He was a fool, an idiot. None of this was her business, anyone's business.

"You were going to marry a girl who wanted you only for your money?"

He laughed, this time a low, vicious laugh from deep inside him, and the words tumbled out. "Oh no, I far exceeded your paltry betrayal, Miss Carrick. I picked a girl who would have killed my father if Corrie hadn't shot and killed her." He couldn't stand himself. He'd poured all that out just to make this outrageous girl feel better. Thank God there was nothing else to burst out of his damned mouth. A pity one couldn't retrieve hasty words and stuff them back down one's throat. He turned on his heel and left the town house.

Hallie Carrick stood on the stairs for a very long time. She'd heard all sorts of gossip about why Jason Sherbrooke had abruptly left England and gone to live with the Wyndhams, but nothing close to this. He was right. She was hurt and humiliated because one dishonorable man had tried to get his hands on her money. What had happened to her was common, but what had happened to him—the way he'd been used, it would rot the soul. He had run away to America; he'd tried to run away from himself. She didn't think he'd succeeded. She turned to go up to her bedchamber. He would never trust another woman. She would wager her substantial dowry on that. She couldn't blame him.

CHAPTER 11

❧

❧ At lunch the following day, Douglas said, "I'm very sorry, Miss Carrick, but Mr. Chartley is selling Lyon's Gate to Jason for the sum he himself paid for it."

"And a paltry amount it was. Yes, it is what I imagined would happen," Hallie said. "Isn't it interesting that after all of this, you, Mr. Sherbrooke, have gained what you wanted and paid only a pittance for it?" She rose slowly. "I would like to thank you for your hospitality, my lord, my lady. I'll be leaving in the morning for Ravensworth. I must pack now."

She nodded to each of the Sherbrookes in turn, and walked out of the drawing room to see Willicombe standing at the foot of the stairs, clearly blocking her.

"Yes, Willicombe?"

"I just wanted to tell you, Miss Carrick, if you'll

forgive my impertinence, that I have a cousin who worked for Lord Renfrew. My cousin said his lordship was a smarmy, mean-spirited man, the kind who would seduce a parlor maid and pat himself on the back for his virility. Never said a thank-you to any of his servants. It was my cousin Quincy who told Lord Renfrew's tailor, Mr. Huff, that his chances for gaining money owed him were not good. Quincy had no idea, of course, that Mr. Huff would come to you with his hand out. Still, it turned out for the best, didn't it?"

"Yes, indeed it did. What a very small world it is." Willicombe gave her a small bow and she walked up the stairs, only to stop again halfway up. "Do you know what happened to Lord Renfrew, Willicombe?"

"His lordship married a Miss Ann Brainerd of York. Her father owns many canals criss-crossing the north country, and made his fortune carrying goods up and down those canals. Now trains are making the canals obsolete because goods are transported much more cheaply and quickly that way. It's rumored Lord Renfrew hasn't gained as much from the marriage as he'd expected. Evidently, his wife's father realized quickly enough that Lord Renfrew wasn't a man of sterling character."

"Well, that's some justice, isn't it?"

"Except for her poor ladyship."

"There must always be someone who loses, Willicombe."

"Yes, miss, isn't that the truth?"

"Your cousin, what did he do for Lord Renfrew?"

"He was his lordship's lead coachman both here in London and at his estate in the country."

"What is your cousin doing now, Willicombe?"

"He is a junior coachman for Lady Pauley, Miss Carrick, over on Bigger Lane. She is quite fat, is Lady Pauley, fair to makes the horses groan when two footmen shove her up into the coach, Quincy says. It's a pity."

"Is Quincy a strong fellow?"

"Nearly as strong as Remie, my nephew."

"Thank you, Willicombe. I must think about this." She left Willicombe looking up after her. The young lady had lost, right and proper, proving what she'd said—someone always had to lose. It was the way of the world. He wondered what would happen to her now. He wondered why she was interested in Quincy.

At dinner that evening, Douglas eyed a silent Hallie a moment, then said, "Let me tell you more about Mr. Chartley. As we suspected, there is a Miss Chartley. We met her when we visited Mr. Chartley at Twenty-five Park Lane, a lovely corner mansion that Lady Bellingham's heirs rented to him for the season.

"Miss Chartley has just turned eighteen. She is, ah, not terribly toothsome, rather she's on the plump side and her teeth are a bit long and forward, and her laugh, well, it made my nerves jump."

Jason looked at Hallie, whose head had been bent over her plate until his father had begun to speak. He saw her jaw drop. He burst into laughter. To her surprise, Hallie joined him, the first sounds out of either of them since the family had sat down to an excellent dinner of braised beef and onion-dunked potatoes, two of Cook's specialties.

The earl nodded at them, pleased. "Now, the truth of the matter is that Miss Chartley is quite lovely. She has been raised well, has lovely manners, and will do well now that I will allow her into society."

Alex said to her sons, "Your father hasn't had a chance to be charmingly ruthless for a good while now. Everyone is in awe of him; some actually quake in their boots, and it has become too easy for him to get his own way outside the portals of Northcliffe. Inside those portals, however, it is a vastly different matter."

Douglas raised his glass of Bordeaux and toasted her across the long expanse of table. "Behold what happens to a man when he's been married close on to forever."

"You look quite splendid, sir," Corrie said. "It occurs to me that perhaps I should take lessons from my mama-in-law. James gets his own way far too often for my tastes. If it continues, he will be a domestic tyrant within another year, maybe two."

"I will give you lessons, Corrie," Alex said. "It is perhaps more needful since James is so very beautiful. Given how their aunt Melissande is still so glorious, I fear that James and Jason will continue to season well, and that could be a female's downfall. Yes, lessons you must have, dearest."

Hallie said, "When my stepmother is angry at my father, her face turns red, she calls him wonderfully inventive names, and tells him he can sleep in the stables. I remember one morning I walked into the stables to see them asleep together in a stall. Hmm. Perhaps, my lady, I can pass the lessons along to Genny."

But she was leaving in the morning, Jason thought.

The following morning at precisely ten o'clock, Mr. Chartley rose to face a lovely young lady who stood in the doorway of the drawing room. "My butler tells me you are the daughter of Baron Sherard and the niece of the earl of Ravensworth."

"Yes, Mr. Chartley, I am. I am here to buy Lyon's Gate from you."

"This is quite remarkable, Miss Carrick. Do come in, won't you? Some tea perhaps?"

"No, sir, but it is kind of you to offer. I am offering you ten percent more than Jason Sherbrooke is offering you. Plainly, I am offering you more than you paid Thomas Hoverton for Lyon's Gate. Selling to me, you will make a profit."

"You know, Miss Carrick, that I have already agreed to sell Lyon's Gate to Jason Sherbrooke."

"Yes, sir, but you haven't yet signed over the deed to him. It isn't yet legal."

"I don't know what to say." Mr. Chartley brushed his fingers through his thick black hair. "This is quite remarkable," he said again. "Young lady, how long do you think I would retain my reputation if I failed to carry through on an agreement I made? No, you needn't say anything, that is something that concerns you not one whit." Mr. Chartley sighed. "If I don't sell you Lyon's Gate, your uncle will prevent my precious daughter from entering society. On the other hand, if I don't sell Lyon's Gate to Jason Sherbrooke, his father will prevent my precious daughter from entering society. I believe that I am between the proverbial rock and the hard spot."

"That is correct, sir. I am the rock. I suggest you accept my offer since the hard spot isn't in sight. That way you will make a profit." She gave him a fat smile. "Ah, my uncle—the earl of Ravensworth—looks upon me as a daughter. He was a military man, you know. I wouldn't want to cross him, were I you. As for my father—"

"I know all about your father," said Mr. Chartley. "As I do the earl of Northcliffe. Indeed, I see very clearly now. If you will take a seat, Miss Carrick—"

The drawing room door burst open and Jason strode in, the butler behind him, flapping his hands.

Mr. Chartley said, "I believe the hard spot just entered, Miss Carrick."

Hallie leapt to her feet. "I was so very quiet, I didn't tell anyone—what are you doing here?"

Jason gave a brief bow to Mr. Chartley. "Forgive me, sir, for barging in like this, but I followed Miss Carrick here." He stood there, hands on his hips, looking like he wanted to throw her out the wide drawing room windows.

"You can leave, Jason. No one asked you here. Mr. Chartley and I are conducting business."

"He has already agreed to sell Lyon's Gate to me. Give it up, Miss Carrick, give it up."

"No, never. Two can play the same game, Mr. Sherbrooke. You have only your father to pound nails in Mr. Chartley's social coffin, whereas I have my father and my uncle to use as, er, leverage—"

"Mr. Sherbrooke, Miss Carrick, I see that I must make a decision. If the two of you would excuse me." He was out the door, closing it quietly behind him.

Jason and Hallie stared each other down from the length of the drawing room.

"How did you know?"

"I asked Remie to keep an eye on you. If one trusts a woman, one should leap immediately into the Thames and drown oneself."

"I saw Lyon's Gate first!"

"That doesn't merit a response, Miss Carrick. Go away now. You've lost. You admitted it last night. Go home."

"My threats are just as potent as yours, Mr. Sherbrooke. Why don't you—"

"I could hear the two of you in the hall." Mr. Chartley stood a moment in the drawing room doorway, then walked in, smiling at both of them impartially, and held out an envelope to each of them. "Now, this is the very best I can do to ensure my daughter's social success. I trust that neither of you will feel compelled to seek my destruction."

"What have you done, sir?" Jason asked, taking the envelope. "You've already accepted my offer."

"I did, Mr. Sherbrooke. But now I have a new understanding of the situation. I suppose you and Miss Carrick could bid on Lyon's Gate until I was close to making a fortune, but I am not a stupid man." He smiled impartially at both of them. "Call me Solomon."

"What is this, sir?" Jason asked.

"Sir, surely we can come to an arrangement that will prevent the earl from ruining you. What is in this envelope?" asked Hallie.

"Ah, would you just look at the time. I must meet my precious daughter on Bond Street. She has a fitting today at Madame Jordan's. Your father so kindly recommended her to me, Mr. Sherbrooke. May I have tea sent in?"

"No," Hallie said, clutching the envelope to her chest. "I must be going."

But Mr. Chartley was faster. Jason and Hallie faced each other again, both holding a sealed envelope.

"Mr. Chartley says he's Solomon?" Jason said.

"I don't like this. I don't like this at all." Hallie picked up her skirts and left Jason standing alone in Mr. Chartley's drawing room, the envelope still unopened in his hand.

Thirty minutes later, Douglas folded the paper and slid it back into the envelope. "Well, I think I wish to share a bottle of wine with Mr. Chartley. This is quite well done of him."

Hallie paced the width of the estate room, a small, thoroughly masculine room of rich brown leather with a mahogany desk and matching bookshelves. Both Douglas and Jason watched her. She stopped at the window and shook a fist in the direction of Mr. Chartley's rented house. "He's a scoundrel, no better than Thomas Hoverton. He's sold the property to two people."

"No," Douglas said. "He sold two people each a half a property."

"Well, yes, he did, but—"

"It was very clever of him. You, Miss Carrick, placed him in an utterly untenable position."

"No, it was you who did that, sir. I simply played the same cards. You threatened to exterminate the poor man and his poor daughter if he didn't roll over like a dead dog and do exactly what you said. I merely followed your example, and look at what it has brought us." She waved the deed and the draft on the Bank of England in his face. Her own face fell then, and she sat down hard in one of Douglas's big leather chairs and put her face in her hands.

Jason said to his father, "I'm gratified. She didn't pull an elegant stiletto out of her sleeve and plunge it through your arm."

Hallie's head jerked up. "I didn't think of that. If you'll excuse me, I'll get my knife. But there is a problem. These sleeves are so blasted big you can't hide anything in them. A knife would clatter to the floor."

"Don't move, Miss Carrick," Douglas said. It was

his turn to pace the room, his eyes on his boots. He stopped, turned to face the two young people. "I suggest we think of Mr. Chartley as an agent of fate.

"The fact is, the both of you now own Lyon's Gate. I further suggest you both sit down like the two adults you are, and figure out how you're going to make this work. I hesitate to destroy Mr. Chartley, given his ingenious solution." Douglas walked to the door, then turned to face them. "Miss Carrick, using my tactics on Mr. Chartley was an excellent strategy. You are a woman of backbone. I must admit that Jason and I were both gloating last night, not blatantly, naturally, since that would be rude."

"I knew you were gloating."

But the earl was gone.

"Quietly gloating," Jason said, frowning at the empty doorway. He heard his father's boot steps receding down the corridor toward the front of the town house. His father was a smart man. Jason eyed Hallie Carrick. "What the devil are we to do?"

"Sign over your half to me. I will pay you for it, naturally. I will even give you a profit."

"You managed to get more money from your bankers?"

"Oh yes. I went to Mr. Billingsley's house on Berkeley Square. Mr. Billingsley tried to hem and haw, but his wife has known me since I was born. She told him to hie himself into his study and write me out a bank draft. I was smart, she said, and wasn't my father always telling him how very smart I was?"

"Sometimes I don't like fate," Jason said. "I'm going riding in the park. Hopefully I will gain some inspiration from the swans in the Serpentine."

It was dinnertime on that drizzling May evening when Jason opened his bedchamber door to find Hallie Carrick standing there, her fist up to knock, a determined look on her face. "Mr. Sherbrooke, I have a solution. You will sleep in the stables. We can fashion a lovely suite of rooms there for you off the tack room. It will be no problem. You can take your meals with me in the house."

He didn't move, didn't look away from her. "No."

"We can't very well share the same bloody house, you know that."

"You can have the stables then. You can have your meals with me in the big house."

"If you were to inhabit the big house, you wouldn't do a thing to make it beautiful again. I will get rid of the mildew, I will put new draperies on the windows and new carpets on the floors. I will buff those floors and replace what is necessary to replace."

"Wherever did you get this blighted notion that men don't care about their surroundings?"

"My stepmother told me that men would be perfectly content to live in a cave. Throw them a meaty bone and give them— Well, never mind that. The stables are perfect for you."

At his hoisted eyebrow, she said, "Very well. Step back."

She nearly walked over him, her hand out, pressing

against his chest. He backed up in her wake. She came to a stop in the middle of his bedchamber and waved her hands. "Just look. A monk could be living in here. The only reason this lovely room isn't covered with dust and muddy boot prints is because of the servants' diligence. This is pathetic, Mr. Sherbrooke. This is how Lyon's Gate would continue to look were you to live in the big house."

"May I remind you that I haven't been here in five years, Miss Carrick?" He should tell her that he'd selected most of the furnishings for the Wyndhams, chosen the fabrics for the new drawing room draperies, and arranged every single interior item.

She thought he was defeated, and she laughed. "I'm right, admit it. You will do just fine in the stables, Mr. Sherbrooke." She nearly danced out of his bedchamber. Jason stood in the middle of the room, his arms crossed over his chest, wondering what was going to happen next.

CHAPTER 12

Northcliffe Hall
End of May

"We should have brought blankets," Jason said and vigorously rubbed his arms with his hands. In addition to being cold, he was beginning to think the ground was a graveyard of rocks. James considered this warm?

"You've become soft in your years away," James said. "This is the first perfectly clear night we've had since you arrived home. Would you look at Orion's Belt, Jase—it looks like diamonds sparkling."

They were lying atop the cliff above the Poe Valley, James's favorite star-gazing place. Jason said, "You've been showing me Orion's Belt since we were six years old. I remember you used the word *sparkling* each and every time."

"And I remember I nearly had to tie you down so you would hold still long enough. At least you're nice and quiet now, except for the complaining."

"If I don't move, maybe I won't freeze to death."

James laughed, came up to a sitting position, and turned to look down at his brother, lying on his back, his head now pillowed on his crossed arms. "Jase, are you certain you want to actually share your house and your stables with this girl? You scarcely know her. She could be a harridan."

"She is." Jason's face was calm, and he looked nothing more than sleepy.

"You're telling me that you're knowingly going to share a house with a disagreeable female who will make your life miserable?"

"That's it. Think of it as an arranged marriage." Jason came up to clasp his arms around his legs. "What other choice do I have?"

"You tried to buy her out?"

"Oh yes. She very nearly gulleted me." Jason suddenly smacked the side of his head. "Come to think of it, maybe I could still have her kidnapped and taken to the West Indies. What do you think?"

"Mother wanted to send her farther away. She'd do it now in a flash. I remember Father left the room, telling her over his shoulder that he believed there was a ship in port bound for Charlotte Amalie."

Jason laughed. "She would. He would." He rubbed his arms again. "Come to think of it though, Hallie'd probably be running the island within five years. Damn, James, I can't believe you think this is warm. Has my blood thinned that much being in America?"

"It would appear so. However, you were bred from hardy English stock, you'll get used to it again. I'm wondering what Miss Carrick's aunt and uncle—not to mention her father—will think about this arrangement, sharing a house with a man who isn't her husband."

"If there's one thing Miss Carrick does well, it's argue. Interesting you should bring up the earl of Ravensworth. I don't believe she plans to tell her aunt and uncle until we've actually split the house in half, her far-removed great-cousin Mrs. Tewksbury is installed, and the three of us have moved in. *A fait accompli,* as it were."

"She's not twenty-one until the end of the year. I suppose her aunt and uncle could order her to move back to Ravensworth Abbey."

Jason arched his left eyebrow. "That is possibly the stupidest thing you've said since I've been home, James. Can you honestly imagine giving Miss Carrick orders to do anything she doesn't want to?"

"Well, where do her aunt and uncle think she is?"

"I believe she's allowing them to assume she's still with Melissa's parents in London. I don't suppose they realize that Melissa's parents have already returned north. And now we'll have Miss Carrick for a guest until Lyon's Gate is ready for us. She arrives tomorrow."

James brooded on that awhile, then said, "Speaking of Melissa and Leo, did I look as besotted as Leo when I married Corrie?"

"No, nothing like that."

James moaned. "Don't ever say that in Corrie's hearing. She'd lock me in a small room with the twins."

"You looked like you wanted to rip off that lovely wedding gown she was wearing and take her right there in the central aisle of the church."

James's head jerked around to face his brother, an eyebrow arched a good inch. "Well, then. You can tell her that." He paused a moment, took the plunge. "That was a time, wasn't it?"

Jason said nothing, continued to rub his arms.

James felt his brother withdraw, though he didn't move a muscle. He backed off. "All right, you puny lad, let's go home. I don't want you whining to Mother that I tried to freeze you to death."

After the twins rose and dusted themselves off, James took one final long look at the heavens. Jason felt the pull of it in his brother, something he couldn't begin to understand. On the other hand, present James with a stud farm to run and he'd probably stare at you, baffled.

James said as he mounted Bad Boy, "Corrie is wonderful, Jason. She's a brick, you can always count on her, and the good Lord knows she makes me laugh. She gets along famously with Mother, Father adores her, only Grandmother maligns her, but that doesn't upset her overly. Do you know that she and I lie on the cliff looking up at Andromeda and find myself blessing all the stars that circumstances threw us together?"

"I heard the two of you yelling this morning."

"She does have a knack for making me so mad I want to lock her in her armoire. In the next instant, I've got her pressed against the wall and she's got her legs around my waist and— Well never mind the details. Hmm. I'll never forget over a dinner of buttocks of beef she thanked Father for educating me so splendidly."

"Don't tell me he knew what she meant?"

"He pretended he didn't."

Jason tapped his boot heels into Dodger's muscular sides. "Just as you will teach the twins."

"That boggles my brain. Here they were this afternoon, left alone for but a moment. When Corrie came back into the room, they'd stuffed three apple tarts in their mouths. They looked up at her, innocent as angels, all the while filling dripping off their chins."

"I wish I could have seen that. I imagine we did the same thing at their age. Are you and Corrie thinking of more children?"

James paled, making Jason reach out his hand to grab his brother's arm. "What's the matter?"

James drew a deep steadying breath. "Corrie had a very bad time of it with the twins. I don't want her pregnant again. It could kill her. She squeezed my hand so hard she broke a bone."

"You stayed with her?"

"Oh yes. She said since I got her into this mess I could very well see her through it. Then she cursed me, but she didn't know that many curses, so she had to keep repeating herself. Between the contractions, I taught her meaty new ones. She uses them today—usually on me. It was scary, Jason. You would not believe the number of good deeds I promised if she would survive, and I've done every single one of them."

"I didn't know. She appears so sturdy, she glows with good health."

"Yes, but the twins were big. It—it was terrifying, Jason. As terrifying as when I thought you were going to die and there was nothing I could do about it except pray. If you hadn't survived, I probably would have curled up next to you. It was the same with Corrie."

Jason never turned in the saddle to acknowledge his brother's words, though they struck him deep. He felt the old rancid pain filling his throat, the bitterness of it making his belly churn. His head began to ache because his brain didn't want to think about the past, simply couldn't.

Jason said, "Damn, the wind's come up—a cold wind. Don't you dare claim that you're still as warm as the back of Father's knees when Eleanor the Third is tucked there at night."

James forced a laugh, but it was difficult. He had to give his twin more time. At least he was home, and that was the most important thing. "Just a nip in the air, nothing more. Eleanor the Third now has a brother, William the Fourth, a big black tom who keeps the back of Mother's knees warm."

"I saw the two of them trotting into our parents' bedchamber, tails high, ready for the knees. Any racing cats around?"

"Mother had hopes for William, but the truth is, all he likes to do is eat and sleep and allow Eleanor to wash him, which she does, endlessly."

"I'd like to have a racing cat. I remember all cousin Meggie's triumphs."

James laughed. "Remember Ellis Peepers, who's now our head gardener? He's all wiry and long, red-haired, full beard that's so bright it looks like his face is on fire?" At his brother's nod, James went on, "He was schooled by the Harker brothers in training techniques and how to select good racing cat owners. Maybe he'll deem you worthy."

"Ellis will find me to be the most responsible of racing cat owners. But I suppose it will have to wait. Just now, what with my partner coming tomorrow, there's simply too much to do."

"So you and Miss Carrick will be spending all your days at Lyon's Gate, repairing the house and the stables."

"Yes," Jason said, voice now grim. He turned to face his brother as they drew in their horses at the stable. "Can you begin to imagine the fights we will have? And unlike you, I won't be able to kiss her until she forgets her own name."

"Or until she's wearing a silly grin and forgotten why she wanted to rip your throat out."

"Now there's a thought." Jason laughed and smacked

his brother on the arm. "It would be so much easier were she a man."

Late the following afternoon, Jason was pleasantly tired after working all day at Lyon's Gate. The stables were nearly ready for their tenants. Perhaps he could list out for Miss Carrick the joys of being close to her horses, both day and night. Or perhaps not. He'd just placed his boot on the first step of the ten broad, deeply set front steps of Northcliffe Hall when he heard a carriage rolling up the long drive. He stepped back down, knowing it was Miss Carrick.

Despite the fact she was a thorn in his flesh, and that fate had planted her right in front of him with no rhyme nor reason, Jason realized he felt good. He crossed his arms over his chest and watched Miss Carrick lean out the window, waving to him. He hoped she didn't leap out before the driver stopped the carriage. He watched the coachman draw in smartly right next to him. Jason saw it was a rented carriage, an expensive rented carriage. There were two outriders.

He started forward when the door flew wide and Miss Carrick jumped down before either he or the coach driver could assist her. He wasn't particularly surprised.

"Mr. Sherbrooke! I'm here. How nice of you to be waiting out here for me to arrive."

CHAPTER 13

❦⚬❦

❦ She was the height of fashion in a dark hunter green gown with wide sleeves tapering to fit snugly at her wrists and a belted waist that looked the size of a man's fists bunched together. Her hair was tucked up under a bonnet of the same dark green, several curls lazily floating down in front of her ears. And in her lovely little ears were sparkling diamond studs. "I see that you are, Miss Carrick. Both you and your equipage look quite grand."

"Yes, the carriage cost me very nearly all the money my father's banker would give me, the dolt. I must write my father and have him send instructions."

"Unlimited funds for you, Miss Carrick?"

"Don't be a knothead. Oh, thank you for the compliment to my person as well as to my carriage. The gown is from Madame Jordan, who tells me that your father selects all your mother's clothes, and your brother selects all of Corrie's. I've never heard of gentlemen dressing women. Isn't that rather odd? Is it some sort of tradition in your family?"

"To be honest, I've never thought about it, although the men in this family have excellent taste— Hmm, now that I think about it, I don't know that I would have selected such a very dark green for you, Miss Carrick. I could, of course, be mistaken—perhaps the late afternoon sun shining too brightly in my eyes—but is *bilious* the right word?"

She let the bait dangle in front of her nose for a moment, then laughed aloud, a bright, quite lovely sound. "That was well done." She turned to the carriage. "Come along, Martha. We're here at Northcliffe Hall. Isn't it beautiful? Look at all the colors."

Her maid hopped out of the carriage, landing lightly on very little feet. She couldn't be more than seventeen, Jason thought. She was very small, her pointed chin trembling in excitement. "Oh yes, it be glorious, more than glorious. So many thick trees, jest like in the park. I didn't know you was acquainted with such grand folk, Miss Hallie."

"Only the grandest folk for me, Martha."

Jason laughed as Hallie rolled her eyes. "Let me see to your coachman and your outriders." Jason turned to the coachman. "Any problems?"

The coachman gave Jason a smart salute. "None, milord. Benji and Neally, our outriders provided by Miss Carrick's banker, well they wanted a highwayman or two to break the monotony, but nary a rascal showed hisself."

"He's twenty-eight minutes too young to be a lord, John," Hallie said. At Jason's raised eyebrow, she added, "I overheard Melissa telling her mother about how close in time you and James were born."

Hallie turned when Martha lightly tugged on her sleeve. "Yes, Martha?"

Martha whispered, "Who is that god, ma'am?"

"God? What god?"

"The young gentleman, ma'am. Oh Lordie, is he ever a beaut. I've never afore seen such a glorious young gentleman, meybe more than jest plain glor—"

"Yes, yes, I understand, Martha. We will look into getting you spectacles."

"But I gots eyes wot can see birdseeds, Miss Hallie."

So both he and the Hall were glorious? He saw Hallie open, then shut her mouth. Routed by her maid. He said to the coachman, "That is Hollis standing in the front door. He will see that all three of you have dinner and beds for the night. Thank you for taking such fine care of Miss Carrick."

The three men stood gazing up at Northcliffe Hall and Jason knew what they were seeing. One of England's great houses, three stories, with three wings coming off the back of the house, making it look like an E. The first earl of Northcliffe had built the Hall, quarrying the lovely gray stone at Hillsley Dale some three centuries before, mellowed now to a soft cream color in the late afternoon light. Northcliffe would look utterly stark and coldly formal like so many of the other great houses of England if not for the current countess who'd planted oak, lime, larch, and maple trees all along the drive and throughout the grounds more than twenty-five years before. As for the myriad bushes and flowering plants, they crept close to the stone walls, softening the lines of the house even more, and presented so many colors and blossoms in the summer that the Northcliffe gardeners would find small groups of strangers on the grounds staring at the incredible summer foliage. It looked like a great house conjured up in a fairy tale.

"Thank ye, milord," the coachman said and turned when Hollis called out, his old voice firm and steady, "Come along, lads, Bobby here will take you to the stables to see to your horses and the carriage, then you'll go to the kitchen."

The three men, leading the horses, with Bobby three strides ahead of them, disappeared around the side of the house. Hollis said as he came down the deep, wide steps to stand beside Jason, "You are Miss Carrick?"

"Yes," Hallie said, staring at the old man with his sharp blue eyes and his flowing thick white hair. "I saw a painting of Moses once. I would accept your Ten Commandments before I would accept his, Hollis."

Hollis gave her a lovely smile, showing a mouth still filled with sufficient teeth to chew his mutton.

Jason, serious as a judge, said, "James and I believed he was God. You never corrected us, Hollis."

"You and his lordship never disobeyed me when

you believed I could smite you both with but a flick of my finger."

"James and I feared more than smiting, Hollis. We feared you would give us pustules all over our bodies."

Hollis looked thoughtful. "Pustules. Hmm. That never occurred to me. I suppose it is too late now?"

"It's perfect for the twins. Ah, would you please see to Miss Carrick's maid, Martha? I will take care of the disposition of Miss Carrick."

Hollis, who'd been studying Hallie, said in a low voice that Hallie could hear perfectly well, "You will not cause her bodily harm, will you Master Jason?"

"You mean as in tossing her into Reever Lake? No, I'm too tired to do away with her today."

He heard a gasp from young Martha and smiled down at her. "I won't strangle your mistress. Don't worry."

Hallie said, "I'll tell you when to worry, Martha. Go with Hollis now." She watched small Martha walk very slowly up the stone steps next to the ancient butler, her hand ready to steady him if he faltered. Both Hallie and Jason saw Martha look up at him, and heard her whisper, "Ye're glorious, Mr. Hollis, meybe even more than glorious."

Hallie laughed, couldn't help herself. She was still very nervous. "And here I wondered if Martha and I would suit."

"Since she makes you laugh, she'll suit you well enough."

"I didn't meet Hollis when I came here after Melissa and Leo's wedding."

"I believe he was in his bed nursing a cold. He is quite well now, thank God."

When Hollis and Martha had negotiated the steps and disappeared into the house, she looked up at Jason. "I don't know about glorious, but you are a beaut. Such a pity that you know it too well."

An eyebrow shot up. "You are something of a beaut yourself, Miss Carrick. However, unlike you, I am not vain. I do not array myself in such a way to draw attention to my attributes."

"And what would you do if you wished to draw attention?"

She had him, and she knew it. She grinned up at him shamelessly. "You really couldn't push your chest up and out, now could you? Hmm. As for rice powder on your face, I daresay you'd sweat it off in the middle of your first waltz."

He quickly took the opening she gave him. "And ladies don't sweat off their rice powder?"

"Certainly not. Ladies are made of fine porcelain, not porous mud."

Since that was exactly what he felt like at the moment, Jason threw back his head and laughed. He realized in that moment he'd missed that fast brain of hers, not to mention her tongue.

"Ravensworth Abbey is as grand as Northcliffe Hall, but it's very different. You have a beautiful home."

"Lyon's Gate is now my home."

"*Our* home, Mr. Sherbrooke. *Our* home." She lightly patted his white sleeve. "Twenty-eight minutes.

Not even half an hour and your fate is decided."

"Please believe me, Miss Carrick, I would rather share a house with you than one day be the master here."

She noticed then that he wasn't dressed like a son of the house. Odd that she hadn't noticed how sweaty and dirty he was, his old boots scuffed, his white shirt open at the neck and a bit down his chest, and she wasn't about to stare, not when all that lovely dirt meant he'd been at Lyon's Gate and she hadn't. "You've been spending the past three days at Lyon's Gate, haven't you?" Her voice rose an octave. "What have you done?"

He'd have to have been dead not to hear the outrage, and was tempted to string her along. No, better not, since her eyes were already bulging in her head. Besides, his precious mother might hear her shouting at him and come down and shoot her. "Nothing you would disapprove of," he said mildly. "I hired three men from the village to help me clean out the stables. We nearly finished today. I've already spoken to the man who will decide what is necessary to repair the house and he and his workers will begin tomorrow. You can speak to them then. Oh yes, my mother sent over a half-dozen gardeners, who are all pulling the ivy from the house and getting rid of the weeds. It begins to look much better."

Hallie chewed this over a moment, nodded. "All right. You are lucky you didn't paint any rooms, Mr. Sherbrooke."

"Paint, you say? I was picturing a lovely bright crimson for the drawing room, perhaps one wall a pale blue. What do you think?"

She looked up into those incredible lavender eyes of his and said, "You surprise me, sir. An excellent choice. And lovely crimson draperies, don't you think? Or perhaps the pale blue?"

"Crimson, with thick braided gold tassels looping them up. Velvet would be utterly charming. How nice. We should have no arguments at all." He offered her his arm. "Let me take you inside to greet everyone. I imagine they should be assembled by now."

She laughed as she walked beside him up the steps. "May we leave early tomorrow to go to Lyon's Gate? I want to see everything."

She was as excited as he was. He hated it that she lusted after Lyon's Gate as much as he did.

He called out, "Hello, Mother. Look who's arrived."

Alex stood just inside the imposing front door, eyeing the young woman who'd had the gall to ruin her son's dream. She knew her duty, gulped once, and presented a smile. Sometimes being well bred was the very devil. "Miss Carrick. How very lovely to see you again."

Hallie curtsied. "Thank you, ma'am, for having me. It is very kind of you."

What to say when she'd really had no choice in the matter? Best to keep her mouth shut.

Hallie gave her a shameless grin. "I do hope you don't have a gun behind your back."

Alex felt an unwanted tug of liking. "Hmm. Be very deferential to me, Miss Carrick, nod in modest agreement at everything I say, and you might survive."

"Sorry, Mother. Even if she tried, I can't see that happening," Jason said.

"In that case, then you must come into the drawing room, Miss Carrick. My dear mother-in-law, Lady Lydia, the dowager countess of Northcliffe, is here for her weekly visit. You can meet her and have a lovely cup of tea."

Jason groaned.

Hallie looked suddenly wary.

Jason tried to catch his mother's eye, but she'd taken Hallie's arm and was steering her in a straight line toward the drawing room. He'd rather be tossed on the back of a wild two-year-old, with no bridle, perhaps even boiled in oil. A firing squad was a good option.

His grandmother hated every female in the known universe except for his aunt Melissande, including his mother and Corrie, and that was why his father had finally moved her into the dowager house at the end of the lane five years before.

He said from behind them, "Mother, perhaps you should reconsider this particular course of action. She's a lamb to the slaughter."

"Nonsense. You are a bit on the dirty side, dearest, but your grandmother won't mind. And Miss Carrick surely is a well-enough behaved girl to sail smoothly through, don't you think?"

"No. Miss Carrick, do you know Wilhelmina Wyndham?"

"Oh dear."

CHAPTER 14

꙳

꙳ Jason would rather empty chamber pots than walk into that drawing room with the tethered goat, but he simply couldn't leave Miss Carrick to his grandmother alone and unarmed. It would be too cruel. Not that his presence would make much difference. She would be crushed by that malicious aged tongue; his grandmother would look at Hallie and see fresh meat. Odd how she never turned her cannon on either him or James or his father. Just those unfortunate enough to be female.

Jason saw Corrie seated in a wing chair, James standing behind her, his hand lightly on her shoulder, doubtless to keep her from leaping up and kicking over his grandmother's chair when she started shooting insults.

His grandmother's eyes lit up when she saw him. "Dear Jason, what a sight you are, my boy, but that certainly isn't important, now is it? What's a little dirt in the flow of time? Come and give me a big kiss."

Jason grinned at the old woman, leaned down and kissed her parchment cheek. She lightly touched his hair and whispered, "I have some nutty buns Hollis brought me this morning. Come later and I will share them with you." Jason gripped her veiny old hands and whispered back that indeed he would.

When he stepped back, the dowager countess looked up to see her daughter-in-law, the red-haired hussy, gripping the arm of a young lady she'd never laid eyes on before.

Jason saw it in her eyes as clearly as if she'd spoken aloud: *new prey, bring me new prey.*

"Who are you?"

Alex dropped Hallie's arm. "This is the young lady who is moving into the neighborhood, Mother-in-law. I fear"—she cleared her throat—"that is, it *appears* she will be staying with us for a while. Isn't she lovely? Don't you think she's beautifully gowned? And observe how gracefully she moves. Miss Carrick, this is Lady Lydia, the earl's mother."

"Well, come here, girl, and let me look at you."

There was a moment of stark silence in the drawing room. Hallie saw that everyone was staring from her to the old woman, and not breathing.

She looked at the little old lady, with her shiny pink scalp showing through her white hair, and couldn't imagine her being the least bit like Wilhelmina Wyndham. Surely not; Jason was joking with her. Lady Lydia was by no means frail, nor did she have the look of a placid old lady to have her hand patted and pillows settled behind her ancient back. She looked as substantial and solid as Hallie's mare, Piccola, and surely that wasn't a bad thing. On the other hand, Piccola could bite her and whip her with her tail at the same time. The dowager's old eyes gleamed, her mouth opened, and suddenly out of Hallie's mouth came, "Do you remember the French Revolution, my lady?"

Lady Lydia froze. "The *what*, girl?"

"When the French people rose up against the king and queen and guillotined them?"

Lady Lydia studied that lovely young face for a very long time before saying quietly, "I remember it like yesterday. None of us could believe the French rabble had locked their king and queen in the Conciergerie. There were reports the king and queen would go to the guillotine. We waited, wondering how such a thing could come to pass. And then one day they cut off the king's head.

"I remember so many people tried to save the queen after that, but you know, she'd become quite dotty toward the end, and the final escape failed. She insisted on the coach stopping so she could smell some flowers. Do you know something else, girl? I also remember Waterloo."

"Did you ever meet the duke of Wellington,

ma'am?" As she spoke, Hallie sat down on the foot cushion at Lady Lydia's feet.

"Certainly, a clever man is Arthur Wellesley. When he returned to London in the summer of 1815, he was fêted every evening; ladies threw themselves at him, gentlemen wanted the honor of being seen with him. So much gaiety, and such relief that the monster was finally vanquished."

Hallie leaned up. "It must be so wonderful to have lived as long as you have, through so many amazing happenings, and you know the duke of Wellington. Did you also know George III before he went mad?"

"Oh yes. There were rumors, of course, but in 1788, it was finally announced that the king's reason had flown the royal head. George got better, but of course, the illness struck him again until finally it never left him. Poor man, shamed by his son and heir, but his queen, Charlotte, ah, such strength she had. Such a pity, such a pity."

"I cannot imagine being as old as you are. You are so very lucky."

Lady Lydia would have liked to arch an eyebrow, but she didn't have any left. "No one has said anything like that to me before. Hmm. I've never looked at all my decades in precisely that light. My daughter-in-law is right. Your gown is lovely even with those ridiculous big sleeves that make you six feet wide."

"At least they fit at the wrist now. You wore those lovely Regency gowns that fit up high and fell straight to the ground."

"Aye, they were lovely, all that light muslin, no corsets or petticoats to weigh you down, but so many ladies caught dreadful colds because they wore so little. At least today you won't catch an inflammation of the lung. Hmm. I find it unusual that you know how to dress since you don't appear to have a husband to select your gowns for you, like these two."

"I have a fine sense of style, ma'am. Thank you for remarking upon it."

Alex was utterly baffled, as were the rest of the people in the room. There was utter silence save for Hallie and the dowager's low voices. The door opened and Douglas came striding in, evidently on a mission to save Miss Carrick. Alex grabbed his sleeve. "Don't move," she whispered. "I can't believe this, but you're not needed." Douglas looked at Miss Carrick, and saw his mother's hand lightly caressing her green sleeve. He froze as had everyone else in the drawing room, his jaw dropped.

Lady Lydia looked over and smiled at her eldest son. "My darling boy, have the red-haired girl pour the tea. At least she's learned how I take it now."

"And you appreciate that, don't you, Mother?"

What was going on here? Hallie wondered. Lady Lydia's mouth was a tight seam. At the earl's continued silence, she nodded. "Yes, I am most appreciative." She turned back to Hallie. "Are you here to marry Jason? My poor precious boy is in need of a good steady girl, a strong girl with nerves of oak. Yes, that is probably the most important requirement of his wife."

"Why, ma'am? Is he of such a delicate disposition?"

"Oh no, it's entirely something else. Well, are your nerves strong as a carriage wheel?"

"Yes, ma'am. But why?"

"Both my beautiful grandsons are gentlemen to their quite well-shaped feet, more's the pity. Jason's wife must be able to protect him from all the hussies who continually hunt him down with the intent of taking advantage of him." She shot a look over at Corrie, who was staring fixedly at her, her mouth open. "What is the matter with you, Coriander? You look like a landed trout. It is not attractive. It will give your husband a disgust of you."

Corrie shut her mouth.

Lady Lydia said to Hallie, "My James's wife is many things, Miss Carrick, but I will say this for her, she's strong as the stoutest oak branch. James rarely goes about without her. He knows she will protect him. She has learned to throw herself in front of him when ladies hurl themselves in his path to gain his attention. Coriander tells him his attention is all he will ever bestow, and then only if the female in question has gained her fiftieth summer."

Jason said, "Grandmother, Miss Carrick is not here to marry me. We barely know each other."

"I believe the best marriages begin with the exchange of names, nothing more," said the dowager. "Look at you, my dearest boy, no female with eyes in her head would not try to hunt you down. Poor James now—"

The earl cleared his throat loudly.

"Humph," said the dowager.

Jason didn't understand why she hadn't yet blasted Hallie, but since no one had drunk any tea as of yet there was time for her to change her mind and decide Hallie was an encroaching hussy, like his mother.

"Then why are you so dirty, my boy, if you weren't chasing her all about the grounds?"

"And she caught me several times and dirtied me up?"

"That's it, yes."

"Sorry, Grandmother. You know I bought Lyon's Gate. I was working there today. I had no time to change my clothes. Forgive me."

"You were working like a common laborer?"

"Yes, ma'am."

Lady Lydia accepted a cup of tea from her daughter-in-law. Douglas watched her shake it around in the cup for a moment, saw that she wanted desperately to complain about it, but she knew if she did, she would not be invited back until the hussy herself invited her back, and she could be dead by that time. Hollis passed a lovely large tray filled with scones, lemon tarts, tiny seed cakes, and small cucumber and ham sandwiches, sliced into myriad shapes.

Jason saw Miss Carrick place her tea and plate containing two lemon tarts on the floor beside her. She looked perfectly content to remain at his grandmother's feet. Just you wait, he wanted to tell her, just you wait until she decides your hair is brassy, or those lovely eyes of yours are sly, or God knew what else.

The dowager sipped her tea, grimaced only a little bit, then announced, "No matter Coriander's faults, and they are multitudinous, she has presented James with two lovely boys, the very image of his beautiful aunt Melissande, who should have been wedded to—"

Douglas cleared his throat, watched his mother poke a tart into her mouth and chew it vigorously, and said, "Jason, you have the look of a contented man. Tell me how everything is going at Lyon's Gate."

Jason sat forward, clasped his hands between his knees, forgot that he was dirty and smelled of dried sweat, forgot that Hallie would be living with him and that she was half owner of Lyon's Gate, and said, "Oh yes. I want you to come over soon, Grandmother, and tell me what you think of my home. The stables are a perfect size, and once we got them all cleared out and cleaned up, we could see the excellent workmanship." He continued to speak, and everyone smiled at him, nodded, asked questions. It was as if no one else in the room existed except Jason, Hallie thought, eyeing him. Not a word about her, but she'd quickly realized that no one wanted to shock the dowager. And, of course, he'd just gotten home after being away for a very long time. Were they all afraid he would leave again? This time for good? So no one said anything to bruise his tender feelings?

When Jason wound down, a silly grin on his face, Hallie said in a quiet voice to the dowager, "Perhaps you and I could visit Lyon's Gate together."

The old lady chewed slowly on her ham sandwich,

which had been shaped by Cook to look like one of the full oak trees outside the drawing room window. Slowly, she nodded. "Yes," she said, patting Hallie's sleeve, "I should like that very much."

Hallie finished a lemon tart. "We will visit early next week." She grinned. "Do you know when I first saw Hollis only a while ago, I asked him if he was Moses?"

"Moses? That crickety old man? Hmm. He does look rather like some ancient prophet, doesn't he? I can remember the days when he chased down James and Jason, tucked them under his arms, and delivered them to their tutor, he was that strong. They were ten years old, I remember. What did Hollis tell you?"

Hallie's lip quivered. "He said no, he wasn't Moses, he was God."

The old lady laughed, a cackle really, but it was full-bodied, even though it sounded like rusty nails grinding together. "Did you really, old man?"

Hollis, who was serving some cream onto Corrie's scone, finished what he was doing, then raised his head and smiled at the dowager. "Certainly, madam."

CHAPTER 15

❧·❧

❧ Five mornings later at the breakfast table, Alex said, "The messenger you sent to Mrs. Tewksbury returned today with her reply." She handed Hallie a pristine white envelope, for the messenger had carefully wrapped the letter in a white cloth. She wanted to tell Miss Carrick it was her responsibility to pay the messenger, but that might be a bit heavy-handed.

"Jason, listen. Angela is arriving at the end of the week!"

Douglas said, "You know, Jason, you cannot move into Lyon's Gate until it's habitable enough for the ladies."

"I agree. However, I can."

Hallie said without missing a beat, "You're going

nowhere near Lyon's Gate with a pillow and a bed unless I'm with you."

Douglas choked on his coffee.

"My lord, are you all right?" Hallie was on her feet in an instant and sending the heel of her hand into Douglas's back.

"I'm fine, Miss Carrick," Douglas said at last. He looked at Jason, who rolled his eyes.

Hallie reseated herself. "I plan that all of us will move to Lyon's Gate together."

Jason said to his relatives, "She doesn't trust me. It's an insult to my mother, Miss Carrick, and surely you would wish to rethink that."

"I beg pardon, ma'am. It is my experience, however, that sometimes the fruit falls some distance from the tree, through no fault of the fine tree."

"Is this a reference to rotten apples, Hallie?" Corrie said.

"Oh no, surely not," Hallie said, and grinned like a sinner.

"As the tree in question, Miss Carrick, I forgive you," said Alex, "However, I do not appreciate your insulting my fruit. You must realize that a tree will go to any length to protect her fruit, no matter how far away it falls. A tree can cast a very long shadow."

The twins and their father stared at the countess in awe. Jason said, "Ah, speaking as a cherished fruit, I thank you, Mother. Well, Miss Carrick, would you like to graciously ask my parents if they would allow Mrs. Tewksbury to spend some time here?"

Hallie smiled at the countess of Northcliffe, who, she was certain, would prefer her to move to Russia. "My lady, I would be very grateful if you would allow both my cousin and me to remain here for a little while longer. It won't be much more than a couple of days after she arrives. We've visited Mr. Millsom's furniture warehouse in Eastbourne. We've selected fabrics and styles. Truly, well, perhaps three more days after Friday."

Such a bright, charming girl, Alex thought, wishing she could strangle her and toss her body in Cowper's well. But it was not to be. "Certainly, Miss Carrick. That will be our pleasure."

Corrie said, "May I visit Lyon's Gate today, Jason? See how everything is coming?"

He nodded. "Don't bring the twins yet. There is too much danger of them getting hurt. You know, Miss Carrick, three days might be about right. Perhaps four. Not everything will be finished, but enough."

"Oh that would be wonderful! It's actually going to happen!" She jumped from her chair, grabbed Jason by the hand, pulled him up, and began to waltz him around the breakfast parlor. She was laughing and hopping about, and nearly struck the back of a chair. Suddenly she stopped cold. She was panting a bit. "Oh goodness, I don't know why I did that. Do forgive me for making a spectacle of you."

He was laughing at her enthusiasm. "I didn't mind. I haven't danced with such enjoyment since just after dawn this morning with my nephews."

"What is this?" his father said.

"They fetched me out of bed at five-thirty this morning. Actually, they jumped on me and began dancing on the bed." Jason shrugged, grinned. "We had a fine time of it. Thankfully the little devils collapsed after about ten minutes and all three of us went back to sleep."

James said, "Their nurse was frantic when she discovered the boys were gone. Corrie and I didn't panic, however. She stood in the dark hall and said to me, 'Listen,' and sure enough there was this muffled singing coming from behind Jason's bedchamber door. We opened the door very quietly, and there he was dancing with the twins. We left. The next time we saw him was an hour later, one twin tucked under each arm, their heads on his shoulders, sound asleep, all three of them."

Jason's smile slid off his face. "Corrie, er, you didn't really look into the bedchamber the first time, did you? I mean, you didn't actually see me dancing, did you?"

"Oh yes." She had the gall to giggle.

He felt the flush rise to his eyebrows. He'd been naked. The twins' nightshirts had left their feet uncovered, and those small toes had been cold.

Corrie said to the table at large, "Neither James nor Jason wear nightshirts."

"Thank you for informing everyone of that fact, Corrie," her husband said, now as red-faced as his twin.

Hallie said, "It can't be that embarrassing, Jason.

You are your brother's twin, and Corrie's been married to him a good long time. No surprises, surely."

Jason's eyebrow went up. "Isn't that a tad indelicate for the breakfast table, Hallie?"

"No more indelicate than what your sister-in-law said."

"But she lives here, has lived here since she was nearly three years old."

"Oh dear, you're right. I am very sorry. Sometimes I speak before I think."

"I think all of us would like some more tea," Alex said.

Douglas said, "Did you dance with James and Jessie Wyndham's children?"

"Oh yes. We had competitions. I believe that Alice and I won the last one, only three days before I left."

"Alice?" Douglas asked. "Oh yes, she's the youngest, isn't she?"

Jason nodded. "She's all of four years old, has a mop of red curls, and a precious lisp. She sang the American anthem at the top of her lungs, all of it while we danced, demanded that I sing it along with her. Everyone was laughing so hard when we finished that Alice claimed the prize while everyone was too weak to argue."

Hallie said when everyone stopped laughing, "And what was the prize?"

He opened his mouth, then closed it. "Nothing much of anything, really. Now, when was the last time you saw Mrs. Tewksbury?"

"I was all of seventeen. My father and Genny asked her to visit Carrick Grange for the Christmas season. She's in love with my father, but every woman is since he is the most beautiful man in the world. Genny paid it no mind since Angela is of the age to be Genny's mother. She is something of an original."

"You honestly believe your father is more beautiful than James and Jason?" Corrie asked, her fork stopped six inches from her mouth.

"Certainly. If the three of them were walking down the street, the ladies would all try to chase my father down. If my father were too fast to be caught, only then would they turn to James and Jason."

James said quickly, before Corrie hurled a forkful of eggs at Miss Carrick, "No matter. I am looking forward to meeting the original Mrs. Tewksbury."

Alex said, "As for me, I want to meet Hallie's father."

Douglas said, eyebrow hoisted up, "You, my dear wife, may observe Alec Carrick from a distance if ever he chances to appear. Is that clear?"

"You always order me about so prettily, Douglas."

James said, before Corrie could accuse Hallie of being a blind moron, "Now, Jason, you've had ten men hammering, painting, carrying wood, not including the three of us, and ten women scrubbing, with Hallie supervising all of us. You've agreed on furniture, have you not?"

Jason said, "Surprisingly enough, we managed to come to agreement, for the most part, and that includes draperies and paint colors as well. I scarce remember how bad the house looked when I first saw it. And the paddocks, all freshly painted, the tack room—" and on and on he went, his family so very pleased they smiled and nodded and asked questions even though they'd heard this nearly same recital every evening. When finally no one could think of another question to ask him, James turned to Hallie, "When are you taking your mare to Lyon's Gate?"

She said, "Piccola's stable is all ready for her, but she will remain here until Jason and I actually move to Lyon's Gate. Did I tell you—"

Unfortunately, Hallie wasn't the long absent son of the house, and was cut off by Corrie. "Oh yes, you told us all about her, Hallie. Goodness, Jason, another week and even the furniture will be there. This is marvelous. And less than an hour's ride from Northcliffe. We are all so very pleased, particularly my husband." She beamed at him only to see that Hallie and Jason were now arguing in low voices. It was so common to see them going at it, she said something sure to snag Hallie's attention. "Hallie, you're very nearly as beautiful a woman as Jason is a man."

Hallie turned in her chair so quickly, she knocked over her teacup. She stared at Jason's sister-in-law and found herself without a word to say. As for Jason, he was laughing.

Hallie said, "Well, thank you, Corrie. However, truth be told, I am only a very vague copy of my father."

Corrie said, "Come now, Hallie, he's your father, thus you see him with less objectivity than you would another man. Come now, admit it."

But Hallie shook her head. "Wait and see."

As everyone filed out of the breakfast room, Alex placed her hand on her husband's arm. "Do you know, everything has changed so utterly since Jason came home. I'm quite enjoying myself."

Douglas looked ahead at Hallie and Jason, still arguing about God knew what, and said thoughtfully, "I wonder."

Alex said, "Don't wonder, I beg of you. Can you believe that Hallie and your mother had a fine time visiting Lyon's Gate? Hallie told me later that when she confessed to Lady Lydia her partnership with Jason, your mother told her to take the upper hand as soon as possible because her two precious grandsons were stubborn as stoats. But then again, she told Hallie, all gentlemen were stubborn and used to getting their own way. Since, she told Hallie, she'd lived eight decades she'd witnessed this many times and Hallie would be wise to take note of it."

Douglas laughed. "If you had been the one to tell her, she would have accused you of fostering immorality and God knows what else."

"Well, I must say I'm relieved that Hallie was the one who told her. I thought that at last she'd blast her."

"Don't sound so disappointed."

"I can't help it. Do you know that Hallie took both

Lady Lydia and Hollis to Lyon's Gate yesterday in the carriage? She even thought to bring a picnic lunch."

"Yes, I knew. Hollis was grinning from ear to ear, told me about everything going on, just as Jason does every single evening."

Alex sighed. "Why would Lady Lydia like Hallie Carrick so very much and detest me?"

"I've thought about that. I think it's because Hallie jumped her before she could get the bit in her mouth and chew on it. I think it would behoove both you and Corrie to learn a lesson from this. It might be too late, but who knows?"

"Hmm. Are you going to work at Lyon's Gate today?"

Douglas shook his head. "With James gone all the time, I must see to business here."

She went up on her tiptoes, drew him down to her, and whispered against his ear, "I haven't minded rubbing down your sore muscles, my lord."

"I married a baggage, thank God."

CHAPTER 16

✣

Lyon's Gate
Five Days Later

✣ "Everett! Don't eat that nail!"

Three adults and Martha ran toward the little boy, but his mother was the fastest. Corrie whipped him up in her arms, pulled the nail out of his hand, spit on her handkerchief and wiped his mouth. "No, no, no!" she yelled in his face and shook him for good measure.

Everett stared at his mother, screwed up his face, threw back his head and yowled.

His twin, Douglas, grabbed his mother's skirt and yanked hard. Corrie, both hands trying to hold Everett still, crooned down to Douglas, "Just a moment, baby, just another moment, and Mama will pick you up too."

Everett's voice went up another octave. Douglas screwed up his face, opened his mouth and matched his twin's volume. Martha patted their hands. "Heavenly groats, my lady, me own little brother niv—never—made so much racket as these little nits."

Jason called out, "Who wants to waltz with me?"

There was an instant of complete silence, then, "I do!"

"I do!"

"Me first, Uncle Jason!"

Everett was trying to pull away from his mother and Douglas was jumping up and down, now pulling on Jason's dirty pant leg.

Jason, laughing, picked up Douglas and gathered Everett to his other side, and called out, "I need some music, please."

Hallie, who'd come running out of the house at Everett's yells, didn't hesitate. She started singing one of Duchess Wyndham's ditties, written some twenty years before and still a favorite in the king's navy. She sang it in three-quarter time to a popular waltz tune so the words fit the rhythm of a waltz, for the most part, making anyone listening laugh his head off.

Jason whirled and dipped and glided. The twins laughed and shrieked. Every adult within one hundred feet stopped working to watch, and listen.

> "'E ain't the man to shout 'Please, my dear!'
> 'E's only a lout who shouts 'Bring me a beer!'
> 'E's a bonny man wit' a bonny lass
> Who troves 'im a tippler right on 'is ass.

And to hove and to trove we go, my boys,
We'll shout as we please till ship's ahoy!"

Three of the workers knew the ditty and began singing along with Hallie. They were all swaying, then Mackie, a bricklayer, yelled to one of the women, "Meg, come dance wit' me!"

Soon there were at least four couples waltzing, Martha herself doing very well with young Thomas the blacksmith's son, who had just celebrated his tenth birthday. Alex heard her say, "She's my mistress, she is. Jest listen to those beautiful pipes inside her purty self."

The dowager countess, Lady Lydia, hummed and swayed in her chair, in blessed shade beside the front door, Angela Tewksbury at her side, laughing, trying to clap her hands in three-quarter waltz time.

Hollis stood in the doorway smiling benignly, foot tapping. He caught Jason's eye and pointed to the platter and formed the words *lemonade, biscuits.* Jason whispered in Everett's ear, then in Douglas's. To his astonishment, both little boys grabbed him around the neck and yelled,

"Dance!"

"Dance!"

It required another full rendition of the sailor's song before the twins decided they wanted lemonade, all because Hollis was drinking a big glass, letting a dribble run down his chin, not three feet from them.

Soon they were seated on a blanket in the shade next

to Lady Lydia and Mrs. Tewksbury, a plate of cakes and biscuits on the blanket between them. They were jabbering in twin talk, each trying to grab the most cakes.

"Give me water, Hollis," Jason said, breathing hard. "Merciful heavens those two have more energy than Eliza Dickers. I don't think even she wore me out as much as those two."

One of his father's eyebrows kicked up. "A Baltimore belle?"

Hallie sneered, her expression condemning as a nun's. "Ah, yes, my lord. I understand that Jason's belle, Eliza Dickers, could perhaps be considered something of a virtuous widow, once upon a time, before your son's arrival to Baltimore."

Jason stiffened straight as the new fence poles he'd hammered into the ground only an hour before. He gave her a look to curdle butter and a voice to freeze the outskirts of Hell. "Eliza Dickers is a lady who is one of Jessie Wyndham's best friends. She, unlike you, Miss Carrick, is an adult. She hurts no one, either with actions or words."

He turned on his heel and walked back to his brother.

Hallie stared after him. "Oh dear."

Douglas said, "Why do you dislike my son so, Miss Carrick?"

"Oh dear," Hallie said again. "I didn't mean—truly I didn't, it's just that I'm—"

"You're still furious with him because he owns half of Lyon's Gate?"

"No," she said, staring at Jason whilst he spoke to his mother now, his hand on her sleeve.

"Ah," said Douglas's father, and smiled at her.

Hallie stilled. "I don't like what you're thinking, sir, even though I don't know what it is, and I don't ever want to know what it is."

She watched Jason raise a glass of water and down the entire glass, his strong throat working. His shirt, open halfway down his chest, was sweated through and clinging to him. The hair on his chest was dirty and shiny as well with sweat, which she wasn't going to think about.

If Douglas wasn't mistaken, and he never was about things like this, Hallie Carrick was staring at his son with a rather alarmed expression on her face. He would wager a bundle of groats that she'd been jealous. Yes, she'd given a display of nice, raw jealousy, as low and human as could be. It was difficult to see another side to her, Douglas thought, a charmingly human side, since he'd wanted to strangle her for so long.

He watched Jason toss his glass to one of the workers standing near Hollis. Douglas said to Hallie, "Your voice is good and strong. Do you know that Duchess Wyndham is James Wyndham's cousin-in-law?"

"Oh yes, she's very famous in Baltimore. I believe Wilhelmina Wyndham quite hates her, although she hates a goodly number of people so that's no particular distinction."

"I can't believe you made that ditty fit waltz time, sort of. Well done."

"Thank you, sir. I suppose it's time for me to get back to hanging the new bedchamber draperies."

Douglas watched her walk into the house, her eyes on her shoes, and, if he wasn't mistaken, her shoulders a bit slumped.

James came up behind his brother, his arms folded over his own sweaty shirt. "Hallie hasn't worn breeches since that very first time we met her."

Jason, no hesitation at all, laughed. "I'm not about to say anything. She'd strip off her gown and pull on breeches just to spite me. Blessed hell, it's hotter now than it was a minute ago."

James took a glass of water from one of the workers, took a sip, then dumped the rest of the glass over his twin's head. "Better?"

Jason yelled, then groaned in pleasure. "Much better. Why don't we swim later?"

"You'll freeze your parts off," said their father.

"I can't wait," Jason said. He heard an ancient cackle and looked over at his grandmother, sitting close to Mrs. Tewksbury, an elderly lady herself, but not by any means an octogenarian. She couldn't be older than seventy. She had white hair threaded with soft brown strands, a sweet round face with few lines. She seemed utterly unflappable, and the greatest shock of all—his grandmother seemed to like her immensely. Not five minutes after they'd met, Jason heard them yelling at each other in the drawing room. He'd never heard a single person yell back at his grandmother before. He was nailed to the spot.

His grandmother sailed out of the drawing room some minutes later, saw him standing there, and gave him a sweet smile. He'd hugged her to him. "You don't like Mrs. Tewksbury, Grandmother?"

She eased back from him and patted his cheek. "Angela? I do believe she's got a nice wit, my boy. You may call Horace. I wish to go home now and speak to Cook. Angela's coming to dinner."

James's voice brought him back. "I like Angela. You never know what's going to come out of her mouth. I do believe she fascinates Grandmother, and vice versa."

"It is a miracle," said their mother, hugging both of them even though Jason was wet and dirty, James only dirty. She stepped back and raised her face to the sky, her eyes closed, her lips moving.

"Mother, what are you doing?"

"Ah, James, I'm praying this miracle doesn't disappear with the arrival of nightfall."

Douglas said, "If the miracle fades away, I'll do my best to cheer you up tonight."

His boys looked at each other, then down at their boots, not a word coming out of their mouths.

That evening, after dinner, the weather continued warm, a sickle moon hanging high in the sky. Jason walked into the east garden where all the naked male and female statues cavorted in timeless pleasure. Strangely enough, he was thinking of the last race he'd run against Jessie Wyndham. He'd been on Dodger, she on Rialto's son, Balthazar. Dodger's head was down, he was dead serious, focused on the finish line in the distance. With not more than twenty feet to go, Jason turned to look over his shoulder to see exactly where Balthazar was. His heart fell to his boots. Jessie wasn't on his back. Oh God, she'd fallen. Jason, terrified she was hurt or even dead, immediately wheeled Dodger about only to hear Jessie laugh. Laugh? He watched numbly as she hoisted herself back straight in the saddle, dug her heels into Balthazar's sleek sides and galloped past him, over the finish line a moment later. She whipped a rearing Balthazar around and called out between shouts of laughter, "Jason, I'm sorry to do that to you, but Balthazar can't bear to lose a race. He stops eating. Once he nearly died he was so distressed over a loss at the McFarly racetrack. I had to do something."

And Jason said mildly, "It's no problem at all, Jessie. That was an excellent trick."

"I've been doing it since I was twelve. I've never had to fling myself sideways with you before. I'm surprised James didn't warn you."

"No, James never said a thing."

"I wonder why the children kept mum."

"There was no reason for anyone to warn me since I've never before beaten you in a race."

She'd given him a fat smile and nodded, recognition that if she hadn't done him dirty, he would have won. When she dismounted, praising Balthazar, Jason rode up to her, smiling, and let Dodger at him. He bit Balthazar's flank, hard. Dodger hadn't been as philosophical about the dirty trick.

He was smiling absently as he looked up at Corrie's favorite statue, a kneeling man frozen for all eternity between a woman's legs.

He turned quickly when he heard a gasp. "Hallie. You found your way in here." She didn't look at him, only stared around at the various statues.

Jason said, "There are fifteen statues. Each, I suppose you could say, with a different approach to the theme. I believe it was my great-grandfather who brought them back from Greece."

She didn't say a single word. Her eyes did not waver.

He pointed up at the statue. "Most women prefer this one, once they are married, but only if their husbands aren't clods."

She looked more closely and blanched. "Oh dear, what is he doing?" Her voice shook, but she didn't look away from the statues. Jason said, his hand on her arm, "Come along." When she still didn't move, he grabbed her hand and pulled her away. He left the east gardens, still pulling her back toward the glass doors that opened into his father's—no, James's—estate room.

"No, no, please, Jason, please, let's not go in yet."

"You shouldn't be looking at those statues. You're too young and too ignorant." He said nothing more, merely looked down at her, his arms crossed over his chest. He watched her tongue rub over her bottom lip.

"I'm not young nor am I particularly ignorant, but I will be honest here. It was difficult to break myself away."

"You'd still be there, staring up, your mouth open, if I hadn't dragged you away."

"Probably true. Please, don't go in yet. I wanted to talk to you, and it's not about the statues."

A elegant brow went up.

She was scuffing her slipper against a small rock.

Finally, after the silence dragged out, he sighed. "Spit it out, Miss Carrick."

Her head came up and she said, all stiff and cold, "Please don't call me Miss Carrick in that awful formal voice again. You've called me Hallie for a good week now."

"Ah, the princess gives a direct order."

She wrung her hands. "No, I didn't mean that, truly, I only meant that when you speak in that tone it makes me feel lower than a slug. I hate it when you use my last name like you despise me so much you don't even want to acknowledge Hallie."

Jason leaned back against a sessile oak tree older than his grandmother, arms folded over his chest, and waited.

"I wanted to talk to you— All right, I really wanted to apologize. I was wrong to speak like that about Mrs. Dickers. It was such a shock to know that you and she—"

"You're ruining it, Miss Carrick."

Hallie sucked in her breath. "You can freeze someone with that voice."

"Yes. I learned it from my father. James as well."

"Don't you see? She's so much older than I am, and

I simply couldn't imagine you and she were, well—"

"This is getting better and better. How long do you plan to make excuses for yourself?"

She took a step toward him, reached out her hand, then dropped it again at her side. "We're going to have to live together, Jason. I can't live with you freezing me like this, like you're still angry, perhaps still disgusted with me. Oh, very well, I'll spit it out like you want. No more excuses. What I said was mean, it was petty, I'm a horrible person. Are you content now?"

"Hmm," he said, turned on his heel, opened the door to the estate room and disappeared inside. She stared after him, angry that he'd walked away and wanting to fall to her knees and beg him to forgive her.

Jason turned back to see her still standing where he'd left her, her face pale in the moonlight. He called out, "If I were a man who wished to marry, something I will never wish to do again in this lifetime, I would be strongly inclined toward Eliza Dickers. She is warm and kind and very funny." He didn't look back again.

And she wasn't.

Well, all right, so perhaps she wasn't warm and kind and funny all the time. She doubted strongly that Eliza Dickers was either. How could one be all those good things all the time? Surely even Mrs. Dickers had moments of pettiness. A pity her husband was dead, or he could be consulted. Surely she'd occasionally called him a bonehead or a fleabrain.

Hallie turned and walked back to the east gardens.

It took her a while to find the entrance even though she'd already been in there. She supposed it made sense to keep these awesome statues well hidden. She wondered at what age James and Jason had found them. She stood in front of the married woman's favorite statue—if the husband wasn't a clod—whatever that meant.

The fact was, she was a jealous bitch. She shook her head. No, she wasn't jealous, that was ridiculous, she was simply a bitch, no jealousy involved. She had imagined he'd bedded every woman he'd wanted to in Baltimore, that Eliza Dickers had been one of many. But maybe there hadn't been a long line of women, and that he, like a sultan, had to merely crook a finger to the one he wanted for the night. Maybe she'd been wrong about him, and he only shared himself with Eliza Dickers. He was certainly fond of her. But the fact of it was, he was so beautiful, so finely fashioned, she couldn't imagine him not taking what was offered. After all, he was a man, and her stepmother, Genny, had told her candidly that every man Hallie met would think of little else other than bedding her, that it was simply the way of the species, and that they couldn't help themselves. But Jason, he'd never shown any lecherous tendencies around her, and how could that be? Surely she was pretty enough to warrant at least one interested look, wasn't she? Perhaps he was simply very good at hiding what apparently all men wanted.

"You're a fool, my girl," she said, looking up at the

woman lying on her back, her mouth open on some sort of scream. Why was she screaming? Was the man hurting her? A woman would willingly allow her husband to embarrass and hurt her?

She continued to study the statue. The man's mouth was where she couldn't imagine a man's mouth being anywhere near, particularly not all settled in like he appeared to be.

Well, no matter. Jason Sherbrooke never wanted to marry. That was good. That was fine with her because she didn't want to marry either, ever.

She ran back to the Hall, aware that she was feeling warm, but not all over. No, not all over at all.

She found Martha curled up in her chair, sound asleep. She'd told her to go to bed, but naturally she hadn't. Hallie led Martha into the dressing room where she slept, took off her shoes and covered her. She'd worked as hard as any of the women, jumping around, exclaiming over this and that, happy as a lark.

Hallie wondered, as she lay in bed that night, exactly what had happened to Jason five years before.

CHAPTER 17

꙳

꙳ Two mornings later, all the male workers moved the furniture from the very clean stables into the house. They grunted and carped, stretched and sweated, but were stoic and nicely silent when Hallie asked them to move a piece more than once. Hallie seemed to be enjoying herself, so Jason didn't say a word until he walked into the room as she directed the men to move the main sofa in front of the windows. He stared. Hallie called out, all delighted, "Yes, that is perfect, simply perfect. Thank you. Now, I'm thinking a chair should sit in front of the fireplace, perhaps that lovely brocade wing chair that Master Jason likes so very much. No reason to be cold, is there? Of course it's very warm now since it's summer. Oh, hello, Jason. What do you think, should the chair still be in front of the fireplace so visitors will know that they'll be warm when the cold hits?"

He was amazed and disbelieving, at what she had wrought, but he said in a straightforward voice, "There is something to be said for reassuring visitors, but I'm thinking the sofa and chair should be together, don't you?"

"But there isn't enough room in front of the windows for both."

"Well then, why don't we try the sofa and chair somewhere else. Perhaps to the left side of the fireplace."

Hallie heard one of the men say to another, "It's about time the master got involved. The next thing she'd want us to do is block the doorway with a hassock."

"Of course I wouldn't want a hassock in the doorway. A hassock can't be separated from its chair. Everyone knows that."

The men shuffled their feet. They didn't notice the twinkle in her eye.

"They didn't mean anything, Hallie," Jason said. "However, you do have some rather curious notions about furniture placement."

Hallie sighed deeply. "The truth is, my father and Genny quite despaired of me six years ago when I tried to redecorate my own bedchamber. I selected lovely colors and furniture, but when it came to placement, I put my bed with its back to the one big window. At least I sometimes recognize when the furniture is placed correctly." She sighed and stood in the doorway.

After Jason had finished with the downstairs furniture, the men grinning, he said to Hallie, "Should we let Cousin Angela make decisions about her own bedchamber and sitting room?"

"After she sees what you've done, she'll probably beg you to do it for her."

"All right, I'll arrange her furniture. If she doesn't like it, I'll change it myself. Now, don't whine and act pathetic. Everyone has things they can do and things they can't do."

"Oh yes? What can't you do?"

He stroked his fingertips over his chin. After a very long march of moments, he said, "Do you know, I'll have to keep thinking about that."

She said something under her breath and stomped away.

"What did you say?"

She mumbled something else, something rather unpleasant, he fancied, about his antecedents. She turned at the front door to see him grinning after her, a lovely white-toothed grin that made her want to both smack him in the head and fling him to the ground. Now, where had that come from? So she flung him to the ground—what would she do then? She'd kiss him until he swooned, that's what she'd do. How long, she wondered, eyes glazed, would it take him to swoon? Oh dear. She kept walking.

After Cousin Angela's bedchamber and sitting room

were charmingly arranged, Jason went back downstairs to see Hallie standing in the open doorway looking off at something in the distance. He called to her, "Come back in, Hallie. Let's take one final look."

"A storm is coming. Do you know when it will hit?" When he stood next to her, she pointed.

"Any minute now. Those are fast clouds and black as a pit. Come, let's look at our handiwork."

He'd even done a perfect job in her bedchamber. She started to sigh, but refused to give him the satisfaction. They walked into each of the other rooms, Jason telling her what an excellent job she'd done selecting the fabrics and design of the draperies. It didn't take long before she was smiling and nodding.

"Didn't you select the hallway carpet?"

She beamed. "Isn't it lovely? It won't show much dirt."

"No, indeed." If someone had told him he would like a dark yellow rug with dark green vines, he would have puked, but oddly, it looked lovely running the distance of the corridor.

When they looked into Jason's bedchamber, at the opposite end of the house from hers, Hallie said, "And this carpet you selected is very distinctive. Very masculine."

"In short, very manly." Actually, it was a lovely Aubusson his father had selected for him.

The floors were buffed to a high shine, the furniture and fabrics light, making all the rooms look airier and larger.

When at last they walked into the drawing room, Callie discovered her throat was tight.

"What's wrong? You still want the chair in front of the fireplace?"

"Oh, no, it's just that this is my first home." She blinked up at him. "My very own first home." She whooped, grabbed Jason, and soon they were waltzing around the room and out into the entryway. They were laughing, then suddenly Jason stopped in his tracks. Hallie, looking up at him, saw something close to panic on his face, and quick as could be, she locked her arms around his neck. She was still waltzing in place when she went up on her tiptoes and kissed him.

For an instant, he kissed her back. Then suddenly, he grabbed her hands and pulled them away from his neck. "No, no, Hallie, I will not dishonor you nor will I— Never mind, you're a lady." He paled, something akin to terror dilating his beautiful eyes, turned on his heel and left the house, nearly at a dead run.

It began to rain, hard.

After dinner, their final evening at Northcliffe Hall, Hallie found Corrie in the nursery, softly singing a lullaby to the twins, who lay like two small spoons, front to back. Hallie watched her lean down and kiss both of them, then pull a light cover over them. She straightened to see Hallie at her elbow. "Goodness, I didn't hear you. What are you doing here, Hallie? Ah, aren't they absolute loves?"

Hallie said, "I've been watching them. Their

fingers fell out of their mouths when they fell asleep."

"Yes, that's always the giveaway. They've tried to fool me into thinking they're asleep, but it's the fingers that do them in. James will be here in a moment. What is it? There's nothing wrong, is there?"

"Oh no. Well, perhaps. Could I speak to you for a moment, Corrie?"

Now, this was interesting, Corrie thought, as she motioned Hallie into a small sitting room down the corridor that overlooked the spectacular back gardens. They heard a man's step in the corridor. "That's James. He'll probably pick both boys up and rock them. They always smile at him in their sleep when he rocks them. Now, tell me what this is all about."

Hallie sat forward in her chair, realized she wasn't certain how to introduce the subject of Jason and what exactly had happened five years before. What came out of her mouth was, "Jason said the statue where the man is kneeling between the woman's legs is your favorite. He also said it was every married woman's favorite so long as her husband wasn't a clod."

Corrie's left eyebrow shot up. She laughed, couldn't help it. "Well, that's the truth. Oh, I see, forgive me. You don't understand. But didn't you look closely?"

"Well, no, not really. It looked to me like the woman was screaming. It looked to me as if that sort of married thing was painful for the woman."

Corrie stared at a young woman who was only two

years younger than she. Well, she'd be ignorant as dirt herself if she hadn't married James. And thank the good Lord, James wasn't a clod. She grinned. "No, there's no pain involved. When you decide to marry, I promise I'll have James make certain the man you've chosen knows what he's doing. That's all I'm going to say about it."

Hallie sucked in a deep breath. "That isn't really what I wanted to ask you. The thing is, well, do you think you could tell me exactly what happened five years ago? Why Jason swears he'll never marry?"

Corrie's face tightened, she tightened all over. She hated thinking of that awful time, and the memories were always there. She saw that Hallie wasn't asking out of simple curiosity, that there was something else at work. But what? Corrie said, "Was it spoken of in Baltimore? What do you know?"

"In Baltimore there were rumors that Jason and James had loved the same woman and she'd chosen James." Hallie shrugged. "He gambled too much, he angered his father, anything you can think of. People talk and gossip because they must, I suppose. All Jason told me was that the girl he loved betrayed him and he was responsible for nearly getting his father and brother killed."

"I see." Corrie fell silent. "I'm surprised Jason said that much to you."

"At the time, I told him that my betrothed was with another woman. I suppose Jason told me what he did to make me feel better."

Corrie was astonished. "You're joking, surely. This idiot man was your future husband and he betrayed you?"

"He must have believed I was very stupid. Actually, he was right. I found out he was marrying me for my money. When I confronted him, he admitted he'd been with this other woman, though only one time, the lying worm swore to me, and then proceeded to promise it would never happen again. I'm not that foolish. It was then that I told him I knew he was a fortune hunter."

"Did you shoot him?"

Hallie sighed. "I would have enjoyed that, perhaps right through his ear, but instead I locked myself in my bedchamber and licked my wounds."

"What happened to him?"

"He married a rich merchant's daughter last year. Poor girl." She paused a moment. "And that's why I don't ever wish to marry."

Corrie rose and smoothed down her skirts. "Well, that's bad enough. I'm sorry you had to care for a man of that ilk. You never suspected?"

Hallie shook her head, saying as she did so, "Not for a moment. Goodness, I was naïve. However, Jason's experience must have been much worse than mine. But the thing is, I can't imagine any girl betraying either James or Jason. They're both so beautiful and, well, they both appear quite honorable."

"Yes, they are. The fact is, I loved James from the moment I first saw him at the advanced age of three.

Do you know that most people can't tell James and Jason apart?"

Hallie shook her head. "No, that's not possible. They're very different from each other. Please, Corrie, tell me what happened."

"It was a very bad time, Hallie, for all of us." Corrie patted her shoulder. "I don't think it's right for me to say anything. You must ask Jason. Shall we go downstairs and play whist? Or perhaps we can waltz."

CHAPTER 18

❧·❧

❧ The move to Lyon's Gate occupied a good three hours, an additional two to install both Martha and Petrie, who had begged Jason to allow him to be both his permanent valet and Lyon's Gate's butler, since Hollis had taught him everything over the past five years. Jason had to admit that occasionally he'd missed Petrie's services in America. He agreed to Petrie continuing as his valet and Hallie agreed to Petrie as their butler. Jason knew she was accepting Petrie in all goodwill and innocence. Well, she'd find out soon enough what a misogynist he was. They hadn't been in Lyon's Gate more than an hour before Petrie told Martha she was a mouthy girl with no respect for his craft and skill. Jason had seen seventeen-year-old Martha, hands on hips, chin out, tell him he was an insufferable prune-faced old tick, and he wasn't even that old yet.

Old tick or not, it was nice to have someone looking after him again. Jason could always smack Petrie if he stepped over the line with any of the females in the house.

Good God, he'd moved into a house with a woman he hadn't known more than two months, and Cousin Angela, whom he'd known a week. His world had turned sideways.

As for Martha, she was so excited she danced in and out of every room, saying over and over, "Our first 'ouse, er, house. Heavenly groats—ain't—isn't—it jest grand, Miss Hallie?"

"It's the grandest," Hallie agreed, and realized she was moving into a house with a man who looked like a god. In the dark hours of the night, she knew she would be quite content to drop him to the floor, hold him down, and kiss him, forever.

The house was quiet. Jason lay in his bed, the first time he and his new bed had been together. He stretched, pillowed his head on his arms, and stared up at the dark ceiling. There wasn't much of a moon tonight, so little light came through the windows. Some minutes later, from downstairs, came twelve mellow strokes from the lovely Ledenbrun clock, a gift from his grandmother.

His first home. Hallie's first home. Oh yes, he'd heard Martha's excited voice, anyone who'd been in the house at the time had, much to Petrie's tight-lipped disapproval. Yes, the house was just grand. He smiled, but it soon fell away. She'd wanted to kiss him. She'd held on until he'd jerked her arms from around his neck.

Their cook, Mrs. Millsom, so bosomy she could probably balance a vegetable or two quite nicely, had prepared them an excellent dinner—some fish and mutton, if he remembered right, but he'd been so wrapped up in sitting in the master's chair at his own dining room table in his own dining room, that he really didn't remember what he'd eaten. Perhaps there'd been some peas as well. He'd been aware of Cook watching him and so he'd complimented her extravagantly. Mrs. Millsom fluttered her fingers and removed herself back to the kitchen, singing if he'd not imagined it, and Hallie had said, "Oh no, not Mrs. Millsom," but he hadn't asked her what she'd meant by that.

He frowned at one memory. Hallie had said as they'd shared a glass of port after dinner, "I'm so excited I can scarcely keep myself from bubbling over—my first home, my first dinner in my own home."

And Angela, seeing that he was ready to open his mouth, said quickly as she raised her glass, "I propose a toast: to yours and Jason's first home and our first home together."

It was her home too, dammit. Her dining room table in her dining room. Not his alone. He'd seen her looking about, in tearing spirits, and he'd known she'd wanted to ask him to waltz again throughout the house with her. But she hadn't, probably because of his blatant rejection of her—and that brought Judith McCrae from that hidden part of his brain out in front of his eyes, the girl who'd been a monster, the girl who'd nearly killed him. Yes, whenever he dredged Judith up, his mind settled back into its proper path.

When he fell asleep, he dreamed of that afternoon again, saw himself jumping in front of his father, felt the bullet tearing into his shoulder, and the endless pain that had drawn him deep into himself, almost killing him. He jerked awake, breathing fast and hard, sweat covering him. He hadn't had that dream for many months. Now, tonight, in his new bed, it had come and brought it all back. He didn't want to go back to sleep. He didn't want to fall back into that nightmare. When he fell asleep again, he slept soundly, nothing at all coming into his brain to break him.

The next morning, as Jason walked down the stairs, the events of that long-ago day tucked back into the shrouded darkness, he heard Petrie saying, "Your step is entirely too light. It shows lack of respect for your betters. You are nearly dancing, Martha, and a lady's maid shouldn't dance. Her step should be slow and stately. Her eyes should be looking upon her feet. I won't have your high spirits in my house."

Petrie's house? Well, why not? It was damned near everyone's house. Jason started to call out when he saw young Martha standing right in front of Petrie, hands on hips, foot tapping, a lovely sneer on her thin young face. "Well, now, you itchy old codswallop, you're not even fat and jowly yet, and 'ere—here—you are acting like a stern grandfather without even a flicker of laughter in him. Dear Mr. Hollis must be ten times your age, yet he's never tight-mouthed and disapproving, and what's more, he quite likes females, unlike you, who would like to bake all of us in that wonderful new oven the mistress bought.

"Listen to me, Mr. Petrie. Of course I have a light step, I'm only seventeen years old. Go away now, I heard your master stirring ever so long ago. You do tend to him, do you not?"

Petrie stared down at her, mouth agape. "I am not an itchy old codswallop."

"My ma always said that sour and stiff and nasty is an old man's sack, no matter you've still got all your teeth."

Jason realized in that moment that Martha hadn't dropped a single *h* and she'd spoken all fluently and fast, her diction and grammar perfect. Anger did strange things to people. He had nothing to do. Martha had quite taken care of Petrie herself. He wondered if Petrie was ready to commit murder. He wished he could simply slip past them. He didn't want to see his valet/butler when he was mortified. But Lyon's Gate wasn't near the size of Northcliffe Hall, so Petrie would have to see him, feel guilt, and suffer.

"Good morning, Martha, Petrie. No, Petrie, I didn't need your services. I'm having breakfast now. Martha, is your mistress up and about?"

"Oh yes, sir. She's an early riser, that one is, fair to made me turn around me—*my*—'ours—*hours*."

"Cheeky and fresh," Petrie said under his breath, but of course, it wasn't under enough.

Martha turned on him, recalled the master was three feet away, and gave him a lovely curtsey before she seamed her lips.

"That was quite well done, Martha."

"Thank you, sir. Miss Carrick, she taught me. She's ever so graceful when she curtsies."

"Possibly," Jason said and walked into the breakfast room. When he sat down, his plate piled high with eggs, bacon, kidneys, he said to Hallie, who was sipping a cup of tea at the other end of the table, "We need a housekeeper, else Petrie will be murdered in his bed by all the female staff."

"Cousin Angela wanted to be the housekeeper but she is my chaperone and a gentlewoman."

"I will ask Hollis to recommend someone for us."

Jason ate while Hallie continued to sip her tea, her fingertips drumming lightly on the tablecloth.

He missed the London paper he would normally have at Northcliffe Hall. "What's wrong with you this morning? Didn't you sleep well?"

"Oh yes. Actually, I would very much like you to give me permission for Dodger to cover Piccola, er, without charge for his stud services."

An eyebrow went up. "No charge for Dodger's services?"

"Since we're partners, I deserve a bit of consideration, don't you think?"

He'd handled Piccola several times since she'd arrived. She was a Thoroughbred, a glossy bay with four white socks and a slash of white down her face, a long graceful neck, a sound chest. "Yes," he said. "If her first foal is a filly, she's yours, if it's a colt, he's mine. All right?"

"Hmm. If it's a colt, can I have the next colt?"

"All right."

She gave him a big grin. "Very well, I'll go speak to Henry. I think she'll be in season very soon now. As you already know, summer is the best time for mating, so we need to hurry. I asked your uncle Tysen to bruit it about that we were open for business. My uncle Burke as well. Dodger will be very busy."

"We are lucky to have Henry back with us again. He told me about the last few years of Squire Hoverton's life, how Thomas was always—" His voice dried up when she suddenly rose, and he nearly fell off his chair. He couldn't believe it. She was wearing black breeches, a loose white shirt covered with a black vest, and shiny black boots. She'd tied her hair back with a black velvet ribbon. It was quite obvious that everything she wore was new and well-made. He remembered the first time he and James had seen her at Lyon's Gate. She'd been dressed in dusty old boy's clothes. Now that he thought of it, he'd never seen her off Charlemagne's back, either.

He found his voice as he roared out of his chair. "Don't you move, Miss Carrick!" For an instant he couldn't think. Her long legs were on very nice display, leaving very little to a man's imagination. Her rear end—

Thank God Hallie slowly turned to face him and he could make himself look up at her face. He leaned over, splaying his palms on the table. He hit his fork and it flew across the breakfast room, but he paid it no heed. She said, eyebrow arched, "What do you want, Mr. Sherbrooke?"

He tried to get ahold on himself. He wasn't her father, dammit, nor was he her husband. But the outrage rolled out; he simply couldn't hold it in. "You will go upstairs this minute and have Martha put you in a proper gown. You will not show yourself outside until you are properly dressed, more or less like a lady. You will not wear men's clothing ever again. Is that perfectly clear to you?"

"Since you're nearly yelling, yes, of course, it's clear. Excuse me now, Mr. Sherbrooke, I have work to do in the stables."

"Don't move, Miss Carrick!" His face was red, the pulse pounding in his neck. Luckily his brain was holding on and told him to retrench. "Damn you—" No, no, try again. Calm, he needed calm and control with her. His voice slowed, deepened, surely a master's voice, a serious man's voice. "Don't you realize that everyone in the district will hear of your man's charade? Don't you realize you will be labeled loose?"

"That is absurd. I already have an interesting reputation in the district simply because I am living with a man who isn't my husband. But let me assure you, no one believes me at all loose."

She'd started out all light and dismissive, amused even, but by the time she'd finished, her voice had risen an octave and her face was red. Well, Jason thought, she was an uncontrolled female, what was one to expect? Where he was calm, his reason sound, she was a stubborn uncontrolled twit. He actually flicked a bit of lint off his coat sleeve. "You can't see yourself from the back, Miss Carrick, whereas I can see every curve—your backside in particular is finely outlined, and your long legs, nicely shaped they are. Trust me on this. Every man who manages only the slightest glimpse of your shadow will be positively delighted. He will immediately see his hands cupping your bottom." Actually, he was seeing himself doing that, and he would swear his hands tingled.

She shook her head at him. "I looked at the back of myself in my mirror. My britches are loose. There's no hugging, no outlining. You're being ridiculous. Now, good morning to you, Mr. Sherbrooke."

He spaced his words out for maximum effect. "If you try to leave the house dressed like that, I will carry you back upstairs, and change you into a gown myself." He shuddered then. "Do you realize what you look like from the front?" He shuddered again.

"I look just like you do, like all men do. There's nothing at all diff—"

"Would you like me to press yourself against me, Miss Carrick, so you can feel the difference between us? Would you like to simply look at me at this very moment to see the differences?"

He stepped from behind the table and walked toward her. "Look, Miss Carrick."

She looked. "Oh dear." Then she brought shocked, excited eyes back up to his face and took a step back. "So this is what happens to you when you look at the front of me?"

"Or the back of you or, I fancy, the side of you, perhaps even from fifty feet."

He stopped not an inch from her, took her upper arms in his big hands and shook her. "You're my bloody partner and you're a nitwit."

She jerked away from him.

He should simply haul her upstairs, strip off her clothes, burn all the breeches she'd had sewn up for herself without his knowledge. No, it wasn't possible. Well, it was—Angela would probably be on his side— but no. Better to try a different tack. Shame, that was it. He drew in a deep breath.

"Attend me, Hallie"—he saw her ease immediately at the use of her first name—"the men working here will tell their wives and their friends how the mistress of Lyon's Gate prances around dressed like a man. The wives will be horrified, they won't want their husbands working for us. As for the men who remain, they will sneer at you, they will be insolent, they will look at you every chance they get and trade jests with each other about your endowments and very probably your lack of character. Is that what you want?"

"The wages we're paying are far too good for any of the men to quit. Also, I can deal with any insolent man in the world."

He nodded. "Possibly you can. But here is the truth of the matter, Hallie. Your reputation will suffer irreparable damage—" He slowed, his voice deepened. "As well as mine. I will be known as the flagrantly debauched earl's son who openly lives with a woman who is nothing more than his lightskirt. And every man and woman in the district will believe I'm rubbing their noses in my open philandering. It will redound upon my parents and on my twin and Corrie. Do you begin to understand the consequences of your britches?"

Hallie grew very still. She'd simply not considered this. "Your parents?"

"Oh yes. As for Angela, she'll be snubbed. She will be regarded not as a respectable chaperone, but a procurer, no better than a madam who owns a brothel in London."

"Surely not. That makes no sense. I simply want to take care of my horses, nothing more than that. It's so much easier in britches. I could fall and break my neck wearing a wretched gown, you know it. All know it."

"I understand your plight, but it can't be helped. It is the way of the world. Given our very irregular living arrangements, neither of us nor our families can afford any more questionable actions. Britches are beyond questionable. Do you believe me now?"

Hallie folded; she looked ready to burst into tears. "The three shirts have beautiful stitching and the britches—they're the finest knit. Oh goodness, and would you look at the boots? You can see your face in them." She raised eyes now sheened with tears. She looked kicked and broken. "Three outfits, Jason, two pair of boots. They cost me a lot of money to have everything made. It isn't fair, you know it isn't."

"Yes, I know. I'm sorry. Everything looks quite fine, and I say that as a man, not a fashion judge."

She cocked her head to the side. "Does seeing me in these britches really drive you mad with lust?"

Jason laughed, not about to remind her that she saw proof of his lust. "Perhaps there is a bit of lust mixed with the outrage. Does that make you happy?"

She searched his face for a long moment. "You truly feel that I will ruin all of us if I step outside wearing britches?"

"When you saw Petrie this morning, what did he do?"

"He's not the one to ask about, Jason. He quite detests women." She grinned. "Actually, he closed his eyes tight, clutched his heart, and looked ready to swoon."

Jason could also imagine Petrie's eyes rolling back in his head. She was fortunate Petrie hadn't forgotten himself and blasted her. "Let me ask you another question. When I first met you at Lyon's Gate you were wearing dirty old boy's clothing. Did my aunt Mary Rose or my uncle Tysen see you?"

Her eyes fell to her shiny boots. She'd used her own recipe, one she'd experimented with endlessly to get just right. She'd wanted to look perfect.

"I didn't think so. What did you do, change in the woods before you came here?"

"Perhaps behind a lovely maple tree." She looked up and smiled. "Then I was riding like you ride, firm in the saddle and not hanging on for dear life in those idiot sidesaddles, and I rode like the wind. It was wonderful."

Jason paused. It was true, everything she'd said. "Jessie Wyndham always claimed sidesaddles were the invention of the devil."

"She always wears britches."

"Jessie isn't really Jessie unless she is wearing britches and racing, she's done it all her life. People are used to it. They don't expect anything else. I'm sorry, Hallie. Perhaps when we are alone—"

There was a shriek from the doorway.

"Goodness gracious, burn a feather beneath my nostrils!" Angela slapped her palms over her chest. "My dearest girl, I've never before seen a young lady's, er, *after parts* in such great detail."

CHAPTER 19

❧

❧ Angela finally stopped patting her lace-covered chest. "Oh dear, Hallie. It's not that you don't look delightful in those exquisite pants—I daresay the gentlemen will surely think so as well, as will those males who aren't gentlemen at all. And that doesn't include all the men at Lyon's Gate with the exception of dear Jason here, and I saw that even he was looking at—well, now, never mind that. I'm sorry, dearest, but the men's britches aren't possible. However, I have an idea. It's been done before, at least I've heard that it has. Go change into an old gown, and I will see what I can do. Yes, dear, you must. Trust me."

Jason, whose eyes were firmly fixed on Angela's face, and not on Hallie's britches, said, "Wouldn't you like some breakfast before you go off to see what you can do?"

"Oh yes, dear boy. That would be quite nice. Do have my Glenda bring a tray up to my room. Jason, I am very fond of the furniture arrangement. It is so cozy, I feel like I've lived in those rooms for a good twenty years." And she glided out on her fairy feet, humming.

"Whatever is on her mind," Jason said, "I fancy it is going to be something very clever. Pick your lower lip off the floor, Hallie. Have faith."

Hallie wasn't so sure. All she knew was she had to give up her wonderful britches. She sighed deeply. "I don't know what clever can do about this. Oh, all right, I'll go change into one of my ancient gowns."

She sighed again and strode like a young man from the breakfast room, eyes down, shoulders slumped, which meant, he supposed, that her lower lip was still scraping the floor.

He heard Petrie gasp and choke, a gurgling sound from deep in his throat, which meant he was in extreme distress.

Jason looked upward. Thank God for Angela. What was she going to do? Whatever it was, he couldn't imagine it would make Hallie happy. But then again, wasn't Angela now his grandmother's cohort? Surely even the good Lord couldn't have predicted that miracle. Indeed, they visited together at least three times a week.

He saw Hallie's britches again in his mind's eye and nearly groaned. Didn't she realize she was going to have enough trouble gaining acceptance without adding her quite lovely bottom to the mix?

Lord Brinkley from Trowbridge Manor in Inchbury, Sussex, brought his mare Delilah the following morning.

Petrie, elegant in full black regalia, showed him ceremoniously into the drawing room, announcing him in a low, mellifluous voice Hallie had never heard before. She supposed it was because he was more in control of his vocal cords when Martha wasn't around.

"Miss Carrick, is it? Delightful to meet you." Lord Brinkley, a man her father's age, who could have passed for her father's father, bowed, quite gracefully for such a portly man.

"Hello, Lord Brinkley. Welcome to Lyon's Gate."

He smiled at her, thinking she looked quite dashing in her full skirt, blouse, and lovely vest. Rather exotic, actually. He pulled his eyes from the vest. "I knew old Hoverton before he passed on. Fine stables, a bit of corruption I heard at the racetrack, but so long as it doesn't happen to my Delilah, I'll live and let live."

Hallie, who doubted that horse racing would ever be free of corruption, said, "Delilah is a wonderful mare. I saw her last spring in a race near Spalding, one I might add that all the owners agreed to run fairly."

"Did you now? Delilah didn't win that one, lost out

to the most beautiful mare I've ever seen, truth be told. I don't remember her name."

Hallie grinned from ear to ear, showing beautiful white teeth that Lord Brinkley envied to his boots. "Her name is Piccola and she belongs to me. That's why I was at the race."

"Well, now, is that a fact? I don't remember you voting for an honest race."

"I voted in absentia."

"Ah, probably a good thing to have a man dealing with such things since you're a female. Is Mr. Sherbrooke here?"

"I believe so. He's probably at the stables tending to Delilah. Would you care for tea, Lord Brinkley, or would you like to meet Dodger?"

"Did you know it was Lord Ravensworth—your uncle I believe—who told me I couldn't do better than a foal off Dodger? He said Mr. Sherbrooke raced him in Baltimore for five years and he rarely lost."

Hallie nodded. She wasn't about to tell him that Dodger, with Jason on his back, couldn't ever beat Jessie Wyndham. "Come with me, my lord."

"Er, you are coming with me, Miss Carrick?"

"Of course. I am Mr. Sherbrooke's partner, you know. Didn't my uncle tell you that?"

"Well, yes, but I thought it was all an uncle's pride, didn't really take him all that seriously, you know."

"He was quite serious, as am I. Come, Lord Brinkley."

She actually heard him debating with himself as he

trailed after her. "*—damndest thing, a girl, nothing but a young girl—yes, she'd fill a man's dreams and really she looks striking, lovely vest—but here she thinks she knows about breeding racehorses? Well, that Piccola of hers won, now didn't she? Maybe all Miss Carrick did was wave her ribbons around the mare to encourage her. It just isn't right for a young girl to see horses mate. So blatant it all is, so immensely intimate, so disgusting actually. Oh dear.*"

Hallie didn't know whether to laugh or scream as she listened, striding fiercely ahead of Lord Brinkley, forcing his lordship to take some double steps. Jason looked up from reassuring Delilah to see Lord Brinkley trailing Hallie, his head shaking, seemingly talking to himself. She'd already argued with him? Jason had been expecting this. He quickly gave over Delilah's reins to Henry, their head stable lad, former head stable lad of Squire Hoverton. Henry stood back from Delilah, told her what a purty girl she was, his voice soft as silk, then finally, he lightly stroked the base of her neck, scratching gently here and there, always speaking quietly to her. He slipped her a lovely fresh carrot, a donation from Cook.

"Aye, would ye look at that, I've got me a friend for life, I do. Mr. Sherbrooke, ain't she a lovely one? Jest look at them ears o' hers, all turned forward."

Jason turned and smiled. "Yes, she's alert and interested." Jason was grateful for Henry. He and Hallie had found him living with his widowed sister in Eastbourne, drinking too much ale because he suffered from melancholia. Jason couldn't recall any individual ever being so excited before at an offer of a job. He had rubbed his hands together, grinning like a loon. Henry indeed had magic hands and a soft country voice that made every horse in the stable whinny and come trotting to him. He'd discovered four additional stable lads for Lyon's Gate. He gave a quick bow to Lord Brinkley, told him not to worry, and turned back to Delilah. "Here now, beautiful girl, ye just come with Henry, he'll feed ye all right 'n' proper, let yer munch on another carrot or two. Jest ain't ye a fine, fine girl. Yer going to like ole Dodger, he's going to make a fine pa for yer baby."

"Lord Brinkley," Jason called, as he strided to the elderly man. "I am Jason Sherbrooke." As he shook Lord Brinkley's hand he continued. "I see you've met Miss Hallie Carrick. Henry will settle Delilah. We will continue with Dodger tomorrow morning."

"Ah, may I see the stables, and Dodger?"

"Certainly. In a while Henry will turn her loose in this small paddock, and you can see how she likes her temporary home."

Hallie let Jason give Lord Brinkley the stable tour. Well, she'd nearly gotten through her first dealing with a gentleman whole hide, or almost. It hadn't been too bad. At least not yet. She was forced to laugh now, thinking back over his monologue. She wondered which one of him had won the argument. Probably the outraged one. She wondered if Lord Brinkley was staying for the mating tomorrow if he found it so disgusting. She knew if he did, he would be embarrassed to his toes if she were also present.

When the two men emerged, Henry had just loosed Delilah, a lovely chestnut Thoroughbred of perfect size and proportion, only fifteen hands tall. She had a refined head, a long arched neck, sloping shoulders and a deep chest. The only thing she didn't have was hard legs. They were on the thin side and that was why Piccola had beaten her. She didn't have the endurance in those too-skinny legs. Naturally, Hallie wasn't about to say that to Lord Brinkley. Then, to her surprise, Jason said, "You saw that Dodger is immensely strong. His ancestry goes back to the Byerley Turk. Dodger's endurance is legendary in America. He has dominant characteristics that appear in all of his foals—the most important one for Delilah's foal is his thick muscled hindquarters and his hard legs. Dodger is bold and spirited, his will to win is unmatched."

"Well, he hasn't won here in England," said Lord Brinkley. "Hmm, that does make his stud fee cheaper, and that is a good thing."

Hallie nodded. "That is true. You are lucky, sir, for as soon as Dodger begins winning races here in England, his stud fee will rise quickly."

After a moment Lord Brinkley announced, "Her legs look hard enough to me." Neither Jason nor Hallie said anything to that, and after a pitiable sigh, Lord Brinkley admitted, "I heard someone say her legs were too skinny, but I ignored it, put it down to spite and ignorance. Her dam was crossed with Sultan, but her beautiful legs didn't breed true. Still, I've always thought her legs quite elegant."

Jason said, "Yes, they are elegant, but too skinny as well. But she is sturdy; look at that short strong back. With Dodger, she will birth a foal with his additional endurance. Just look at her. She's ready."

Delilah was prancing, as if for Dodger, back and forth in the paddock, head high, ears forward, tail up, whinnying. Lord Brinkley swelled with satisfaction.

Hallie said, "Look at the pride in her, my lord, and the graceful line of her neck. The intelligence in her eyes—yes, that will doubtless breed true."

Lord Brinkley continued to puff out his chest until he chanced to look down. "My God, young woman, you're wearing a man's boots!"

Hallie immediately removed her booted foot from the bottom paddock rail.

She said mildly, "Slippers really aren't the thing for stable yards, my lord. All the mud and muck and scattered pebbles everywhere. These boots were made by G. Bateson, a longtime apprentice of the great Hoby himself."

"Hmm. It offended me when Hoby had the gall to die, fell over a boot he was fashioning, face landed in a pile of leather. Aye, I always gave Hoby my custom until that fateful day. Look at those boots of yours. I can see my face in the shine. Don't tell me your maid knows how to shine a man's boots?"

Jason rolled his eyes, but Hallie said, her eyes shining nearly as clear as her boots, "Actually, my lord, I take great pride in the appearance of my boots so it is I who polish them. It takes me a good half-hour, you know, sometimes longer, until I can see myself clearly in the shine."

"I must ask your recipe, my dear. I'll give it to my man."

"It's all in the size of the hand that measures out the vinegar, and my very special ingredient, anise seed. Does your man have large hands?"

"Oh, aye, Old Fudds has hands bigger than my mother-in-law's, God rest her soul as of two months ago, amen. Used to sport in the ring, you know, Old Fudds did, not my mother-in-law. Oh dear, what am I to do? That is really a marvelous shine. Anise seed—who would have ever thought it important for anything save making your breath smell strange and sharp? I can see my eye twitching back at me, clear as day in that shine. My eye—been twitching like this for a good twelve years now, drives my wife quite distracted, particularly in company, She believes I'm winking at other ladies."

"What do all the other ladies think, my lord?"

He grinned at Hallie. "They think I'm winking too. Quite dizzies them up."

"Then it's a good twitch, don't you think?"

Jason said, "Er, Lord Brinkley, could you care to see Dodger out of his stall now?"

"What? Oh yes, certainly." Lord Brinkley gave a wistful glance back at Hallie's boots, then turned to follow Jason.

Hallie called out, "I will provide you with an exact measure, my lord, for Old Fudds."

Lord Brinkley stopped in his tracks and gave her a charming bow. If she wasn't mistaken, he winked at her. Hallie didn't believe for a moment it was a twitch. She heard him say in a lovely carrying voice, "Nice girl, Mr. Sherbrooke. Does she know a single thing about horses or is she only good at shining boots?"

"She trained Piccola, my lord."

"Hmm. That would raise a man's confidence, now wouldn't it? Or terrify him out of his wits. Ah, but it's still difficult—I don't like books that don't fit their covers."

"Sometimes the books in question turn out to be unexpectedly interesting though, don't you think?"

CHAPTER 20

❧❧

❧ The next morning it rained enough to make everyone, horses included, hunker down to stay warm and dry. Lord Brinkley sent them a messenger who looked nearly drowned when he knocked on the kitchen door.

Jason read the short note, then looked at Hallie. "Lord Brinkley is leaving for Inchbury, doesn't want to wait until the rain stops. He sends you his direction so you may send him the recipe for his boot polish. He mentions you're not to forget the exact amount of anise seed for Old Fudds." He grinned over at her. "That was very well done of you, Hallie."

"If he accepts me because of my dandy boot shine, then I'll willingly accept it. Jason, I don't suppose Delilah or Dodger have any interest in getting on with the business today?"

"Not a dollop, at least not when I saw them earlier. Henry came to the back door a few minutes ago, said Dodger was napping, said the nap looked to be a long one. The fact is, Dodger has no interest in females when it's raining, unlike gentlemen, who are interested in females even when the snow is piled to their noses and—never mind that. Ah, where was I? Oh yes, Henry covered Dodger with a blanket he'd warmed on his own stove top, and kissed his forehead."

"What you said, Jason—no, I'm not even going to think of snow all the way to gentlemen's noses and why—no, I'm not." Then she laughed. "Oh dear, I can picture Henry lovingly laying that blanket over Dodger's back, and kissing him. What about Delilah?"

"When I looked in on Delilah before breakfast, she was eating. Henry said he'd allow her to eat as much as she wanted today. She was frustrated, he said, and eating helped her—all females actually—get through the dry spells."

"Henry said she was eating because Dodger wasn't interested in mating with her?"

"Oh yes. He also told me that was why ladies who didn't have good men or were in what one might call a desert of, want, tended to be on the plump side."

"I have never been in any sort of desert of want—indeed, I have no notion of what you're talking about. Nor do I have a good man, if such a thing is possible—and I'm not plump."

"You're young and ignorant, so you don't count. Angela's plump."

"Not much, and her husband's been dead for years—that is—no, this is absurd. You're making it all up."

"Not a bit of it. As for Piccola, according to James Wyndham, she's pregnant—she's rubbing her belly against the stall door, a sure sign. Not that I ever observed a mare rubbing her belly, mind you. Have you?"

"No, never even once. What does Jessie say?"

"She said she always rubbed her stomach on doors when she was newly pregnant. James used to say it was ever so delightful to watch, but it wasn't really good for anything except more play, that is—never mind that."

Hallie punched him in the arm. "You're making all this up, I know you are." She looked down at her flat stomach. "Imagine rubbing your belly on something when—" She realized what she'd said and turned red to her hairline.

"You doubtless will be rubbing in the not-too-distant future."

She stared up at him, said not a single word, looked at his mouth. She blinked. "Ah, I didn't see you when you came in."

"I went right to my bedchamber."

"So you got soaked going to the stables this morning?"

He shrugged, took a step back from her. "Of course. But only one of us needed to get his bones soggy, and I did draw Angela's shortest knitting needle.

If anyone croaks of an inflammation of the lung, it will be I. You're safe."

"Well, you're all dry now, and your wit is overflowing. You had more fun than I did, sitting around here in a blasted gown and ever-so-dainty green satin slippers."

"Dainty? Do you really think so, Miss Carrick? I believe your feet are nearly the size of mine."

She threw her empty teacup at him, grinned as he snagged it out of the air not an inch from his left ear. "You have very fast reflexes. What will we do today?"

"We will improve upon our bookkeeping. I've spoken at length with James and his steward, McCuddy. We will incorporate some of their practices, change others that fit our operation better. Come along, I'll show you."

They worked, heads together, until late afternoon when Angela knocked on the estate room door. She heard some arguing, laughter, solid silence, and she frowned as she knocked. She didn't open the door until she heard Jason call, "Enter."

"Children," she said to them, quite on purpose. They were sitting too close together, but on the other hand, neither of them looked the least bit guilty or embarrassed, a huge relief.

"Yes, Cousin Angela?"

"Now, my boy, you may call me simply Angela. I'm here to fetch you both so you may beautify yourselves for dinner. I believe Petrie was moaning over the state of your clothes, Jason. Martha told him to get a grip on himself, his whining didn't set a good example for the staff. And what, she said, would our new house-keeper, Mrs. Gray, have to say about it?"

Hallie said, "What did Petrie say to that?"

"I didn't hear, but I'll wager his mouth closed and his shoulders straightened right out. You've met Mrs. Gray. She'd straighten the shoulders on God."

For a moment, Jason frowned down at his tapping pen. He looked toward the far wall, its big window now sporting lovely new pale golden draperies. He heard the rain slapping in windy gusts against the clean glass panes.

He rose quickly, smiled at Angela, and said, "It's nearly five o'clock. I had no idea. We have accomplished nearly everything we set out to accomplish. Thank you for fetching us, Angela. I won't be here for dinner this evening. Hallie, let's put away our new record books. We've worked hard enough."

Hallie sat back in her chair, crossed her arms over her chest. "That is the truth. You are very good at mathematics, Jason, excellent indeed. I've always done much better with musical notes."

"Your entries are much neater than Jason's, dear," Angela said. "You could also set your entries to a jaunty tune if you wished. Jason couldn't."

Hallie laughed. "I had my knuckles rapped by my governess if every line and curl wasn't perfect. How-ever, I'll get the hang of all of it. Jason, where are you going tonight? To Northcliffe Hall?"

"No," he said, not looking at her. "I've an

appointment in— Well, that's not important. I will see you ladies in the morning."

"But look, Jason, it's still raining hard."

He nodded and left the estate room.

"How very odd," Hallie said to Angela. "He suddenly seemed very distracted. I wonder why. I also wonder who would agree to an appointment on this perfectly dreadful evening, and where it is."

"You could follow him, I suppose," Angela said.

"Hmm," Hallie said. "I could, but this time I don't think I will. With my luck, he'd see me—"

"—and toss you in a ditch to drown."

"I was thinking something else, but no matter. I'm starving, Angela. What did Cook prepare for dinner?"

"Lovely baked sole, I believe, and some fresh green beans. It's a pity Jason won't be here. I do believe Cook excels when he is present."

"He toadies up to her."

"No," Angela said. "He's polite and he smiles at her. That's all it takes. She told me that looking at him made her recipes take wing."

Hallie said slowly, nodding, "I heard that every cook in Baltimore wanted to feed him; it was a competition of sorts to gain his attention. Absolutely ridiculous. They did the same thing for my father. Genny always said she couldn't believe he never became fat as a stoat. He doesn't gain flesh, you know. I hope I am like him."

"You are his female image. Ah, two such glorious men, that's the truth."

Hallie grunted.

Angela said, "It's better I don't speak to Cook. Maybe she won't find out Jason's not here, and we'll enjoy the fruits of his bonny self. Also, I must tell you that Petrie was telling Martha that her English is not what a lady maid's should be, and thus she should keep her mouth shut until it improves."

Hallie laughed. "Did Martha smack him?"

"It was close, but she said smartly that she could only continue to improve if she practiced all the time, and why wasn't he smart enough to figure his way to that conclusion? And if he was going to continue as an old trout-tooth, she might forget her lessons on purpose. Then she flounced off with Petrie huffing and puffing behind her, without a word to say. Poor Petrie, a misogynist all these years—though he isn't old at all, is he?"

"No, Petrie isn't old at all, just a trout-tooth, Martha's right about that." As she walked upstairs to her bedchamber to change—and why should she bother anyway?—she wondered yet again where Jason had taken his bonny self. It must have been dreadfully important for him to go out in this weather. Maybe she would ask Petrie. She excelled in subtlety. He didn't stand a chance.

She saw her prey just before she went into the dining room, coming out of the drawing room, humming, oblivious of his looming surrender. "Petrie," she said, all smooth and guileless, "I wished to ask Mr. Sherbrooke about a matter of importance. Do you know when he will return home?"

The hum died in Petrie's mouth, his face turned to

stone. Chin going up just a bit, he said, "He did not confide in me, Miss Carrick."

But he knew, damn him. Petrie wouldn't let Jason out of the house if he didn't know where Jason was going and with whom he was meeting. What was he hiding? How to pry it out of him?

"It concerns the Dauntry mare coming tomorrow, an urgent matter we must discuss as soon as possible. Surely he said something."

"My master spoke only of the bloody rain, Miss Carrick. Ah, he did mention he might ask you to shine his boots for him tomorrow."

"Surely you didn't agree with that, did you, Petrie? A female shining your master's boots?"

Petrie said slowly, "I have never before considered anise seed. We will see. Oh yes, Mrs. Gray sent a message saying she wouldn't be with us tomorrow. It seems her brother has a broken leg and she must tend to him. She believes the first of next week will be all right for both her and her brother."

Hallie realized she was stumped. What else could she ask? Better to quit the field with some dignity. "Ah, well, no matter. Thank you, Petrie."

"Of course, Miss Carrick. I am at your service, naturally, at any time at all."

His slyness smacked her in the back of the head. She would never give him the exact measure of anise seed. "You gave me no service at all," she said over her shoulder as she marched, with not much dignity, into the dining room.

Cook burned the sole, mashed the fresh green beans, and placed lovely warm rolls on the table with doughy centers. The promised blancmange for dessert never appeared, probably a good thing. Angela remarked that she heard Cook singing a funeral dirge, and who knew funeral dirges for heaven's sake? Who had told her of Jason's defection? Hallie decided she should have tried a little toadying. Maybe it would have worked as well as male beauty and Jason's smile.

Or maybe not.

CHAPTER 21

⚜

❧ The following morning was sunny and warm. No one would guess it had rained hard enough to fill the rain barrel unless they slipped in an occasional three-foot mud puddle.

It had taken Hallie and three stable lads to hold Delilah still and keep her calm while Henry and Jason controlled Dodger, who was snorting, wild-eyed, nostrils flaring. He was so well-rested and excited, saliva was dripping from his mouth, but he didn't hurt the mare, which was a relief.

After Dodger had performed his duty with Delilah, Hallie wondered how Delilah could have enjoyed herself at all. It was a messy business, sometimes dangerous. The thing was, Henry told Hallie, that Delilah was no longer interested in her food. Dodger was something, wasn't he, he'd rescued Delilah from a desert of want. Hallie had no answer for that.

Everyone was exhausted and tired and sweaty when it was over. The men hadn't even seemed to notice she wasn't one of them there toward the end of the business what with sweat running down her brow.

As Hallie wiped Delilah's sleek neck, she said, "You're a brave girl, Delilah, a stoic princess faced with a toad, not a prince. Yes, you were able to bear that clod of a horse with that disgusting spit hanging out of his mouth." She was reaching for a damp sponge when she saw Jason standing in the stall doorway, arms crossed over his chest, an elegant eyebrow arched over wicked eyes, grinning at her.

Her chin went up, her voice defensive even as she willed it not to be. "Well, it's the truth. Dodger wasn't at all, er, graceful and considerate, as he was to Piccola."

"As I recall, Piccola nearly slept through it."

"Well, Delilah wanted to kill Dodger. She was quivering, her eyes were rolling, and she looked really mad. The more upset she became the more of a brute Dodger was."

"Some men are as well," Jason said, realized what had come out of his mouth, and bit his tongue. What was the matter with him?

That made her frown at him. She started brushing Delilah too vigorously and was nearly bitten. She jumped aside even as she said with a lovely sneer in his ever-so-lovely smiling face, "Well now, haven't you been in a deliriously happy frame of mind since the moment Petrie dragged you out of bed this morning? Very late, wasn't it? I do believe that Angela and I had long finished eating. If it wasn't for your damned face, you would have gone hungry."

"Well, I didn't since our cook is excellent and ever so flexible. She served me fresh nutty buns, scrambled eggs and, I do believe, bacon crisped just as I like it. We are very lucky to have her."

"Go ahead, trade on your wretched looks. It means nothing."

"Careful, Hallie, you're not exactly a knotty stick, you know. Hypocrisy isn't attractive. Also, what do you mean by that? I don't trade on anything, much less my damned face, it's absurd."

"None of that is to the point."

"And the point being?"

"Look at that grin on your sorry face—all vacuous and silly, like you're so pleased with yourself. What sort of meeting did you go to? Who made you so happy? No, I see, you drank a lot, didn't you? Gambled away our profits?"

"Perhaps a bit of brandy. I couldn't gamble because we don't have any profits yet." He scratched his belly and leaned against the stall wall. "Delilah will try for another bite if you don't stop rubbing her so hard. Use the sponge on her. I'm not about to say anything more about that."

"What do you mean about men being clods?"

He seamed his lips, shook his head. She could pull out his fingernails, but he wasn't doing any explaining, particularly since he'd never meant to say it in the first place to a young lady who was as unbroken as a newly born filly. "Sex," came out of his mouth, followed by, "It's a fine art. Some men are too selfish or simply uninformed, well, never mind. Curse me again for opening my mouth. When you're through with Delilah, Henry said Angela wanted us to know that Cook has outdone herself for lunch, though I have no idea why she would do that since every meal she's prepared for us has been quite excellent."

Hallie stared at him, swallowed, managed to get herself together and say, "She cooks for you."

"What does that mean? No, don't even think something so utterly ridiculous. She's always cooked for the three of us."

"Never mind. You're quite conceited enough. Go away. I'm starving. What is she preparing?"

Jason looked blank. "I don't know, I never asked. Normally she usually stands there, saying nothing at all, when I speak to her."

Hallie snorted.

The shaved ham was lovely, sliced as thin as Cook's at Northcliffe Hall, and so Jason told her after luncheon, only Mrs. Millsom didn't thank him, simply continued silent, staring at him. He thanked her once more, and left the kitchen, shaking his head. The woman might be dim-witted, but she was magic with the cook pans.

* * *

Angela was taken aback when Petrie, voice rich and formal, announced a gentleman was here to see Miss Hallie.

She said, "This is odd. It can't be any friends or relatives or they'd know she was likely at the stables. Hmm. Show this gentleman in, Petrie."

A very handsome man indeed, Angela thought as the gentleman in question walked with a gentleman's saunter into the drawing room. He paused a moment, stared all about before focusing his attention on the only occupant, namely Angela.

He sketched her an elegant bow. "Ma'am, I'm Lord Renfrew. I'm a special friend of Miss Carrick's."

Angela, who didn't know a thing about Lord Renfrew's nefarious marital schemes for Hallie, rose, her smile welcoming, and stretched her hand out to him.

Lord Renfrew took her hand, raised it to his lips. Ah, a very graceful gesture, Angela thought, feeling her heart trip for a moment. He must have met Hallie during her season. What a very lovely man indeed. Why had Hallie never mentioned him?

"Won't you sit down, my lord? Hallie is riding, I believe."

Lord Renfrew eased his elegant self into a high-backed chair with lovely patterned brocade cushions. "I have been out of town, ma'am, and thus didn't hear until I returned to London a short time ago that Miss Carrick had moved here to run a stud farm with a gentleman she met not two months ago. I cannot imagine her doing such a thing. Miss Carrick is a lady.

Since you say she is riding, that rather puts a period to that ridiculous rumor, doesn't it? A lady rides, after all."

"Well, yes, of course a lady rides. Actually, though, my lord, there is much more than riding involved. Are you familiar with the Sherbrooke family?"

Lord Renfrew nodded, laid a graceful hand on the chair arm. "Certainly everyone in society knows the Sherbrookes, ma'am. However, this son, Jason Sherbrooke . . . I understand he's not been in England for many years."

"He's home now. He's here, to be more specific. He and Hallie are partners. I am her chaperone."

"Chaperone? What is this? I don't understand. This makes no sense."

Angela said, "The reason they're here together is because they both wanted Lyon's Gate. Neither would sell out to the other. It's a bit more complicated than that, naturally, but that's the essence of it." She paused a moment, then added, "Anyone in London could have told you that."

"As I said, I did not believe it." He looked around the drawing room. "This is a charming room, and the grounds and paddocks look prosperous, but still, why would Miss Carrick wish to own this particular property? It is not as grand as she is used to. You know she lived at Ravensworth Abbey for many years. Surely she wouldn't be content coming so far down—" At that moment, Petrie, knowing the gentleman's worth, wheeled in a fine old tea cart donated by Lady Lydia. Petrie's entrance was a good thing, and Lord Renfrew realized it. He'd been unmeasured in his criticism of this undistinguished property that smelled of stables. He bowed his head and said nothing more.

What is all this about? Angela wondered as she gave him a cup of tea with three sugars, and two small cakes. She said, as she sipped her own tea, "During the mornings, Hallie and Jason are always working at the stables or exercising the horses."

"Do you know when Hallie will be coming back to the house, ma'am?"

They both heard the front door open and close, and Hallie's voice calling, "Martha! Come quickly, I've had a dreadful accident!"

"Oh dear." Angela was on her feet and running. Lord Renfrew rose more slowly. His instincts were excellent. He waited, saying nothing. He heard a young girl say, "Heavenly groats, Miss Hallie—look at that tear. Petrie said the Dauntry mare was arriving this morning. Did the beast snag your skirt?"

"Her name's Penelope and she's fast."

"I can fix it. Come along, Miss Hallie."

Petrie said, "It's a large tear, one more suited to the skills of a seamstress, not a poorly educated young lady's maid who should, at best, be a tweeny."

"Now, you see here, Mr. Sweaty-Breath, I can do almost anything at all, I—"

Hallie was laughing. Lord Renfrew heard that sweet laugh quite clearly. He'd always liked her laugh.

Toward the end, though, she hadn't laughed as much. He waited.

"It's all right, Martha. Petrie will soon see how very talented you are. Let's go upstairs. Don't worry, Angela, the mare got the skirt, not me. I should have been paying more attention. I left Jason holding his stomach, laughing his head off, the moron."

"A moment, Hallie. You have a visitor in the drawing room."

Petrie inserted himself between Angela and Martha. "I was going to inform her, Mrs. Tewksbury. Indeed, I am standing right here, preparing to inform her of her visitor in the drawing room. You did not give me a chance, and Martha here—but all's well, really." He pumped up his lungs. "Miss Hallie, there is a visitor to see you in the drawing room."

"A visitor?" Hallie asked. "Oh, you mean Corrie is here to visit? Yes, I remember. Give her some tea, Angela, and I will join her in but a moment. I am not ready to be seen."

"But Hallie—"

"I'll be right back, Angela."

Lord Renfrew heard her quick steps up the stairs. Or maybe that was her poorly educated, too-young lady's maid. The older lady with all the lace marching from her waist to her neck hadn't told her his name, nor had the butler with the lovely voice. She would probably find out though before she came back downstairs. He didn't know if that would be good or bad, though he always preferred surprise. He always had the advantage when he did the surprising. He walked to the fireplace, looked at himself in the mirror, knew that he looked elegant, beautifully garbed and as handsome as a minor god. He seated himself again, sipped his tea, and waited.

To his surprise, it wasn't ten minutes before Hallie appeared in the drawing room doorway, a bit out of breath. She saw him and stopped dead in her tracks.

"You're not Corrie."

He gave her a smile that had once burned her to her toes. She looked strange. It was that full skirt, that strange-looking shirt and vest she was wearing. Why was she dressed like a Romany gypsy?

She said, "I hurried because I thought it was Corrie visiting. Both Angela and Petrie are in the kitchen trying to fix Cook's new stove. Had I known it was you, I would have taken my time."

"It is all right, Hallie. You look lovely."

She hadn't meant that at all, the conceited buffoon. "Lord Renfrew. What the devil are you doing here, sir?"

Not an auspicious beginning. On the other hand, he would have been a fool to expect otherwise. "It is wonderful to see you again, Hallie. Won't you call me Elgin again, my dear?"

He strolled over to her, forcing her to look up because he was tall. He took her hand before she realized what he was about, and kissed the inside of her wrist, licking where he'd kissed. Hallie jerked her hand back. Before, so long before, she would have gone pale and hot with excitement. "What are you doing here, sir?"

He wanted to slap her. "I am here to see you, naturally. I have come to beg your forgiveness for my errant stupidity."

She nodded. "Yes, you were excessively stupid. I suppose it means something that you can admit to your perfidy now and apologize for it. However, I have no intention of forgiving you for the entire length of my lifetime, so take yourself away."

"No, not yet. Give me but another moment, Hallie. You were always a kind girl, sweet-natured—"

"Don't forget naïve."

He sighed deeply, walked back to the fireplace, knowing he presented an excellent impression, knowing she would be blind if she didn't admire him, and turned slowly to lean back against the mantel, his arms crossed over his chest. "How very sorry I was for the loss of your trust in me. It was all a mistake, a dreadful mistake that happened because I was taken in by a woman who was more experienced than I, a simple man from the country. I was weak, I admit it. This is no excuse, pray don't think it is. The fact is that I was weak and was led astray. That woman is no longer in my heart or in my mind."

"That was certainly fortunate, since you then married that poor girl in York. Do I have that right?"

"Ah, my poor little Anne. She died nearly a year ago, you know, so unexpectedly, leaving me and her father bereft."

"I am sorry. I had heard she died late this past fall."

"The time has passed so slowly, my despair so deep,

it could be ten years," he said. "After her tragic death I could not look backward or forward. Only recently have I felt the moments of life flicker again within me."

"I had forgotten how very lovely you speak. Such eloquence, such grace."

"It is not kind to mock a man who's known such pain. What I said is true."

"Was she as young as I was when you married her?"

"She was eighteen, a woman who knew her own mind, a woman grown."

Hallie shook her head. She picked up the teapot on the side table and poured herself a cup. She sipped it as she looked over at Elgin Sloane, Lord Renfrew. "I have been thinking that females shouldn't be allowed into society or into the company of men until they are twenty-five."

He laughed, a dark brow climbing up to what she'd always considered a highly intelligent forehead. "A marvelous jest, my dear. You know very well that no gentleman would wish to wed a female that old."

"How old are you?"

"I am thirty-one."

Hallie sat down and drummed her fingertips on the arm of the chair. "My uncle always said that men needed more years to leaven than women. One could think you were far too leavened now."

"I am considered a young man."

"And twenty-five is old for a woman?"

He had to regain control, not that he'd had any sort of firm control over her yet, truth be told.

She toasted him with her teacup. "Goodness, you were far too old for me before, but I was such an infatuated young fool I never even noticed those wrinkles around your eyes. Or perhaps they weren't there a year and a half ago."

His hand flew to his face, then, not looking away from her, he slowly lowered his hand back to his side. "I have always loved the way you joke. You will keep me humble, Hallie, a good thing for a man."

"This is really too much, sir, since—"

There was a horrible crashing sound from the back of the house. Hallie was out of her chair and through the drawing room doorway in an instant.

The kitchen, Lord Renfrew thought, that dreadful noise had come from the kitchen. A man didn't appear to best advantage in the middle of a mess in a kitchen. Best to remain here, above all the chaos, calm and clear-eyed.

"Good grief, who are you? What's going on?"

CHAPTER 22

✢

✢ "I, sir, am here to visit Miss Carrick. I believe she just ran back to the kitchen, some sort of female disaster."

Female disaster? Jason stared long and hard at the elegant vision standing at languid ease in front of him, thinking that he didn't particularly care for the latest gentlemen's style. The waist looked too nipped in, the tails too long, altogether unpractical, at least if one were mucking out stalls.

Jason heard a shriek. When he ran into the kitchen, it was to see Cook, Petrie, Martha, Angela, and Hallie bent over coughing, covered with the settling smoke still billowing up from the new Macklin stove. Since he and Hallie had been assured that this modern wonder would be in use until the turn of the century, Jason didn't believe this to be a propitious beginning. He saw that there was no fire, only smoke. He opened the kitchen door and the three windows and waved.

"Is everyone all right?"

Black tears streaked down Petrie's face. He was wringing his filthy hands. "Oh, Master Jason, look at what that smoking monster has done to my linen, all spotless only three hours ago, and now look."

Martha poked Petrie in the shoulder. "Here now, Mr. Petrie, don't cry or I'll tell Mr. Hollis meself— myself. Get yourself together—be a butler."

Jason hoped Petrie wouldn't throw Martha onto the still-smoking stove.

"Anise seed won't help get us clean, I'm afraid," Hallie said, wiping a hand across her face. "Don't worry, Petrie, Martha is good with all sorts of stains. Angela, your face is a bit black."

"So is yours, dear. Do you know this lovely gown was once green?"

Hallie grinned, shook her head. "Jason, I believe we were cheated by that lovely man who talked us into buying this modern marvel."

Angela said, "Perhaps it's simply breaking itself in, getting itself used to our house."

Jason said, "I'll have One-Armed Davie look at it once it's cooled down. The wood is embers now; it won't take long."

Angela said, "It amazes me what that man can do with only five fingers and his teeth. Cook, are you all right? You're not hurt, are you?"

Mrs. Millsom had forgotten her stinging hand. She stared, eyes fixed, at Jason, who was standing right in her kitchen, not three feet away. "Mr. Sherbrooke saved us," she whispered.

"Oh dear," Angela said.

"Well, actually not, Mrs. Millsom," Hallie began, but Mrs. Millsom appeared not to have heard. She continued to stare at Jason, who continued to look splendidly male, hair windblown, white shirt open, leaving his brown neck bare, his britches lovely and tight, his boots dusty, and Hallie could only roll her eyes. "Actually, all he did was open the door."

"And the windows," Mrs. Millsom said, still in a whisper.

Jason stretched out his lovely brown hand and came to within a foot in front of her. "Cook? Mrs. Millsom? Are you all right? Ah, you've burned your hand."

Cook stared at him, shook her head as she held out her hand, which he gently held between his own. "It's not bad. Angela, hand me some butter, we'll cool it down. Petrie, fetch some bandages." To his astonishment, Cook looked down at her hand held by both of his, and fell into him, almost knocking him down. He caught her even as Hallie grabbed his arm, pulling him upright.

Angela called out, "Ah, Jason, be careful of the—"

Jason went down on the large spoon covered with some sort of batter, pulling Hallie with him, Cook on top of him.

"Oh dear," Angela said.

Jason felt flattened. As gently as he could, he rolled Cook onto her back even as Hallie came up onto her knees over him. Jason said, "Why did she swoon? Is she in pain?"

Hallie could only laugh at his utter bewilderment. "Jason, you are such a moron. You touched her, that was all it took."

He patted Cook's face even as he shook his head, and everyone began to laugh. Cook's eyes fluttered. She stared up into the delicious young master's concerned face. Concern for her. The breath whooshed out of her. "Oh, Mr. Sherbrooke, oh, sir, I only wanted to make you a lovely ginger cake."

"Ginger cake." Angela fell against the kitchen table she was laughing so hard. As for Petrie, he found himself slapping Martha on her thin shoulder, telling her that her face was black as one particular All Hallow's Eve he remembered as a boy.

"I say," came an astonished voice from the doorway, "there is no more tea in the pot."

Hallie looked at the elegant man she'd once believed she'd loved, once believed was as near a perfect man as her father. She said to the kitchen at large, "Heavenly groats, was I mad and blind, or simply stupid?"

"Oh dear," said Petrie, trying to wipe his face and clean off his linen all at the same time, "I should be hung perhaps, but not drawn and quartered. My lord, I pray you will forgive my unforgivable negligence in my duties. I will fetch you tea immediately, sir, well perhaps not exactly immediately, if you will see and comprehend this niggling obstacle that confronts me."

"Of course my good man." Lord Renfrew gracefully inclined his head. "Good God, Hallie? Is that you on your knees? The only thing left white about you is your teeth. What are you doing in here? Surely—"

"Sir," Hallie said, not moving, "please take yourself off, or if you must, at least take yourself back to the drawing room."

Angela said, "She's right, my lord. I would never forgive myself were you to get a single black speck on your beautiful pearl-gray tailcoat."

"It's true that a gentleman should not take careless chances with his appearance," said Lord Renfrew and backed quickly out of the kitchen.

"I wish I could stick his head in the oven," Hallie said, rubbing her arms, streaking the soot.

Jason wrapped Mrs. Millsom's hand in a soft washing cloth, assisted her to her feet and eased her ample self into a chair. "Martha will take care of you, Cook. Rest for a moment."

Mrs. Millsom looked ready to swoon again. Martha quickly stepped close, propping her up.

Jason began backing out of the kitchen. "I will see to the dandy in the drawing room."

"Elgin a dandy?" Hallie said, a newly blackened brow arched. "Surely not."

Jason grew very still. "Did you say Elgin? Wasn't he the fellow who brought back the marbles from Greece?"

"Well, yes, but Elgin is Lord Renfrew's first name."

To her surprise, Jason's face turned grim as any reaper's. "He's the one, isn't he, Hallie?"

"Well, yes."

"What the hell does he want? Why the devil is he here?"

"Stop tearing into me. I don't know why he's here."

"You didn't invite him?"

Hallie threw the spoon he'd tripped on.

He caught it not six inches from his forehead. "You nearly nailed me with that spoon," he said, and was gone from the kitchen.

"Don't kill him, Jason," she called after him. "You wouldn't like Australia."

Angela grabbed her arm before she could take one step.

"Who is Lord Renfrew? Why is Jason angry?"

"He was the bounder I was going to marry when I was eighteen."

"But dear, I don't understand why the man is here—"

Hallie was gone. She paused at the open doorway to the drawing room, and watched in bewilderment as Jason, who no longer looked like he wanted to hurl Lord Renfrew through one of the sparkling front windows into the newly planted primroses, was jovial and welcoming, shaking Elgin's lovely strong-looking hand, the hand that had once skimmed over her breasts, something for which he'd apologized profusely. She hadn't understood at the time, but now she did. She crossed her arms over her chest, leaned against the open door, and tapped her foot. What was Jason up to?

"How very nice to finally meet you—did Hallie say your name was Eggbert?"

"Elgin."

"A distinguished name."

"Yes, yes, it most certainly is." Lord Renfrew wondered at Mr. Sherbrooke's bonhomie. But then again, why not? Jason Sherbrooke was a second son, twin or not, and probably didn't have much money, given how paltry this property was compared to his father's vast estate. The man doubtless saw Lord Renfrew as the embodiment of what he wasn't. Yes, that was it, and he wanted to lick his boots. Lord Renfrew would allow it.

On the other hand, Mr. Sherbrooke was sharing the property with Hallie, and she was rich—his solicitor had confirmed that. Hmm, he didn't like the sound of that. *Sharing*. Lord Renfrew cleared his throat. "It is an unusual situation you and Miss Carrick are in, Mr. Sherbrooke."

Jason gave him a white-toothed smile, a sort of man-to-man smile, if Lord Renfrew wasn't mistaken, and no man was ever mistaken about that. "Not really," Jason said. "Miss Carrick is, ah, a very accommodating girl, you know."

Hallie's jaw fell two inches while Lord Renfrew's jaw tightened.

Jason, cheery as an octogenarian with a new bride of eighteen, said, "Won't you sit down, my lord? Our servants aren't at all well-trained yet—really, such a small problem in the kitchen—but I imagine some more tea will be along shortly."

Small problem? They were all black as newly polished boots and Cook had swooned on him, knocked him over. That was small? Petrie not well-trained? He had been trained by Hollis himself. What was going on here?

Lord Renfrew seated himself, made certain his coattails were smoothed neatly beneath him. "What do you mean, 'accommodating'?"

"Why Miss Carrick is always anxious to please, to do whatever one wishes her to do."

What did he mean, anxious to please? She could be bad-tempered in the morning. Maybe she was anxious to please when she wanted something badly, Hallie thought as she looked up to see Petrie carrying the lovely silver tray Jason's mother had given them, his face still black as night. Oh dear. She ran to look in the mirror over the small table and nearly shrieked. She'd known what had to be in the mirror, but the fact of her black face—she raised her skirts to run to her bedchamber when she stopped cold. She smiled at Petrie. "We," she said, patting his arm, "will make an entrance. Ah, do I look as toothsome as you do, Petrie?"

"Surely you must consult the dictionary, Miss Hallie. We both look like critters escaped from the mud flats. There was no time for me to set myself to rights since one can't leave a gentleman waiting for his tea.

Oh dear, oh dear, your face, Miss Hallie, my face—This is disastrous. Whatever will the gentleman think?"

"I, for one, can't wait to find out." She walked into the drawing room, her stride long as a boy's, all possible because her full skirt was slit like very wide-cut trousers, giving Jason a smile scary enough to curl his toes. "I had Petrie bring the tea. Ah, does that please you, Jason?"

CHAPTER 23

Jason nearly fell over. A siren's voice coming out of a filthy face. Lord Renfrew rose quickly to his feet, nearly *en pointe*. He said in a loud voice, "I am very pleased, my dear, very pleased indeed. I always believed you were delightfully accommodating."

"Did you really, my lord? How very gallant of you to say so. May I ask why?"

Lord Renfrew gurgled deep in his throat.

She preened, black face and all.

So she'd heard that, had she? Jason walked to her, stopped not a half-foot from her nose and reached out his hand. He began twisting a long tangled hank of hair that fell nearly to her breast. He leaned closer, his warm breath on her cheek, lust in his eyes. "You smell like smoke."

She batted her eyelashes, but didn't move, felt his fingers wrapping round and round her hair. She said, "Does it displease you, Jason, the smoke? I do so ever wish to please you."

"I will think about that." He tugged her hair, then stepped back. "Please don't sit down in that dirty dress, Hallie. Our furniture is new and it would be a shame to dirty it up so soon."

Lord Renfrew pulsed with questions, none of which he could ask in Hallie's presence, dammit. He cleared his throat. She looked over at him. A witch, she looked like a witch. What if she wanted to touch him? Perhaps he should step back so she couldn't easily reach him. "Perhaps, Miss Carrick—Hallie— you'd best go to your bedchamber and prepare yourself."

"Prepare myself for what exactly? Oh, you mean the way I do for Jason?"

Jason shook his head, wagged his finger at her. "You baggage, where are your manners? You will shock poor Lord Renfrew. Who did you say you were, Lord Renfrew? A longtime friend of Miss Carrick's? Perhaps a friend of her father's? You don't have a grandfather still living, do you, Hallie?"

"No, my father's father died many years ago, long before I was born. My father became Baron Sherard when he was only seventeen. Genny's father died when I was only five."

Lord Renfrew said, "I came into my title two years ago. I am Viscount Renfrew, you know."

"I didn't know," Jason said, "but it has a nice ring to it."

"I would like my tea."

"Certainly," Hallie said, pouring a cup and nearly spilling it in his lap when Lord Renfrew said to Jason, "I am a very close friend of Miss Carrick's. Indeed, it would be more accurate to say that we were beyond close. I never met her father, although I would have met both her parents if things had progressed in the smooth way they were meant to progress."

Hallie said to Jason, "It's hard to be smooth when one is picking flowers in another garden, don't you think?"

The air pulsed with hot silence, until Jason said, voice limp as a dead lily, "So you excel at growing flowers, my lord? Perhaps you will give us advice on what to do with our gardens. My mother planted the primroses beneath the front windows. Alas, neither Hallie nor I have much of an eye for blooms."

"I don't either," Lord Renfrew said, and added a fourth spoonful of sugar to his tea.

"Then why would you be picking flowers? Oh, I see, you are a romantic, not a connoisseur."

Lord Renfrew stirred another spoonful of sugar into his tea. It was nearly painful to watch him drink it, but Jason nodded and continued to smile.

"Look here," Lord Renfrew said, waving his teacup, so full of sugar Hallie was surprised he could lift it, "none of this is to the point."

"What is the point?" Jason asked politely.

"It is very strange to have a lady standing whilst the two of us are sitting."

"Possibly so," Jason said. "However, unlike you, I am not slurping tea in a lady's presence. I think Hallie must realize how thoughtful and polite I am, thus making her more accommodating." He gave her a smile that would have made Mrs. Millsom swoon again.

Lord Renfrew saw that smile, knew there was power in that damned smile, and it burned him to his feet. Bastard, damned toad of a second-son bastard. He'd always recognized that the Sherbrooke twins were considered very handsome men, but since he himself wasn't an affliction to the female eye and had always been admired by both men and women—perhaps women a bit more than men, as he'd been told many times—he hadn't begrudged them their additional dollop of physical beauty. He did now. He saw the clout of that beautiful face aimed at Hallie, and hated the man to his toes. He wanted to seduce her, he wanted her money. This wasn't to be borne. "Miss Carrick, I am Lord Grimsby's guest, Viscount Merlin Grimsby of Abbott Grange. I am here to ask you to attend a ball this Thursday evening, a ball in my honor, and you would be my special guest."

Jason leapt to his feet. "A ball? Did you say a ball? I haven't been invited to a ball since my return to England. I would be delighted to attend, my lord. I shall bring Hallie with me. Do you have a suitable gown, Hallie?"

"Will it be a costume ball, sir?"

"No. It will be a regular sort of ball. Actually, Mr. Sherbrooke, I only—"

"I believe I packed away a lovely medieval maiden's gown in one of my trunks. A pity it isn't a costume ball."

"I am certain the gown is lovely, Miss Carrick—Hallie—but it is, as I said, a regular sort of ball. Mr. Sherbrooke, about the ball, I can only invite—"

"I know what you are thinking, my lord," Jason said, "and you are right to be concerned that I have been out of civilized England for too long, that I have nothing fashionable to wear. I will ask my brother. He's the viscount, you know, and he is always a well-dressed fellow. Sometimes he gives me his last-year britches, sometimes even his coats. Very few stains since his valet is such a superb fellow.

"As for Hallie, I believe my brother's wife could lend her something. Don't worry, my lord, both of us, I fancy, will look quite dashing."

"Miss Carrick is rich; she has many gowns, all lovely. Besides, since she is rich, surely she wouldn't lower herself to borrow anything from your blasted sister-in-law."

Hallie said, "I must say it's ever so predictable you remembered the groats in my pockets, though I'm not surprised. I think a ball would be delightful. Thank you for inviting us. Jason, do you know Lord Grimsby?"

"Oh yes, though I haven't seen him in a long time,

since James and I were at Oxford and observed him with a delightful young lady who, I believe, was no relation to him at all."

"Now, see here, Mr. Sherbrooke. Lord Grimsby wasn't all that old then."

Hallie said, "Isn't Lord Grimsby married?"

"I was being indelicate," Jason said. "When James and I were quite small, Lord Grimsby let us ride his prize pigs, big pigs, you understand, so fat they could barely walk and thus weren't hazardous to the health of two three-year-old boys."

"Your father let you ride pigs?"

Jason nodded. "He said if we could stay on Ronnie and Donnie's backs for three minutes without sliding off, we would be ready for our own ponies."

Lord Renfrew said, disdain radiating from his lovely tall self, "I have never ridden a pig in my life."

"Well, I haven't since I was three-and-a-half and my father set me on my first pony. How about you, Hallie?"

"I wish I had the memory of a fat pig from my childhood, but alas—you know that my father and I sailed everywhere when I was little and the deck rocked too much for livestock to roam about." She turned to Lord Renfrew. "Perhaps you were too young to remember your pig-riding."

"Of course I would remember. I don't." He shut his mouth. He was in Bedlam. This was absurd, ridiculous. Both his host and hostess were smiling at him, ready to offer him more tea, ready to misunderstand what he said. He rose, bowed in Hallie's direction, sighed, knew there was no hope for it. It was either both or none. "I will see you Thursday night. Mr. Sherbrooke, it's been pleasurably irksome to meet you."

He bowed again and nearly ran from the drawing room. They heard Petrie's rapid footsteps toward the front door. "Oh, my lord, do give me just a moment. The door is heavy, it must be opened just right. I am re-prepared, and at your endless service."

They didn't hear a word from Lord Renfrew. The front door closed, a bit on the loud side. A moment later, Petrie appeared in the drawing room doorway. "How very odd, Master Jason, the gentleman didn't take his hat or cane, and you can be sure I held them both out to him."

Chapter 24

The Dauntry mare, Penelope, was made at home in the stall next to Delilah's, where it soon became apparent that they didn't like each other. Jason and Hallie watched Henry jerk Delilah back before she could sink her healthy yellow teeth in Penelope's lovely chestnut neck.

"It's because of Dodger," Jason said to Hallie. "Both Delilah and Penelope want him. They know they're beautiful, used to winning, and have sharp teeth. What will we do?"

"Let them tear each other's manes out," Hallie said.

Jason laughed. "What a sight that would be. No, it's a sight I never want to see again in my life. Put her in the end stall, Henry."

Henry looped Penelope's lead reins around his

hand. Her new accommodation was probably too close to Dodger's stall because Delilah whinnied, tossed her head, and kicked out, making the wood shudder. As for Piccola, she continued to chew on her hay, her eyelids heavy. Dodger looked up to see what the excitement was about, saw Penelope swaying toward him, and nodded his big head. "I swear his ears perked up," Jason said, "when Penelope came into his view."

Henry called over his shoulder, "I will take his sultanship into a paddock so we'll have no more carryings-on between the ladies."

Hallie said slowly, "I don't think I have laughed so much in a very long time."

"With Elgin hanging about, I can believe it. You're lucky to be rid of him."

She shuddered. "I once thought he was very amusing." She turned to leave the stables, paused a moment, turned back to him. "But not now. I am going to try to balance our expenditures with our profits. Will you check my figures later?"

He nodded, watched her stride back toward the house. He remembered the Wyndhams—the laughter, the shouting, the arguing, natural to a house with four young children. He missed that very much.

Both Jason and Hallie met at the top of the stairs at eight-thirty the evening of the Grimsby ball. They stared at each other.

Jason, because he was older, more experienced, more used to dealing with ladies than Hallie was dealing with men, said easily as he took her arm, "I don't know, Hallie. Corrie has this lovely pale green gown that is the perfect shade for you. But this blue? Don't mistake me, it's lovely, and I'm sure the style of the gown is fashionable, but the truth? That particular shade of blue makes you the slightest bit sallow."

She poked him in the stomach with her left fist.

He grinned down at her. He was so beautiful in his formal evening clothes it would make any living female so dizzy with excitement, she just might fall over, or vomit. "All right, not a sallow patch can I see on you. You look quite the thing. I'm glad Martha kept your hair simple, the braids look very fine on you."

"She told me she's the best braider this side of London, that the profusion of crimped curls defeat her. She patted my hair when she was done with me, said better braids for me than little sausages. As for you, Jason—" She drew a deep breath. It wouldn't be wise to tell him the truth—that he looked like a god, so absolutely perfect, every artist in the world would have wanted to sculpt him, or paint him, or murder him when their wives got a look at him.

Thankfully, Petrie called out from the foot of the stairs before she could say something stupid, "Ah, Master Jason, every lady between the ages of fifteen and one hundred and five will believe you have the best valet in the entire world. It's a treat you are to the senses, sir, a treat. Forgive me, Miss Hallie, you look as lovely as one could expect a female to look. Ah, isn't this exciting? Our first ball in the neighborhood."

"As for me what, Hallie?" Jason asked.

"I had a temporary affliction of my brain," Hallie said. "Forget it, Jason."

He was grinning as Angela came out of the drawing room looking like a fairy queen, all in pink and white lace. "Oh my dears, both of you look splendid. Oh dear."

"What's wrong, Angela?" Jason asked her, taking a quick step toward her. Since he hadn't released Hallie's arm, he pulled her with him.

"It's Cook."

"What about her?"

"She's breathing hard. I fear the worst."

Jason spun around to see Mrs. Millsom standing not two feet from him, staring up at him. He caught her before she hit the floor.

Jason, Hallie, and Angela didn't arrive at Lord Grimsby's lovely old manor house, Abbott Grange, built during the early years of Queen Anne's reign, until nine o'clock. The night was warm, little gusts of wind stirred the oak branches, and the moon nearly full.

"What a perfect night to be out and about," Angela said, and patted Hallie's knees. "Or inside and about, for that matter. And you will have a lovely visit with your family, Jason. How very nice of your father to lend us one of his carriages. I hear that your father has known Lord Grimsby forever."

Hallie said, "Will your grandmother attend as well, Jason?"

"Yes, I believe so. Do you know, I've never seen her

dance? My father told me once when she was young, she danced until the sunrise. However, since Angela will be there, who knows?"

Angela said, "Lydia told me yesterday she was coming. I told her you would dance with her, Jason. James as well."

"If she can meander around the dance floor with her cane, we should have no problem," Jason said.

Hallie said, "I plan to ask James if he has fond memories of the pigs."

"He will," Jason said. He gave Angela a grin to smite her dead.

"Poor Cook," Angela said.

"Don't encourage him, Angela. His head is already so big—not much heft up there to speak of, just air—it's ready to float."

Abbott Grange sprawled over a half acre, every window filled with light, probably a good five hundred candles lit, Hallie thought, wondering at the expense and the sheer number of fingers required to light that many tapers. There were more carriages than Hallie could count lined along the entire perimeter of the long drive. After Angela and Hallie were handed down by two liveried servants who looked to Jason as if they'd come directly from a boxing match, he thanked John Coachman, whose name was really Benjie, and slipped him a bottle of Mr. McFardle's fine ale from his tavern in Blaystock.

"This could be in London," Hallie said behind her hand as the three of them joined another dozen guests wending up the wide, deep stone steps past liveried servants holding flambeaux high above their heads. They were no sooner announced to the sixty or so guests in the Grimsby ballroom, than a young man's voice said, "By all that's wicked, isn't it Jason?"

A lady's voice said, "I believe it must be since the girl with him isn't James's wife."

"Jason, is that really you? You're home at last?"

"This is the young lady who—"

"Jason, you look tanned as we ever did in the summer as boys. Remember that time at Punter's Pond?"

"She's far too pretty to be a partner. Look at that gown."

"My God, man, it's been too long. Welcome home."

Jason was laughing, shaking hands, clapping backs, a huge smile on his face, and he didn't let go of Hallie's hand. He introduced her and Angela to all the gentlemen and ladies who crowded around him. Hallie curtsied, nodded, presented her right hand to be kissed a dozen times, and smiled. The ladies were a bit on the cool side, but as Jason had said when they'd first walked in, "They're my friends. They'll accept you fast enough."

"Goodness," Angela said from beside Hallie, fanning her face. "Our Jason certainly knows everyone. He's very popular, Hallie. Is this ball really in honor of Lord Renfrew?"

Hallie said, "Difficult to believe. Now, a lovely get-together for his hanging, that I can believe. He's over there, Angela, speaking with that young lady with all the black hair. Drat, he's coming this way."

Lord Renfrew swept down on her, ignored Jason, and took her hand in his. She gave a little tug, but he wasn't about to let go. He gave her a man's look that she recognized quickly enough, and asked her to waltz.

She chanced to see a half a dozen ladies, none of them older than she was, coming straight at Jason in the form of a wedge, the lead girl a lovely blonde, no more than eighteen, with an impressive chest that was on prominent display. Jason was trading jests with a man he appeared to have known since he was born, unaware of the approaching armada. She smiled up at Lord Renfrew. "I am sorry, my lord, but I have already agreed to dance with Mr. Sherbrooke. I will need my hand. Would you please escort Mrs. Tewksbury over to Lady Lydia?"

The wedge was nearly on him. She heard one gentleman say, his voice near a squeak, "I remember this all too well. The devil take it. Why, I—"

Hallie grabbed Jason's arm. "I'm saving him, sir. Jason, come along quickly or you will be swept away."

Jason knew female determination when he saw it, grabbed Hallie's arm, and laughed as he let her pull him through the crowd to the dance floor. The musicians had just started up a rousing waltz.

"I've seen your prowess on the dance floor, sir; I am ready to be impressed."

Jason smiled down at her, clasped her firmly, and whirled her around in wide circles for nearly five minutes. Hallie was panting when he finally slowed. "That was quite wonderful, Jason."

"My father taught James and me that a lady always forgave a gentleman for even the most stupid remark if he danced well."

He whirled her about, deftly avoiding other dancers until she was laughing.

CHAPTER 25

❧❦

❧ When Hallie caught her breath, she said, "Your father must be right. I haven't wanted to call you a moron once since our feet started moving. Oh dear, I do believe the ladies are surrounding James as well. Will the two of you never be safe?"

"James said he truly appreciated being married to Corrie. He said she protected him, like grandmother told you."

"I wonder if Corrie ever fears being shot? Oh dear, I don't believe Lord Renfrew is glad you're here, Jason. He wanted to dance with me, you know. He's giving you a remarkably nasty look. Ah, good, he's asked that black-haired girl to waltz. That's a relief."

"She's fluttering her eyelashes at him," Jason said.

"She's not doing it well, but she's young yet. She'll learn."

"I think she's doing very nicely. Ah, you're very graceful. That would make sense if a gentleman wanted to be successful with the ladies. However, you could dance like a clod and it wouldn't make any difference."

"I was thinking the same about you, Miss Carrick." He gave her a white-toothed smile and whirled her about until she would swear under oath that she was flying two inches off the floor.

When they slowed a bit again, he said, "I can't imagine why Lord Grimsby—he's the elderly gentleman standing next to the lady with the huge ostrich feather—would give a ball especially for Lord Renfrew."

"It makes no sense to me. I did meet Lord and Lady Grimsby; you simply weren't aware of it. They told me how Lord Renfrew could speak only of my grace and loveliness. Nausea nearly flooded me. You, unfortunately, weren't available to deter them. You were surrounded by too many well-wishers. It appears everyone missed you, Jason."

"It's good to see old friends."

"You know, Lord Grimsby was giving me the eye—not a flirtatious eye, mind you, but an assessing eye—perhaps to evaluate if I'd do or not."

Jason said slowly, "I wonder if your Lord Renfrew has some sort of hold on Lord Grimsby. I shall have to ask my father. He knows everything, which is odd, since he refuses to listen to gossip, but still, information finds its way into his ear."

Hallie could only marvel at him. "I will tell you, Jason, I am used to being drowned in compliments, but not to the extent the ladies try to corner you. It is, naturally, the same with my father. Perhaps more so."

"You haven't noticed all the gentlemen salivating, Hallie. That's why I tried to keep you close, to protect you."

She laughed, couldn't help herself. He whirled her around and around. When the waltz finally came to an end, once she could suck in enough air, she said, "Another dance, please, sir. You do it very well."

"All right, but not a third waltz until much later, Hallie. I don't want your reputation to suffer."

She didn't care, but acquiesced. After the second waltz, Jason left her at Angela's side. He turned to his grandmother, bowed formally. "My lady, would you condescend to waltz with a grandson who, upon three different occasions, stole your nutty buns?"

The old lady rapped his arm with her fan, gave him a huge grin. "Ah, I knew, I always knew. Take me to the floor, my boy."

Alex Sherbrooke couldn't believe her eyes. She clutched at her husband's sleeve. "Douglas, goodness, I didn't think the old bat could move so spryly."

"A potted palm would move spryly if dancing with one of my sons," Douglas said. Actually, Lady Lydia was swaying in place, Jason smiling down at her, holding her as gently as he would one of his nephews, telling her that particular shade of pale yellow was perfect with her complexion. The old lady preened.

"She always loved Jason best." Alex sighed. "As many times as I still want to kick her, she looks lovely, and so very happy. Why can't she be happy all the time? Why can't she ever smile at me like that?"

"Give it up, my dear," Douglas said, and drew her to the dance floor. "I doubt not that when she finally croaks in the next century, she will still insult you to your toes, be it Heaven or Hell. All six remaining teeth on full view. Do you think we'll still have some teeth when we're her age?"

"Oh dear, Douglas, I don't wish to visit that thought at this moment. My lord, you dance as gracefully as ever."

"More than three decades of inspiration keep the spring in my step," Douglas said.

An hour later, the entire Sherbrooke family sat at three tables in the lovely dining room off the ballroom, eating shrimp patties, drinking champagne, and delighting in the Grimsby's cook's incredible olive bread, a recipe she claimed had come from Sicily itself, from her grandmother the ancient Maria Teresa. Lady Grimsby was heard to say that every olive in a twenty-mile radius would be residing in her guests' bellies before the night was over.

"Father," Jason said, "tell me why Lord Grimsby is giving a ball in Lord Renfrew's honor."

"Hmm. Lord Renfrew seems a pleasant enough

man, despite his need to be shot," Douglas said, nearly sighing over another bite of the olive bread. "Fact is though, Lord Grimsby and Elgin's uncle—Bartholomew Sloane—were first cousins on the mother's side. Grew up together. One of Barty's sons died in Greece some ten years ago. Grim told me the boy traveled with Lord Byron."

Hallie said, "My lord, perhaps a large dinner party with whist afterward would be more appropriate than a ball. Why would Lord Grimsby go to this sort of expense for his cousin's son?"

"Ah, that's an excellent question," Douglas said. "Didn't I hear that after you gave Lord Renfrew the boot, Hallie, he married a girl up north? Her father was a wealthy merchant or such? And she died?"

"How did you know that, sir? I swear I never told a soul."

Douglas shrugged as he snaffled the last slice of olive bread off his wife's plate. "And now he has no money. It all makes very clear sense, don't you think?"

"But I'm living with Jason!"

There was only a bare moment of appalled silence.

"You're his partner, Hallie," Corrie said. "You're not his mistress."

"Of course I'm not his mistress," Hallie said. "I am too rich to be any man's mistress."

"Be that as it may," Douglas said, "it would appear that Elgin Sloane wishes to see if he can't reattach you, my dear."

"But I found out he was marrying me for my money, my lord. Do you know what else he was doing? He was sleeping with another woman."

"Not quite so loud, Hallie," Alex said, patting her hand.

Corrie said, "That doesn't make much sense, does it? He was doing both? Doesn't he have a functioning brain?"

Hallie said, "He must have believed he could get away with it."

"All girls except Corrie are stupid at eighteen," Corrie's mother-in-law said. "Did you know that she saved James's life?"

"She's got more guts than brains," James said.

Hallie said, "Well, no, and I should like to hear all about it. Didn't Lord Renfrew get a good look at Jason, sir? Is the man blind?"

Jason waved away her words. "He thinks I'm poor, jealous of my brother, and something of a buffoon." Jason grinned. "It was quite an enjoyable visit with him, as a matter of fact."

"You're wicked, my boy," Lady Lydia said, staring at the shrimp patty that lay in the center of her daughter-in-law's plate. She wanted that shrimp patty. Alex knew it. She speared the entire patty on her fork and raised it to her mouth. Then, cursing herself, she cut it in half and set one half on her mother-in-law's plate.

Lady Lydia eyed the half shrimp patty. "I'll wager you licked it, didn't you? You did it very fast so I could see only the shadow of movement of it, so I'd know what you did, but not be able to prove it. And that's why you gave it to me. You want Douglas to believe you are selfless, but you licked it."

"Yes," Alex said. "I licked it." She stared the old woman down until she ate the shrimp patty. "It tasted strange," Lady Lydia said as she set down her fork. "I don't know your particular taste as my poor son does, but—"

"Mother," Douglas said, his voice icy enough to freeze the champagne, "If Alex licked the shrimp patty, it will bring you luck."

"All this dancing, I must keep up my strength," the dowager said.

Her fond son said, "You've more strength than two prize bulls, Mother. You're quite remarkable."

Angela rolled her eyes. "Lydia, do visit Lyon's Gate tomorrow. You and I can oversee Cook making nutty buns. You said she still doesn't do it right."

"They are barely edible," Lady Lydia said.

"We will keep Jason out of the kitchen so she won't be distracted."

"One cannot expect everything," Hallie said, "Her braised buttock of beef is outstanding, at least when Jason is at the dinner table. That makes me think you need to have Jason simply stand in the middle of the kitchen while she makes the nutty buns. They will be heavenly."

"Hmm," Angela said. "Hallie has a point. The only problem is that she will probably swoon."

Jason choked on his champagne.

"You're right," Hallie said. "You must simply tell her that the nutty buns are Master Jason's most favorite treat. They will be ambrosia. I'm willing to lay a wager on it."

Lady Lydia said, "Your cook swoons? How very odd of her."

"Why the devil does the woman swoon?" Douglas asked.

"It's your dratted son, sir," Hallie said.

Corrie said, "How much would you like to wager, Hallie?"

"Use your head, Corrie. Jason is the image of James."

"Oh. I'm a dolt. Forget the wager. We have a male cook and let me tell you, he's never once swooned when he's seen either me or Mama-in-law."

There was laughter then. "How very delightful to find all of you together," Lord Grimsby said from beside Douglas's elbow. "I have brought another loaf of olive bread so that I would be welcome to join you, and my dear Elgin as well."

CHAPTER 26

⁂

"Delighted," Douglas said, and watched servants tenderly ease two chairs to the table. He wondered as he watched them why a man couldn't pull his own chair to the table. He knew well enough it was the way things were, but he didn't like it very much. Never again, he decided, would he allow someone else to get him a damned chair.

"My wife said it was the last loaf. She said to use it wisely." Lord Grimsby bowed and presented the loaf to Douglas.

Hallie wanted to spit. Lord Renfrew smiled down at her as he said, "Here, bring the chair closer," and squeezed in next to hers, on the other side of Jason. Smart man, Douglas thought, knowing well the look on his son's face—Jason would smile while he pounded the man into the ground. "Hand me the bread, Grim," Douglas said to Lord Grimsby, who sat next to Alex— too close, Douglas was thinking. As Douglas reached for the loaf, he looked around the table hopefully. "I don't suppose everyone is full?"

Every relative held out his plate.

Douglas asked a servant for a cutting knife. The next three minutes were spent with every eye focused on the width of each slice Douglas cut.

When everyone, including Lord Renfrew, had a slice, Douglas said, "A lovely ball, Grim."

Lord Grimsby laughed, waved his half-eaten slice of olive bread at James and Jason. "My wife told me that every lady in the district would be smitten, and she is right. You invite these two, and every other man in the room feels like donkey dung."

"A father's cross to bear," Douglas said.

"My father also had a cross to bear," Lord Renfrew said in a very loud voice.

Hallie arched an eyebrow. "I should think so."

"Yes, of course you are a fine-looking boy, Elgin," Lord Grimsby said. "Now, Miss Carrick, it is a pleasure to meet you. I have heard all sorts of tales about your partnership with Jason."

"What sorts of tales?" Lady Lydia asked, her old eyes sharper than a vampire's teeth.

Lord Grimsby waved a negligent hand. "Oh, nothing really, just one story that struck Lady Grimsby very forcibly. She heard that a visiting servant who saw Miss Carrick kick over a bucket said there was a seam down the middle of her skirt and so she wasn't really wearing a skirt. Never heard of such a thing myself. I told my wife the man must have been mistaken."

"It boggles the mind what a man will see when confronted with a lady kicking a bucket," Jason said. "A seam? As in her skirts were divided into two parts, two different parts? I can't imagine such a thing. Can you, Angela?"

"No, my boy, never."

"Laughter," Lord Renfrew said. "I heard too much laughter, not coming from the stables, but from inside the house."

Lady Lydia said, "Angela has told me all the laughter comes from Petrie—the butler, Lord Renfrew, not from anyone else. Hallie's lady's maid is always telling Petrie jokes."

As a distraction, Jason thought, it was well done.

Corrie, her head cocked to one side, said, "Petrie laughing at something a woman says? That doesn't sound like the Petrie I know. Petrie is a misogynist. Grandmama-in-law, why are you rolling your eyes at me? Why, Petrie even claimed I didn't really save you, James, that as a female I am only capable of cowering behind a hay bale. He said it was you, James, who saved the day, that because of your extraordinary bravery, you disremembered what miraculous deeds you performed."

"None of this is to the point," Lord Renfrew said. "Of course you did not execute any sort of rescue, my lady, such a thing would be in very bad taste. Now, this Petrie fellow, he did serve me tea, but his face was stove-black and he stole my hat and cane."

"No, that's impossible," Jason said. "Petrie told me himself that he disliked the new style in men's hats, although the cane was all right, save for the ridiculous eagle's head."

"My father selected that eagle's head!"

"Perhaps Petrie sold the hat and cane," Alex said.

"Hollis always said that Petrie had an excellent eye for goods, that were he a criminal, we would be in trouble."

Lord Renfrew threw his napkin on his plate. "You are all jesting. I do not like it. My lord, I wished to visit with Miss Carrick, but all these people are interfering."

Lord Grimsby leaned over to pat Lord Renfrew's hand. "Simply smile and nod and you will get through it."

Lord Renfrew said, "I also saw my former head stable lad, Quincy. I can't imagine how he came to be working for you. He was a shiftless fellow—"

Hallie said, sarcasm dripping out with her words, "Perhaps one should pay one's servants, Lord Renfrew. That is probably the best solution to any problem."

"How is Quincy with you?"

"I informed Willicombe, the Sherbrooke butler in London, that we had need of an assistant head stable lad. Quincy was at our door within a day, grinning from ear to ear. He is quite good, you know."

"Yes, I know. The fellow was good, but he had no loyalty—"

The earl said, "If a man doesn't pay his dependents, he should be deported to France."

"Then *she* should be deported, not I," said Lord Renfrew, nodding at Hallie. "It is her fault that poor Quincy wasn't paid. His pay could have been her wedding present to me."

Hallie was ready to leap over the table and gullet Lord Renfrew with his own fork, when Douglas lightly laid his hand on her sleeve. "I think it's time I told everyone about my grandsons. Their names are Douglas and Everett. You should see Jason waltz with them—"

Lord Renfrew smiled. "Oh, I see. Well done, my lord. You are endeavoring to show Hallie the glories of having children in the house. Listen, Hallie. I would be a spectacular father. Only imagine this delightful domestic picture: a handful of children waltzing with their proud papa. Ah, yes, it warms my heart."

There was a cloud of appalled silence over the table until Lord Grimsby said, "Tell me, Douglas, how much longer do you think King William will last?"

"It's what follows William that gives me pause, Grim. Oh, who is this now at our table? Another friend of yours, Jason?"

Jason looked up at the distinguished gentleman who bowed, snagged Hallie's hand, and kissed her fingers. He grinned like a bandit and licked his lips. "Olive bread. It is quite good, isn't it?"

Hallie raised the fingers of her other hand to her mouth and licked them. "Yes, quite good."

"I am Grandison, you know."

James said, "Charles, what on earth are you doing here in the wilds of Sussex? Last I heard you were sailing off the coast of Portugal."

"No, not Portugal. Ah, James, what a picture you present. Why don't you gain flesh? Perhaps lose your teeth, shed a bit of hair? And Jason? It has been far too long."

The twins rose, shook the gentleman's hand.

Charles Grandison looked closely at Jason. "You look content."

Jason laughed. "I will be content after Dodger leaves your tired old nag, Ganymede, snorting and sweating in the dirt."

"Stuff dreams are made of, my boy. Elgin tells me you and Miss Carrick own Lyon's Gate. Together. I should like to hear how that came about."

"A simple enough tale, sir," Hallie said. "Both of us wanted the same property."

"It shouldn't have happened," Lord Renfrew said. "Hallie should be married to me, all settled in a lovely house in London, planning our next soiree."

"That could be possible, I suppose, were you another man altogether," Hallie said.

Charles Grandison laughed. "Ah, that's a grand wit you've got, Miss Carrick." He turned to the earl of Northcliffe, bowed. "My lord, forgive my interruption. I am Charles Grandison. My father vastly admired you."

"I remember your father and his antics," Douglas

said. He didn't add that he'd believed Conyon Grandison had been more incompetent than evil, which was the only reason he hadn't been hung.

Charles said, "Just so, sir. To my dying day I will rejoice that my father didn't manage to shoot that bullet into Miles Sinifer's head." He turned, bowed to Alex. "I spent many hours convincing my sister she didn't want to fling herself from her mare's back on the off-chance that James here would catch her before she landed on a yew bush. She's expecting her third child now. Screamers, the first two are."

He was too charming, Hallie thought, watching him joke with Angela and the countess. She sipped at Lady Grimsby's champagne punch, potent enough to knock a girl on her bottom and not care. She watched Charles Grandison, Lord Carlisle, bend over Lady Lydia's ancient veiny wrist and treat her to an intimate smile to make her remaining teeth tingle.

"Who is Miles Sinifer?" Hallie asked.

"Ah, a gentleman who tried to seduce my mother. My father picked up his gun and shot it from no more than three feet from Miles's head. As I said, thank God he missed."

Where the devil had Charles been, James wondered, watching the man he and Jason had always admired make his way charmingly from lady to lady at their table. Until he got to Corrie. He stilled. James knew when a man was looking at a woman with lust in his eyes. James stiffened in his chair, but said pleasantly enough, "Keep away from her, Charles. I'm younger, stronger, and meaner than you. Unlike your father, I wouldn't miss."

"This is your Viscountess, James? The innocent young girl who saved you from kidnappers and herself from Devlin Monroe?"

"Oh goodness," Corrie said. "I haven't seen Devlin in far too long. He is well? He is married? Does he still avoid the sun?"

Charles Grandison laughed and took Corrie's chair when she slid over onto her husband's lap to make room for him.

"Devlin quite likes all those whispers about his being a vampire, all naturally behind polite hands. I believe you were the one who started it—"

"Perhaps I was the first to say vampire out loud," Corrie said, "but Devlin always admired his pallor. Now, you, sir, and my husband have known each other for a very long time, have you not?"

"Since he tried to beat my gelding, Horatio, in an impromptu race. James was riding his pony, Jason cheering him on. They were five years old as I recall, and I was an ancient eleven or twelve."

"In that case, please call me Corrie. I miss Devlin and his pale face. He was quite amusing." She sighed and James wanted to smack her. Instead, he eased beneath her gown and slid his hand up her leg.

Always the charmer, Jason thought, content to sit back and watch Charles charm his family, but what was he doing here? He appeared to know Lord Renfrew, and surely that wasn't in his favor. Charles had been racing mad as a boy, and now owned one of the largest racing stables in northern England. It was heard he would shut himself in his bedchamber for three days and nights if he lost a race, which wasn't that often. No one tried to cheat Charles or poison his horses, or cripple his jockeys—the price Charles made the miscreant pay was too high. And that, Jason decided in that moment, was the reputation he was going to nurture as well. Maybe his would even be more fearful.

Jason, Hallie, and Angela didn't arrive home until nearly three o'clock in the morning. Both Martha and Petrie were in the drawing room, Petrie, head thrown back on the back of the sofa, snoring, Martha huddled in a chair, one stockinged toe sticking out from beneath her gown.

When they walked into the drawing room, Martha jerked up and yelled, "Tell us everything!"

Petrie's nostrils pinched as he jerked awake, and he nearly stumbled off his feet he jumped up so quickly. He was quick to wave his nanny's finger at her. "Martha, a lady's maid doesn't demand gossip from her mistress. You will lower your head and inquire if Miss Hallie wishes to have you remove her stockings."

Angela said, "Goodness, Petrie, isn't that rather indelicate of you? Martha, after you have assisted Hallie, do come to my bedchamber. I appear to have more buttons than fingers to do the task."

"I will, Miss Angela." Martha whirled around on Petrie, hands on hips, "As for you, Mr. Stump-Chops, don't you tell me what to do with Miss Hallie's stockings. It pains Master Jason to hear such private matters spoken of in his drawing room."

"Actually, I believe Jason is standing in my half of the drawing room," Hallie said.

"But—"

Jason raised his hand. "Be quiet, Petrie, let it go. No, no more from either of you. No, Martha, heel." Jason turned to Hallie and Angela. "You see? I put a stop to the hilarity just as you asked."

"Hilarity?" Petrie said. "Hilarity is not at all the thing in a gentleman's household."

"All we need," Angela said, "is Cook to complete the picture."

"But, Master Jason," Petrie began, knowing he had an important point if only he could find the ears to hear it.

"No, Petrie. We'll tell both of you everything in the morning. Everyone to bed now. Petrie, you're with me."

"Martha," Hallie said, "I will tell you all about Mr. Charles Grandison, who will probably be visiting us in not more than seven hours from now."

"What a lovely name," Martha said. "Is he a gentleman wot—what—looks like his name like Master Jason does?"

"Indeed. Master Jason said Charles Grandison was ruthless when it came to all the scoundrels and the corruption in the racing world. So much money involved, you see."

"We are going to be more ruthless, more feared even than Charles Grandison," Jason said. "We will make anyone who tries to hurt our horses or cheat or threaten us, pay so great a price they'll never try it again."

"And our reputation will spread." She rubbed her hands together. "My father taught me how to bring a man to the ground with very little effort."

"Very little effort? Do I wish to know what you're talking about?"

"Well, it involves my knee, Jason. My father said a man couldn't bear that sort of pain, whatever that means."

Jason and Petrie looked appalled.

Martha said, "Well, more power to a lady's knee, I say. Now, Miss Hallie, it's very late. Time for me to see to you and Miss Angela."

Jason said, "I, as well, learned a lot with the Wyndhams in Baltimore. Americans can stand more pain, and they don't whine as much, I found. Jessie asked me to exercise desperate measures on three occasions as I recall."

Hallie said, "What kind of desperate measures?"

"A competitor bribed a stable lad to poison one of the Wyndham horses. I made him walk through downtown Baltimore—it wasn't raining, as I recall— carrying the tub of the poisoned grain he would have fed Rialto. Every three steps he had to announce what he'd tried to do."

Hallie nodded in approval. "I heard from my father that you once sliced a jockey's face with your whip when he was going to stick a knife in your horse's neck."

"Nearly to the bone."

"My father also said you nabbed another jockey as he was coming out of Mrs. O'Toole's tavern and beat the stuffing out of him for trying to shoot you off your horse in a race the week before."

Jason smiled at the memory, flexed his fingers without conscious thought. "I should have waited until he'd sobered up. It would have been more fun."

"Just so," Hallie said. "No one will go against us more than once."

"Heavenly groats, Miss Hallie," Martha was heard to whisper as she walked between her mistress and Miss Angela up the staircase, "this is so exciting. Do ye—you—think you'll have to resort to some of these desperate measures Master Jason was talking about?"

"It's possible," Hallie said, as serious as a nun wielding a three-pronged whip.

"And yer—your—knee, Miss Hallie. I want to hear all about your knee."

"That thought would make the blood move swiftly through a man's heart, wouldn't it?" Angela said, as she lightly patted the very feminine white lace over her bosom.

CHAPTER 27

❧❧

❧ Charles Grandison said, "I want to buy Piccola. She's magnificent. I'll pay you very well for her, Jason."

"She's not my mare to sell."

"Ah, so Miss Carrick is her owner. A lady enjoys having lovely things—"

"I've noticed that gentlemen enjoy lovely things as well," Hallie said, coming around the corner. She strode, Jason thought, like a boy with more arrogance than brains. What would Charles make of that? What would he say if he noticed her gown was really a pair of fat-legged trousers? Ah, and the shine on her boots.

Hallie patted Piccola's forehead while she nuzzled a carrot off Hallie's palm. "She will win me many more races before she retires, my lord. Unfortunately, we have no horses for sale at this time. We've not been in business all that long."

Jason said, "James and Jessie Wyndham will be visiting in August. They're bringing us stock they've selected themselves."

"Yes," Hallie said. "Come see us in September."

"I will," Charles said. "It will interest me to see what an American considers good breeding and racing stock. Ah, Miss Carrick, Lord Brinkley told me about the shine on your boots. Said his man Old Fudds still couldn't get it just right."

"Practice," Hallie said.

"That is true of most things, I've found," Charles said, and turned to Jason. "You've begun well, Jason."

"Thank you," Hallie said.

Charles Grandison laughed. "I would like to meet this misogynist butler who stole Elgin's hat and cane."

It was later, over Cook's lovely tea and gingerbread that Hallie asked, "Lord Carlisle—"

"Call me, Charles, please."

She smiled, inclined her head. "Have you and Lord Renfrew known each other long?"

"Elgin is horse mad," Charles said. "He has asked me to assist him in buying quality horseflesh."

"It is an expensive undertaking," Jason said, and chewed a raisin Cook had put in the gingerbread.

"Oh, you don't think Elgin has enough pounds in his pockets?"

"I really don't know," Jason said. "Nor do I really care."

"I suppose you told Jason, Miss Carrick, that Lord Renfrew would very much like to marry you?"

"No, I did not tell him that. Why would I?"

"He is your partner, ma'am. Were you to wed Lord Renfrew, why then, it would be he who would deal with Jason here and your horses."

"I hadn't realized that marriage went hand in hand with incompetence. Marriage would make me stupid, then?"

"A lady as lovely as you are could be as stupid as a chamber pot and it wouldn't matter."

Jason, in mid-drink, spewed the tea out of his mouth and began coughing. Hallie walked to him and smacked him hard on the back. He finally caught his breath. He grinned up at her. "Ah, thank you for the brute assistance."

"I have four young siblings. One is always prepared to do anything, including cauterizing a wound. Now, Lord Carlisle, about Lord Renfrew."

"Charles, please."

Hallie picked up her teacup and saluted him, and yet again she inclined her head. "I don't suppose Lord Renfrew asked you to come to Lyon's Gate to, er, soften me up a bit?"

"I scarcely know the gentleman."

"You and he are of an age," Hallie said.

"Surely he is older."

"I don't believe so, unless he lied to me. I believe Lord Renfrew is thirty-one years old."

"Hmm. Yes, Elgin lied. It is a nasty thing, a lie, but

some feel compelled to do it, particularly when the young lady is of tender years."

"I'm no longer tender, sir."

A very handsome dark brow arched up. Charles looked toward Jason, then back at her. "You must take care, Miss Carrick, this young gentleman here is known for his prowess with the fair sex. Tender or no, it has never mattered. Why, stories are legend about—"

"I've been gone five years, Charles. The legends are good and dead."

"But new ones are well begun in Baltimore," Hallie said. "So many females running toward him in the rain, bumping umbrellas."

Charles burst out laughing. "Good God, I can picture that."

Hallie said, "I, myself, sir, saved Jason from a bevy of eager ladies at the ball last evening. Their strategy—a lovely narrow wedge headed by a very determined young lady—was excellent, but I was faster."

Jason rose. "All of this must be amusing to the two of you. I, however, have work to do, work that will make me sweaty and dirty and completely unappetizing to the fairer sex."

"Not Cook."

Lord Carlisle's lovely eyebrow went up again. "Cook? What is this?"

Hallie said, "Cook swoons whenever she sees Jason. He's caught her twice now, one time she took him to the floor. When he is at the table, we eat very well indeed. If not, why, both Mrs. Tewksbury and I lose flesh."

Jason threw up his hands and walked out. Hallie, without pause, said, "It took me long enough to arouse him. Thank you for your assistance, sir. Now, you will tell me what is going on with Lord Renfrew. There is no reason for Jason to have to suffer through another recital of the man's mental and moral failures. He told you our history, I presume?"

Charles nodded slowly. "He told me he was foolish, that he didn't realize the value of the precious jewel in his very hand."

"Surely you're making that up. Elgin really said such an idiotic thing?"

"Well, perhaps not. It's difficult to know, Miss Carrick, whether to flatter, to soften, or to spit things right out into the open."

"Spit, please, sir."

"Only if you will call me Charles."

"No, I don't know you well enough yet. Please don't ask me until sometime next week, if, that is, you're still in the neighborhood."

"You wound me, Miss Carrick."

"I doubt that. Like Jason, I have a lot of work to do."

Charles finished off his tea, sighed, and sat back in his chair, legs stretched in front of him. "Elgin's father drank, his mother took lovers—he had a very difficult family—"

"You will not make excuses for him. Elgin Sloane is a man, he must be held responsible for his actions. That he obviously believed me to have less mental aptitude than a cow—well, now, that's a painful tonic to swallow. However, when I discovered the truth, I would have shot an arrow through his gullet if I'd had my bow with me."

"As I said, Miss Carrick," Charles said, "Elgin made some bad decisions, decisions he bitterly regrets. He has changed. He has grown into his years, although it has taken him longer to grow since he lied about his age."

"How old is Lord Renfrew?"

"I know for a fact that he is thirty-three."

She laughed, simply couldn't help herself. "Twenty-four months, he lied about twenty-four months. He believed that to an eighteen-year-old-girl head over boots in love, twenty-four months would make a difference?"

"One never knows about females. My own wife was a mystery to me until the day she died. I see you are still feeling the pain of the blow he struck you."

"What blow was that?"

"What he did isn't all that dishonorable, Miss Carrick. Elgin desperately needed money to restore his uncle's estates. The old man was a wastrel, unworthy of his lands and title. Elgin knew he would have to make the ultimate sacrifice."

"The ultimate sacrifice," Hallie repeated slowly, savoring the words. "I had no idea I had achieved such status. That's the only blow he told you about?"

"Good grief, there's another?"

"Indeed. The thing is, Lord Renfrew was bedding another woman at the same time of our betrothal."

Charles winced. "I can see why he wouldn't want to admit that to me. That does make him appear in a rather stupid light, doesn't it?"

"Oh yes. Now, you can't buy my mare and you can't push Lord Renfrew's suit. You've drunk your tea. Would you like to leave now, sir? Perhaps take Lord Renfrew's hat and cane to him?"

Charles slowly rose. "I knew that messengers were always kicked, yet still I came. That second blow, he didn't tell me about that one. Next time I will know better."

"Lord Renfrew must have a hold on you, to actually convince you to come here. To be his emissary, that is certainly sinking oneself very low."

"Oh yes, certainly he has a lovely hold over me. If he didn't, can you possibly imagine I would be here to push the nitwit's suit with you?"

She laughed, felt a tug of liking. "What is the hold he has on you?"

"I don't believe I'll tell you that, Miss Carrick. May I call you Hallie?"

"No. Perhaps next week. If there is a next week, which, given the company you keep, is highly unlikely. Jason and I are very busy. I do not like to have to spend time sipping tea when there are stalls to muck out."

"A lovely thought, that," he said. He walked to her, his stride strong and graceful, making Hallie wonder just who Charles Grandison was. He collected her hand, turned it over and kissed her wrist. "Such soft skin," he said.

"If you lick me, I shall kick you out the front door."

He laughed. "Oh, no, I don't lick a lady's flesh, at least not in the drawing room, Miss Carrick. It has no finesse, only the value of shock. I dislike such artifice."

She wondered what he was thinking when he mounted the lovely gray Andalusian gelding held by Crispin, their youngest stable lad, all of thirteen, and watched him accept Lord Renfrew's hat and cane from Petrie. She watched him ride the Andalusian through the open gates and down the drive. An excellent riding horse—proud, agile, calm. She wondered what his name was. She wondered what hold Lord Renfrew held over Charles Grandison.

Hallie wanted to work her horses, she wanted to sweat, to perhaps sing a ditty. She didn't want a man to make a fool of her ever again.

Ten minutes later, she was walking quickly toward the stables. She could still hear Petrie and Martha arguing, hear Cook singing as she prepared Master Jason a Spanish frittata, and Angela humming as she sewed another divided skirt for Hallie.

She whistled until she wasn't more than twenty feet from the paddocks, and heard a scream.

It was Delilah, and she was loose. So was Penelope, and both were in the paddock running after Dodger, who, with a tremendous jump, cleared the paddock fence to race off into the distance.

"What the devil happened, Henry?"

Jason came running around the corner, a hoof pick still in his right hand. He gathered what it was all about.

"Bring me Charlemagne. He's the only one fast enough to catch Dodger."

But Hallie was faster. "He's my horse," she said, slid the bridle into place, grabbed his mane, and pulled herself up. "I'll fetch Dodger home, sir. You calm the mares."

Jason watched her ride that brute of hers bareback at a gallop. He watched Charlemagne take a fence in full stride. He shook his head and went to the paddock.

"The little missus sure can ride," Henry said. "I ain't niver seen a female ride like that 'un."

"It's a pity Charlemagne's bloodlines aren't worth spit, else we could make a lot of money off him."

"Old feller's an accident o' blood, Master Jason, an' that sometimes 'appens. He niver shoulda been so mean nor so fast."

Not five minutes later, Corrie and James rode up to the stable. "We saw Hallie riding like the wind. What's going on?"

"Dodger's ladies were fighting over him. He escaped, and Hallie went after him."

James handed his brother Bad Boy's reins. "You'd best make sure she doesn't break her neck."

CHAPTER 28

❖

❖ It was the fault of Major Philly's cow, who was wandering free in her pasture, chewing placidly on the fresh summer grass as she stared after Dodger, who was still running faster than the wind. The cow was unaware that Charlemagne was running right at her, all his focus on Dodger, who was still a good thirty yards ahead of him.

When the cow saw Charlemagne, eyes wild, head down, she mooed loudly in alarm.

Charlemagne heard the moo but didn't see the cow, but Hallie did. In a last-ditch effort to avert disaster, she threw herself against his neck, grabbed the reins close to his mouth, and jerked as hard as she could to her right.

Charlemagne ripped the reins out of her hands,

jumped straight into the air, slashed out at the cow with his hooves, missed, and sent Hallie hurtling over his head.

Jason saw the whole thing. He was so frightened he cursed until he'd run out of both human and animal body parts. He leapt off Bad Boy's back, dodged the cow's butting head, and fell to his knees beside Hallie.

She was pale except for two bloody scratches on her cheek. He felt for the pulse in her throat, couldn't find it. "Don't you dare be dead, damn you. I want Lyon's Gate, but not over your dead body. Open your eyes, you bloody female, now. You don't wish to be the first buried here in this cow pasture, do you? There, I found your pulse. You're alive, so stop pretending you're not. Wake up, woman."

"I wonder where all past owners of Lyon's Gate are buried?"

Her words were slurred, but he understood them. "Good, you're here. Keep your eyes open. How many fingers am I waving in front of your nose?"

"A blurry fist. You're shaking your fist at me. What nerve."

"Hold still." He started with her arms, then skimmed his hands lightly over her, ending with squeezing her toes in her riding boots. "Do you have pain anywhere else other than your head? Don't lie there with a vacant look on your face, answer me. You didn't groan, is it only your head?"

"Yes, it's only my head. Get that fist out of my face."

"My fist is two fingers. Keep your eyes open, Hallie. I saw what happened. Ah, here's Dodger, come back to see what trouble he caused. I tried to shout after you that Dodger always came home by himself, but you were off to save the day rather than pause for just an instant to see if your assistance was even needed."

"He comes home by himself?"

"Look at poor old Charlemagne. He's blowing after that adventure you put him through. Charlemagne could have hurt that cow, and you have no idea how much Major Philly loves his cows."

"Would Dodger really have come back since Delilah and Penelope were after him?"

"Hmm."

"You don't know either since this is the fist time two mares wanted him. He was frantic, Jason. He wanted only to escape. Charlemagne doesn't come back. Can you teach him to come home?"

"Maybe. Right now, all three horses are standing no more than six feet from me, wondering why you're lying here on the ground."

Jason felt in his pocket and gave each horse a sugar cube. "You want one too?"

Hallie looked at him, then at the horses, all three of them still staring down at her, chewing on their sugar cubes. She was glad she didn't know what they were thinking. The cow mooed. Jason gave the cow a sugar cube too.

"This is humiliating," she said, and closed her eyes.

"Open your damned eyes!"

"No," she whispered and turned her face into his hand. He felt her warm blood against his palm. "Can I have a sugar cube?"

He wanted to laugh, but he didn't. He felt her warm breath, then he realized she was asleep, or unconscious, he didn't know which. He felt the lump behind her left ear growing bigger. She wasn't going to like the way she felt when she woke up. Jason sat back on his haunches, popped a sugar cube into his mouth. Dodger, seeing him do that, whinnied. "Well, my fine fellows, what the hell do I do now?"

He looked up when he heard Major Philly say from behind his right shoulder, "I say, Mr. Sherbrooke, what are you doing with my sweet Georgiana? Why is Miss Carrick—she is Miss Carrick, isn't she?"

Jason nodded. "She was thrown." He turned back to Hallie to see Major Philly's Georgiana butting her head, licking her hair and face.

"Get that fist out of my face."

"It's Georgiana, not my fist," the major said. "Is Miss Carrick all right, Jason? She doesn't look at all the thing, you know. There's blood running down her face."

Hallie moaned and didn't breathe in. She didn't move.

"Here's a sugar cube," Jason said and stuck it in her mouth. "Suck on that and I'll get you home."

"I say, Mr. Sherbrooke, poor Georgiana is overset. Her eyes are rolling in her head."

"Give her another sugar cube, sir, she'll be fine."

When Jason carried Hallie into the house, Martha yelled, "Heaven's groats! There's blood dripping off her face. She's dead!"

Petrie, to Jason's surprise, said as placid as a vicar who's drunk the sacramental wine, "Calm yourself, Martha. Master Jason would have told us if she was dead. She looks bad, though. Shall I fetch a doctor, or is it too late?"

"I suppose it would be best to have her head checked. Send Crispin. He knows where Dr. Blood lives."

"Yes," Corrie said, coming into the drawing room, "he can ride Petunia, my mare. Dr. Blood is such a good physician, but such an unfortunate name."

"Hello, Corrie," Jason said. "You and James came for a visit? Everything's all right at home, isn't it?"

"Oh yes, but Hallie—"

Before Petrie took himself off, he said to Corrie, "I can see her chest moving, my lady. Well, since she's a female, it's not quite accurate to say chest, but you know what I mean—"

"Everyone knows exactly what you mean, Petrie. Go." Jason sat beside her, held her hand, told her that even though Major Philly wasn't pleased with her for scaring the bejesus out of his cow, Jason had talked him around. "Keep those eyes open and listen to me. Twenty years ago, James and I helped him herd his cows into another pasture when his dog, Oliver, was ill and couldn't do it. He always called us Mr. Sherbrooke."

"Because he couldn't tell us apart," James said.

"Probably not, but it was a nice touch, made us both feel very important. The thing is that Georgiana is a very sensitive bovine. It's possible her milk has been adversely affected."

"All right, if it isn't her fault, then it's Dodger's fault."

Jason tucked the lovely afghan his grandmother had knitted over her. "Do I recall preaching about taking responsibility?"

"You listened to what I said to Lord Carlisle about Elgin Sloane, did you?" asked Hallie.

"I had to remove a pebble from my boot. My ears didn't stop working. When you're upset, Hallie, you're loud."

When Dr. Blood, a Scotsman from John O'Groats, so far north that throwing people into the frigid sea was the preferred method of murder, arrived and looked down at Hallie, he stroked his chin. She still smelled like cow, sugar cubes, and carrots, and had a blinding headache, but Dr. Blood was pleased she was awake and alert. She looked up at him with narrowed eyes. "I don't want any man named Blood near me."

"Too late, young lady," said Jonathan Blood. He finally had to shove Jason out of the way. "Do you want to vomit?"

Petrie said, "See here, she can't vomit, not in the drawing room where there's no chamber pot in sight."

"No, Petrie, I'm not nauseous, thank God."

Dr. Blood felt the lump behind her ear, looked at her eyes, kneaded her neck, felt her ankles after he'd removed her boots, frowned at her torn stockings, and ordered strong tea without sugar. "You'll do," he said. "Nothing like a woman to have a hard head. You remain lying there, Miss Carrick, all limp and female and let Jason here wait on you. Jason, you can give her some laudanum now. The headache should be gone when she wakes up."

"The master doesn't do that," Martha said from the doorway. "I do that."

"No, it is I who dole out the laudanum," Petrie said. "I am the one ultimately responsible for curing Miss Carrick's headache. I am the butler."

Hallie groaned.

"Oh dear," Petrie said.

"She's not going to vomit," Corrie said. "Are you, Hallie?"

"No."

James said, peering down at her, "Now that we know you're all right, Hallie, my wife and I will see ourselves out. You've enough to deal with without family hanging about, even though Bad Boy saved the day, and I've yet to hear a single thank-you."

Jason threw a wet cloth at his twin, who caught it out of the air, and said, "It smells like cow. Not good."

Corrie laughed, took her husband's hand, and dragged him from the drawing room. "Rest, Hallie. I will come back in a couple of days to see how you are doing. Angela, don't worry, your fallen chick will be just fine."

By eight o'clock that evening, Hallie was so bored,

she was ready to tear raw meat apart. Not a minute later, Jason obligingly came into her bedchamber, whistling and carrying a tray.

She eyed the teapot. "I hope Cook made the tea for you. If not, it will taste like hot water with oak bark in it."

Jason set the tray down, poured a cup and tasted it. "No, not oak bark. Hmm. Elm bark, if I'm not mistaken."

She laughed, drank some delicious tea, eyed the single scone he handed her. "You lied to her. Well done."

"I told Cook I needed sustenance to see to your care. She commiserated; not verbally, of course. She didn't swoon."

"This is the first time I've seen your face since you carted me upstairs."

"Someone has to work around here," he said, and handed her the scone. "Don't stuff it in your mouth. I don't want you getting sick to your stomach."

"Petrie came here three times, and each time he pointed out the chamber pot to me. Everyone else was nice enough not to mention it."

"Angela told me you didn't look too bad. The scratches on your cheek, I don't think they're deep enough to scar."

"My father always told me I was like him. I could get knocked about, even stomped on, and never show a mark. I like Bad Boy. Do you think James would sell him to me?"

"Not in this lifetime. But he is talking about breeding him. I'll come to an agreement with him. How do you feel?"

"You know that Normandy church in Easterly? I feel like the bells are clanging inside my head."

"Good. They're lovely, those bells. Would you like some more laudanum?"

She shook her head. "Are the horses all right?"

"Dodger seems quite content to whinny over his stall door at both Delilah and Penelope. As for Charlemagne, he got extra oats and a good brushing. Henry told him even though he had a rotten bloodline, he was a steadfast lad, one could count on him."

"I want to race him next week at Hallum Heath."

"I'm riding Dodger in that race."

"You're too big. You'll lose."

"I know, it simply sounds nice to say it. We've a jockey arriving early next week, in time for that race. He's ridden for the Rothermere racing stables for seven years now, ever since he was fifteen. He's marrying a local girl, moving here, and we are the ones to benefit from Rothermere's loss. His name is Lorry Dale. Phillip Hawksbury, he's the earl of Rothermere, said Lorry stuck to a horse's back like a tick. He only weights eight and a half stone."

"Hmm."

"We can both attend, make certain nothing bad is taking place, shout ourselves hoarse, and have some fun. Dodger will win with Lorry on his back."

"I weigh eight stone."

"This isn't Baltimore, and you aren't Jessie Wyndham. You will not race here, Hallie. Living with me is difficult enough for people to accept, and they only do it because of my family. Your riding in a horse race wouldn't be tolerated. You'd have to shoot yourself dead to be forgiven that transgression. The winner's purse is one hundred pounds. Money we can well use."

"But—"

He lightly placed his fingertips over her mouth. She froze. Jason did as well. Neither moved. Suddenly, Jason took three steps back from her bed, stuck his hands behind his back. He looked toward the door. "I'm going out."

Hallie felt as if she'd been punched in the gut. She watched him walk backward, looking at her like he wanted to—what? She didn't know. He was flushed, his eyes looked funny. He wanted to leave? He'd touched her mouth and he couldn't wait to get away from her? "What do you mean you're going out? You said nothing before. It's nearly nine o'clock at night. Jason, wait, where are you going?"

"I'm going out now." And he was gone in the next thirty seconds. It wasn't the first time he'd absented himself abruptly in the evenings, for no particular reason that she knew of. Four times now, five? And when did he come home? That was a good question.

Hallie heard him walk by her bedchamber near dawn. She jumped out of bed, nearly fell over at the drumming pain in her head, but managed to stumble out into the corridor. She saw him with his hand out to grasp the door handle on his bedchamber door.

"You just got home. You're whistling? It's almost daylight!"

He jerked around like he'd been shot. He saw it was her, saw she was weaving in her open doorway, and started walking back to her. "Yes, I'm home. Let's get you back to bed, Hallie. What were you doing awake?"

"I was nearly awake when you walked by. Oh dear, where's the chamber pot?"

CHAPTER 29

✢

✢ He held her while she heaved and shuddered and felt her belly clench in on itself since there was nothing to come up.

His guilt was heavy; he never should have left her. It was all his fault. He'd been only concerned with himself. And so he pulled back her hair now and yelled at her bent head, "Why the hell didn't you call for help if you felt ill? Why did you leap out of your bed when you heard me outside? Have you no brain at all?"

She finally stilled. He pulled her back against him. The weight of her breasts on his crossed arms felt very nice, but he could take it now. He'd worked himself nearly to death last night to be able to take it now.

Her breathing was calmer, she was relaxing more against him. Her hair was tousled and smelled of jasmine since Martha had washed out Georgiana's scent. "How do you feel?"

It was the oddest thing. He could feel her thinking. Finally she said, her breath warm against his arm, "I don't want to die at the moment and that's good. But my belly feels like it's raw."

"You're far too obstinate to die anytime in the next fifty years. All right now, I'm going to heave you back into bed."

When he'd pulled the covers to her waist, he gave her some tea that had steeped since the previous night. She sipped it and nearly rose straight off the bed. "Oh goodness, that tea has vampire teeth."

"Yes, I thought it might do the trick. Cleared your head right out, didn't it?"

She breathed through her nose as the world tilted, then felt her belly calm. Jason eased her head down on the pillow. "I'm all right now. I don't know what happened—"

He said, "I'm thinking now you weren't feeling ill. You got out of bed to come and spy on me, didn't you?"

"Well, yes, it doesn't sound very noble, but that's the way it was. I'll tell you now, Jason, I wouldn't have if I'd known what would happen."

"Consider it the wages of sin." He stood beside her, pulled the covers to her chin, and realized his arms were still warm from her breasts. He frowned. Everything, he'd learned, was temporary in life, and sometimes, like now, it was a damned nuisance.

He was backing away from her bed again.

"What is the matter with you, Jason? Are you going out again?"

"What? Oh, no, I'm going to bed. I added a bit of laudanum to the tea. You should be asleep in two minutes. Don't worry about anything." And he was gone from her bedchamber, closing the door quietly after him. She heard his boots in the corridor.

She was asleep, belly and head calm, within the next minute.

It was a hot morning in July. Jason could smell the freshly scythed grass from the open breakfast-room window. It filled him with contentment, that, and the fact that there were now six mares in the stables, hopefully all of them pregnant, all of them sent by friends or friends of friends or friends of relatives.

"Isn't it nice having such lovely big families?" Angela said at the breakfast table. "This is a note from your aunt Arielle, Hallie. She writes that the duke of Portsmouth will be contacting you and Jason about two mares to be covered by Dodger. He also wants to breed his favorite stallion with Piccola next year." Angela raised her head.

Jason appeared distracted. "Yes, Angela, lovely."

Hallie licked some gooseberry jam off her toast, looked at him, and sneered. "What is this? You wish to run away in the morning?"

Jason tapped his fork on the plate, picked up a slice of bacon and ate it. He rose. "I have work to do," he said, and was gone.

"The young master seems to have a lot on his mind," Angela said. "Perhaps Petrie will know what's going on."

"Petrie is a clam when it comes to Jason. As wily and subtle as I am, even I couldn't get a thing out of him."

"Perhaps Petrie needs a more mature hand, one that makes a lovely fist."

"Hmm. I never thought about threatening him," Hallie said.

"I will begin with wearing a soft glove over the fist." Angela left the breakfast room humming.

Hallie looked down the short expanse of breakfast table and saw that Jason had left most of the food on his plate. What the devil was wrong with him? He seemed jumpy lately, as if, somehow, he were in some kind of distress. This wasn't good. She had to find out what was going on with him. After Angela was done with Petrie, Hallie would push her own gloved fist in his face.

But Petrie was nowhere to be found. As for Jason, Lorry, their new jockey, told her, he'd ridden off in the old gig.

An hour later, nearly high noon, Hallie dressed in one of her split skirts, grinned down at her reflection in her shiny boots, and took herself to the stables. There was always so much to be done.

There were only two mares in the paddocks, both asleep where they stood, their tails flicking gently. It was later than she'd thought. All the lads were out exercising the horses. She walked around the corner of the stable and stopped dead in her tracks. Jason was forking hay into the back of an open wagon, his movement rhythmic and graceful.

He wasn't wearing his shirt. In point of fact, he was naked from the top of his head all the way to his waist, well, perhaps even a bit lower than that. There was a line of hair that trailed beneath the waist of his trousers. She saw a faint line of sweat. He paused a moment, and stretched.

She nearly expired on the spot.

Jason walked back into the stable. She walked quickly after him, not even realizing that her feet were moving. She came to a stop in the open doorway, heard the mares whinny, watched him stroke each nose as he gave each mare a sugar cube.

When he wiped his palms on his breeches, he turned, whistling, and froze. He hadn't heard her, hadn't known she was anywhere near. She was standing not six feet from him, her arms at her sides, staring at him like a halfwit. "How is your head?"

"My head? Oh, fine." She gulped, trying to bring her eyes to his face, which was always a treat, but unable to this time. "Just fine. Lorry said you had left in the gig."

"I had to deliver two saddles to the blacksmith in Hawley."

"That's nice. The gooseberry jam Cook made you for breakfast was wonderful."

"Well, yes, it was. Hallie—" He scratched his

chest—his bare chest. He hadn't realized he'd taken his shirt off. Bright sunlight shone through the open stable doors, and he saw it on a tree stump twenty feet away. He looked toward the shirt, back at her face. "Hallie," he said again. "My shirt—let me fetch it."

"You don't need to do that. I've seen men without their shirts before."

"Why don't you go back to the house? Or I can go back to the house and pick up my shirt on the way."

"Actually, the only man I saw without his shirt on was my father. He grabbed his shirt really fast so I didn't see all that much, which is a pity since he is so beautiful and a girl needs to know what's what. I have younger brothers—I bathed them, went swimming with them—but to be honest here, that's not really the same thing."

"No, it's not. If would be best if you turned around now."

"That isn't necessary, Jason. You are very lovely to look at."

"Do you think you could look me in the face when you say that?"

She began walking toward him. The mares whinnied. Jason stood nailed to the spot. When she was no more than three feet from him, she hurled herself at him, threw her arms around his neck, and pressed close.

She nearly knocked him over backward. He grabbed her arms, tried to peel her off him, but it was no good, she was strong and determined. He couldn't believe he was panting, but he was. "Hallie, for God's sake, you've got to stop, you've got to get hold of yourself—" He felt the length of her hard against him. "No," he said into her mouth. Oh God, her mouth was so very soft and her breath tasted sweet. It was the hardest thing he'd ever done in his life, but Jason kept his arms stiff against his sides. One of her hands stroked down his chest. His breath whooshed out when her finger slipped beneath the waist of his trousers. She didn't know what she was doing, she couldn't know. No, he wouldn't seduce her, no, it wasn't going to happen, he refused—

"What the hell is going on here?"

A man's voice, sharp, appalled, a voice vaguely familiar, a voice he'd heard before, but not here, not in England. Oh God, that voice was from Baltimore. That was a father's voice, a voice ripe for murder.

Hallie's father's voice. Baron Sherard. Bloody hell and back.

"Hallie, step away from the man."

She turned to Lot's wife. Her breathing was hard and fast, but she didn't move, if anything, she pressed closer, warm, soft, all of her pressed so close, too close, and her father was spitting distance away. "Er, Father?" She sounded out of breath, like she was walking on a tightrope and was going to fall at any moment, like she wanted to fall, and—

"Yes. Hallie, I'm your father, and I'm here, not more than eight feet behind you. I want you to listen to me now. Take your arms from around Jason's neck. Do it now. Step back."

"It's hard," she whispered, breathing in the scent of his flesh. "Very hard, Papa. He doesn't have a shirt on."

"I can see that. Step back, Hallie. You can do it, I know you can."

She felt her father's hand on her arm, tugging her, but still, it was so difficult. Slowly, she managed to put an inch between herself and Jason, then two. She wanted to weep at the distance.

Her father was here, not three inches behind her, his hand on her arm. Sanity returned with a solid thunk. She turned. "Papa? You're here at Lyon's Gate? I mean, you're here at this specific time, which is really very unfortunate for me. Should you like to come to the house for a cup of tea?"

His little girl, he could see her all of five years old, sitting cross-legged and barefoot on the quarterdeck of his brigantine, practicing her knots, clad in denim dungarees, a straw tarpaulin hat covering her head. Dear God, here she was nearly twenty-one years old and her eyes were glazed with lust. It was hard for a father to accept, but no matter, it was up to him to remain cool and calm, to remain in control, to save his daughter from herself. He cleared his throat. At least she wasn't pressed against Jason Sherbrooke like a second shirt any longer. He cleared his throat again, this time for himself. "First, you will tell me why you're plastered against Jason Sherbrooke."

Hallie licked her bottom lip. Her father saw that tongue of hers and knew to his toes that if he'd been five minutes later, Jason would have had her naked under him on the stable floor. Or she would have had Jason naked and on his back on the stable floor. His little girl had tied the best rolling hitch on board his ship, but that little girl was no more.

"Jason," he said, never taking his eyes off his daughter's face, "go get your shirt and jacket on."

Jason nodded.

Alec Carrick took his daughter's arms and pulled her slowly against him. "Hello, sweetheart. May I say you're always surprising me?"

"I'm sorry. I couldn't help it."

"No, I could see that you were completely involved in what you were doing. Could you tell me exactly what you were doing, Hallie? What you were planning to do?"

She blinked up at him. "I'm not really sure. It's just that I saw Jason without his shirt on, and I fell off the cliff."

Alec Carrick didn't need to ask which cliff.

"Oh dear. I've never even thought to do anything like that before. I was getting used to his face, and that's taken some doing, I can tell you that, but then to see him from his head to his waist—it was like a blow to the belly."

Alec Carrick closed his eyes a moment. He'd learned all about blows to the belly at age thirteen.

"Baron Sherard," Jason said, his shirt buttoned to his throat, his jacket buttoned as well, looking ridiculous in the heat. "Welcome to Lyon's Gate. We weren't expecting you."

"No, I planned a surprise," Alec said slowly, eyeing the young man who'd left scores of female hearts cracked when he'd steamed away from Baltimore to return home.

"I apologize, sir, for this particular surprise. I swear to you this hasn't happened before, and it won't happen again."

A gentleman, Alec thought, he was a gentleman, taking the blame off his daughter's head. As for Hallie, she was staring at Jason like the village idiot, lust still blooming bright on her cheeks, still glazing her eyes.

"Hallie," her father said, "I would like some tea. Go into the house, fetch Angela, and Jason and I will be coming along soon."

Both men watched Hallie walk slowly back toward the house, head down. It soon became obvious she was talking to herself. She waved her right hand, which meant she'd made a good point and the other part of her brain had to accept it.

"She'll lose this argument."

That brought Alec up short. "You know what she's doing?"

Jason shrugged. "She was arguing with herself about me once. I was relieved that the side of her who'd taken my part that day, won. She didn't bash me on the head. Sir, about what you saw—"

"Yes?"

"As I said, this has never happened before. It happened this time because I was forking that damned hay, and it's really warm this morning. I just didn't think. I took my shirt off. I'm sorry."

Alec Carrick stood not three feet from Jason, his arms crossed over his chest, legs spread. He looked perfectly capable of drawing a pistol and shooting Jason between the eyes.

"Would you like to tell me why one of my daughter's hands was straying down to your belly?"

Jason nearly shuddered, felt again quite clearly those long fingers of hers on his flesh, tangling in his hair. He'd wanted to jerk and quake. "No, sir, both hands were around my neck except for the very shortest of moments. I swear to you I hardly noticed her hand. Or her fingers."

That was a lie of the first order, but Alec didn't nail him. "Thank God you didn't or I imagine my daughter—what's this? Oh yes, the stable lads have returned from exercising the horses. No one was about. That's fortunate. I hate to ask myself what my daughter would have done if the stable lads were in the stables. Would she have controlled herself? As a father, I pray so. Shall we continue this at the house?"

"Certainly." Suddenly, Jason grinned. "I wonder what Cook will do when she sees you."

An eyebrow went up as the baron strode next to him. "Why the devil should your cook do anything?"

"If she swoons at the sight of you, my lord, do catch her, else we won't eat well for dinner."

Cook looked at both gentlemen, standing side by

side, and burst into a vaguely Italian aria, both hands clasped over her breast. She never stopped singing as she skipped back to the kitchen, an amazing sight, given her bulk.

"Heavenly groats, Miss Hallie, and me poor whirling eyes, this is too much bounty for a simple female. Two perfect gentlemen, both of them standing right here in our house, right next to each other. Are you perhaps Master Jason's older brother, sir? Oh my, did Cook swoon?"

"Cook sang," Hallie said. "Actually, she is still singing. This is my father, Martha, Baron Sherard."

"Lawks, sir, ye—you—can't be a father. You're a god."

CHAPTER 30

❧❦

❧ That evening, after a delicious dinner of turbot of lobster with peas and asparagus and a savory roast saddle of mutton, Cook delivered up a chocolate cream for dessert to make the angels sing.

It was still light outside, so the draperies in the drawing room weren't pulled, and several windows were open to the sweet night air.

Hallie poured her father tea, added a dollop of cream, just as he liked it, and handed it to him. She could still smell Jason on her skin. How was that possible, since she'd bathed before dinner? Her hand trembled. She couldn't think about Jason, at least not now. Her father was telling an amusing story, she had to pay attention. She said, "So what did Genny do to this Mr. Pauley?"

Alec laughed. "I believe she asked him if he played the piano, which he did, of course—she'd found that out before she asked the question. She then patted his hand and told him despite the fact that playing the piano, just like painting watercolors or sewing samplers, was a distinctly female pursuit, she still believed he looked manly enough, well, perhaps not quite as manly as he could if he eschewed the piano keys, for say, billiards and cheroots. He looked at me, studied himself for a moment in the mirror, coughed, then asked her very politely to design his yacht."

Jason, who knew Genny Carrick, Lady Sherard, nodded when Hallie said, "I never saw her back down from a fight. And she's so smooth. I still get so mad I want to spit nails in a man's face when he tells me I'm too pretty to be out in the mud."

Alec said, "Genny was the same as you at one time. However, since she married me, she's learned to deal with businessmen with far more finesse."

"That's because if she could deal with you she could deal with the devil himself."

Alec laughed and toasted her with his teacup.

Angela said to Jason, "Baroness Sherard taught Hallie to stand firm when the ground was firm enough to stand upon, otherwise, she was to step back quickly."

Alec Carrick looked at his watch, looked at his daughter, and rose. "I believe Jason and I will have a short conversation. If you ladies will excuse us."

Hallie jumped to her feet. "Oh no, Papa, don't you

dare take him outside and shoot him or break his head. He didn't do anything. It was all me. I attacked him. I nearly knocked him over I wanted to get to him so quickly. You cannot blame him, it isn't fair."

"I cannot very well call my daughter a blockhead and knock her in the jaw, now can I?"

"You've called me a blockhead many times."

Alec Carrick sighed. "I forgot."

"Listen, Papa, he was helpless, he was polite, there was nothing he could do except maybe kick me away. Besides, all the stable lads were out with the horses. Angela won't tell anyone, will you?"

"Certainly not, my dear, but you know these things have a way of oozing out of cracks in the walls."

"No," Hallie said. "No, it's not possible."

"Hallie, go to bed," Jason said. "Sir, it's quite a lovely night. Would you like to see Piccola prance around the paddock? It is one of her favorite pastimes."

"Prancing on a moonlit night?"

Hallie said, "She refuses to prance if the sky isn't clear. I don't want to go to bed. I want to speak to my father, set his mind on the right road, assure him that if anyone did happen to see anything at all, I would bury him under the willow tree."

Alec Carrick walked to his daughter, clamped his hand over her mouth, and said quietly into her ear, "There will be no bodies buried anywhere. You will not open your mouth again. You will go upstairs and you will stay there."

Angela took Hallie's arm. "It's one of those times when the ground isn't firm enough to stand on, my dear. Come along."

Five minutes later, Alec Carrick was smoking a cheroot and thinking about this very odd day. He said as he watched the smoke curl up into the clear night sky, "My daughter is one of the most self-contained individuals I have ever known. Even when she was small, she looked at those around her with a dispassionate eye. However, she was not at all dispassionate today in the stables."

Jason had never seen her dispassionate, indeed, did not recognize this woman her father spoke of. Hallie, dispassionate? Never. He said, "It is true, sir, what I told you. Nothing like that has ever happened before. I would not dishonor your daughter."

"No, the shock on your face, the desperation, was as stark as the white moon. The initial letters my daughter wrote to her mother and me after the both of you wanted Lyon's Gate—she was quite ready to tear your head from your body. When she wrote of your male beauty, I could picture the sneer on her face. What do you think of my daughter, Jason?"

"She has more guts than brains."

Baron Sherard nodded, remained silent.

"This is something that shouldn't have happened, my lord. I never wish to wed, you see."

Alec said slowly, "I heard rumors to that effect, rumors that you'd exiled yourself from England, spent nearly five years of your life living with the Wyndhams. You did this because of a woman?"

Jason shook his head.

"I had heard you were shot, nearly died. I will admit, I wondered what happened."

"I didn't die."

Alec Carrick waited.

Jason said, "It's been over a long time, yet when I close my eyes it seems just a moment ago. I was responsible for the near-murder of my father and brother."

"How can that be?"

Jason shrugged. "It was a bad time. Know that I was the one responsible for it."

Alec let it go. "I repeat, Jason, what do you think of my daughter?"

Jason looked out of the paddock, listened to Henry's low, soft voice as he spoke to Piccola, who was lightly tapping one hoof against the ground. Moonlight washed over the two of them, made the white paddock fence look like a painting. "This is my home. When I first saw Lyon's Gate, I knew it would be mine, that I would live my life here and race and breed horses."

"My daughter felt the same way."

"Yes, I came to realize that. I will tell you that my family, because they love me, tried to get rid of her, but she never faltered. Thus we have this partnership of sorts. It has been difficult, I won't lie to you, my lord. Your daughter is lovely, she is bright, she works until she's cross-eyed, and she can walk into a room of people and bring laughter or create chaos. We have yelled at each other, nearly come to blows, all in the past two months, including the day I first saw her. Both of us have learned to bend a bit. Did you know that Lord Renfrew was in the neighborhood?"

"That ass? Did she hurt him?"

"It was close, but she decided to laugh instead, at how stupid she'd been. Do you know what really angered her? Evidently, in addition to bedding another woman during their betrothal, the buffoon lied to her about his age."

Alec Carrick threw back his head and laughed at the moon. Piccola raised her head and whinnied. She broke away from Henry and began to dance around the paddock, coming nearer and nearer to where Jason and Hallie's father stood, booted feet on the wooden railing. Her eyes never left the baron's face.

Jason said, "I hadn't realized Piccola liked laughter so much."

Alec said slowly, smiling toward Piccola, "After she found out about Renfrew, my daughter told me she never intended to marry. She said she didn't have good judgment in selecting gentlemen. I reminded her that she was only eighteen years old, and what could she expect in the way of seeing behind the masks people wear?"

"You're never smarter in your life than when you're eighteen," Jason said.

"I assume you're right. It's been too long for me to remember. Now, so you'll know how serious she was, Hallie wanted to make a blood oath with one of her brothers that she would never wed. Her brother was eleven years old and would do anything she said. I put a stop to it before she could cut her palm with a knife.

"After turning down a good half dozen gentlemen, four of the six quite satisfactory, I believed her."

"Hallie and I suffer from the same bad judgment in potential mates."

"I see. I think it's time you told me a bit of what happened, Jason."

Jason saw no hope for it. He said slowly, "Unlike Lord Renfrew, this very smart and beautiful young lady did nothing so paltry as lie about her age. She was a monster and I never saw it. As a result of my poor judgment, she nearly killed my father, and her brother nearly killed my twin.

"The fact is, I am not good husband material, my lord, because I can't imagine ever trusting a female again in my life. I couldn't give a wife what she'd deserve. I couldn't make her happy."

"Because of this lack you see in yourself."

Jason nodded. "It's there and it's deep, part of me now, and a wife would come to resent me, even hate me."

Baron Sherard said nothing more. He patted Piccola's nose, remembering how she'd struggled to stand after her mother had finally birthed her six years before at Carrick Grange. He watched her prance about in the paddock beneath the moonlight. He smiled. Youth, he thought, was always such a serious business. There was a lot to think about. He wondered what the earl and countess of Northcliffe thought of his daughter. Had they known what would very probably happen if two young, healthy people were put together like this?

Jason was lying on his back, his head pillowed on his arms, staring up at the shadowy ceiling. Moonlight poured through the open window. The air was still and sweet. Sleep was a million miles away.

He watched the doorknob turn slowly. In an instant, his body was poised to fight. The door opened quietly.

A halo of candlelight appeared. "Jason? Are you asleep?"

"It's after midnight. Of course I'm asleep, you twit. What do you want, Hallie? Don't you take another step. You will not come in here, not with your father sleeping twenty feet down the corridor. Go away."

She slipped through and quietly closed the door. "When I was little, I practiced walking on cat feet since I excelled at eavesdropping. The only person who would ever hear me was my stepmother. She told me it was a good skill to develop but I must promise not to use it on her. I never did."

"I heard you. Go away."

"Jason, I'm not going to jump you again," she said, and she sounded both mortified and excited. She tossed her hair behind her, long thick hair, which he had no intention of thinking about, how it would feel rubbing against his cheek, a curtain over his belly.

"Stay there, Hallie. I have no nightshirt on."

"Really? You don't sleep in a nightshirt? Yes, I remember Corrie saying something about that. Do you know the moon is flooding through that window, Jason? If I come only five steps closer, I'll be able—"

"If you come one step closer, I'll personally throw you out that window. It's a nice drop to the ground."

"All right, all right, I'll not move from this spot. Tell me, did my father try to break your arm?"

"No, he didn't."

"Do you know what my father is thinking? He wouldn't tell me a thing, patted my cheek, bid me good night, and walked away. And here I've known him all my life."

"I saw you slide your right foot forward. Step back, Hallie."

She took a very small step back. He saw she was barefoot. "If my father didn't hit you, then I know what he wants, Jason, but believe me, you don't have to agree. What happened was my fault, I've told him so a good dozen times. He says nothing, only looks patient. I wish he would believe that no one could possibly know. It's as if it simply never happened. Poof, it's gone."

Jason sighed. "Nothing's gone. He's your father. That makes all the difference in the world. I don't think there's going to be any choice here, Hallie." He gave a short laugh. "At least our questionable partnership will be over."

"No, don't say it. I wanted to apologize to you for what I did, though I don't remember thinking anything at all while I was doing it."

"Usually it's gentlemen who lose their wits and can think only of getting a woman flat on her back."

"I hadn't gotten that far," she said. "I mean, your shirt was off and that gave me quite a lot to think about. When my hand made that very brief foray down your chest, well, perhaps I did think that getting you out of your trousers might be a very nice thing." She paused, took a sideways step. "You're out of your britches now."

He sat up.

She stared at him.

He pulled the sheet around him, then a blanket up over his shoulders, pulling it together over his chest, like a shawl.

Alec Carrick said from the doorway, "Hallie, I cannot believe you are here. Have you no sense at all?"

"Is that you, Papa? Oh dear, I believe it is. I'm not touching him. See, I'm at least seven feet away from his bed."

"Did you count the bloody feet?"

"Well, yes, perhaps I did, and how fast it would take me to cover those feet if I ran. Papa, I'm only here to make Jason tell me what you said to him. See, he's all covered up. He's safe."

Alec Carrick laughed, couldn't help himself. "You're going to chase him out of his own house if you're not careful, Hallie."

"He's been chasing himself away lately," she said to her father. "We'd be speaking, then he'd up and leave and not come back until dawn. I know it was dawn the other night because I was nearly awake, and so I told him."

"I see," Alec Carrick said. "How often does Jason simply leave like that?"

"He's left a good half dozen times. Never a warning, he ups and leaves."

Jason wanted to dump her into the horse trough. "My lord, nothing would have happened here, nothing at all."

"I believe you. So you left, did you? How long do you think you could have kept that up, Jason?"

Jason felt like a fool. He was lying naked in bed—his bed—minding his own business, and she tracked him down, and now her father was looking at him with a good deal of understanding and determination. He said slowly, "Perhaps we could speak in the morning, sir? Make decisions, settlements, that sort of thing."

"Yes," Alec said. "That would be fine." He took his daughter's hand and dragged her from Jason's bed-chamber.

"Wait! What is going on here? What do you mean, decisions? Listen, just because Jason leaves the house a lot, you want to talk about settlements? No, I won't do it. I don't wish to marry, I've told you that again and again, Papa. Look at Lord Renfrew. I shudder to think of him. Can you begin to imagine what his children would have been like? Papa, I won't do this! Didn't Jason tell you he didn't want to wed either? He was really hurt, Papa, burned to his feet, not singed like I was. This can't happen."

Alec Carrick quietly closed the bedchamber door.

Jason, wide awake, knowing he was facing his doom and seeing no hope for it, jumped out of bed, dressed quickly, and within five minutes, was riding Dodger away from Lyon's Gate. Hallie sat at her window and wondered again where he was going.

CHAPTER 31

᛭

Corrie was dreaming about the day she finally gave her grandmother-in-law her comeuppance, a loud, thoroughly satisfactory comeuppance it was. In her dream she was standing there, her hands on her hips, staring down the old besom, who, for the very first time in her life, had nothing to say. Something skittered along the back of her brain. The dream folded itself away in an instant. Something skittered again.

Corrie's eyes flew open. She'd heard something that didn't belong in her bedchamber. What was it? She saw a shadow in the window. Oh God, someone was trying to get in. James grunted in his sleep as she eased out of bed. She saw another movement. She grabbed the poker from the fireplace and yelled as she ran toward the window, "Bloody hell! A woman lets her guard down, even dreams a lovely dream, and look what happens—a bloody man is climbing into her bedchamber, uninvited. Come in and make it fast else I'll clout your head!"

James jerked awake. "Corrie, what the devil is wrong?"

"Shush, Corrie, it's just me, Jason. Don't crack my head open with that damned thing."

Corrie lowered the poker, her heart still pounding wildly. "Jason? It's you? We have doors. What are you doing coming in through our window?"

"I want to speak to James. I didn't want to wake the household."

Corrie helped Jason into the bedchamber, and tossed her husband his dressing gown. She stood back, eyeing her brother-in-law. "What's happened, Jason?"

He ran his fingers through his hair. "Listen, Corrie, I don't mean to be rude, but I really need to speak with James."

"But you haven't told me anything—"

James studied his brother's shadowed face, his look of desperation. He felt horrible alarm.

"Sweetheart, Jason and I will go down to the estate room. Get back into bed."

With James carrying one lit candle, the twins made their way down the wide staircase, down the long corridor, to the eastern side of the house, and into the estate room. James poured them each a brandy.

Jason took a sip and set his glass down. "Hallie's father is at Lyon's Gate."

James said, "Yes, he visited with us here first, said he wanted to surprise Hallie. He's very charming, and a man I'll wager has few go against him."

"He certainly did surprise his daughter. And me. He came into the stable and saw his daughter all over me. I'd taken off my shirt to work."

"Ah, well, that's that, isn't it? When is the wedding to be?"

"Probably as soon as the baron can manage it. We did nothing, James. I, in particular—"

"You're saying Hallie attacked you? Just because you didn't have your shirt on? I thought she barely liked you—"

"Dammit, James, she doesn't have a clue about sex and she wants it. She wants me."

"And you? Do you like her?"

"Most of the time. If I like her too much, I simply leave, and visit the three charming ladies I know in Eastbourne."

"That could exhaust a man's resources, all those nights spent away from home."

"You know better than that. She's so bright, James, and stubborn."

James said, "Father thinks she's got grit and backbone, said she's the image of her father, who is very handsome indeed."

"What does how you look have to say to anything? What's important is what you're made of inside. Well, yes, sometimes I look at her and I ache. I want to touch her hair, maybe wallow in it, there's so much of it and it's this marvelous mixture of shades, from the lightest blond to a rich wheat color."

James marveled at his brother. He didn't appear to realize what was coming out of his mouth. He sipped at his brandy, leaned his hip against the mahogany desk.

"She makes me laugh, James. She makes me feel important—no, it's more than that. She makes me feel that what I do is important." Jason paused, took a sip of brandy. "She makes me feel like I have value."

"You do. You always have."

Jason shook his head, began to pace the estate room. "A man who's a blind idiot can't have much value," he said over his shoulder.

"She makes you feel important to her."

"Yes. Then that fool Lord Renfrew comes back and I truly wanted to kill him for her, but then, James, it was all so funny, particularly the way she looks at him now, that it was all I could do not to laugh. Do you know the idiot lied to her about his age?"

"No, I didn't know that. Hallie laughs at him too now?"

"For the most part. I've determined to keep her from all weapons when he's anywhere near, though. Then Charles Grandison came over to plead Renfrew's case. Kept asking her to call him Charles, and she kept saying no."

"Ah, Jason, it sounds to me like you're a happy man."

"No, certainly not, at least not in the way you're thinking. It's just that I'm where I'm supposed to be and doing what I want to do. I don't wish to wed, James, and neither does Hallie. Renfrew stomped her into the dirt."

"Well, Judith burned you to your soul. It seems to me the two of you will do well together."

"No, I'd be no good for a woman, no good at all. There's nothing deep inside me. I'm empty there. Lust is something a man must bear. But the sort of sharing you and Corrie have, it's impossible for me, James."

"Well then, perhaps it's impossible for Hallie as well."

Jason paused in his pacing. He gave his twin a sharp look. "No, it's not impossible for her. Lord Renfrew was a dolt, a greedy man, but there's no evil in him, not like there was in Judith."

"Judith's been dead for five years, Jason. You can't continue to let her control your life. Don't give her that sort of power."

"If she'd murdered Father, if her damned brother had murdered you, then what would you expect me to think?"

"It was you who saved Father's life, you who nearly died, and I survived. It's long in the past. It's over."

"I don't want to marry her. She deserves a man who can give her more than I can. Damn, but she does say the funniest things, words just pop out of her mouth and you want to hold your belly you're laughing so hard. You should have seen how she was arranging our furniture—the sofa facing the window. What the hell am I to do?"

Jason slammed out of the estate room through the French doors that gave onto the garden, leaving his brother to stare after him, tapping his fingertips thoughtfully on the desktop.

His father said quietly from the doorway, "We will see, James. You did well."

"He is so very hurt, like there's this deep wound that won't heal."

"He won't let it heal," Douglas said. "I think he's so used to the pain, to the infernal guilt, that he would feel bereft without it."

James handed his father a snifter of brandy.

The earl said thoughtfully as he swirled the brandy about, "I think the day you and Jason met Hallie Carrick at Lyon's Gate was the day that might bring your brother back to you, and my son back to me."

Late the following morning, Hallie paused outside the drawing room door when she heard a familiar female voice say, "I had it from my own maid, Angela, and a maid always knows exactly what's true and what isn't. She had it from her cousin who's a stable lad here. It's true, and I can tell from the look on your face that you know it's true. Oh dear me, dear me."

"Nonsense. Would you care for some tea?"

Lady Grimsby said, "No, I want to know what you're going to do about this, Angela. You're her chaperone. This has got to stop."

Angela said, "Have a nice cup of oolong."

Hallie stood nailed to the spot. Angela had been

right, things like this oozed through cracks in the wall.

Hallie heard the rattle of teacups. Then silence, then Lady Grimsby said, her voice now louder, "I have a solution that should please everyone. It's said that Jason Sherbrooke will never wed. And that leaves Hallie with a reputation in ruins." She drew a deep breath. "My dear Elgin. He's the answer."

"Lord Renfrew? You don't mean the dishonorable fellow who—"

"No, no, don't say it, Angela. Elgin has changed, both Lord Grimsby and I agree on that. Charles also insists he's changed. Elgin loves Hallie. He would make her a fine husband."

"Lord Renfrew doesn't assume that Hallie has been bedded by Jason Sherbrooke?"

"Surely Miss Carrick hasn't gone that far! It was just that single embrace."

"How can Lord Renfrew know that for sure?"

"As I said, my dear Elgin loves her. He's willing to overlook certain matters. He's willing to mend her reputation, give her the protection of his name."

Dead silence, then Hallie heard the rustle of skirts. She quickly walked toward the back of the house. She heard Angela say, "I shall certainly speak to Hallie about this, Lady Grimsby. But she was very overset when she learned Lord Renfrew had lied about his age."

"Lied about his age? Why would a gentleman do that? It's absurd, only ladies lie about their age. A man is supposed to be a girl's senior by a number of years and proud of it since he is the one who must provide his young wife with proper guidance, a firm hand, wise counsel—"

"So I may assure Hallie that Lord Renfrew plans to hunker down in front of his own hearth, not avail himself of her money and begin to celebrate birthdays again?"

"You are treating this as a joke, Angela. You know that a woman's money becomes her husband's upon her marriage. It is always the way things are done. You must know that as soon as this news gets out, Miss Carrick won't be invited anywhere.

"Jason Sherbrooke won't marry her. Lord Grimsby assures me that he won't. If she has a brain, she's to thank the good Lord for sending Elgin here to save the day. As for her ridiculous partnership here at Lyon's Gate, everyone knows it's Jason Sherbrooke who runs things, it's—"

Hallie said, "Good morning, Lady Grimsby. How very lovely of you to visit. Ah, if you would be so kind to tell Lord Renfrew I will be by at precisely midnight with my ladder. I will climb up to his bedchamber and rap smartly on his window. I will take him to Gretna Green. What do you think of that?"

Lady Grimsby looked her up and down. "I don't care if your boots are shiny, Miss Carrick, you cannot continue living in this house with a man who isn't your husband."

"So if I were to wed Lord Renfrew, he would move in here too?"

"Why, as to that, I don't know. Perhaps he would simply have Jason Sherbrooke leave and take over the management of the stud."

"Jason won't sell out, Lady Grimsby. If I were Lord Renfrew, I would think seriously about sitting across from Jason Sherbrooke's beautiful face every morning at the breakfast table."

"Elgin will see that that doesn't happen. He's older than Jason Sherbrooke, he will take care of him, you'll see."

"Elgin and who else?"

"I do not find you amusing. Good day, Miss Carrick. Good day, Angela. I shall tell Elgin you're ready to hear his suit now."

"A moment, Lady Grimsby," Hallie said. "Did you know my father, Baron Sherard, is staying here with us? If Elgin wishes, he can certainly speak to my father."

"Your father is here? How long has your father been here, Miss Carrick?"

"Why don't you ask your maid. She can ask her cousin. If he isn't certain, why he can come to the house and I will give him the straight facts. Good day, Lady Grimsby. Oh goodness, which is Lord Renfrew's bedchamber? I should hate to rap on your window by mistake."

Lady Grimsby turned back as her footman prepared to hand her into her carriage. "You will come to a bad end, Miss Carrick. This levity, it doesn't bode well for a lady's future." Lady Grimsby swept into her carriage. The driver gave Hallie a mournful look as he gently closed his mistress's door.

Hallie heard Jason's whistle coming from the stables, and heard her father's voice. She called out, "Jason, do we have a nice tall ladder?"

CHAPTER 32

❧❧

❧ Jason caught Hallie eavesdropping, her ear pressed to the drawing room door. She didn't act embarrassed at being caught, rather she smiled, motioned him to her and whispered, "I can't believe he actually screwed his nerve to the sticking point and came here to face my father." She gave Jason a sideways look. "Hmm. Perhaps I've misjudged poor Elgin."

"He came again?" Jason said. "Lord Renfrew must need money very badly."

"Ah, so you don't believe his courage is because he's lost himself in love for me?"

"No."

She sighed. "At least in his case the truth doesn't hurt."

Seven minutes later, Hallie jumped back from the

door. Three seconds later, Lord Renfrew, looking both pale and philosophical, preceded Baron Sherard out of the drawing room. He saw Hallie standing beside Jason Sherbrooke, the bastard with his angel's face that he didn't deserve, and a male form he didn't deserve either. Elgin knew he ruthlessly used both to his advantage, because it would be the reasonable thing to do. As for Hallie, this girl he'd tried yet again to secure as his wife— He nearly shuddered. She was wearing those ridiculous boots that were so shiny he could see the sweat on his own brow. Her hair was windblown, and there was a dirt stain on the side of her nose. She looked frowzy. He said to her, "I don't know why you're standing there holding a bridle."

"It's broken. I'm going to fix it."

"You're a female despite those shiny boots of yours. You can fix a cup of tea but you can't fix anything important, certainly not a bridle."

"Tea isn't important?" said Alec Carrick, a brow shooting upward. "I find nothing so inspiring as a bracing cup of tea. A dollop of milk, nothing else."

"Oh no. One must add lemon so that the tea obtains the most select depth of flavor, not milk. Very well, tea is important, but for her to fix a bridle? No, girls don't do that sort of thing."

Hallie said, "You may be right. I certainly couldn't fix you, could I?"

"You never tried. You never asked me to explain, never showed me a moment's compassion, you just booted me out the door. And now I understand from your father that you will marry this man who doesn't want you, this man who compromised you only because you are here and willing, and that makes him worse than me."

Jason asked, "How could I be worse than you?"

"I never tried to seduce her so she would be compromised."

Hallie wished she could whirl that bridle about in her hands and aim for Lord Renfrew's head. "You didn't have to compromise me. I swam right into your net."

"Well, yes you did, but that's not what's important here. What's important here is manhood and the use of it. I would have done all those things he probably did to you, but only after you became my wife, when it would be proper to do so. You could have had me, Hallie, and all my devotion and all my skills as a renowned lover."

"Jason did not compromise me," Hallie said.

"Ha. He's a man, isn't he? It's obvious he wanted to enjoy your fair person without having to sit across the dinner table from you for the rest of his life."

"Since we are partners, my presence at the dinner table is a regular occurrence. Nothing would change there."

"I would have wanted to sit across the dinner table from you, Hallie, perhaps feed you bits of my dinner roll. He doesn't want to. He is trapped only because your father is here and would kill him if he didn't marry you."

"Maiming might have been an alternative," Alec said.

But Lord Renfrew ignored him. "I can't imagine being your partner; it doesn't bear thinking about. Having to put up with your impertinence without enjoying the benefits of your womanly self at night—perhaps, were I he, I'd flee back to Baltimore. As for his marrying you, it is to gain your money, all know that. You are not wise, Hallie. You could have had me with my heart in my hand."

"That is a thought that stirs the hairs on my neck. Good-bye, Lord Renfrew. Whenever I think of what I could have had, I shall doubtless be saddened, for the rest of my life."

"Your father is right. You would have not made me happy."

"I didn't say exactly that," said Baron Sherard.

"No, Papa, probably not," she said. "Consider yourself a lucky man, Lord Renfrew. Good day to you."

He shook his head, said to himself as he clamped his hat down upon his head, "I cannot believe I let Charles talk me into wasting my time here," and he was gone.

Jason frowned after Lord Renfrew: *Charles Grandison wanted that dolt to marry Hallie?* Charles never did anything without a reason. Jason wanted to know what that reason was.

Alec Carrick said, "There goes a man who will have a rich wife by the end of the year, maybe even by fall.

He's really quite believable when he sets his mind to it. I can see how you were taken in, my dear."

"Not any longer. I do wonder why he came." She watched Lord Renfrew mount his horse and ride away, not looking back. He rode well, tall and arrogant in the saddle. "Did he think I would forgive him what he'd done? Is this what Charles Grandison thought?"

"Yes," Angela said. "What I don't understand is why Charles Grandison wanted him to marry you so badly."

Jason cleared his throat. "Hello, Angela. You move very quietly. Were you eavesdropping from outside the drawing room window? No, don't tell me. Lord Renfrew is gone and that's all that matters now. As for Charles and his part in this, I will pry the reason out of him the next time I see him. Hallie, I believe you and I should take a walk now."

"Why? Is something wrong with one of the mares? Father, why are you shaking your head at me like that?"

"Sweetheart, do not be obtuse. Face up to the facts. Go with Jason. There will be a lot to do. Oh yes, your aunt and uncle will be staying at Northcliffe Hall."

"Father, all that talk about Jason having to marry me, I thought you were joking, that you were torturing Lord Renfrew, and I will admit that I thought it was well done of you. You really believe I should marry Jason? That's ridiculous." She whirled around to face Jason. "Listen to me, I will not marry you. You don't want a wife. You wouldn't trust a wife."

"Come along, Hallie."

"No. You said you never wanted to marry. I don't want to marry either. That makes two of us. We have the majority opinion here."

Alec Carrick roared, "You had your hand down his damned britches, Hallie! You would have had him on the stable floor in a matter of moments if I hadn't pried you off him."

"*Pried* me?"

"No, sir," Jason said, heart pounding, the specter of doom sitting on his shoulder. "I would have stopped her. Well, perhaps not."

"Exactly," Alec said. "This is called consequences, Hallie. Get a grip on yourself." He said to Jason, "She once denied a downpour because she wanted a picnic. Denying the need for a husband would be nothing for her."

"But—"

"Shut up, Hallie." Jason grabbed her hand and jerked her toward the front door. "Let's talk about a picnic in the rain."

She said, "That particular picnic was pretty dreadful, truth be told—" Jason dragged her out of the house.

Angela said to Alec, "I am worried about this, my lord. She's always been stubborn."

"I have confidence in young Mr. Sherbrooke. I saw him surrounded by children several times in Baltimore. They adored him. They obeyed him. He will bring Hallie around. Did you know she found out who the stable lad is who told his cousin, who is Lady Grimsby's maid, about Jason and Hallie in the stables?"

"Oh dear, is the fellow hanging from a stable beam? Will we have to hide the body?"

"Nothing so final. She told me she was going to lock him in the closet beneath the stairs, keep him on a diet of bread and water until he repented his loose tongue."

Despite knowing better, Angela looked back over her shoulder toward the stairs.

Alec Carrick laughed, buffeted her shoulder. "Life is never what one expects, is it, Angela?"

"Their children will be beautiful," Angela said.

Alec Carrick looked like she'd slapped him. He was still shaking his head as he walked to the stables. He saw Jason and his daughter walking toward the maple copse to the east, and stopped. No, he wasn't needed. If Jason didn't have the wherewithal to bring her to reason, it would take the Devil himself. How strange that she was so like her stepmother—bullheaded wasn't far off the mark—and not at all like the woman who'd birthed her. He wondered what Jason would say to her.

Jason didn't say a word. He pulled her to a halt beneath a lovely summer-leafed maple branch and dove his fingers into her hair. She closed her eyes. How could massaging her scalp make her want to rip off her stockings and boots? "Surely that is sinful. It feels too good not to be bad."

"What comes after my rubbing your scalp is what's bad." She leaned toward him so he could rub her head better, not because she wanted to throw herself on him. She was firm with herself about this, she was in control of herself. She would see this through, she would not bow to parental pressure. When he released her, she pulled a maple leaf off and began twisting it around her fingers. She said, "I will not marry you, Jason. I will speak again to my father, tell him that—"

Jason growled low in his throat, grabbed her, and kissed her hard. He said into her mouth, "Be quiet. It's done. You've got me. We've got each other. I will do my best to be a good husband to you, Hallie, I swear it to you. Now stop being a mule."

He raised his head and she was forced to look into his incredible eyes, a woman's downfall, those eyes of his, and his mouth—well, she wasn't going to look at his mouth, or his eyes, she wasn't that great a fool. She wanted to ram him against the tree. No, she was strong, in control of herself, she knew what was right. Forcing him to wed her wasn't. Her heart, though, it was pounding so hard and fast it nearly hurt. She wanted him to press his fingers to her racing heart. She felt his fingers stroking through her hair again, this time pulling out the pins. She felt his mouth again on hers, and finally, thank the good Lord above, felt his fingers lightly cup her breast. Her wits fell out of her head. She saw things very clearly in that moment, looking up at him, seeing his determination, and yes, lust as well. Perhaps there was caring as well, mayhap a dollop of tenderness. It was enough. It was more than enough. Without another thought, she jumped off the cliff. "All right," she said. "Yes, perhaps marrying you would be a very wonderful thing."

Over dinner that evening, Jason invited all the staff into the dining room for a glass of champagne.

"What is this, Master Jason? Have we a new mare to be covered by our virile Dodger?"

"No, Petrie. Miss Carrick and I will be married. Very soon. Don't tell me you haven't heard the rumors. The rumors will cease once my uncle Tysen says the hallowed words over our heads."

Martha accepted her glass of champagne, beaming. "Oh, Miss Hallie, how very exciting, to actually have Master Jason all to yourself! But you nearly had him in the stable, didn't you? Well, perhaps it's best not to speak of that."

"To the joining of partners," Baron Sherard said loudly, and everyone cheered and drank the rather decent champagne, all except Petrie, who looked like he would burst into tears.

"Give it up, Petrie," Jason said. "Drink your champagne It will make you feel more resigned to the inevitable."

"Is that what you have become, my poor master? A guzzler?"

"That is quite enough, Petrie," Angela said. "Trust me on this."

Petrie wasn't stupid. He saw the warning in the master's eyes, knew he was dead serious, and gulped down the champagne. "Don't let her rearrange the furniture in your bedchamber, Master Jason."

Hallie said, "Oh goodness, I hadn't thought about that."

"Please, don't, miss," Petrie said.

"Not the furniture, you dolt, I hadn't thought about sharing his bedchamber. I like mine better. Why can't he move into mine? Why can't we each keep our own bedchambers?"

Jason patted her hand. "Don't worry about it now. We will figure things out."

Angela said comfortably as she accepted another glass of champagne from Lord Sherard, "Perhaps I can move to your bedchamber, Hallie, and we can tear down the wall between mine and Jason's bedchambers. You'll both have enough room and Jason can arrange the furniture. What do you think?"

Hallie looked like she might bolt. Jason himself wanted to bolt, but he said, "We will consider this. However, right at this moment, I believe we should stick to well-wishes and toasts."

Petrie moaned again, and it wasn't at all discreet. Martha rounded on him, waved her glass in his face. "You don't amuse me, Mr. Petrie. Look at my mistress—a beautiful lady she is, nearly as beautiful a lady as Master Jason is a gentleman. It's close. Maybe not really close— Yes, you've hurt her feelings with your sour little female slurs that smack of a female-having-blighted-your-heart, something that probably happened years ago."

"Not that many years ago," Angela said. "Petrie isn't that old."

Hallie said under her breath to her father, "I wonder if that can be true. Is Petrie's dislike of women because his heart was broken?"

"No," Jason said. "Petrie came into this world disliking the fair sex. His mother never chided him, never abused him. She adores him. She still does."

"She doesn't love me deep inside where it counts," Petrie said and everyone looked at him.

"That's the silliest thing I've ever heard, Mr. Petrie! Have you told your mama this?"

"Of course not. It would upset her and a female who's upset does scurrilous things."

Jason rolled his eyes. "I will tell your mother you feel this way, Petrie, so any curses she has are heaped on my head, not yours."

Martha said right in his face, "You're a petulant stick."

Petrie opened his mouth to blast her. Angela said, "Goodness, all this excitement makes me hungry. Cook, why don't you bring out your blancmange?"

Petrie said, "But I—"

Martha rounded on him again, this time her voice black with warning, "You say another word and I'll stuff the blancmange up your nose."

"Martha, you must show me proper respect, you—"

Angela said, "You don't want to waste the blancmange on Petrie's nose."

As for Cook, she had seemed perfectly content to stand quietly and look from Jason to Alec Carrick, not a single aria bursting out of her mouth. "Petrie's nose? My blancmange, Miss Angela? Oh goodness me, that's a sort of food, isn't it? How could I forget? Ah, two such lovely gentlemen. I must ease my parched gullet." She drank down her glass of champagne, carefully set the glass on the sideboard, and went to the kitchen, saying over and over, "How can I make both lovely gentlemen stay right here so I can feed them until they swoon on my kitchen floor?"

"I'll drink to that," Hallie said. "Father, I've never seen you swoon."

Alec's eyes met his future son-in-law's. "It happens," he said. "Believe me, it happens."

Petrie moaned.

CHAPTER 33

❧❦❧

❧ Jason and Hallie Sherbrooke spent their wedding night under the distinctive curved eaves of the master bedchamber of Dunsmore House, Georgian in mood if not in style, set gracefully on a broad tree-covered promontory just outside Ventnor on the southeastern coast of the Isle of Wight, the summer residence of the duke of Portsmouth. After a two-hour steamboat ride from the mainland, they'd arrived at Dunsmore House, windblown and sunburned, smiling from ear to ear at the housekeeper, Mrs. Spooner, and ready to tear each other's clothes off.

Once upon a time, Mrs. Spooner had been intimate with lust, having five grown children to show for it, and not to mention being three months shy of a half dozen grandchildren. She certainly recognized it when it stood in front of her, though she wasn't certain which of the two had greater lust for the other. The simple beauty of this couple would warm the coldest heart, which hers wasn't. "Well, now, His Grace told me you were two special young people and so you appear to be. Come in, come in. You'll have the large bedchamber that looks out at the harbor and all the fishing boats. It's Her Grace's favorite bedchamber and the sheets are all fresh for you. What a fine day to begin your married life."

Because she wanted them to eat, Mrs. Spooner herded them into the breakfast room, smaller and more intimate than the grand dining room, and quickly served them cold chicken and warm bread for dinner, and fresh peas from her own garden in Ventnor. She said comfortably as she passed Mr. Sherbrooke the platter of chicken, "Only I will be here to see to you." She passed Hallie another small loaf of hot bread, whispered close to her ear, "Eat up, my dear. One will need strength with that one."

Hallie gave her a blinding smile. "Yes, I certainly hope so."

Mrs. Spooner patted her arm. "The duke and his family always like their privacy, and so you'll have it too. Maids will come during the day, but they won't bother you."

"Thank you, Mrs. Spooner. I've never had privacy before. I have three brothers and a sister and—" Hallie blinked and shrugged. She'd looked at Jason. "I forgot what I was going to say."

"Well, this is your honeymoon, now isn't it, Mrs. Sherbrooke? It's not a time for brains."

"Mrs. Sherbrooke," Hallie repeated slowly, staring at Mrs. Spooner. "Isn't this the oddest thing—from one day to the next I lost my name."

"The new name—Sherbrooke—is charming, though I'm certain your father prefers Carrick, just as Mr. Spooner prefers his name over mine, which was equally unique."

"What was your maiden name, Mrs. Spooner?"

"Why, I was Adelaide Bleak, certainly of a pessimistic bent, that name. Now. I'm thinking that the last thing you and Mr. Sherbrooke would want is tea served in the drawing room, so I'll bid you good night."

Hallie and Jason looked at each other. She said as she chewed on a buttered hunk of fresh bread, eyes nearly closed in bliss, "We've been married for seven hours now."

"Yes."

"Mrs. Spooner is very nice."

"Yes. Are you through with your dinner, Hallie?"

She gulped down the bread. "Yes. Oh yes, Jason. Do you know my aunt Arielle told me to let you take the lead, to try to restrain myself? She advised me against taking you to the floor. She assured me that men enjoyed that, but not at first. She blushed while she said this—I'll tell you, that took me aback. She said men liked to be in control during the first romantic encounter, which is a good thing since they know more about the business—and she blushed again. I told my father her advice, and he laughed and laughed, told me he doubted you'd mind being jumped at any time, on the boat or on dry land or on a dining room table. Hmm. This table is very nice and long and—"

He was nearly shuddering himself out of his boots, his hands clenching and unclenching. It hurt him to say it, but he finally managed it. "No table tonight. Your father is right. You have my permission to jump me whenever the mood strikes you. I won't ever mind." He drew in a deep breath and Hallie would have sworn he shook a bit. "It's going to be close."

She wasn't a fool. She knew what that look meant. It was delicious, that look; it made her heart race, her skin tingle. She raced from the small breakfast room, up the wide front stairs, down the corridor, to the large corner bedchamber. It was light and airy, not that she cared a whit, and she knew the furnishings were perfectly arranged—well, perhaps those two big chairs would be better pushed together and placed at the foot of the bed in case one was so tired one couldn't make it all the way. She started to ask Jason what he thought about the chairs, but stopped cold.

Jason came into the bedchamber at that moment, closed the door, locked it, and leaned against it. "I left the house all those times because I wanted you so badly."

"You what?"

"I visited other ladies, they took care of me, sent

me home exhausted and back in control of myself, for a few days at least."

"That's quite the oddest thing I've ever heard. I wouldn't have minded you kissing me, Jason, with or without your shirt. You're telling me you went to other women because you thought I wouldn't like it?"

"No, that's not it at all. You're a young lady, Hallie, a virgin, and a gentleman doesn't seduce a young lady who's also a virgin. But that's over now. Don't ever think I'm another Lord Renfrew. I'm now your husband. I will be faithful."

"Were those other ladies enthusiastic? Like I was in the stable?"

"Well, yes, why wouldn't they be? I've known all of them for years."

"You don't have all that many adult years, Jason."

"A man gets started as soon as he's able, Hallie. All the ladies are older than I am, not that it matters at all."

"I have yet to get started."

"I know." He pushed off the locked door, pulling off his vest and cravat as he walked to her, then tossed them on the arm of a chair. So that was the purpose of the chairs being on the way to the bed. He paused a moment and pulled off his boots and socks. He never took his eyes off her.

"I can see that you're uncertain about this now that we've reached the sticking point. It's quite all right. Trust me. I'll take care of everything." He unbuttoned his shirt, shrugged out of it, let it fall to the carpet.

He was naked to the waist, just as he'd been that morning when her father had paid a surprise visit to the stables.

"Oh my." She cleared her throat, tried again. "Do you know, I rather liked you all sweaty."

"It's a warm night. Perhaps I'll sweat for you before it's over. Perhaps you'll sweat too." He held his arms wide. "Take me down, Hallie."

It was the longest jump she'd ever made in her life, true, but he took a step forward to catch her, settled her legs around his waist. She cupped his face between her palms and kissed him all over his face, until, laughing, he pressed her against a wall, and lifted his hand to cup her jaw. "Hold still," he said, and kissed her, really kissed her, not nipping little bites, piddling little licks, but a deep kiss, one that blurred the world and made her legs slip. He cupped her bottom before she fell off him and carried her to the bed.

He grinned down at her. "Don't move. Let me get the rest of my clothes off and then I'll start on yours."

"No, let me do it." She bounced to her feet and fell to her knees in front of him, her eyes on those buttons. Jason's breath whooshed out of his lungs. His wife of now close to a third of a day was kneeling in front of him, her hands on his britches' buttons, and she was kissing his belly.

"Hallie, the damned buttons. It's important to unfasten the damned buttons."

She said absolutely nothing, looked up at him through the veil of her hair, her eyes so filled with excitement, fear, and lust, he wanted to laugh, then he didn't because she unbuttoned three buttons in a flash and was kissing his belly, and lower. Her fingertips touched him, stroked him, held him, and he felt her warm breath on his flesh. "Oh God," he said, and knew it was going to be very close. "You've got to let me go, Hallie. No, don't kiss me, not now, I can't bear it. Take your hands away." He didn't want to, the good Lord knew he didn't, but he grabbed her beneath her arms and hauled her up, grateful that she'd released him at the last moment. "That's very nice, really, don't get me wrong, a man loves for a woman to touch him with her hands and her mouth, rub her cheek over his belly, her hair all tangled, her breath hot, but I can't take it at this particular moment, Hallie. There are other things now." He shuddered, gulped down a deep breath. "It's your turn."

"You mean there's a certain order to this business?"

"Not really, but a man doesn't want to maul, well, never mind that. Trust me."

"But I want to touch you again, and your taste, Jason, it makes me want—"

"Be quiet. Your words make me see things and start shaking. Close your mouth. I know what's to be done." Even as he got her out of her clothes, she touched, tried to kiss him. "Stand up." When finally, she was naked, he took a quick step back. He knew she'd be beautiful, hadn't doubted it for an instant, but the reality of her, the fact that they were here together, married, for God's sake, and she belonged to him now and forever, made him look at her differently.

"I will try to make you happy, Hallie," he said, and then there were no more words. He got his breeches off, picked her up and laid her on her back, coming down over her, his mouth on hers, the length of him against her soft flesh.

"Don't worry about any of this," he said into her mouth. "Just do what I tell you."

"What do you want me to do first?"

He shuddered like a palsied man. "Open your legs for me." She parted her legs, just a bit.

"That's right, that's exactly what I wanted you to do. Mayhap a bit more. That's it." He wondered how a man could bear this. Pleasure, he thought, drugging pleasure, but she was a virgin, she didn't understand what all this was going to feel like, even if she knew what happened between Dodger and the mares. He knew he couldn't simply take her, he had to do things right. His twin had confided in him that he'd mucked up his own wedding night, and when he'd awakened, he was afraid Corrie had left him. "It was an awful feeling," James had said, shaking with the memory. "If I'd had a sword I would have run myself through. Force yourself to back off. Don't fall on her and yell like a wild man."

Jason backed off, came down on his knees between her legs. He held her ankles, slowly pulled her legs farther apart. Her legs quivered. "You are so bloody beautiful." He was looking at her, between her parted legs, and she was so embarrassed and so excited, both at the same time, that she lay there, staring at him. "Tell me what to do, Jason."

He never looked up, merely shook his head slowly. "Nothing at all, just let me do what I want."

"What do you want?"

"First I want to put my mouth on you. If you don't know what I mean, don't worry about it, only know that I'm going to make you scream. Yes, I can do it without trembling myself off the bed." But he didn't have a chance. Hallie lurched up, knocked him backward and came down on top of him, covering all of him she could manage. He was laughing so hard it gave him a measure of control, thank God.

"Oh my," she said into his mouth, "tell me what to do, Jason, but be quick about it."

He sat her upright to straddle his belly, told her not to move, to watch his hands stroke every beautiful inch of her. "Know these are my hands, Hallie. They'll be on you for the rest of our lives. Ah, the feel of you, the smoothness of your skin. I am a very strong man." He grinned, pulled her down again. When his tongue was in her mouth, he whispered, "This is how I'm going to be inside you, like my tongue, but first—"

She was frantic when at last he caressed her with his mouth. He'd told her he was going to do this, but she hadn't been able to grasp the reality of it, what it made her feel, and he knew it, and didn't stop. When he felt her stiffen, felt her back arch, felt her pulling out his hair, he was a king. Her scream and her shudders, her hands fisting on his arms, her hot breath against his neck, it turned his king's brain to mush. He drove inside her in the next moment, felt her maidenhead give, felt her jerk of pain. He touched his forehead to hers when he was against her womb. "I know it hurts. I'm sorry. Lie still, let yourself get used to me."

"It's hard."

That was certainly the truth. "I know, but try. It will get better." She was still holding herself stiff, but when he didn't move, her body began to ease around him. He felt himself deep inside her. Soon he was moving, slowly.

She lurched up, stared at him, her eyes blind. "Ohmigod, ohmigod, ohmigod, it's happening again, Jason. This is too much, simply too much, and surely we will both die of it. Please, don't stop."

When he himself yelled above her, feeling that delicious soft body of hers twisting and heaving beneath him, he was glad he hadn't mucked things up. He'd given her pleasure twice, it was well done of him. And they were both sweating. It was very well done of him.

Hallie lay in the darkness that had finally swallowed up the midsummer day not more than ten minutes earlier, and listened to Jason's deep, even breathing. He'd fallen over her, given her a silly smile and fallen asleep. She remembered as a child how she'd slept with her father, realized now how careful he'd been to wrap her in her own covers first.

To sleep with a man, to lie naked with a man, to feel him against her, his cooling flesh, the inner heat of him that didn't lessen, it amazed her. She wondered if

Jason was dreaming, and if so, what he was dreaming about right now. About her?

Probably not. She remembered Lady Lydia, now her grandmother-in-law, her veiny old hand lightly patting Hallie's as she leaned close, smelling like ironed lace and the fresh lemon wax she rubbed into the eagle head of her cane, and whispered, "Jason is a fine young man. Give him what he needs, Hallie."

"What do you think he needs, Grandmama-in-law?"

"He needs to have his heart rekindled."

He needed to have his heart rekindled? What did that mean? He needed her to love him?

Was what she felt for him the same as what she'd felt initially for Lord Renfrew? She didn't think so. This was deeper, richer, more urgent.

Did she love Jason? Well, if it was love she was feeling leaping out of her, she wasn't about to blurt it out to him. No, she realized, lightly laying her hand on his belly, feeling the muscles tighten unconsciously, what he really needed was to trust again. To trust her. And maybe that would rekindle his heart.

Her new father-in-law approved of her, she knew that, and he'd said as he'd touched his fingertips to her cheek at their wedding breakfast, "Trust is a precious commodity, fragile yet binding once it's accepted by both the heart and the intellect and has burrowed deep inside. Be yourself, Hallie. All will be well. My son isn't a dolt."

"No," she'd agreed. "He isn't." What trust was, she thought now, was an elusive commodity.

It was a meaty goal, this trust and rekindling business, after what this Judith woman had done to him five years before. She snuggled next to him, wondering if it would be all right to wake him up. Why not? He'd told her she could jump him any time. She eased down his body, kissing every inch in her path. When she took him into her mouth, he nearly arched off the bed, fisted her hair in his hands, and groaned like he was in mortal pain.

When he came into her, still not entirely awake, she pulled him close, felt all of him deep inside her, closed her eyes, felt his whiskers against her cheek, and thanked God for sending her to Lyon's Gate that particular day two months before.

Once again, early the next morning, Hallie lay on her back, panting for breath after the cataclysm, her eyes nearly crossed. She felt she could sink through the bed, perhaps sink through the floor as well. What room was beneath the bedchamber? She didn't want to move. Her eyes jerked open at Jason's appalled voice. "My God, it looks like I killed you!"

"Wha— what?"

"Oh God, how many times did I take you?"

"What a strange way to say it. Take me—like I didn't have any say in it."

"Hallie, it doesn't mean anything. Wake up."

"I don't want to wake up right now, Jason. My brain isn't working well, only my mouth. I certainly remember the last time you, ah, took me—just five minutes ago. How can you even talk?"

"Hallie, are you all right?" He sat down beside her, grabbed her shoulders and shook her.

Her head fell back against the pillow, and she moaned. "I feel like my bones have faded out of me. Let me lie here in endless bliss, Jason. I'm all right, I must be since I did speak to you."

"Yes, but you looked ridiculous while you spoke, grinning like a loon with no sense."

She giggled. He looked harassed. She watched him rake his fingers through his hair, stroke his whiskered chin. She realized he was now looking down at her belly, perhaps even lower, and somehow the covers were gone. She yelped, trying to pull the covers over herself. He stayed her hand. "Ah, damn me and damn my randy self. Forgive me, sweetheart, I had no idea, I mean, I know that virgins bleed the first time, but—oh God, blink your eyes at least three times at me if you're really awake and not just grinning like that because you've fallen back asleep and are dreaming."

"I'm awake now, Jason. What are you doing? Don't look at me. Please, it's very embarrassing. What do you mean, bleed?"

"Nonsense, I'm your husband. Don't move. I'm going to clean you up. It's just a bit of blood, nothing to worry about. I'm sorry about waking you up that third time, Hallie."

"It was the fourth."

"That's right, you woke me up the third time. I'm innocent of that one. Hmm. The second time as well if I remember rightly. Four times? Well, that's nice now, isn't it?" He looked immensely pleased with himself, looked at the blood smeared on her thighs again and paled.

"Oh yes," she said. "I did. Don't worry, I'm all right. I am, aren't I?"

"Yes," he said and prayed he was right. He'd never heard of a bride bleeding to death from her wedding night.

When he went to fetch a cloth and the basin of water on the commode, she jerked up, pulled up the sheet, and said, "You really don't need to do this. I'm fine, at least I think I am." She tented the white sheet over her head and looked down at herself. "Oh dear, perhaps I am a bit of a mess. But I don't think I'm dying. I feel wonderful. You said I was supposed to bleed?"

"Yes."

"Well, then, all right. Hand me that cloth."

He watched her hand slide out from beneath the sheet and placed the damp cloth on her palm. He heard her talking to herself, probably discussing both sides of this problem, although he couldn't imagine how there could be a second side. He wished he could make out her words. He had a feeling that if he could, he'd be howling with laughter.

"You won't leave the house ever again, will you, Jason?"

"Oh no," he said. "Oh no." And because he was worried, he pulled the sheet off her and made certain she was all right himself.

CHAPTER 34

❧❧

Northcliffe Hall
August 10th

❧ Hallie sent a blinding smile out to the table at large as she said to her father-in-law, "You wish to know about the Isle of Wight, sir? Hmm. Well, yes, I have it—Ventnor is quite picturesque. It lies on the southeastern coast, I believe. I have sent the duke and duchess of Portsmouth a watercolor of Dunsmore House to thank them."

Corrie said, "I didn't know you did watercolors, Hallie."

"Well, I do, actually, but I didn't do this one. There simply wasn't enough time. I commissioned it from a young man we found painting on the beach."

"What do you mean, you didn't have time?" Hallie's father asked, his fork still over his plate, an eyebrow up. "I found two weeks more than ample time for me to do everything I wished in London."

"You forget, Alec," Douglas said. He snapped his fingers. "At certain times in life, time goes by that fast."

Baron Sherard said, grimmer than any reaper, "Not when we're speaking of my daughter, it doesn't. Whenever I thought about her with your damned son, knowing what damned sons are like, since I was one once, my belly cramped." Alec sent a look of acute dislike to his new son-in-law.

Lady Lydia announced, "I never had a honeymoon worth speaking of."

"I don't speak of mine either," Angela said.

"When we finally had a honeymoon," Alex said, beaming at her husband, "I believe we spoke French the whole time."

The earl rolled his eyes.

Lady Lydia snorted. "Always after my boy, you were—still are—don't think I didn't know what you were doing when I was visiting on Wednesday, laughing behind the estate room door. It's a disgrace."

Hallie sat forward, all earnest, her eyes on her father's face. "Two weeks on the Isle of Wight is nothing like two weeks in London, Papa. There was so much to do—"

"Like what?" her father asked.

"Well, like eating and sleeping now and again, and watching the sun rise, not to mention the sunsets."

Douglas caught his wife's eye, then smiled at his new daughter-in-law. She looked glorious, she glowed, her eyes were bright, she sparkled, she was complacent.

And she couldn't seem to stop laughing. What she was, Douglas thought, was a pleased woman. As for his son, Douglas realized Jason looked content, perhaps he even looked at peace. He wondered if Hallie was pregnant yet. He wouldn't be surprised.

Corrie, far more innocent than she'd ever believe, said, "I visited the Isle of Wight only once, as a child. Uncle Simon got vilely seasick, so he swore he wouldn't ever leave his dinner in The Solent again. You remember, Hallie, The Solent is what they call the strait in the English Channel between Southampton and the Isle of Wight."

"Of course I remember. Hmm. We didn't leave from Southampton, did we, Jason?"

"No, we left from Worthing."

Corrie said, "Is the bright red house still on the hill overlooking the harbor?"

"Red house, you say? Jason, do you remember a red house? On a hill overlooking the harbor?"

Jason looked perfectly blank.

His twin said, "That's all right, Jase. What's a red house in the big scheme of things? What did you do besides visit Ventnor?"

Jason continued to look perfectly blank.

"We went down on the beach," Hallie said, and raked her fork along the tablecloth just like she was raking sand. She paused and her hand trembled. Jason knew exactly what she was thinking.

He cleared his throat, couldn't think of a single word to say. His mother obligingly said, "Oh, you mean the beach off the right side of the promontory, not fifty yards from Dunsmore House? Did you swim?"

"Yes," Hallie said. "we were there most nights, except when it was raining."

"Nights?" Lady Lydia asked. "My dear child, you and your precious new husband went swimming in the evenings?"

"Oh yes," Hallie said, beaming. "There was no one about after the sun went down so we—oh dear, never mind that. Fact is, we did plan to swim one day after we'd eaten a lovely picnic lunch on the beach beneath a lovely tree, but then—" In a flash of inspiration, Hallie said, beaming at her mother-in-law, "We were invited to Lord and Lady Lindley's house twice. Very charming people. Weren't they, Jason?"

"I believe they were. Yes, of course they were. Lord Lindley admired you, perhaps overmuch as I recall."

"What about Lady Lindley? I believed she would try to bite your neck she got so close to you. Not to mention those three girls who attempted a very old tried and true stratagem—"

"The wedge," Corrie said.

"Yes, they tried a very nice wedge to get a clear path to you."

"What did you do?" Corrie asked.

"I executed what I now call my counteroffensive. Jason, do you remember when I asked you to look at that particular painting on the drawing room wall?"

"Yes, you nearly had me walking backward a good six feet as I recall."

Hallie nodded. "That's it. It quite flummoxed them. Their wedge vanished, they fell into disarray." She frowned. "However, this one young lady was determined but I whisked him off to a waltz."

"I like that counteroffensive," Corrie said. "I'll try it when James and I attend our next party."

Alex said, "Hallie, other than Lucille admiring my son's neck, didn't you find she has exquisite taste?"

"Well, the inside of her armoire—it smelled quite fragrant, but that's not important, now is it?"

Alec Carrick choked.

Hallie's mother-in-law leaned over and smacked him between his shoulder blades.

James said, "Mother, why should Hallie have remarked on Lady Lindley's taste in particular?"

"She sings beautifully, her voice has much the same rich tone of Hallie's. But it's louder, much more volume."

"But what does her voice have to do with her taste?" Angela asked.

Douglas said, a dark brow raised, "She manages to shatter a crystal glass at each of her concerts, so I've been told."

Alex said, "The goblet she broke when we were last there was made specifically for her by the Waterford artisans."

Jason said, "Lady Lindley did sing for the group, so I heard later. Hallie and I didn't happen to be in the drawing room at that particular moment to witness the goblet shattering. Grandmother, what are you and Angela fighting about this evening?"

Angela said, "She is more selfish than my one and only husband who would stick out his hand for a plate of food, never looking away from his bloody Greek textbooks."

"He was a very learned man," Alec Carrick said. "He was also a demanding tyrant."

"Hear, hear," said Angela. "I do wonder sometimes where he resides now." As she spoke she lightly tapped her slipper against the floor. "I will not speak more about my husband, his spirit is still too near. You will not believe this, my dear," she continued to Hallie, "but this withered old bat"—she waved a hand toward Lady Lydia—"allows that in certain lights, she just might look younger than I do, and here I am young enough to be her daughter, almost."

"Ha!" said Lady Lydia. "Unlike her, I still have beautiful hands, elegant hands, look at my hands, lovely blue veins, so close to the surface. They're of remarkable beauty, don't you agree, dear boy? My sweetest Hallie?"

"I was remarking to my wife that you had extraordinary veins, Grandmother."

Alex marveled at the meaty insults, all given and accepted in high good humor. She wondered what her mother-in-law would say if she called her a shrunken old bat.

"You're both amazing," Hallie said, looking from one to the other.

"My dearest girl," Lady Lydia said, "tell this woman

you don't want her at Lyon's Gate now that you're married and sharing so many lovely activities about which I have little or no memory at all. Tell her that she's to come and live with me. I'll give her a bed in the attic."

"You don't have an attic in the Dower House, Lydia. Your memory is like this lamb chop, nearly all chewed up. Were I to consider moving in with you, I would want that lovely yellow room that faces the back of the house, overlooking the garden Hollis oversees. Then I should want to take over the gardens, plant dill and thyme."

"I don't like dill," Lady Lydia said, then leaned close to Angela. No one could make out what she whispered.

Corrie said to her mother-in-law, "Such wonderful insults and they're all for show. Were she to say them to me or you, she'd mean each and every one. Whereas this one"—Corrie turned to Hallie, an eyebrow arched—"walks in the house, says something absolutely ridiculous to her, and she's charmed. You can do no wrong, Hallie, and it galls me. Mama-in-law and I are forced to listen to her sing endless praises about you, how Jason is so very lucky to have you for his wife. It's quite provoking."

"I'm lucky to have you, Hallie?" Jason said. "Hmm, do you really think so, Grandmama?"

Lady Lydia looked up and blinked. "Oh, my dearest little Hallie. She is doubtless an angel, unlike Corrie here who behaves like a hoyden—imagine, I watched her slide down the banister to fall into poor James's arms. They both went to the floor, playing and laughing, certainly not something to happen in the entrance hall of a nobleman's estate. But the truth is, Hallie and Corrie are the lucky ones."

Hallie said, "Thank you, Grandmama-in-law. I have wit. I like that. And since I'm new and fresh, don't you think I'm worthy of Jason, ma'am?"

Lady Lydia eyed Hallie from her lovely braided hair atop her head to her lovely thin nose to her low-cut evening gown that framed breasts Lady Lydia couldn't remember ever having that high up on her chest. "Yes," she said, "you are worthy. For the moment. My birthday is next month."

Corrie said, "I gave you a lovely marquetry table for your last birthday, but you never said a single word about my being worthy of James."

"I am still thinking about it," Lady Lydia said.

Corrie wanted to tell her not to think about it too long or she just might finally croak. She said, "By the way, Hallie, did you and Jason see anything at all of interest on the Isle of Wight during that long two weeks you were there?"

There was silence the length of the dinner table, then perhaps a giggle from one of the women. Was that Lady Lydia?

James said, "You are one to talk, Corrie. We spent nearly a month in Edinburgh and yet you don't even remember much about the castle. You hemmed and hawed when the twins asked you about it."

"That," Corrie said, "was different. It rained all the

time. We couldn't go out very much. Don't you remember? I sprained my ankle—"

Jason asked, "However did you sprain your ankle, Corrie?"

James said quickly, "Neither of us remember. It's not important. I told her not to hurl herself—well, never mind."

"Listen, James, I do remember the castle. I remember very clearly how you carried me into that tunnel that led to the dungeons—"

James's eyes dilated.

"Oh goodness, James, let me fan myself."

James waved his napkin in her face. "Well, the tunnel was nice and private, not a soul around."

"Oh yes," Corrie said and gave him a smile to curl his toes. She turned to her sister-in-law. "You haven't yet answered my question. Did you see anything at all of interest during your very long fourteen days on the Isle of Wight?"

Hallie never looked up from the lovely asparagus spears in the middle of her plate. "Well, now that I truly think about it, Corrie, I must say no. Jason, can you remember anything we saw that was of any interest, for longer than say, eight minutes?"

"Longer than eight minutes? No, I don't believe so. For the most part, we admired the architecture at Dunsmore House."

CHAPTER 35

❧•❧

*The Beckshire Race
One Week Later*

❧ *Dodger will win; Dodger will win; yes, Dodger will win.* It was his litany, Jason thought, as he looked out over the Beckshire race course.

The prestigious Beckshire race, one half of a mile, four laps around the roughly shaped oval track, open to the first dozen owners who ponied up the fifty-pound entry fee and discreetly handed over a hefty bribe, was run on August the seventeenth beneath a cloudy sky on a cool day that required the ladies to wear light wraps.

The maximum of twelve horses were entered in the race today, not surprising since the Jockey Club members not only offered a healthy prize purse of five hundred pounds, but also the opportunity for owners to compete again against many of the great racing studs that had run their prize horses at the Ascot races in June and the Hallum Heath winners at the end of July. Unfortunately, Dodger hadn't run at Hallum Heath since his owner had been on his honeymoon.

They had not bothered to widen the width of the stretch, so it could be a dangerous race. But that didn't matter. Everyone who was anyone fought to get entry into this race. Dodger was running in the race not because of bribery but because Jason was very good friends with one of the Jockey Club member's sons.

Lorry Dale, head jockey of Lyon's Gate Stud Farm—indeed the only jockey of Lyon's Gate Stud Farm—proudly wore a shiny new livery of gold and white, sewn by Angela, his black boots shined by Mrs. Sherbrooke herself using her own special recipe. He stood, speaking low to Dodger, who stomped and waved his head, doubtless agreeing with what Lorry said, obviously ready to run his heart out. Dodger, Jason said, was at his very best when he was racing or mating. Or one followed by the other. An uncommon combination, Jason admitted, but then again, Dodger wasn't a common horse. Jason nodded toward Charles Grandison, who was running his Arabian bay gelding, Ganymede, then frowned at Elgin Sloane, who stood beside him, a young lady on his arm, the young lady's father standing next to her, obviously pleased with Elgin.

"His heiress?" Hallie said behind her hand to Jason.

"So it would appear. Her father, Mr. Blaystock, owns a large stud near Maidenstone. See that brute of a horse trying to kill his jockey? It's fitting that his name is Brutus. Brutus belongs to Mr. Blaystock. It looks like your father is right. He said Elgin was a man who learned from his mistakes, said you would probably be his first and last big one. It's true that his coming to Lyon's Gate to try to regain your affections was indeed a miscalculation, but it didn't cost him anything but his time."

"I wonder if the poor girl knows his first wife died not a year after he married her," Hallie said. "You don't think he killed his first wife, do you, Jason?"

"No, I don't."

"That Brutus does look vicious. It's the shape and size of his head, the way his eyes roll around. I wouldn't want to be around him."

"He'd be a handful. He's a beauty, though, isn't he? That white star is perfectly formed. Elgin is eyeing that stallion with a good deal of possessiveness if I don't miss my guess."

Hallie said something rude beneath her breath, then pointed to Lord and Lady Grimsby, who had just moved to stand next to Lord Renfrew. "They all appear to be here together."

Charles Grandison waved at Jason, but made no move to come over. Lord Renfrew looked over and laughed too loudly. As for Lord and Lady Grimsby, they smiled at Jason and Hallie because they lived in the neighborhood, mingled socially, and Jason's father was the earl of Northcliffe.

Included in the hundred-some people at the Beckshire race were a dozen Sherbrookes, all there to yell their heads off for Dodger. "We must be very careful of Dodger," Jason had said to Henry.

"Like you, Master Jason," Henry said, "I've put the word out that any attempt to harm Dodger or our jockey will lead to unpleasant consequences."

"At the very least."

Henry grinned. "I heard ye were more specific than that when you put out the warning, Master Jason."

"Yes, a bit more. We will see if anyone is foolish enough to test me. Keep your eyes sharp, Henry." Jason looked out now over the dozen horses coming up to the starting line, most of them bucking and rearing.

Charles Grandison's Ganymede stamped his right front hoof over and over again. Ganymede was favored to win the race, which pleased both Hallie and Jason, as they stood to make a good deal of money with a victory, what with the four-to-one odds the bookies had set. And all because Dodger was an unknown. He'd had made his name in Baltimore, not here in England.

Ganymede, two horses down the line from Dodger, continued his stamping. Jason watched Dodger's ears flick back and forth. It didn't appear to make him uneasy, unlike the big gelding between Dodger and Ganymede who was rolling his eyes, his jockey trying to calm him and failing. That was it, Jason thought, the hoof-stamping was to intimidate.

Lamplighter, Lord Grimsby's huge bay Thoroughbred, was snorting so loudly the horse beside him tried to back away.

At last, the moment of truth. Lorry sent Hallie

and Jason a salute with his whip, hugged himself to Dodger's neck, held him steady and calm, stroking his neck, speaking quietly to him, until Mr. Wesley shouted, "Go!"

Then he stretched himself out, kicked Dodger lightly in the ribs, touched his whip to Dodger's ears. The dozen horses kicked and bucked and heaved forward. Whips slashed down, horses slammed into each other, trying to take over space, jockeys shoved and kicked out at other jockeys. The ground was dry, and dust flew thick in the air. Lorry, prepared, pulled his handkerchief up over his nose.

Dodger, as was his wont, kept his head down, all his attention on covering that track. Lorry, coached by Jason for hours, continued to hold himself low over Dodger's neck—"eating his sweat"—and ignored the other horses.

"Keep his head down, Lorry," Jason said over and over again. "Yes, that's it." He was squeezing Hallie's hand hard. Suddenly Jason saw a flash of silver from the corner of his eye, not twenty feet away, off to his left, from the copse of oak trees beside the track. He'd seen it before at the Hinckley racetrack outside Baltimore—it was the silver of a gun stock glinting off the sun when the man brought it up to fire. Jason yelled to Henry, but he didn't hear him, his eyes on Dodger. Jason picked up a good-sized rock, prayed, and hurled it. He didn't hear anything over the crowd noise, in fact, none of the people standing near him even noticed what he'd done, but the gun stock suddenly disappeared.

"That was an excellent throw," Hallie said, holding his arm tightly. "I wonder which jockey the poltroon was going to shoot?"

Horace, one of the stable lads, sixty years old, hoary and seamed and agile as a mountain goat, yelled, "Ye got 'im! I'll see to the blighter, Master Jason!"

"Dodger's gaining on Lamplighter," Hallie yelled. "He's going to get him, I know it. Lamplighter is fast, damn his eyes. Run, Dodger, run!"

Lamplighter, the big muscled bay Thoroughbred from Lord Grimsby's stable, had taken the lead from the start.

Hallie grabbed Jason's hand, yelling, "Dodger, come on, Dodger," over and over again.

"It's the fourth lap. Dodger will make his break, any second now," Jason said, and held his breath. The field was close, the horses nearly on top of one another the track was so narrow at this point. Nothing but yelling, louder and louder, but Jason didn't hear them. He was concentrating on Dodger and on Lorry Dale riding so low on his neck they almost looked like one. It was time. *Break, Dodger, break now.* It was as if Lorry snapped a spring. Dodger leapt forward—exactly like a racing cat, Tysen Sherbrooke was to tell everyone later—and in the space of three seconds there wasn't more than three inches between him and Lamplighter. He was gaining, gaining, nearly there. Soon Dodger and Lamplighter were nose-to-nose.

Charles Grandison's Ganymede was moving up on Dodger's left side. Unless Dodger could get past Lamplighter, he'd be trapped between the two horses, a favorite ploy.

"You've got to move up, Dodger. Run."

"He's head to head with Lamplighter," Jason said, "Dodger's got to get ahead of him." But Dodger wasn't past Lamplighter when Ganymede's jockey managed to pull alongside Dodger and began to press inward. Jason thought he'd never breathe again. Suddenly Mr. Blaystock's Brutus was directly behind Dodger, sweat spuming off his neck. He looked mean and vicious and as strong as the Devil. Lord Renfrew and the young lady were yelling their heads off, her father as well, looking nearly apoplectic. Charles Grandison stood quietly, his hands fisted at his sides, his eyes on Ganymede. His lips were moving.

Jason clearly heard the girl's father yell, "Bite him, Brutus, bite him now!"

Elgin yelled, "No, use your whip! The whip!"

Bite? What was this? The horse couldn't get past the wedge of three, all of them so close together, keeping the rest of the pack behind them, until one of them broke to the lead, or the middle horse was squeezed out. Brutus's jockey leaned forward, and slashed his whip on the flanks of all three horses. He nearly overbalanced when he struck Lamplighter, but held on, and kept slashing.

Lorry Dale, unlike the other two jockeys, didn't look back, kept his head down, kept talking to Dodger. In the next moment, Lamplighter moved to his right to escape the jockey's whip. It gave Dodger a precious second and he pulled quickly ahead of both Lamplighter and Ganymede, a half length now. Brutus came between Lamplighter and Ganymede, running hard, harder, moving ahead of them, only Dodger in his path now.

"BITE HIM, BRUTUS!"

Brutus stretched out his neck and bit Dodger on his flank.

Dodger's ears flattened, his tail slashed in Brutus's face, and he put his head down and ran hard.

Ganymede's jockey kicked out at Lamplighter's jockey, his boot connecting with his leg. If a jockey didn't practice this, he'd go flying off his horse's back with one good hard kick, but Lord Grimsby's jockey held on tight. Then Ganymede's jockey raised his whip and brought it down hard on Brutus's rump. Brutus, enraged, ignored his jockey, kicked out his hind legs, slowing him down, but he missed Ganymede, who was now beside him, pushing forward.

Dodger, run, run, run.

Once again Lamplighter and Ganymede came up on either side of Dodger and tried to press inward again, crowding him. Lamplighter's jockey struck his whip out at Lorry then again at Dodger. Dodger screamed and reared, and Jason watched Ganymede pull ahead. Lorry appeared rattled. Jason knew the blow from the whip must hurt. He'd taught Lorry what to do and stood there, helplessly, praying that Lorry would remember, that he'd act before Ganymede. Lorry Dale stood straight up in the saddle, kicked out his left leg and connected with Ganymede's jockey. The jockey went flying. Ganymede veered in front of two horses and the three of them tangled to the shouts of their jockeys toward the side of the race course.

Lord Grimsby's Lamplighter was closing again on Dodger, but the finish line was close now. Almost there, almost.

There was a popping sound.

It was a gun firing, Jason thought blankly, and watched in disbelief as Lorry grabbed his right arm. But he didn't fall. He tucked himself closer to Dodger's neck. To Jason's surprise, very few of the spectators appeared to know one of the jockeys had been shot.

Jason's hands were fisted at his sides as he watched Dodger run nose-to-nose with Lamplighter. Time slowed, seemed to stop altogether. Then Jason smiled as Dodger stretched out his powerful neck and shot forward. He sped over the finish line a full half-length in front of Lamplighter. Brutus came in third, for which there was no prize money at all.

He heard a loud curse from Lord Grimsby, a yell of fury from Mr. Blaystock, and nothing at all from Charles Grandison. Was that weeping he heard from Lord Renfrew?

CHAPTER 36

> ❖

❖ There was a moment of stunned silence. It wasn't every day an unknown thoroughbred won the Beckshire race, or any other big race for that matter. Many of the spectators had lost a goodly number of groats. Then, with all the Sherbrookes leading the way, the air began to thicken with cheers, louder and louder still. Those who had taken the chance on the long odds and the unknown Dodger soon out-shouted the Sherbrookes. Jason heard his twin, could see his father's grin splitting his face. Hallie was in his arms, hugging him, squeezing his arm, laughing, then rose to her tiptoes and kissed him hard right in front of everyone. She laughed into his mouth, kissed once, twice more.

Jason stood there watching Lorry slow Dodger. He watched him pat his neck continuously, just as

Jason had taught him, holding him firm with his knees, holding his right arm, the blood oozing out between his fingers.

"Oh God, he's been shot," Hallie said blankly. "I didn't see. Oh, blessed hell. Jason, who would have shot at Dodger?"

It was then that the rest of the spectators realized that Dodger's jockey had a bullet through his arm. There was a chorus of outrage, and of curses.

Jason said, "Someone who wanted to win badly. Everyone is upset about this now, but truth be told, it won't change anything. You know what, Hallie, I'm thinking the owner who hired the first man to shoot also hired the second. And we've got him. We'll see if Henry and Quincy and our other men can find the man who shot Lorry." Excitement pounded through him. Dodger had won and Lorry appeared to be all right.

As it turned out, the bullet had barely nicked him, but Jason knew it must hurt badly. He and Hallie stood over Lorry as the physician bound him up. After thanking the doctor, Jason and Hallie turned to find themselves surrounded by a dozen excited Sherbrookes, laughing all of them and slapping both Hallie and Jason on the back. Jason realized, as he looked into all those beloved faces, that they were all so very happy he'd won because they still saw him as the wounded man who might bolt again. Fact was, Jason thought, hugging his aunt Mary Rose close, he hadn't thought about that horrible day for a while now, perhaps nearly a month. He looked over at

Hallie, laughing with his uncle Tysen. She was enjoying herself immensely, but he saw her looking around whenever she thought she could get away with it.

She was looking for him. He was suddenly filled with warmth and a soft sort of pleasure that made his chest two inches wider. Jason turned, grinning, at a tug on his sleeve. It was Henry. "Master Jason, we've got the blighter over there by Dodger's wagon. The second blighter, the one wot shot Lorry, I'm sorry to say he got away."

"We'll find out all we need to know from the first one, Henry." He went over and grabbed his wife. "We have some business to attend to, Uncle Tysen. Excuse us for a moment."

"Well, at least Henry got the first villain," Hallie said. "I want to question this fellow myself, I want to grind him into the dirt. How could he do that? As for that other fellow—to shoot a jockey, it's disgraceful. Jason?"

"Yes?"

"You told me that no one tried with Charles Grandison because of the consequences. Lorry kicked Ganymede's jockey off his back."

"I don't think Charles is going to say anything since his jockey tried to take Lorry down first. Charles should have realized I'd teach Lorry to fight as dirty as needed."

"If Charles does try anything, I'll have something to say to him. Now, Jason, I want to beat Charles's consequences."

Jason hugged her, felt her heart against his chest. "Yes, we will. Ah good, James is bragging on Dodger like the proud papa. He'll keep everything under control whilst we deal with this idiot."

The idiot was young, that was Hallie's first thought, his clothes filthy, as if he'd slept in this field for a good two days before the race. Probably searching for the best spot from which to shoot, she thought, her hand clenching at her side. He was sitting on the ground, his back against the right rear wheel of Dodger's traveling coach. Henry stood on one side of him, Quincy and Horace on the other.

Hallie stood over him, hands on hips. "Your boots are a disgrace," she said, and kicked his right foot.

He looked up at her, eyes widened. "Aren't ye a purty little thing, missus, all that lovely hair on yer head, sweet breath flowing over me, each word ye speak like bells chiming beautiful music. I appreciates beauty, so the beauty should appreciate me, don't ye think?"

"No."

"Now yer're saying ye don't like me boots?" He gave her a young man's cocky grin. "Ye want to polish 'em all up fer me?"

"No, I'm going to have your boots pulled off and you're going to walk over a bed of nails. Hot nails. What do you think of that?"

"Ye're a young lady, I seen ye wi' that fella over there. Now me, missus, I could show ye some real fun iffen ye'd—"

"Are you mad, you moron? Look at that fella over there."

He looked. "Well, meybe not," he allowed. "I don't knows why I'm here. These bully boys grabbed me where I was taking me nap and—"

Jason said, "What's your name?"

"I done forgit," he said and spat. "I demands ye lets me go. I didn't do nuthin', I'm just 'ere to see all the swells."

"Nice gun you've got here," Hallie said. "Are you utterly stupid? Look at how dirty you've let it become. I'll bet you Mr. Blaystock gave it to you all clean and primed, and yet—"

"No, tweren't like that a'tal. I—"

"Mr. Blaystock gave you a dirty gun? He expected you to shoot a horse or a jockey with a dirty gun?"

"No, 'e—well, stick me thumb in me nose. I don't know wot ye're jawin' about. Smart mouth on yer, missus, enough to make a man scurry to 'ide 'is privates. Listen to me, little girl, I don't know no Mr. Blaystock. Who is this fancy cove?"

"You were going to shoot at one of the horses," Jason said. "Were you aiming at any one in particular?"

"Dunno nuthin' about it."

Hallie went down on her knees beside the young man and grabbed his dirty shirt collar in her hand. "You listen to me, you miserable varmint, my husband is going to send you to Botany Bay. Do you know what that is? It's a place halfway around the world that's filled with strange bugs who burrow inside your ear while you're sleeping and suck the blood out of your head—*if* you survive your voyage there. Did you know the sun is so hot over there that you'll explode after a while? That is, if the bugs don't drain you first."

The young man had clearly heard of Botany Bay, and chewed his lips frantically. "I ain't got that much blood in me 'ead to start with. No, no, missus, ye can't send me there, ye can't."

Jason snapped his fingers. "You'll be gone by Friday."

"Think of that sun burning through the top of your bloodless head. It will shrivel right up."

"I thought ye said I'd explode."

"One or the other. It depends on the bugs. Now, which horse did Mr. Blaylock want you to shoot?"

"Jest the jockey, not the racer. Ye only has the one jockey, it'd put ye right out o' business."

"What is your name?"

He gave Hallie a sour look, shook his head.

She said, "Botany Bay. Friday."

"I'm William Donald Kindred, the proud fruit of me pa's loins, now filled with gin, not seed. I ain't niver done nuthin' like this, but ye see, me ma is real sick, me little brother too, an'—"

"You will remain with us until I have verified that you are who you say you are, Mr. Kindred," Jason said.

"I don't want to go to Botany Bay! Don't put me name on no bill of ladin'. Don't ye send me to the bugs!"

Hallie said, "Then you'd best be a very cooperative prisoner from this moment on, don't you think? For goodness' sake, polish those filthy boots."

Jason took her hand, kissed her fingers, saw she was looking at his mouth, and smiled at her. "That was well done, Hallie. An excellent questioning technique. Mr. Blaystock, huh?"

"I saw my father do that once, worked like a charm. Hmm." She frowned, tapped a lovely shod foot.

Jason said, "What is it? You guessed right."

"I know him," Hallie said finally, looking back at the man who was now standing, his hands tied behind him, Horace's big hand around his arm. "Yes, I'm sure of it now."

Jason waited, didn't say a thing.

"I saw him hold Lord Grimsby's horse once when I was in Eastbourne, in front of Mountbank's Stable off High Street."

"Lord Grimsby," Jason repeated. "You're sure?"

"Yes, Lord Grimsby had just spoken a few words to his wife, and was off to a tavern, once she was out of sight. I heard him yell something to this man. I'm sure it was our Mr. Kindred."

"So," Jason said, looking at the man now walking between Henry, Quincy, and Horace. "He's not stupid, our dirty young man with his seedy-looking boots. He realized very quickly he could shift the blame onto Mr. Blaystock. He was quite smooth. Interesting."

"Yes, it is. What are we going to do, Jason?"

Jason smiled down at her, saw her tongue slide over her bottom lip, sighed deep in his throat, kissed her hard, and stepped away from her. "What I'm going to do is try to keep my hands off you until we're home. Er, Hallie, I meant to ask you, do you really want that chair to be at the foot of the bed?"

"You're right. My gowns never land on the chair. I know, I'll move the chair in front of the armoire. It faces the window and such a lovely view it is, don't you agree?"

Jason stared down at her, fascinated and appalled.

"I'm joking, Jason. I'm joking."

CHAPTER 37

❧❧

❧ "This one is too close." Hallie kissed the long thin scar high on the inside of his left thigh.

"Yes, much too close," Jason said, and tried not to think of her mouth caressing that scar he always noticed when he was bathing because it had been too close, of her palm now lying flat on his belly, fingers splayed. He was trying his best not to shudder like a palsied man. He said only, "Hallie." Odd how whispering her name in moments like this flowed so steadily through him now, warm and strong. He said her name again because it felt so good, because her breath was warm against his flesh.

She looked up the length of his body to his beautiful face, stretched up to kiss his belly, then looked at his face again. "Not long ago I would have been

alarmed that I was causing you distress. But not now."
She lowered her head, kissed the scar again, her touch
so light he wanted to cry. "How did it happen?"

"What? Oh, the cut on my leg. James managed to
get under my guard, poked his wooden sword into
my belly, and I toppled backward over a log. A small
and unfortunately very sharp branch was sticking
up, and it tore right through my britches and got
me."

"Were you old enough to be mortified when your
mother wanted to take care of you?"

"Oh yes, but my father saved me, bless him for all
time, cleaned me up himself." And he said her name
again. "Hallie."

She traced the thin scar over his right hipbone, the
result of being thrown off his pony when he was six
years old, he told her. Jason believed it was all over for
him when she licked that scar, her fingers curling
around him now, and he, quite simply, wanted to
drum his heels against the mattress, and die. Thank
God he wasn't eighteen and still had a modicum of
control over himself. Hallie, however, was orderly.
She wasn't to be hurried. After an eternity, she reached
his chest. She was on her knees leaning over him, her
hair loose, veiling her face, her fingers moving to the
scar high on his shoulder. She lightly traced it. "This is
the bullet wound."

"Yes."

"From five years ago."

"Yes."

"Tell me, Jason. Tell me what happened. I think it's time, don't you?"

When he remained silent, she leaned down and kissed the puckered scar. "The pain you must have endured. I am so very sorry."

He felt a catch in his throat, felt a shot of pain so black, so very real, for a moment he couldn't breathe. So long ago that pain, but he still felt it, felt the utter helplessness, and he knew it was payment owed for his appalling judgment. She must have seen that pain in his eyes because she kissed him, kept touching him, nibbling here and there until the pain receded. He wondered how she could ease him so quickly, so absolutely. He said, "She was going to kill my father. I couldn't allow her to do that."

"No," she said, kissing him again and again, his throat, his chin, his mouth, "of course you couldn't, no more than I could allow someone to kill my father, not if I could stop it."

"She aimed at his heart. My father is about an inch taller than I am. He would have died instantly. That blessed inch saved my life."

Her eyes closed though she could still see him throwing himself in front of his father, the bullet tearing into his flesh. She felt such intense, vicious hatred for this long-dead woman, that for an instant she knew what it was like to wish death upon another. It was a pity this woman was already dead and beyond her.

"I don't understand. Why did she want to kill your father?"

He reached up his hand and pulled her hair back. He saw fury in her eyes, making them nearly black, and wondered at it. How could she feel so deeply over something that had happened so long ago, long before she'd known him? It was right and just that he remember, that he burrow into the leaching pain as he would a familiar old shirt. Perhaps he shouldn't remember it with such stark clarity, but he did. "Her name was Judith and I was her cat's paw. She was beautiful, but it wasn't her beauty that reeled me in, it was her wit, her ability to surprise me, to make me laugh and shake my head at the same time. I wanted to marry her. I never saw her treachery until it was too late. I was a bloody fool."

"Tell me," she said, and sat back on her haunches, white and naked, her hair long and loose, falling over her shoulders to veil her breasts, her hands open on her thighs. "Tell me," she said again.

Jason didn't want to call up the memory that was still so hot and stone-hard inside him. He didn't want her to know the damnable details of what he'd done, he didn't want her to realize what a fool he'd been, to see the pathetic young man who'd very nearly destroyed his own family, but words came out of his mouth even as he shook his head. "It was all about the greed of three evil people, three people with absolutely no conscience. My father was caught in this storm's eye." He told her about Annabelle Trelawny, a woman who had fooled them all, including Hollis, about how James had nearly died as well. "He managed to kill Judith's brother, Louis, but it was so close, Hallie." He rubbed his shoulder, feeling again the instant the bullet had struck him, hurling him back against his father. "Corrie killed both women," he said. "Saying it now, it doesn't seem possible, but she did it, she first shot Judith, then Annabelle Trelawny, to save Hollis. I can remember the sounds of the bullets, and I thought how very loud they were, and I knew one of them had struck me, and I thought it very odd since I felt numb. Apart from it, really. I remember my father pressing his palm against the wound in my shoulder, remember him yelling at me, and I was so relieved he was all right. Then I remember thinking that with my luck the bullet could so easily have torn through me and still killed him, but that didn't happen. I wanted to tell him that I was sorry for all the devastation I'd caused, but I couldn't, the words wouldn't come, and then, well, then I couldn't do anything."

"You nearly died," Hallie said. She was stroking her fingers over his shoulder, lightly touching the scar.

"But I didn't. My family was there, they were always there, and when I finally opened my eyes, they were so happy and relieved, told me over and over that I would be all right, that I would live. I wasn't sure I wanted to. All those forgiving, beloved faces, the worry and love for me etched deep, the fear that I would die."

"You couldn't bear it because the blame was yours."

"Yes, it was mine, no one else's."

"Tell me again how it was all your fault."

"If I hadn't been such a fool, so blind and full of my own conceit and invincibility, Judith wouldn't have been able to draw me in, to make me her dupe. She wouldn't have won."

"You say she won? How could she have won, Jason? She's dead. You're not dead, your father's not dead, James isn't dead."

"No thanks to me. They wanted our deaths, Hallie. They wanted the actual doing of it. Worst of all, they wanted the benefit from it. They were monstrous evil. Judith's brother had knocked James out and tied him up. Thank God James is so strong and so smart, but still, it was too close. He could have died so easily."

"He didn't. He saved himself just as you saved your father."

Before he could speak again, she leaned down and kissed his mouth lightly, her palm over his heart. The beat was solid, steady, not fast now with need. "Your father," she said thoughtfully, her brow furrowed, "he must have hated that you, his son, saved him."

"Yes, he did. He told me he was the father, it was he who should protect his son. He was angry that I leaped in front of him."

"That surprises you?"

"No. He's my father. He tried to excuse what I'd allowed Judith to do to me, said if I wanted to apportion blame so badly, then give them all their share." Jason fell silent, aware of her palm now covering the bullet scar, but beneath her palm the damnable pain was still there, pulsing strong and hot. "He said what I would say had I been the father."

"Of course. He was also right."

"You weren't there, Hallie. You don't know what really went on."

"Has your father ever lied to you?"

"Of course not, but this is much different. He wouldn't see this as a lie, he'd see it—"

"As what?"

"As something he'd fight to believe since I was his son and he loved me."

"Do you love your father, Jason?"

He grabbed her wrist and pulled her down to an inch from his face. "Why would you ask something so stupid as that?"

She kissed his mouth lightly, then pulled back a little. "Because you obviously didn't believe him when he told you that you weren't to blame. How can you love someone when you believe they're lying to you?"

"It wasn't like that. He tried to justify it, tried to excuse what I did—"

"This is quite remarkable."

"What is, damn you?"

"You've wallowed in guilt for nearly five long years. You've managed to keep that wound raw and bleeding, always there at the edge of your mind so you won't forget to hate yourself. You've nourished this constant companion of yours, kept it strong and in control for so very long. That is great dedication on your part, Jason. I imagine you would probably feel incomplete without it there, poking you, reminding you what an abominable excuse of a man you are.

"Your father must feel that he's failed you. Actually, I suppose he did fail you. Like I said, it's obvious you didn't believe him, did you? Didn't believe his word that you weren't to blame? Hmm, all this flailing about over long-ago evil and endless bloody guilt, it's made me quite thirsty. Would you like some warm milk? I understand it's Mother's antidote for depressed spirits. My father always rolls his eyes and says brandy is the only drink to realign the humors. Or would you prefer your spirits to remain depressed?"

"It was you who brought all this up, Hallie, you who demanded to know what happened. My spirits aren't depressed, dammit."

"Well, you've certainly depressed mine." She pulled away from him, rose, beautifully naked, only he didn't notice, since his eyes were focused on her neck, how his hands would fit nicely around her neck, and squeeze. He felt the heavy burn of anger in his throat. "I told you part of me was dead, that I wasn't whole, that trust had been burned out of me and that's why I didn't want to marry, that—"

"Oh yes, you did," she said, as she pulled on her dressing gown. "It is all very sad. Just imagine—being part dead. Yes, that is indeed sad." She sighed. "Look at the guilt I shall have to carry around now."

"Guilt? You? You don't have any guilt, you were a girl at the time this happened."

"Oh yes, I do. Don't you remember? I jumped on your poor dead innocent self. I was very ready to plunge my fingers down the front of your britches—my father was right about that. Attacking you like I did, I sealed your doom. Poor Jason. In addition to all that soul-shattering pain that haunts you, you were forced to take a wife, namely me, the very last thing you wanted. Having a wife must seem to you like the final instrument of torture—the iron maiden—sorry, just a little joke. Poor Jason, trapped now with both the memory of failure and blame—and a wife. Do you think that long-dead evil Judith is hanging about as a spirit, rubbing her hands together because she knows she still controls your life? That would please the damnable bitch, don't you think? Hmm. I wonder if her spirit ever believes she won. Would you like some warm milk?"

He jumped out of bed, so angry he was nearly rabid with it, so angry he wanted that neck of hers between his big hands, now. He shook his fist at her, yelled at the top of his lungs, "Don't you try to act all superior and smart with me, Hallie. Don't you bring up Judith's smarmy spirit to make me feel ridiculous. Damn you, don't you dare try to jolly me out of this!"

She saw the pounding pulse in his throat, then stared at his groin. "No, of course not. Sometimes words pop out of my mouth, you know that. I know there's no way I can make you face up to what happened five years ago. It would be like prying the shingles off a roof with your fingernails. Aren't you chilly,

Jason? Should you like me to give you your dressing gown? I believe it's over here on the floor, where you threw it about fifteen minutes ago. Ah, but I enjoy looking at you so very much, perhaps—"

He picked up his own dressing gown and shrugged it on. "Damn you, stop staring at me."

CHAPTER 38

❧❦

❧ "Why? You have incredible stretches of self that quite delight me. Whenever you have me out of my clothes, you're either looking at my breasts or at my belly or my legs, or talking about kissing me behind my knees. It's like you can't make up your mind.

"Not that it's any easier with you. Well, I always know where to begin, but then there's your chest, I can't forget about your chest, but then, your legs—goodness, I love your legs too. I guess the truth of the matter is every time I look at any part of you—even the dead parts—I feel all sorts of delicious little tingles. Would you like some warm milk now?"

"I don't want any damned milk. I want a brandy."

"Hmm. My father would be pleased. Perhaps I'd like a brandy too. Jason?"

"What, dammit?"

"You really don't like the chair at the end of the bed? Perhaps with enough practice, our clothing would end up on the chair rather than on the floor."

She was callous and not at all solicitous of him, despite all her bleating to the contrary. He kicked the chair, cursed because it felt like he'd broken one of his toes, and slammed out of the bedchamber. He wished at that moment that Angela was still here. He'd take her a snifter of brandy, pull up a chair beside her bed, and tell her about how he was going to strangle his wife. Then he'd go take care of Lord Grimsby, but Lord Grimsby was a distant second to his crass, unfeeling wife. But Angela had moved to the Dower House three days before, Hollis supervising the four footmen. He and Hallie were alone in this big house. He'd never believed it was too big before, but he did now. If he strangled her, it would seem even bigger. The entire house would be his. He could do just as he pleased whenever he pleased. Damnation.

Perhaps he'd wake up Petrie, tell him about this bloody uncaring wife of his, listen to him add his own list of female failings to Jason's list. How long would that last? Knowing Petrie, possibly a week. Besides, with his luck, Martha would overhear, rush in, and smack them both in the head.

"Yoo hoo, Jason! The house is very cold, don't you think? Can one heat brandy?"

He turned to face his wife, all smiles, trotting toward him down the corridor. She grinned up at him, took his arm. "The house seems too empty without Angela. What do you think is happening at the Dower House?"

"Hopefully they're sleeping," he said in a prissy voice.

"Oh dear, this is all my own fault. If only I'd not asked you all those soul-wrenching questions that ended up with you walking out on me, why, right now I'd be lying in the middle of the bed, a silly grin on my face, with you sweating beside me, maybe singing a duet."

"Be quiet, Hallie."

She began whistling.

He wished he could whistle as well as she. "Whistle that ditty about the drunken sailors."

She did. She grabbed his hand and began swinging her arm in march time. When she came to the end of the ditty, she said, "I don't suppose you'll want to make love to me on the kitchen table, will you? I could arrange myself, perhaps even lift the corner of my gown so as to focus your lovely eyes—"

"Shut your mouth. You have the feelings of a damned gnat."

It was meaty, that insult. She went on her tiptoes and kissed his cheek. He felt her hand low on his belly through the velvet of his dressing gown, pressing in, touching him. His breath hitched at the quick punch of lust. "Truly? A damned gnat?"

"Get your hand off me, Hallie. I am not in the mood."

Her fingers stilled, but she didn't move her hand.

"It came to my attention during our ever-so-pleasant stay on the Isle of Wight that men were always in the mood. Ah, Jason?"

"What?"

"Why are you so angry with me?"

He realized they'd been standing at the top of the stairs for the last three minutes. It was dark, but there was a swatch of moonlight coming through the front windows. He opened his mouth, shut it, said, "You refuse to acknowledge the god-awful mess I made, you refuse to understand the devastating shadow I cast on so many lives."

"It certainly appears to be a very long-lasting shadow."

"Dammit, Hallie, because of me, my family nearly died! Stop mocking me, you're not treating what happened with the seriousness it deserves."

"No, I suppose not. Had I been there, been your wife, it's possible I would have coddled you and reassured you for a full six months. Then I would have gotten tired of your ridiculous guilty drivel. And I would wonder why you couldn't see that you survived and those evil people didn't. Yes, I would have reached the end of my tether of your attachment to a past that would be forgotten if not for your dreary vow to suffer for the rest of your life.

"Hmm. I've heard of sack cloth, it's spoken of in the Bible. I wonder if one can still purchase sack cloth. Ashes, now, that would be no problem. Wouldn't you look a treat in sack cloth, all dirtied up?"

He growled at her, actually growled he was so angry. He left her at the top of the stairs and headed down. He nearly tripped at the shock of the gloomy voice that came from the thick shadows near the drawing room. "Master Jason? Is that you, sir? Oh dear, what is wrong? I heard voices, arguing voices, mainly that of your new wife.

"Ah, I knew it was a mistake, you're such a fair man and she took full advantage of you. You had to marry her and now she's forcing you to argue."

Another voice, this one much higher and louder, trumpeted from the shadows back near the kitchen. "You miserable fat-tongued dead-witted slug! Don't you dare speak of my precious mistress like that. My mistress is the best thing that has ever happened to Master Jason. She makes him laugh and smile and, well—all have heard him groan."

Petrie, in a dressing gown as black as a priest's robes, puffed himself right up. "And what about *her*, Martha? I've heard *her* groan so loud I feared for the newly hung chandelier. It's disgraceful that a supposed lady would enjoy, well—"

Martha flew at him, her white nightgown whirling around her ankles. She jumped on him, took him to the floor, a tangle of black and white. She grabbed fistfuls of his hair and began banging his head against the tiles. "You wretched water-piddled trout-brain! Like every other man in the universe, all you can think about is this yelling business. Of course she yells, you cracked pot, she should yell. Do you think the master has no skill at all? You think he's a clod of a lover? You think he shouldn't yell as well? You think my mistress is a clod? Never mind that, men don't need to have skill applied to them to make them yell. Have you no working mental parts at all? No feelings in your heart?" Bang, bang, bang. Petrie groaned.

Jason said as he lifted her off Petrie, "No, Martha, don't kill poor Petrie. This thing about men's hearts, I fear in many it's lower, much lower." He realized in that instant that Petrie was staring up at Martha, a very strange look on his face, almost as if he were in very bad pain, which he should be.

"Master Jason, you may drop her back down on me, if you wish, sir. I don't mind, the pain in my cracked head is nothing. Her breath is very sweet, it has quite left me wondering what has happened. I am adrift, waiting for enlightenment."

Martha shrieked, tried to kick him.

Hallie said, "Martha, thank you for standing up for me. Now, both you and Petrie take yourselves back to bed." She paused a moment, staring down at Petrie, who hadn't moved and who looked both baffled and appalled, his dark hair standing in clumps on his head where Martha's strong fingers had nearly pulled them out. "You will go back to your own bed, Petrie. You will think of no other bed except yours. You will not think of Martha's sweet breath. All is well. We are no longer arguing. Master Jason simply wanted some brandy. Perhaps you know. Can one heat brandy?"

Petrie said, "Well, back in 1769, it's said that old Lord Brandon was suffering from an ague. His valet, an ancestor of mine, heated him a snifter of brandy over a small hob in the fireplace. It was told me by my mother that the heated brandy made him well within a half hour."

"I'm going to sleep with Henry in the stable," Jason said, and marched toward the front door.

"You won't be happy walking out there bare-footed," Hallie called after him. "Petrie, why don't you fetch your master's boots, put on your own as well, and the two of you can snuggle down together in the warm straw on either side of poor Henry." Hallie smiled at both of them impartially, and walked toward the kitchen. "Jason? In case your mood changes, I will take a very close look at the kitchen table."

Jason was dressed and on Dodger's bare back within ten minutes.

CHAPTER 39

❧⭒❧

❧ Corrie rubbed the cramp in her leg. She never should have let James arrange her in such a position, ah, but it had been such fun. She rubbed some more. She'd swear she had never used that particular muscle in her life. Perhaps she should rub in some of her mother-in-law's special warming cream that seeped to your bones.

She heard something. She froze, cramp forgotten, instantly as still as James, who was lying on his back, breathing deeply in sleep, nearly dead, he'd told her before falling on his back, an angel's smile on his face.

She heard it again. A noise coming from the window. Good heavens, this was the second time. When Corrie crept toward the window, a poker in her hand, she saw it start to slowly inch upward.

She watched her brother-in-law ease the window up far enough so he could swing his leg over the sill and climb in.

"I was hoping for a villain this time," she said, and gave him a hand. "I was armed and ready."

"Thank you for putting down the poker, Corrie. I'm sorry to come in through your window again, I know it's late."

"Not that late. I felled poor James. That's him, snoring from the bed."

She sounded quite proud of herself. Jason touched his fingertips to her cheek. "I'll wake up the sluggard. He doesn't deserve to sleep."

Jason shook his brother's shoulder. "Wake up, you pathetic excuse for a man."

James, as was his wont, opened his eyes without hesitation, and focused instantly and clearly on his brother's annoyed face above him. "I feel very fine," he said, and smiled.

"You don't deserve to, damn you. Get up, my world has ended and you're lying here, thinking about how wonderful life is. You don't bloody deserve it."

James, still light in the head and heart, said, "All that?"

"What's wrong, Jason? What's happened?"

Jason looked with a good deal of affection at his sister-in-law, whose white hand clutched his sleeve, her worry for him shining in her eyes, though in the dim light it was hard to know for sure. "You look ever so nice with your hair all wild around your face, Corrie."

James bolted upright. "Don't you admire her, you dog. Damn you, you've got a wife of your own. Step away from her before I flatten you."

"What's wrong, Jason?"

"I've left Lyon's Gate," Jason said, and stepped back from his sister-in-law because he knew when his brother was serious. He slid down to the floor, leaned his head back against the wall, closed his eyes and wrapped his arms around his bent knees.

James pulled on his dressing gown, eyed his wife's revealing nightgown, and said, "Get back into bed, Corrie. I don't want Jason to get any ideas."

"Ideas? How could he possibly be thinking about me and this lovely peach nightgown when he's left his home?" Corrie lit some candles, then slipped back into bed, drew a deep breath. "You've left Hallie?"

Jason said, not looking up, "The nightgown is lovely, Corrie, but I'm not thinking about you under it. My life is ripped apart. I meant to go sleep in the stables, but I came here instead. I don't know what to do."

James patted his wife's cheek, tucked more covers over her, then pulled his twin to his feet. "Let's go downstairs and have a brandy. You can tell me what's happened."

"Do you know if heated brandy is good, James?"

When the brothers stepped into James's estate room, it was to see their father pouring each of them a snifter of brandy. He was wearing a dark blue dressing gown whose elbows were worn nearly through. "So,"

Douglas said, trying to sound calm, when in fact, his heart was racing, and he was terrified, "why, Jason, did you leave your home in the middle of the night, and your wife of not yet a month?"

James said, "Actually, it's not all that late, not even midnight yet."

"Don't make me shoot you, James," his father said.

Jason gulped down the brandy and fell to coughing. When he finally caught his breath, his father poured him more. "Slowly this time. Get ahold of yourself. Tell us what's happened."

"I don't think brandy needs to be heated. My belly is on fire. It's Hallie."

Both Douglas and James remained silent.

Jason sipped at his brandy. "I'm very sorry to break in on you like this, but I just didn't know where else to go. Well, like I said, I was going to sleep in the stable, but I was afraid Petrie would come with me."

Douglas said, "What did Hallie do?"

Jason sipped brandy.

"What did she do?"

"She laughed at me."

"I don't understand," James said slowly. "What did she laugh at you about?"

"She wanted me to tell her what happened five years ago, and so I did. She made light of it! Dammit, all three of us still live with that awful time."

James said, "The gall. Here I was growing fond of her. I thought she was nice, filled with kindness."

"She is, usually."

"No, she's obviously cruel," James said, and shook his head. "Hard, that's what she is, and unfeeling."

Douglas nodded. "Indeed. I trust you set her straight, Jason. I am very disappointed in her. I believe I will ride to Lyon's Gate right now, and give her a piece of my mind."

"I'll go with you, Papa," James said. "I'd like to shake her, tell her she doesn't understand what really happened, how it smote you to your toes, Jason, how deeply you feel about it, and your part in it."

"She had the nerve to say that any part I had in it I should have gotten over by now."

"What a coldhearted creature," Douglas said. "I'm very sorry you had to marry her, Jason. I've wondered if perhaps she took advantage of you because she knew her father was there, knew perhaps he was even on his way into the stable."

Jason drank more brandy. "No, she didn't know her father was there. She simply couldn't help herself."

"Well, no matter. Yes, I'll go over right now and set her straight about things. I won't have her hurting you when you're so very hurt already."

"I told her how I was such a fool, how Judith pulled me in so effortlessly, that she'd won. You know what Hallie said? She said Judith didn't win, how could she when she was dead?"

James said, sipping his brandy, "I've never looked at it in exactly that light. Fact is, Jase, she did fool you— fooled the rest of us for that matter, and surely that makes all of us dupes—but I certainly understand how you would feel more like a fool, more like a failure and a loser, than the rest of us. I want to go with you, Father. Hallie needs to be thrashed."

"More brandy, Jason?"

Jason frowned as he stuck out his snifter to his father. "She didn't call me a failure or a loser. I tried to explain it to her, but you know Hallie, she's able to weave in and out of a conversation. She was talking about Judith's spirit hanging about, about how her spirit must be so pleased that she was still controlling my life. That isn't true, dammit!"

"Of course it's not," Douglas said. "Imagine, a woman dead for five years still controlling someone's thoughts and actions. It's absurd."

"Well, yes, it is. It's just that I— Oh hell, Father, you could have died. Do you hear me? You could have died! How can I ever forget my role in that?"

"But I didn't, Jason, you're the one who could have died."

"Well I didn't either, but that's neither here nor there. Do you know she asked if you'd ever lied to me?"

"I don't believe I have," Douglas said. "Hmm. Well, perhaps I did when you were a lad and you wondered why your mother had yelled in the gazebo—"

James would cut his brain out before he'd think about that. He nodded. "Yes, I would lie to Douglas and Everett as well."

"The point is, you haven't ever lied to me about anything important, and so I told her. Then she had the cheek to tell me I believed you had lied to me—my own father."

"Why is that?"

"She said it was obvious I hadn't believed you when you told me I wasn't to take the blame, and thus I did believe you'd lied to me."

"Hmm," said Douglas. "Fact is, Jason, she's right. You didn't believe me. I hate to say it, but Hallie did nail that one."

"It's not that I didn't believe you, Papa, it's just that you could have so easily died and so could you, James, and it was all my fault, no one else's. It hit me between the eyes it was so clear. How could I deny something so obvious? You love me, damn you, and that's why you—well all right, I didn't accept your words, I couldn't because I knew you said them because you loved me."

Douglas said, "Even though I'd like to clout Hallie, let me be honest here. The fact is, Jason, you just admitted it yourself—you didn't believe me. Perhaps you simply weren't able to, but you wounded me, Jason, deeply, I'll admit it."

"Still," James said, "she shouldn't have said such a cruel thing about a son disbelieving his father, a father he admits never lied to him. I hope you set her straight, Jase."

"Yes, certainly. About what exactly?"

Douglas said, "That's all right. Don't tease yourself any more about it. Truth is, I've lived every day for the past five years worrying about you. I can still feel the wet of your blood against my palm. There was so much blood, Jason, and it was you who were bleeding—my son, who was a damned hero. I remember exactly how I felt, how all of us felt, when you were so ill, when we listened to your every breath, praying it wouldn't be your last. That sort of fear is corrosive, it burns into your gut and your heart." Douglas paused a moment, then said quietly, "You weren't the only one to suffer, Jason. Corrie killed two people. It's a tremendous burden she must carry the rest of her life, even though she would never regret what she did. She still has occasional nightmares. We, all of us, live with the past, Jason, you more than any of us. Perhaps it's time all of us consigned that wretched time to the ether. It's time we all let it go."

"I can't," Jason said, then paused. "Hallie said once that the only good she ever saw in remembering a painful event was that it might keep you from doing the same stupid thing again. But it's so much more than that. Damnation—nightmares? I'm very sorry about that. Poor Corrie, in addition to being a fool, I'm selfish. I didn't consider anyone except myself. Oh hell."

James said, "I say thank God for the passage of time. It blurs things, and you begin to realize how very lucky we all are, how very blessed. We all survived. We're here drinking brandy now, aren't we?"

"But I was to blame, I—"

Douglas said, "Tomorrow I will ride to Lyon's Gate and inform Hallie she isn't to treat you so badly again, that she is to comfort you, help you endure your lifelong misery. She is to stop being cold-hearted."

Jason said, "It's not that she's coldhearted. It's that what happened—it's so damned deep inside me that I'll never be free of it. I accept that. She must accept it too, she must."

"I will set her straight," Douglas said. "Trust me, Jason."

"No, please, Father, don't say anything to her. I must go now, I've kept you too long as it is."

"One more thing, Jason," his father said. Jason slowly turned. "Never forget that I love you, that I've loved you since you were in your mother's womb and I splayed my palm over her belly and felt the two of you trying to kick off my hand. When you came yelling your head off into the world, I believed there could be nothing sweeter in life. However, truth be told, at this moment, Jason, I'd like to kick you across the room."

Jason nearly fell over. "I don't understand."

"You don't?" James shook his head at his brother. "You said you left Lyon's Gate because Hallie was making fun of you. Do you mean she can't understand why, after five years, you're still wanting to drown yourself in guilt?"

"The way you're saying it doesn't sound reasonable, James. Surely you must understand that—" He fell silent because he couldn't find the words to say.

"Yes, we do understand," his father said. "I think

that after what happened five years ago, you desperately wanted to free all of us from your pain. You saw leaving England to be the answer. You thought we'd forget you, perhaps? That when we spoke of your triumphs in Baltimore, we'd not also remember you lying in bed with the physician digging that bloody bullet out of your shoulder, not remember that you nearly died? You are a blockhead, Jason."

"But I was the one who—"

Douglas said, "It has always amazed me how you so eagerly gave yourself all the credit for bringing about that particular tragedy. You were nothing more than a young man who held honor dear, who loved his family, who faced evil and didn't recognize it. And why should you? None of us had ever before been thrown into evil such as those three offered up. You ran away, Jason. I wish you had not, it nearly broke your brother, leaving him to deal with a new wife who'd had to kill two people, and every day face a mother and a father who would gladly have given their own lives for yours.

"And you survived, Jason. I believe you've survived fairly well. And now you have a wife who, if I'm not mistaken, would also give her life for you. Go home, Jason. Go face yourself, and the past, and think about your present and future. Both look remarkably fine to me. Oh yes, I got a letter from James Wyndham. He and his family will be here in three weeks and they're bringing you a thoroughbred you trained yourself for a wedding present."

"Which one?"

"I believe James Wyndham said his name is Eclipse, after our own very famous Eclipse."

Jason said absently, "Eclipse never lost a race. He was amazing. Stubbs painted him."

"Yes," Douglas said. "All right. James Wyndham said his little girl Alice named him."

"Yes," Jason said, "yes, she did." He walked to his brother and hugged him tightly. Then he stood a moment, looking at his father from a distance of six feet. He felt tears rise in his throat. "Papa, I—"

"Uncle Jason!"

"Uncle Jason!"

Two small boys, their white nightshirts flapping around their ankles, burst into the room, arms raised.

Jason stared down at the two beloved little boys. Life always moved on. Even as he gathered up both of them tightly against him, the tears dried in his eyes and in his heart. "What are you two devils doing awake this late?"

Everett gave him a wet kiss on the neck. Douglas was squeezing his neck so hard he nearly broke it. "We heard Mama arguing with herself."

Jason nodded. "That would arouse my curiosity as well. Ah, Mother, you're awake too?"

Alex came over to peel one of the boys off Jason's shoulder. "I'm here to rescue you. No, Everett, no waltzing tonight. It's time for the two of you to get back into bed."

After no more than two minutes of whining, at which point James said, "That is enough. You will both be silent. Kiss your uncle good night. You will see him again soon. I will come up in a moment and tuck you in."

Douglas shook his head at his wife. "I believe I said the same thing to him and Jason."

"Very probably. Innumerable times. Are you all right, Jason?"

Jason hugged his mother, stepped back. "Don't worry about me, Mama. I'm off." He paused a moment, then said, "I missed all you so very much when I was in Baltimore, please never doubt that."

James said as they listened to Jason's boot steps receding on the tile floor, "I am going to give Hallie anything she wants."

His father smiled.

CHAPTER 40

❧❦❧

❧ At the breakfast table the following morning, Hallie said brightly, "It's been nearly a week since the Beckshire race. What are we going to do about Lord Grimsby?"

Jason said as he smeared honey on his toast, "Those are the first words out of your mouth since I slammed out of the house last night and left you alone with Petrie and Martha."

"I saw you ride back and knew you were all right."

Of course she would wait up for him. "I slept in Angela's room."

"Yes, I know. I hope you slept well?"

"Not very, but it doesn't matter." He became suddenly very stiff and formal. "I wish to apologize for my melodrama last night, Hallie."

"Yours wasn't the melodrama." Even when he raised his eyebrow in question, she simply shook her head, said nothing more.

"I see, you're going to be mysterious about this. I was hopeful that yesterday would be the day I'd be off to see Lord Grimsby, but it wasn't. I am hopeful, however, about today." He pulled out the watch from his vest pocket and consulted it.

"Now you're being mysterious."

"Yes, I am, aren't I? Well, we'll see. I would imagine he's wondering why the devil I'm waiting this long, particularly since he knows we have Kindred."

Hallie said, "Perhaps he thinks you've forgotten about it since it seems to be the done thing. When will you be ready? What does your seeing him depend upon?"

He only smiled at her.

"Very well, be a closemouthed trout-brain, as Martha would say."

"As mysterious as my wife."

"That's different, but no matter. Now, I have a wonderful surprise for you, Jason," and she beamed at him.

An eyebrow went straight up. "You're pregnant?"

She dropped her slice of toast. "Oh dear, I don't know. I don't think so."

"You haven't had your woman's monthly flow since we've been married."

"Oh blessed hell, is that true? But I'm not always— Jason, that is very private. I don't wish to speak of it."

"I'm your husband. You're to speak to me about everything."

"No, surely not."

"My father always said it's very important for a wife to tell her husband everything. Tell me your surprise."

Pregnant? Her flow was erratic but she wasn't about to discuss that with him. She couldn't imagine such a thing. It floored her that he would bring it up so easily. She took a bite of her toast, cleared her throat, and said, "At the race, you remember the other man, the one who actually shot Lorry, the one we didn't catch—"

"Yes, of course, I can't find out who he is, dammit. Kindred won't tell me a bloody thing. He won't even admit to a bloody thing."

She looked at the clock beside the sideboard, gave him a fat smile. "Because I'm an excellent wife and partner, I am serving him up to you on a platter. Henry and Quincy should walk up to the front door with him very soon now."

"The man who shot Lorry? What is this, Hallie? What are you talking about?"

"Early this morning, I had an informative encounter with Kindred. He told me the other man's name. It's Potter He's also a stable lad for Lord Grimsby. He blamed Potter for everything, of course."

Jason stared at his wife. "You're telling me that Kindred spilled his guts simply because you *asked* him? I can't believe that, Hallie. I threatened Kindred several times with a long voyage to Botany Bay, but still he wouldn't tell me a single thing, claimed over and over, he was smoking his silver pipe when a rock comes flashing through the air to strike him in the head. I can't believe he told you."

"Big threats weren't working on him, so I made a believable threat. Kindred said the 'little bugger must believe he's all safe'—and Kindred spit then—so I don't think he was sorry to give up Potter's name to me."

He could but stare at her, this young woman who'd broken a man's nearly weeklong silence early this very morning. He didn't know whether to be happy or howl because she'd done it and he hadn't. "Hallie, what did you threaten? Not to cut off his manhood, I hope."

"Oh no, that's not believable."

"Tell me."

Hallie sat forward, rested her chin on her steepled fingers.

"I told Kindred that I would strip him naked and have him walk behind my horse, hands bound in front of him, tethered to a rope. I told him we would ride all hereabouts—visit with every soul in the village, see all his relatives, his friends, his enemies, visit Lord Grimsby and the stables, and I would tell everyone what he'd done, and this would be the punishment for anyone who ever tried to harm either our horses or jockeys. He didn't choose to believe me. He laughed, called me a cute little girlie, and surely I couldn't be such a bold chit."

Jason hadn't realized what an excellent storyteller she was. He paused a beat, then, "And?"

"I had him stripped to his dirty hide, his hands tied together and looped to the end of a rope. I rode Charlemagne, holding the other end. He cursed, yelled I wasn't a cute little girlie at all, and called me unnatural, among other charming names. When we were no farther than one hundred feet beyond Lyon's Gate, just getting a good start toward the village, he gave it up. He screamed out Potter's name, swore that Lord Grimsby had told Potter to visit his brother in Cranston until everyone forgot about the race. He cursed again and said it wasn't fair that Dodger still won, that he bet Lord Grimsby wasn't happy about that."

Jason didn't want to picture Kindred naked in his mind, but he did. Not an appetizing vision. Kindred was tall, but he had thin legs and a chest that sank inward. He had hair everywhere. Even on his back? He wasn't about to ask his wife. "So Henry and Quincy went after this Potter fellow."

"Yes. The key is to follow through on the threat. One must even be prepared to up the ante for repeat bad behavior. While I had him naked in the middle of the road, I told him if he personally ever tried to harm any of our horses or jockeys again, I would have his mother-in-law lead him about. The idiot said she didn't like horses, to which I replied that she could ride in my lovely gig on a delightful sunny day, with him trotting behind her. He believed me. I told him to spread this around since it would be the official Lyon's Gate punishment for any trouble at the racetrack."

"Did Kindred tell you Lord Grimsby threatened him if he ever opened his mouth?"

"Oh yes. I simply said that a threat in the hand was worth any number of unseen threats in a bush, didn't he think so? Then I looked him up and down, told him that the bunions on his toes were very unappealing." She threw back her head and laughed and laughed, so pleased she was with herself.

Jason joined her, couldn't help himself. What she'd done was worthy of Jessie Wyndham. When she was hiccupping and sipping water, he said, "Of course he believed you, since he was bare to the hide. Well, that's that. You've taken care of everything." Was that sour grapes in his voice? Jason was appalled at himself.

His wife was grinning at him, shaking her head. "Oh no, I merely scooped up the pawns. You're going to flatten the black king."

"Calling him a black king is giving him too much gravitas."

"He's only the first in a series of black kings who will know your anger." He realized she was perfectly serious. He felt something expand deep inside him, something that made him feel grand, filled with energy and contentment. He realized it was conceit. "I haven't yet been to confront Lord Grimsby because I wanted to know exactly why Elgin Sloane and Charles Grandison and he were so bloody close. I set inquiries in motion six days ago."

"But you didn't tell me."

"You didn't tell me what you were going to do with Kindred either. Don't whine. The fact is that I would prefer to strip Lord Grimsby naked like you did Kindred. Unfortunately I don't think I could get away with it."

"Talk about an appalling sight— Oh well, I think that was very smart of you, Jason." He heard admiration in her voice and it sent warmth flooding through him.

Petrie appeared in the doorway. "Master Jason, there is a small man here to see you. Very small in stature, not, I hope, in character. He says it is urgent."

Jason tossed his napkin on his plate and rose. "That sounds like Mr. Clooney. Maybe I'll be visiting Lord Grimsby this morning after all."

She wanted desperately to go with him; she was his partner after all, but she knew deep in that well of knowledge she was convinced women were born with, that this was something he had to handle himself. She knew it was, simply, men dealing with men, drawing boundaries, meting out retribution for breaking rules.

"What about Elgin and Charles Grandison?"

"I'll be sending a message over to Lord Grimsby, asking him to have them there when I arrive, if, that is, Mr. Clooney has answers for me."

Hallie said, "I wonder if all three of them paid to have Kindred and Potter shoot Lorry."

He smiled. "Elgin doesn't have any money. Would Charles do that? I wouldn't have thought so." She never looked away from his stern face, so beautiful in the morning sunlight streaking through the window that she wanted to weep. Or swoon, like Cook, and sing arias.

She said, "Will you take Potter and Kindred with you to confront Lord Grimsby?"

"No," Jason said, "it's not necessary." He strode to her, leaned down to kiss her mouth, and gave her a blinding smile. "I'm going to nail his butt to the stable door."

"Whose?"

Jason laughed, patted her cheek.

"Master Jason."

"Yes, Petrie? You're still here, watching everything?"

"Certainly, it is my duty. I wished to say that your boots shine much brighter this morning than the mistress's."

Jason looked at his face in his shiny boots presented to him that morning by Petrie.

"It is my opinion, sir, that her use of anise seed is overrated."

Jason said to Hallie, "I told Petrie to write to Old Fudds and find out the exact measurement since I doubted you would tell him."

"That's true," Hallie said. "Still, you did well, Petrie."

Petrie preened.

"Ah, listen. I hear Cook singing, and that means she's scrambling your eggs as we speak, with just a pinch of thyme, the way you like them. Are you coming back to eat them?"

"Hallie," he said. "Do you know that last night I realized how simply saying your name— Oh, Petrie, are you still lurking? Go see to Mr. Clooney's comfort. I will be along in a moment. Go. As I said—merely mentioning your name, even in passing, makes me feel warm all the way to my heels."

"I'm very glad about that. Oh, the devil. I'll tell you, why not? I love you, Jason Sherbrooke, even though Cook will never scramble eggs specially for me like she does for you."

She loved him? It amazed him, nearly brought him to his knees, nearly pulled a shout of pleasure right out of his mouth. He said, "I don't deserve it."

"Possibly not, but what am I to do? It's there, deep inside me, this love for you, and I know it will never go away. You don't have to say anything, Jason. Tell Cook that you're bequeathing your lovely scrambled eggs to me this morning."

"It's done." He gave her another quick hard kiss on her mouth, and was gone.

When Cook came into the dining room a few minutes later, Hallie said, "Master Jason said I could eat his eggs."

Mrs. Millsom nodded sadly. "Yes, the beautiful young master apologized to me, told me it was not to be."

She looked ready to burst into tears.

"He is meeting with a man right this minute, Mrs. Millsom or I know he would be here."

But Cook wasn't listening. She carried the plate of scrambled eggs in her arms like a baby, walked to the windows and looked out. When she saw the master striding toward the stables, she shouted at the top of her lungs, "Master Jason, come back before your eggs disappear down the mistress's gullet! Bring the scrawny little man with you!"

Hallie heard him shout back, "Mrs. Millsom, please let the mistress eat my eggs this morning. She's very possibly with child and I want my heir to grow big and strong."

Mrs. Millsom whipped about to stare at her.

Hallie shrugged. "One never knows. Give me the eggs, Mrs. Millsom. The last thing we want is a paltry heir."

"Eat them all mistress. Soon now you'll be puking up your innards in the mornings."

"That is not a happy thought, Mrs. Millsom."

CHAPTER 41

❧❧

❧ Two hours later, Jason rode Dodger up the curv-
ing, oak-canopied drive to Lord Grimsby's manor
house, Abbott Grange. He imagined lengthening the
drive to Lyon's Gate, perhaps adding a couple of
curves for interest, and planting oaks like these. In
twenty years or so there would be a canopy of thick
green leaves over their heads as well. His father was
right. The future looked remarkably fine to him too.
He wondered if Hallie was indeed carrying his child.
Very possibly, he thought, very possibly indeed. He
grinned like a fool and whistled one of the duchess's
ditties.

It was a warm day, the sun bright and strong overhead, wild roses bloomed over stone fences, and
sweat made his shirt stick to his back. He saw a single

peacock sweeping about on the front lawn, tail feathers spread, and wondered where the recipient of all this glory was hiding. Peahens, he knew, were notoriously fickle.

He left Dodger in the care of a stable lad he'd seen at the Beckshire race. The lad looked nervous, understandably so, given he had to know Jason held Kindred. Jason leaned close. "You must be quite shorthanded since I have both Kindred and Potter. You'll take good care of Dodger, won't you, lad?"

"Oh yes, sir, yes I will. He's a lovely boy, strong teeth he's got, and the Devil's eyes."

"You mean he's got mean eyes?"

"Oh no, sir, he's got eyes that see every sin a man's ever committed."

"I trust he won't see you commit any sins." Jason patted Dodger's neck. He watched the lad give Dodger a carrot while he hummed at him in a lovely deep voice.

Lord Grimsby's butler, a droopy-eyed old man who looked ready to sink to the floor in a stupor, looked Jason up and down and said in the booming young voice, "I don't see why my master is so afraid of you, young man. I imagine you smile and the angels sing, but who cares? Ever since the Beckshire races, you've fair to made him gibber like that idiot peacock."

"Perhaps you will soon gibber as well," Jason said, and gave him a smile meant to intimidate, which only made the old man say, "You're right handsome, sir, too handsome, my master says. Lady Grimsby says his jealousy is pathetic." He paused, cocked his head a moment. "Yes, I hear angels singing right this moment. Follow me, young sir, and let's see if his lordship will see you."

Jason grinned at the back of the butler's bald head as he followed him to the drawing room. He lightly touched his hand to the old man's arm. "You needn't announce me. Allow me the pleasure." Jason tapped once on the closed door and walked in.

He hummed with pleasure at the sight of Charles Grandison and Elgin Sloane, both sprawled in chairs, listening to Lord Grimsby. All three here and accounted for. Since they'd gotten here quickly, it meant they were worried. When they turned toward him, their expressions were identical—boys caught stealing the vicar's sacramental wine.

"Good morning, gentlemen. I am pleased Lord Grimsby got you here so very quickly."

"Yes," Lord Grimsby said, not rising from his chair. He looked wary and ill-tempered. Well, in all fairness, he had been two stable hands short for nearly a week.

"Let me say first of all, my lord, that Kindred is fine, at least for the moment."

"Kindred did you say? I fired Kindred a number of months ago. I don't know who he's working for now. But not me. Now see here, Jason—"

Jason smiled. "Hello, Charles. Elgin. I can see that the three of you are very intent on some project."

Charles said, "May I ask what your wife is doing to poor Kindred?"

"Preparing him for a long voyage to Botany Bay?"

"Botany Bay! That's bloody absurd."

"Who cares," Elgin said. "The silly blighter got himself caught."

Charles Grandison said, "Don't you think Botany Bay is a bit extreme, Jason?"

Jason merely smiled.

"You come here to threaten my former stable lad with deportation to Botany Bay? Good riddance to him. Kindred always was a troublemaker, that's why I dismissed him. There's nothing more to be said. You may leave us now."

"Oh no."

Lord Grimsby eyed him for a moment, then got control of himself. "What do you want, Jason? Why did you want to see all of us? It's a damned impertinence, boy. Oliphant shouldn't have let you in, damned mince-head."

"I intimidated him, my lord."

"That's not possible. The old relic doesn't see well enough anymore to be intimidated."

Charles said, as he lazily flicked a bit of lint off his sleeve, "Surely, Jason, one doesn't ship a man to Botany Bay because one believes he might have planned to shoot a gun at the racetrack. Everyone has discussed it, and all agree that the fellow who shot your jockey is the one you need to find, not this poor Kindred fellow."

"Actually, I'm pleased to tell you that I have the

man who actually shot my jockey." He smiled at Lord Grimsby. "Potter sends his regards, my lord. He isn't very happy at this point because Kindred told him what his punishment will be. According to my wife, it will take a good four hours to complete."

"Potter? That nitwit? He knows nothing, Jason, nothing at all."

"My men found him where Kindred said he'd be—at his brother's cottage in Cranston, scared to his toes. He and Kindred both have told me of your instructions, my lord. At least you didn't order them to kill any horse or jockey, merely disable the horse that looked like it would win, if, that is, any horse was ahead of Lamplighter."

Charles roared to his feet and advanced on Lord Grimsby. "You would have had one of your villains shoot my Ganymede?"

"Don't be absurd, Charles. Sit down. Jason is trying to set us against each other."

Jason said, "Yes, Charles, if Ganymede had been the clear leader, why then, I fancy he or your jockey would have gotten a ball of lead in him."

"No, that's a lie. Elgin, tell him that's a lie."

"It's a lie, Charles. If I were to believe the lie, why then, that would mean Brutus was also at risk. My uncle would never seek to harm a horse that belonged to my heiress."

Jason said, "I fancy Lord Grimsby would shoot whatever needed shooting for Lamplighter to win. But, Charles, feel free to believe what you wish to believe."

Lord Grimsby exploded, "Now, listen here, Jason. This is racing! All sorts of things are done in racing, a bit of mischief, a bit of pain, it's simply part of the sport, it doesn't alarm anyone, it adds excitement and suspense."

Charles said, "Actually, it makes me rather rabid. You know my reputation, my lord. You surely wouldn't be such a fool as to disregard the punishments I mete out if anyone, let me repeat, *anyone* tries to harm my horses."

"Of course I do. I'm not a fool. That's why this is all nonsense. Besides, you're different, Charles, you take it all too seriously."

Elgin said, "Will you punish Jason, Charles? After all, his jockey kicked yours off Ganymede."

"That's true enough, Charles, can I expect a visit from you?"

"No," Charles said.

"Good, since your jockey started the whole business in the first place," Jason said. He turned back to Lord Grimsby. "My lord, what if one of the other owners had shot Lamplighter?"

"I'd kill the blighter."

"Just so," Charles said and took a sip of his tea.

"Dammit, boy, none of this makes any difference. Listen to me now. It was just a flesh wound, nothing of any importance at all. Dodger still managed to win the race, so what's there to say?"

"You wish me to tell my jockey that the bullet wound in his arm added nothing more than some lovely color to his racing livery?"

"A tear through the flesh, nothing more," Elgin Sloane said.

"Ah, Elgin, how did you know it was only a flesh wound?"

"Everyone from here to London knows about it. Mr. Blaystock was quite upset. He wished the bullet had been more true, that it had at least knocked your jockey off that damned Dodger, so that his Brutus would have then won."

Charles tsked. "Ganymede would have won if Jason's jockey hadn't kicked my jockey off his back. No, Elgin, Brutus wouldn't have won no matter how many horses' rumps he'd managed to bite, an interesting ploy, I admit, but doesn't Mr. Blaystock find it somewhat unpredictable?" He turned to Lord Grimsby. "I find myself wondering, sir, if your Lamplighter were to run a straight race if he would beat Ganymede. I tend to doubt it, though Lamplighter is a fine animal. Had there been a straight race between Ganymede and Dodger, I am sure in my own mind that Ganymede would have taken the prize."

Jason said, "Dodger ran as straight a race as he could. It took Lorry time to kick back at your jockey, Charles. I wish it hadn't been necessary, but you know it was. Listen to me, all of you. At the very least all these shenanigans distract the horses and the jockeys. I've always believed it would be better to let the horses run without interference."

"That will never happen," Lord Grimsby said.

"Never in a thousand years. Jockeys like to use their whips, like to kick their opponents, like to squeeze in on a horse until he falls back. As for the horses, they're devious, it's bred into them. Mr. Blaystock told me Brutus was born to bite. Horses would be so bored if they didn't fight that they wouldn't run their best. They need distractions to keep them going."

Jason said, "Dodger doesn't need distractions, he doesn't like them, nor do I." He didn't say that Eclipse, however, kicked up his back legs when he felt a horse getting too close, something he'd done naturally the first time he raced. "However, don't you believe there must be a line drawn?"

Lord Grimsby shrugged. "It happens. It will always happen. If you're serious about racing, Jason, you'll accustom yourself to the way it's done."

Charles said, shaking his head, "Five hundred pounds, that is quite a purse Dodger took, Jason. I imagine you also bet a good amount for Dodger to win. I myself wagered a couple of pounds on him, the odds were so long. Do you mind if I ask what you won?"

"Ten thousand pounds or thereabouts. All my relatives did well too. I've also gotten notes of thanks from others who wagered on Dodger to win."

"That's not fair," Elgin Sloane said bitterly. "No one told me how very fast Dodger was, how well trained. Damnation, you have a female for a partner. Who would believe you would know what you're doing? It's simply not fair. At least there won't be long odds again. Why didn't you tell me, Charles?"

"I myself didn't realize how very fast he was, Elgin. I only won a couple hundred pounds, nothing really."

Jason said, "Do I wish you well, Elgin? Will you be marrying Brutus's mistress?"

"Yes. Thank God she isn't like Hallie. She knows nothing about horses and would be disgusted were she to have to witness a mating. She knows when to yell her head off at the races and that's enough for any woman. Her father doesn't know much more, except biting. He enjoys seeing his horses bite the competition."

"Then you'll have a free hand," Jason said. He walked to the fireplace to lean against the mantel, arms folded over his chest. "Charles, do you recall telling me that no one tried to shoot either your jockeys or horses because the consequences were so painful?"

Charles Grandison nodded.

"Hallie and I agreed that we would outdo you if anyone had the nerve to try to cause us harm. I am here to tell Lord Grimsby of his punishment."

"Now, see here—"

"My lord," Charles said in a sigh, stretching his long legs out in front of him, "did I not tell you not to try your skullduggery on Jason? Did I not tell you that he was a serious man? Look at what he did to my jockey for a small jostle during the race."

"Yes, but he knows nothing about racing, nothing at all! He raced in America, the former *Colonies*, for

God's sake. There is nothing there, nothing remarkable, including horses or jockeys."

"Actually, the Americans have skullduggery down to a fine art. I hated it there as well."

"You won the damned race, Jason. You said you were going to announce my punishment? You young pup, your father won't allow you to do anything to me, why I've known him and your mother since before you and your twin were born."

"That's a very long time, my lord," Jason said, and shook his head. "That's why I am surprised you would be so stupid. Can you imagine my father ever allowing anyone to harm someone close to him?"

"Your father understands racing, understands the risks, the challenges, the little eccentricities. Another thing, you are not your father. All know never to cross him, or there's hell to pay."

"You're right, I am not my father. Actually, both James and I are much meaner. Now, I have weighed both Kindred's and Potter's guilt in this matter. I'm not sending them to Botany Bay. My wife has devised a much more effective punishment. You will see two very chastened men when they return here. I imagine news of their punishment will spread. Everyone will hear about it. It will be more and more difficult for owners to find minions to do their mischief. As for you, sir, as I've said, I've decided upon your punishment."

"Impudent puppy!"

"You won't race for a full year, indeed, not until the Beckshire race next August."

Lord Grimsby jumped to his feet, his face crimson, shaking his fist in Jason's face. "You can't give me orders like that, you young bastard! I won't stand for it. Get out of my house!"

CHAPTER 42

❧❦

❧ Charles said, "Jason, don't misunderstand me, I think it's excellent retribution. But tell me how you will prevent Lord Grimsby from racing for a year."

"You've used beatings against the actual miscreants, Charles, and you wounded two owners in duels when they shot one of your jockeys and one of your horses. I don't like duels, they're too dangerous, the outcome too unpredictable. And they are against the law. I don't fancy having to haul my wife off to the Continent or back to Baltimore because I got caught after shooting some fool racehorse owner. No, I prefer something more bloodless, but infinitely more painful."

Lord Grimsby looked faintly alarmed now. "I will race, damn you! What is bloodless?"

Jason said in a very low voice to Lord Grimsby, "You will not race for a year, sir, or else Elgin Sloane, this precious relative of yours, won't be allowed near Elsie Blaystock. Indeed, her father might shoot him. I will also see to it that every heiress he wants, flies away. And what, I ask you, will happen to Elgin's family if he is unable to provide for them?"

"You can't do that," Elgin said, alarmingly pale now, sitting forward in his chair. "I didn't do anything to your damned jockey—he did. I'm not to blame."

"Then you'd best convince Lord Grimsby to agree to my terms. Just as you convinced him to push your suit with Hallie Carrick."

Lord Grimsby waved his fist in Elgin's nose. "You try to convince me of anything, and I'll break your bloody face, you paltry excuse for a man! Besides, there is no way Jason can prevent you from marrying Elsie Blaystock or any other heiress you choose. I have some power here. I can forestall anything he'd try to do. I know you must have money. I'll see that you wed." He whirled back to Jason. "Of course he must have money for his family."

Jason said pleasantly, "That is the big concern, isn't it, sir?"

"Of course it is," Lord Grimsby said as he began pacing. He paused to shake his fist in Jason's direction, then gave Elgin a look of pure hate.

Charles said, "I fancy, dear Jason, that your father will assist you."

Jason smiled. "He would, if I asked him, but I

don't see the need, at least in Lord Grimsby's case. He will do as I ask, with only my boot lowered to his neck. As for Elgin here, I fancy my father would enjoy speaking to Mr. Blaystock about who his daughter marries."

Elgin Sloane raised his head. "I beg you, sir, agree not to race for a year. I must wed, I must, or all will be lost. A word from Lord Northcliffe, and Elsie's father would shut the door in my face. I need her, sir, very much. I need her now."

"That's true enough, Elgin," Charles said, "but it's the horses you really want. You can see yourself, the proud son-in-law, owning a big stud farm."

"Perhaps that is a part to it, Charles, and why not?"

Jason said quietly to Elgin, "Remind Lord Grimsby about Elaine."

Elgin's jaw dropped. "You know about Elaine? But how?"

"Actually," Jason shrugged, "I know everything."

Lord Grimsby said, staring at Jason, "You do?"

Elgin said, "He's right, sir. You must do as he says, else I won't marry Elsie and my sweet sister will starve in a ditch. Already she has no governess, I can't afford one. She is alone, and will not have a roof over her head unless I wed very soon."

Jason said, "Did you hear him, my lord? Elgin is concerned that Elaine will starve. What do you think, sir?"

Lord Grimsby rounded on Elgin, ignoring Jason. "You damned idiot, you foolish ass! You could have married Hallie Carrick, beautiful and rich she was, but no, you had to sleep with some bucktoothed matron during your betrothal! Naturally she found out and broke it off! Then you were married to Anne Cavendish. Just look at how you mucked that up. Her father tied up her dowry and she had the nerve to die. Now, enough of this. You will bring your sister here to me—rather your half-sister—and that's an end to it." Lord Grimsby waved his fist in Elgin's face.

"Oh no, sir."

"Damn you, she belongs with me. My wife wants her here. Bring her to me!"

Elgin said, "I will never give up my leverage. I'm Elaine's guardian and I will remain her guardian. You will continue to do as I tell you, sir. You will not race for a year."

"I'll kill you!"

Jason said, "No, sir, he's not worth it. I've found there are always reasons for a man's behavior. One must find out what they are. It didn't take me long to discover why you've suffered this idiot in your home, given a ball in his honor, tried to find him a rich wife. How long have you known Elaine was your daughter, Lord Grimsby? Like I told you, I know everything sir, no reason to lie anymore."

He whirled around to Jason. "I would tell the world about her, if it weren't for this bastard making his damned threats. I've known since before she was born, so did Elgin's father. He threatened to make her a servant in his own house unless I paid him well. And now his son does the same thing. Rotters, both of them. My wife wants her with us. We have no children and Elaine is but ten years old. She's ours, she shouldn't be under this idiot's thumb."

Jason said, "And you, Charles? I'm not quite sure how you fit into this puzzle."

"I'm not a big mystery, Jason. I was only trying to help Lord Grimsby. I've always known about poor little Elaine, how Elgin has used her for a bargaining chip, learned it from his father. Poor little girl, I feel for her. I must say I'm impressed with how quickly you've gained your information. You are talented, Jason."

"Just don't ever try to hurt my horses," Jason said. He turned to Lord Grimsby. "You will agree not to race for a full year, my lord. All will know that you are being punished for your misdeeds, and all will know they run a huge risk if they try anything against my jockeys or horses in the future. Do you agree, sir? One year of not racing? I'm perfectly ready to help you gain what you wish."

"What do you mean by that?"

Jason nodded to the open doorway. Lord Grimsby looked up to see his wife standing there. She'd heard everything, he knew it. The woman had ears like Elgin. Lord Grimsby said slowly, "I will agree not to race for a year if you make Elgin give me my daughter. I mean give her to me legally. My wife and I wish to adopt her. Then I won't have to ever speak to this nincompoop again. Can you do it?"

"Of course, sir. Elgin?" Jason's voice was very soft, the voice he always used to gain instant attention and compliance from every child he'd ever met. "You will have Elaine here within the next three days. Lord Grimsby's solicitor will see to the adoption. Then you may marry your heiress."

"No, I won't give up my leverage. My father told me I could dine on this until Lord Grimsby croaked. Oh damn! It's not fair." He fell silent, his hands clasped between his knees. He looked ready to cry. He said finally, "I want that racing stud. Blaystock is a fool, knows nothing about anything. Did you hear the idiot shouting for Brutus to bite the horses in front of him? He has no finesse, no imagination." He turned to Charles. "Do you assure me that Blaystock is very rich?"

"As rich as Croesus until the Persians planted their heels on his neck."

Slowly, Elgin nodded. "I would certainly rather marry Elsie Blaystock than Hallie Carrick. She doesn't show the proper respect for a man, doesn't forgive him for small, really insignificant blunders. She doesn't shut her mouth and she's too smart by half. I am in her father's debt for convincing me she wouldn't make me a good wife."

Jason smiled. "She forgives my blunders."

"That's just because you're so damned pretty," Elgin said, and waved a fist toward Jason.

"Pretty is as pretty does," Charles Grandison said, and rose. "What a morning it's been. I believe I am no longer needed here. My lord, my lady, I wish you the greatest happiness with Elaine. She's charming. Elgin, I doubt I'll be attending your nuptials. I would like to keep Jason as a friend in the future, you see. Jason, I'll see you at the Grantham races next month."

"I'll be racing two horses," Jason said as he shook Charles's hand. "James Wyndham is bringing Eclipse over to me. He was born and bred in Baltimore."

"Eclipse?" Elgin said. "He's been dead for years and years. He wasn't bred in America."

"The same name and, I hope, a similar future. I believe my Eclipse may be as fast as Dodger."

"An American horse named Eclipse, just what we need," Charles said. "What do you say we try to make this one a straight race?"

"I know that Kindred and Potter will spread the word."

"What is your punishment?"

"You'll find out soon enough," Jason said. When he took his leave a few moments later, Lady Grimsby stopped him at the front door. "Thank you, Jason. How I've hated all this deception, hated having to pander to this paltry young man. I have wanted Elaine since she was born, you see. How very grateful I am to my husband for making you his victim. Thank you for what you have accomplished. Give my regards to your lovely wife."

Jason's lovely wife was sitting on the ground, covered with dust, yelling at the top of her lungs at

Charlemagne, who'd thrown her trying to get to the mare who'd been delivered to Dodger.

Jason pulled her up, dusted her off, kissed her nose. "I've been thinking. Why don't we breed a mare to Charlemagne? He's a bighearted fellow, arrogant as his namesake. Who knows, with the proper mare, we might produce a legend."

"Charlemagne, a legend," Hallie said, and laughed.

CHAPTER 43

❖•❖

Lyon's Gate
Ten Months Later

❦ Jason would later swear her scream shook the house. After all these interminable hours, he couldn't imagine she'd have the breath, much less the strength to yell, but she did. He thought the bones in his hand would break she squeezed so tightly.

"She's getting there," Dr. Blood shouted over that scream. "Not long now. A bit over nine hours, not too long at all."

Hallie slitted her eyes up at Theodore Blood, who was racing mad and liked nothing more than to be invited to Lyon's Gate to watch Dodger and Eclipse train, and panted, "Nine hours isn't long, you buffoon? Why don't we trade places?"

He paled—Jason would swear that Theo paled. He didn't blame him. He himself was exhausted, out of his mind with worry, but compared to the pain she was enduring, it was nothing. He leaned close, kissed her. "Theo would apologize for that stupid remark, but he's too close to babbling with fear. Now, sweetheart, that was a really meaty yell. Do it again, that's it. It won't be long now."

She screamed, gone from him for a long moment.

Jason cursed, wiped her sweaty forehead with a cool, wet cloth. "I'm so sorry, curse me some more, that will make it better. Your father said Genny encouraged you to learn new ones just last month."

"I didn't believe her," Hallie said. "I'm as stupid as Theo. I didn't believe her." Her grip on his hand tightened. "Oh damn you, Jason. I hope you rot in the deepest pit in Hell, you and all men, you miserable, horse-breathed toad—" She broke off, panting, then she was gone again, whimpering. Then she screamed again, her back arching off the bed. Jason felt the contraction rip through her. Theo out-yelled her. "You've done it, Hallie! Nearly there. Push, Hallie. Push! Now, that's it."

"Damn you to the blackest pit with the rest of the idiot men—oh God, oh God—"

"Push!"

She gritted her teeth and pushed.

Jason said, "That's it, sweetheart. That's it, my beautiful brave girl."

Hallie yelled at him between pants, "You pickle-eyed Satan, that's what you said to Piccola when she was birthing her foal!" and she yelled again through her gritted teeth.

At a nod from Theo, Jason said, "Again, Hallie, again!"

"I am pushing, curse your black soul and your sinful smiles that landed me in this mess in the first place."

"Ah, I've got him! Ah, yes, it's a boy and he's perfect. Oh my, you should listen to those lungs, loud as his mother's—but wait, what's this, oh my, another one—it's another baby, oh goodness me, this is a surprise, but it shouldn't be now, should it? Oh dear, I didn't think, didn't guess, and I should have. Yes, Hallie, push, but not much. I don't have enough hands! Jason, come here now!"

Jason caught his daughter in his outstretched hands. She opened a tiny mouth and yelled as loud as her brother. He stared down at the tiny being in his hands, at the fingers that were no larger than the splinters Jason had pulled out of Henry's thumb yesterday. Theo and the midwife, Mrs. Hanks, who were both laughing at this unexpected surprise, quickly got themselves together. Mrs. Hanks took the babe from Jason, saying over and over, "Isn't this just grand? Two of them at once, another set of twins in the family. Oh, isn't she beautiful? Just like her daddy."

"And her brother."

Jason looked over at Theo Blood, who held his son, singing to him even as he cleaned him up. Neither of them stopped yelling. He quickly washed and dried his hands, then leaned over Hallie, and wiped the sweat off her face. "They're perfect," he said, and kissed her.

"They're incredible, Hallie, you're incredible. You've given me two babes, a boy and a girl. Oh God, this is too much for a man to take in."

"If you faint, Jason," Theo called out, "I will announce it in the *London Gazette*. Keep yourself together."

Jason laughed. "I won't let you down now, sweetheart, though I do feel a bit light-headed. How do you feel?"

Hallie was beyond words. The endless pain was gone, truly gone. It was over. She was alive, and she, like Jason, was staring over toward the fireplace, watching Theo and Mrs. Hanks bathe and wrap the babes in soft white wool.

Her babes. She'd birthed two babes. She wanted to hold them, to feel their small bodies, have them yell right in her face.

"They're both perfect, Hallie," Theo called out. "Small, but perfect. Give me another moment and I'll make sure you're perfect as well. Ah, what a remarkable exhibition of lung power. Did either of you hear what I said over the yells?"

Jason nodded. He couldn't take it in. He leaped to his feet, ran out of the bedchamber, raced down the corridor to grab the banister at the top of the stairs to keep himself from hurtling down. "We've got twins! Corrie, James, help, we need your hands. Everyone else, don't move! Everything is all right."

Corrie and James came running. Theo handed the little boy to Corrie and Mrs. Hanks handed James the little girl. James had meant to tell her what to do with that tiny screaming creature, but could do nothing but stare. He whispered, "Douglas and Everett were this small, weren't they? It's amazing. Oh God, Jase, we're both fathers."

While Theo tended Hallie, Jason, to distract her, continued to wipe her face with cool, damp cloths and kiss her—her mouth, her nose, her ear. "You've done it, given me two perfect babes, a boy and a girl this time." Jason laughed and wanted to weep. "I'll bring them to you in a moment. James and Corrie are seeing to them. Don't worry, I'll make certain they don't try to steal them, not after all the work you did. They're so small, James could ease them in his jacket pockets. Now, what do you want me to do to this pathetic doctor of yours whom I believed so smart? This brainless fellow didn't think it was two babes. He claimed you were just big. You were quite wrong, weren't you, Theo?"

"I'm a dolt."

"More loudly please," Jason said.

"I'M A DOLT."

"Good. Now, my sweet, sweaty girl, you need to rest. We'll decide later what we should do with this gourd-brained doctor."

Hallie was so very tired she wanted to sleep for at least a year. She felt battered and beaten-down and quite wonderful given that she had been cursing Jason only five minutes before. Her body felt surprisingly light. She moved her hand to her belly. "You said that to Piccola as well."

He grinned down at her.

"My belly's gone down again."

"Yes." He grabbed her hand, kissed her palm.

"Did I say anything to Theo I'll have to apologize for?"

"You don't have to apologize to the dolt."

"True," Theo said. "Besides, I've heard much worse."

Mrs. Hanks said, "Amen to that."

"One can but try," Hallie said.

"You showed good range, Hallie, excellent feeling, and the volume was more than adequate."

Hallie smiled at Theo Blood, their physician with the unfortunate name, who'd become an excellent friend to both her and Jason during the past six months. He took her hand, felt her pulse. After a moment, he nodded. "You're going to be fine. I see no problems, the bleeding isn't bad. I am a superb physician."

Jason leaned close to his wife and shut out the world. He ran the tip of his finger over her eyebrows. "I love you, Hallie. I love you. I mean it now. I'll mean it in fifty years. Sleep now."

"That sounds so very nice. You truly expect me to docilely fall asleep when I want to sing, Jason? Not dance though, I—" In the next moment, she was asleep.

Jason kissed her chapped lips, smoothed her sweaty hair back from her forehead, and rose. "My babes?"

"Beautiful," Corrie said. "And healthy, Jason, even though they're so small. They're all ready to meet their mother. Imagine, another set of twins. Goodness, she's the first little girl in the family. Jason, you must go downstairs and tell everyone before they come storming into the bedchamber."

Theo said as he tucked a soft blanket under Hallie's chin, "I hope you have another name hanging about, Jason."

"Hmm, other than Alec? Yes, I'm thinking—no, I must discuss it first with Hallie. If she ever wakes up."

Theo looked at his watch. "She fell asleep before she saw her babes. She'll be awake in not more than a minute from now."

"No, impossible. She's worked so hard, Theo, nine hours, she's exhausted, you're wrong about this just as you were about twins—"

"Jason, I want to see our babes."

Jason shouted with laughter. He looked over at his own twin. James was holding one of the babies in his big hands, Corrie holding the other one. He didn't deserve to be this happy or this lucky, but God had made it so. He prayed the twins would be all right, that they would grow up to have their own twins. He was blessed. Both he and James were blessed.

He cleared his throat. "Give me my babes. I want to show them to their mother."

When Jason cradled both babes in his arms, he felt his brother's hand on his shoulder. As had happened so many times in their lives, they shared the same thought: Life was sweet. They were the luckiest men in the world.

Theo said, rubbing his hands together, "I have done remarkably well. Everyone is healthy. So what if I was off by one babe?"

Douglas Sherbrooke's hand was raised to rap on the bedchamber door when he heard his sons' laughter.

He lowered his hand. *His* sons. He heard a tiny yell, and smiled. He prayed that life would continue doling out more laughter than tears. Then he heard a chorus of yells.

The yells continued, two distinct yells. Bedamned, another set of twins. The door opened. Jason whooped when he saw his father, and grabbed him close. "Hallie gave me a girl and a boy. I am surely the luckiest man alive."

"I rather thought I was," Douglas said, looking over to see James grinning at him. He nodded at his elder son and called out over his shoulder, "Alexandra, come listen to this lovely duet of yells from your new grandbabies."

EPILOGUE

※

Three Months Later

❧ No rain today, thank God, Jason thought, unlike the previous three days that had the twins yelling their heads off because they liked to lie on a nice thick blanket in the middle of the green lawn at Lyon's Gate, kicking their legs, flailing their arms and breathing the freshly scythed grass.

It was a beautiful day. Jason watched his wife, a babe under each arm, walk to the blankets he'd spread on the side lawn at Northcliffe Hall. The noon sun was bright overhead, and James's brindle racing cat was tearing across the lawn to run around Hallie three times before dashing back to James, who gave him a fresh slice of sea bass, told him what an elegant fast boy he was, and scratched the spot right in front of his tail. Alfred the Great purred like there was no tomorrow.

Douglas and Everett, now four years old, something Jason couldn't quite get his brain around, were sitting as quietly as they ever sat, watching their father train the year-old golden-eyed Alfred the Great.

Jason watched Hallie arrange the twins amid piles of pillows, then lean back on her elbows and raise her face to the blue sky. He felt his throat close as he watched her, such love swamped him. He was a lucky bastard, as his twin had told him just that morning, and he agreed. He was thirty years old, he had Hallie as his wife, and he was a father of two healthy children. Amazing. Even more amazing, or perhaps not, both babies looked like him, which meant they also looked like their cousins and their uncle James, which led back to Aunt Melissande, who'd smiled her incredibly beautiful smile when she'd seen them, while her husband, Uncle Tony, was heard to say, "Yet another generation of nauseatingly beautiful children in my wife's image. It fair to makes my teeth ache. Thank the good Lord that our three boys look like me. It adds balance to the world."

"Thank God you still have all your teeth," Aunt Melissande had said, and poked her husband in the ribs. He then kissed her hard on her mouth and the younger generation turned red to their eyebrows.

Jason heard a horse whinny, fancied it was his father's huge bay thoroughbred stallion, Caliper, who was going to be bred with Miss Matilda out of Charles Grandison's stud in two days. Lyon's Gate flourished. They'd won races, their reputation as a stud was growing. As for Lord Grimsby, he'd asked Jason to take Lamp-lighter, to train him, run him, and breed him, and all the winnings would be his. Lamplighter had won the Beckshire race a month before.

Jason closed his eyes, content for the moment to breathe in the scent of fresh grass along with his twins and his wife when he looked up to see his father and mother, Uncle Ryder and Aunt Sophie come out of the Hall. Soon the grounds would be overrun with Sherbrookes, even Aunt Sinjun and Uncle Colin from Scotland and Meggie and Thomas from Ireland, Meggie bringing three racing cats for the big cat race next week at the McCaulty racetrack, and their three boys, who helped train the cats.

Hallie said, "Jason, I need you as a father. Alec is hungry, again," she added quite unnecessarily.

Jason set up an umbrella to give his wife privacy, then picked up his daughter, grinned like a fool when she blew bubbles up at him, and watched Hallie feed Alec. She looked totally absorbed, crooning to the babe as he suckled frantically. Nesta rooted around Jason's chest to find a breast, and he laughed. "You'll have to wait, sweetheart, your mama's busy with your brother now."

Nesta wailed.

"Uncle Jason!"

"Uncle Jason!"

Douglas and Everett raced across the lawn toward him, dirty, rumpled, grins splitting their beloved little faces. No waltzing for them anymore; they were too old for that. Since Uncle Jason was holding Nesta, they didn't leap on him, but he could tell they wanted to, badly.

"We went fishing in the pond," Everett said.

"What did you catch?"

"Just a toad and a load of dirt," Douglas said. "Don't tell Mama, she'll tan us."

"She told us to stay clean for at least an hour. What time is it, Uncle Jason?"

"Nearly time for luncheon."

"It's nearly an hour, Everett. We're safe. Mama won't yell at us."

"How about your papa?"

"He'll throw us in the air and call us filthy grubs," Everett said. "Do you want to play with us now, Uncle Jason? Douglas has a new cannon that we need to fire."

"Be patient," Jason said. "Your cousins need their luncheon first. Ah, I see your grandmother coming over. She'll beg me to let her play with Nesta. Then we'll go fire that cannon, maybe then I'll take the two of you to the pond and toss you in."

Alex came down on her knees, her arms out. Jason kissed his tiny daughter's forehead and handed her to his mother. "Ah, my precious little sweetheart. You're hungry, aren't you, lovie, and here's your stoat of a brother taking all the lunch. That's right, you just suck on my knuckles." She smiled over at her son, saw that Everett and Douglas were fidgeting. "I heard your uncle tell you to be patient, boys. You may have him in five minutes. Good. Now, Jason, I suppose I'm the one to tell you. Petrie has proposed to Martha. When she confided to Hollis, he told her she'd be far better off marrying him than Petrie, that even though he was approaching his golden years, he wouldn't drive her as distracted as that codshead would."

"What did Martha say?" Hallie asked, looking up.

"I believe after she tucked the blanket lovingly around Hollis's legs, she told him that even though she preferred him to Petrie, she couldn't marry him since she wanted children. She fancied that even though Hollis was surely superior to the codsbreath, she doubted even he would still be on this earth to greet his grandchildren, something she believed very important. She then assured Hollis that Petrie was no different from a racing horse or a racing cat. With a nibble of trout, a bucket of oats, or a smidgeon of a kiss, she could work miracles. Oh, dear, I see Mother-in-law. She's still walking, can you believe that? She can even push Hollis's chair, and believe me, it makes him furious. He even yelled at her once, and do you know what? She laughed, told him since he'd waited on her his whole life, she could at least push him about a bit now." Alex smiled, kissed Nesta's tiny mouth. "Hallie, your aunt Arielle is so pleased you named your daughter after your mother, even though you never knew her. She said that counts."

"Papa got tears in his eyes when I told him her name," Hallie said. "It's odd. He didn't have a single tear when we told him we'd named Alec after him. I saw Angela pushing Hollis's chair too."

Jason was stretched out on his back, Douglas and Everett on top of him, holding him down, jabbering the same twin talk he and James had spoken as boys. He didn't understand them. He wondered what sort of torture they were thinking up for him once they'd fired the cannon and headed to the pond.

He smiled over at his wife, who was kissing the sleeping Alec's forehead, a bit of milk dribbling down his chin.

Hallie looked over at him, grinned at Douglas and Everett, who were trying to pull his boots off.

"Next," she called out.

A note on the **PREMIUM** format

This Premium format paperback is specially
designed for comfortable reading, featuring
remarkable improvements on the interior design
of the traditional mass market paperback.
The book itself is larger, for easier handling.
The type is also larger. The paper is of higher
quality, more like a hardcover. There is more
white space between the lines of text,
so reading is less of an eye strain.

So get comfortable and discover this
innovation in paperback books.

Don't miss our other Premium editions:

Now Available
Nights of Rain and Stars by Maeve Binchy
Lost City by Clive Cussler

Available October 2005
Two Dollar Bill by Stuart Woods
Northern Lights by Nora Roberts

Available November 2005
Night Game by Christine Feehan

New York Times bestselling author

Catherine Coulter
The Sherbrooke Twins

The *Bride* series continues with the story of
handsome identical twins
Jason and James Sherbrooke.

0-515-13654-9

Now available from
Jove Books

catherinecoulter.com
penguin.com